NOT
The I
Raskin

"An exuberantly comic writer."
—*The New York Times Book Review*

Loose Ends

"Lively, immediate, and very readable
. . . It takes an effort of will to consider
Loose Ends as fiction." —Larry McMurtry,
The Washington Post

"Fast and funny . . . Completely convincing."
—*The New York Review of Books*

Hot Flashes

"As important as *The Group* and *The
Women's Room* . . . A female *Big Chill*."
—*Cosmopolitan*

"Funny, perceptive, outrageous and sad."
—*The Washington Post*

"Compelling!"   —New York *Daily News*

"Powerful, moving and hopeful."
—*Cincinnati Post*

BY BARBARA RASKIN

Loose Ends
The National Anthem
Out of Order
Hot Flashes

BARBARA RASKIN

LOOSE ENDS

ST. MARTIN'S PRESS/NEW YORK

LOOSE ENDS

Copyright © 1973 by Barbara Raskin

ISBN: 0-312-91348-6   Can. ISBN: 0-312-91349-4

Printed in the United States of America

Bantam Books edition/November 1973
Revised St. Martin's Press mass market edition/January 1989

10 9 8 7 6 5 4 3 2 1

Because this is an hystorical novel, it is dedicated to the first of my grandchildren—Emily, Zachary and Maggie Ryan Littlewood

CHAPTER 1

Coco was outside on the second-floor back porch where she had spent every day since the first of June on the adjustable nylon lounge chair, which was now set at Semi-Recline and turned westward to catch the strong noonday sun. Everything that she needed was stationed around the long narrow porch. On the coffee table beside her was an ice bucket, two plastic tumblers, half a carton of Marlboro cigarettes, her electric portable typewriter, one oversize ashtray with a sandbag bottom, a Con-Tact-paper-covered English biscuit tin filled with beauty aids, three boxes of kitchen matches, a Snoopy alarm clock, Gavin's transistor radio, a can opener and one economy-size can of Raid insect repellent.

A box of Bond typing paper and two packs of light blue manifold carbons (ripped off from Gavin's office) were tucked under the chaise lounge safe from stray breezes. Along one wall of the porch marched an orderly parade of items led by a gallon jug of Woodley's gin and followed by five six-packs of Schweppes quinine water, a People's Drugstore electric coffee-pot, half a can of Medaglia d'Oro, a jar of Pream and one large plastic container of QT suntan lotion. Three paperbacks, *Play It as It Lays, The Female Eunuch* and *Anna Karenina,* plus four hardbacks, *The Bell Jar, The Journal of Anais Nin Vol. II, Sexual Politics* and *Wonderland,* brought up the rear. The Joyce Carol Oates leaned, prolific and weary, against the fat ends of Coco's looseleaf notebooks, which were stacked in the corner.

A fifteen-foot telephone wire crept under the porch door and meandered along the floor, occasionally crossing and tangling with the ten-foot electric extension cord that Coco used for her various appliances. A small mirror, propped on the narrow ledge beneath the screen, was tilted at an angle so Coco could see herself only when the chaise was set at Semi-Recline or when, on rare occasions, she raised herself to Upright so she could look into the backyard where her children were playing.

For nearly a month now, Coco had spent nine hours a day secluded on the six-by-ten-foot porch. This long period of convalescence was occasioned and guaranteed by the fact that on the last night of May, Coco's husband had confessed his first and only marital infidelity. Although Coco had successfully conducted seven undiscovered love affairs during their twelve-year marriage, she immediately launched a very noisy, minor mental breakdown. This necessitated quitting her job (which she had been meaning to do all year), reestablishing her three-times-a-week psychoanalysis, and renegotiating Mrs. Marshall's salary and hours so Coco could recuperate every day, all day long, on the apple-green-painted screen porch in Recline, Semi-Recline or Upright position.

At various intervals throughout June, Coco went into strategic declines that consisted of hysterical crying jags; these caused some disturbance to the neighbors and much concern to her family. On the weekends, Coco conveniently recovered her emotional stability so she could have dinner out at a restaurant or attend a movie. But her psychological improvements were only temporary and, late Sunday night or early Monday morning, she would suffer a relapse that returned her to the porch where she tanned as much of herself as possible—considering that she could be seen by people living above the third floor in the apartment building across the alley.

During the first week of her exile, Coco read 107 final examinations from her four sections of freshman English, marked the bluebooks, computed semester averages and mailed in her grade sheets to the registrar's office. She then revised her daily List of Things To Do (for the week of June 5–9) and developed her very first Seasonal List, neatly headed THINGS TO DO THIS SUMMER and subtitled "Inventory of Objectives —1972." After contemplating various possible principles by which to rank her intentions, she finally settled on a nonpriority list which read:

1. *Reorganize life*
2. *Write novel*
3. *Do women's-lib stuff for Housing Accommod. Commit.*
4. *Have Affair?*
5. *Find* GOOD *publisher*
6. *Take vacation alone*

7. *Take vacation with children to Yellowstone
   National Park?*
8. *Send children to Mother's!*
9. *Decide what to do in September*
10. *Get pregnant?*
11. *Fix house*
12. *Buy a farm*
13. *Get political—work for new Democratic
    nominee. McGovern?*

Coco placed this list behind Addresses/Telephone
Numbers in her 5×7" calendar notebook and reviewed it periodically to determine if she had suffered any setbacks or made any progress. On the
back side of the same page, Coco wrote:

LEDGER
June, 1972
Income: My salary   *$000.00**

Expenses: Dr. Finkelstein   *$360.00*
          Mrs. Marshall   *$300.00*
                        —$660.00

Coco consulted her ledger several times a week for
budgetary reviews, and one day added an asterisk
and a note at the bottom of the page.

**June 17: Notice the three digits' worth of ze-
roes to indicate my nonsalary. Unconsciously I
know I am professionally worth only three
figures a month.*

The astronomical financial damage done by just one
psychiatrist and one housekeeper depressed Coco

every time she examined her budget, but she dispatched her discomfort by visualizing Gavin in bed with his girlfriend and then balanced off his marital infidelity with her economic deficit. Since Coco was unable to teach summer session, incapacitated as she was by Gavin's adultery, it seemed only fair that he subsidize her domestic and therapeutic needs while she wrote the novel she had been harboring for twenty years, to be titled *Take Heaven by Storm.*

Several days after her Reorganization Effort, Coco began a Writer's Journal in a black-and-white marbleized hardback tablet. On the first page she wrote:

HOW TO TRANSLATE TRUTH INTO FICTION
(a structural plan)

Then she skipped a few pages and wrote:

MAJOR THEMES TO BE EXPLORED

1. *The Fifties—The Fairytale that Failed*
2. *A Chronological Hysterical Novel about the Sixties*
3. *Communal Living and Open Marriages*
4. *The New American Revolution (check in closet to find two old short stories on same subject that cld be used)*
5. *Misogyny in the Movement*
6. *Story about a second wife who is less successful than the first wife—both of whom are writers and the marital trouble this causes*
7. *Hangups of American men which prevent Hardons*
8. *Struggle vs. Resolution. Title? Thunder on the Left?*
9. *Effects on a small town when Hollywood com-*

pany arrives to make a movie. Show impact of culture shock.*

10. The Impossibility of ever finding The Right Mate. Identity vs. Marriage

11. Conflicts Which Avoid Conclusions. (Idea that people cling to the engagement or the process rather than pushing toward a real change which might prove dangerous.)

12. A combination of 10 and 11.

*(maybe Archer City, Texas, and Bogdanovich's The Last Pict. Show)

Whenever Coco reread this list of possible themes, she smoked several cigarettes in rapid succession, because she always felt pleased by the profundity and irony of Number 11. Most of the time, however, she felt drawn to Number 10 because it seemed the easiest.

CHARS. TO USE

1. Someone like Gavin—a man who gravitates toward all radical causes, but who is too insensitive to really understand women's liberation.

2. Someone like me (description of the difficulties, history of using hysteria—since childhood— to escape confrontation with real feelings. The search for intensity rather than simplicity. The unwillingness to maintain One Single Life Style. The inability to achieve success due to sexist society plus unavoidable female insecurity.)

3. Someone like Ann. First wife who casts dark shadow over ex-hubby's new marriage by becoming a chic journalist in New York.

4. Some ex-Peace Corps types

(The different chars. should be brought together at one time or place to show psychodynamics of the group: social, political, sexual implications, etc., etc.)

On the next page was:

UNRELATED INCIDENTS ALREADY WRITTEN
THAT MIGHT BE INCORPORATED
(upstairs in trunk with snowsuits and sleeping bags)

Coco left this page blank until she had time to look through some of her old fiction. Then she turned back to CHARS. TO USE and wrote:

*Find substitute word for "prick"
**Think up good names for the characters!

Coco had already written the beginnings of nine First Novels and at moments of fine astuteness, usually when she was drinking coffee late at night alone in the kitchen, she resigned herself to her fate—that she would never surpass the Beginnings of Unpublishable First Novels stage because she couldn't decide what she really wanted to write about. In her hours of greatest depression, usually during the soggy, delayed awakenings of a Sunday morning, Coco knew she really had nothing important to say. In her bitterest moments, drunk or stoned, she thought of her novels as nothing more than whining come-ons for men, still strangers, to become her friends.

But now, finally, Coco had achieved a kind of enraged resolution; she would not leave the porch until her novel was finished. During the first week of her self-imposed exile, she worked out a system for running her establishment by dropping written messages over the banister for Mrs. Marshall. After two years of an intense love-hate relationship, Mrs. Marshall was becoming more friendly because she thought Coco had come down with incurable lung cancer from smoking too much and was dying on the second floor. Relieved of face-to-face confrontations, Coco could simply fold one of her good sheets of Bond paper into an airplane, like the kind Mike made for Nicky, and sail it down the staircase so that it landed near the front door. Eventually Mrs. Marshall would wander past, unfold the airplane, and read some message about not putting T-shirts in the Bendix dryer anymore please or what meat to defrost for dinner. Coco also developed the habit of ordering all department-store consumer goods by telephone and returning the rejects via the next delivery man for an additional fifty-cent service charge.

Coco only allowed the children upstairs to visit her retreat when disputes erupted which necessitated psychological evaluation and counseling. Otherwise, her contact with the four little Burmans was limited to waving lovingly at them from the porch if they yelled up from the yard for a little attention. Some afternoons, depending upon the length of her previous night's battle with Gavin, Coco would treat herself to an hour-long nap to prepare for her next evening's performance. Coco felt it was necessary to run through a variety of hysterical symptoms every night to reaffirm her mental disorganization and her right-to-retirement-with-a-doctor-and-staff. But even in her authentically irrational moments of rage (and these became progressively more frequent during the month of June), Coco was always conscious of building a nestegg of convalescent time during which she could conclude almost thirty-two years of humiliating literary silence.

Actually, the first thirty days in which Coco labored to deliver her book were of such epic scale that she was never totally aware of all the various levels of her experience. Not only had she agonizingly sentenced herself to five hours of writing OR ten pages daily, but she also had to: produce nervous-breakdown symptoms and relapses; struggle with Gavin about the condition of their marriage; read the *Washington Post*'s book reviews to check out her competition; stifle strong urges to telephone her girlfriend, Glenda, who was in South America; keep applying thick, greasy coats of suntan oil to enhance her tan and erase stretch marks; and assiduously avoid confronting any of her real pathological pain over the possibility that Gavin was no longer totally in her sphere of influence—routinely orbiting like a satellite around her.

After the first trip to Dr. Finkelstein's office, Coco began wearing a bikini, instead of underwear, beneath her summer cottons, and though the tight elastic leg bindings caused her some discomfort while she lay on the blue couch in the doctor's office, the moment she reached home she could dash up to the porch, pull off her dress, and collapse on the chaise without losing any time or tanning potential. Since the weather began to get hot early in June, Coco quickly acquired several heavy coats of golden brown color on her face and body which helped to excavate all of her latent beauty as well as blot out the small pigmentation spots along her hairline which mysteriously appeared, like her mother, after each new baby.

Because Coco would turn thirty-two in August, her physical appearance had begun to interest her now

more than ever before. Involuntarily she studied her
face in the small makeup mirror propped against the
screen—which she always encountered in Semi-Recline front-side tanning position for signs of old age
until she decided (during the second week of her
retreat) to squelch this growing obsession and limit
her beauty-duty to only one half-hour at the beginning of each day. Her reclamation routine consisted
of leafing through inspirational fashion magazines
(she still received *Vogue* on an introductory offer that
she kept recycling under fictitious names), while oiling knees and elbows (neglected since infancy), tend-
ing to cuticles, practicing the surgical gluing-on of
false eyelashes (she owned four pairs that varied in
length and price) with her eyes closed (as preparation for doing it in the dark), brushing the slightest
curl out of her long black hair, experimenting with
various depilatories, testing the tone of her tan
against the two pale patches always protected by
parts of her bikini, studying the circumference and
depths of various enlarged pores near her nose in a
drugstore magnifying mirror, and trying to correct
the contours of particular toes, especially the number fours that flawed the perfection of her feet and
thus her total body.

Although filing, cutting, shaving, trimming, clip-
ping, gluing, plucking, polishing and squeezing became terribly engrossing, Coco still managed to keep
to the schedule that she had plotted out in a denim-
blue looseleaf notebook left over from her history-of-
linguistics course at the University of Chicago. With
great thought she had carefully parceled out her
daily nine hours of freedom into neat (lined with a
ruler) square boxes on an unlined sheet of notebook
paper. Promptly at 9:30 she stopped her Surface Improvements and commenced her physical exercises.

On the rough wooden porch floor she did sit-ups, push-ups, and breast-development flexings while trying to think Eastern to put herself in a productive Western frame of mind.

9:30 to 10:00 was allocated to telephone calls of a nonpersonal nature. These included making orders for grocery deliveries from the most expensive Connecticut Avenue market; discussing her balance with the credit department at Lord & Taylor in Chevy Chase; making appointments for the children to visit friends or dentists; attending to repair needs on large appliances for which she carried Sears Roebuck repair insurance (the dishwasher and the garbage disposal each broke twice in the first eighteen days of June); calling Gavin to tell him to: have the car inspected, pick up his shirts at the laundry, remember Mike's Field Day on the fourteenth (wear tennis shoes), and to save the fifteenth for Jessica's kindergarten puppet show.

Every morning Coco also phoned five names from her Women's Liberation Citywide Calling List to help find housing for the numerous marchers coming to Washington on July Fourth to picket the White House in a Women's Declaration of Independence Day March. Coco felt very efficient about (a) fulfilling her political obligations while flat on her back and (b) staying in touch with demonstration organizers, since one of the possible themes (or basic metaphors) she was considering for her novel was the May Day peace demonstration two years ago. For months now, the Fourth of July had loomed as an important summer landmark. By that time Coco planned to have finished the first draft of *Take Heaven by Storm* so she could take off a few days to participate in the women's-liberation activities. Since she had offhandedly (way back in February) agreed to be co-chairman of the D.C. Women's Liberation Coalition Housing and Accommodations Committee, she had been invited to march at the front of the parade and over a month ago had made Gavin promise to take care of the house and the children during most of the Fourth of July weekend.

Immediately following her thirty minutes of phone calls, Coco would begin to type parts of her life into the Smith-Corona (10:30–4:00), eagerly waiting to see if any part of her past would produce a theme or plot that seemed either authentic or original. She never stirred from the chaise until ten of the projected three hundred pages were finished and, for maximum efficiency, she unplugged the telephone during these hours and assigned Mrs. Marshall the task of taking all the children to the park for a daily picnic lunch. This arrangement meant that around noon everyone disappeared from the house carrying toys, extra clothing, books, blankets, baskets of sandwiches and money to buy Slurpies from the Seven-Eleven store at the corner. Thus Coco ensured silence during her most intense work period and also avoided the temptation of eating a meal, which tightened up the muscles in her stomach that she anyway contracted isometrically at rhythmic intervals throughout the day while she was typing.

But by five o'clock, when Coco resumed domestic duty on the first floor and began preparing another candlelight dinner to initiate her nightly battle with Gavin, the children were always tired, hot and hostile. They would hang around the kitchen, cranky and peevish, persecuting Coco for her day-long neglect by stealing Oreo cookies from the big glass apothecary jar on the counter (impractical—since it was glass—but a definite personality plus) or running through the first floor fighting and howling about

whether they should watch the cartoons on Channel
4 or *Petticoat Junction* on 5. Inevitably the phone
would join the posse in pursuit of Coco's cool, jan-
gling repeatedly so that Coco became cook/opera-
tor, cramming the receiver against her ear with an
aching shoulder while shuffling burning bacon
around in the fry pan, setting the kitchen table, passing out paper cups of Hawaiian punch, writing
checks for the grocery- and/or liquorstore delivery
men, and guiltily letting Josh drink his bottle uncud-
dled in the middle of the kitchen floor surrounded by
the pots, pans and canned goods he inventoried every evening.

As a show of penance, Gavin had begun coming
home from work before six, presumably to establish
his credibility as a good present and future fidelity
risk. Looking sheepish and ill-at-ease, he would play
with the children while Coco cooked dinner, awkwardly help set the table, and then pick up toys after
the kids went to bed. Although for several weeks he
had uncomplainingly submitted to Coco's intensive
after-dinner interrogations, he eventually began to
show some signs of impatience with her nocturnal
prosecution and persecution of him. After three long
weeks, he still would not identify the girl by name or
reveal which hotels they'd visited or what aliases
they'd used or if they had indulged in room service.
He would not describe their mode of transportation,
discuss what time of day they rendezvoused, reveal if
the girl used a douche (if so, she wasn't Jewish), or
entertain any discussions about hotel-inspired fancy
sexual positions, postcoital co-ed showers, or how
much the totaled hotel bills had cost. Although early
in the month Coco had worn Gavin down to a point
where, in a moment of exhaustion and penance for
the nerve of his adultery, he agreed that the Wash-

ington Hilton would have been a convenient location
and that the month of March had been an expedi-
tious one, he eventually began to field or ignore Coco's questions thus igniting her genuine hysteria
which he couldn't distinguish from her simulated
episodes.

During those long June evenings, Coco would
drink gin until she finally exploded into screaming
accusations, charging Gavin with ruining their marriage, her mental health, her social position, and her
new state of political enlightenment achieved
through the Columbia Road Local Consciousness
Raising Group as well as the Northwest Washington
Theoretical Council. Coco insisted that Gavin's affair
was unfair because it was only a last brutal swipe of
chauvinistic terrorism, an attempt at neocolonial re-
pression before the advent of the postrevolutionary
age which would produce a more equitable balance
of domestic power and make extramarital sex totally
irrelevant as well as difficult to obtain. Coco spent a
considerable amount of time and energy trying to
educate Gavin about the counter-revolutionary nature of his infidelity, but she was never totally confi-
dent that he understood and accepted her analysis.

CHAPTER 2

*S*ometimes Coco wondered if everything had gone wrong simply because of a pill she had taken. After many unsuccessful weeks of hunting for uppers on the campus, Coco had finally scored twenty dexedrine spanuals from one of her freshman students who dropped by the office after class to discuss a late term paper. When Coco asked how anyone could possibly complete all the necessary research in the last week of the semester, the girl insisted it would be no problem. Then Coco inquired if college students still used stay-awake pills and, right on cue, Lillian Greenberg produced an enormous bottle of bennies and dex from her Greek fabric shoulder bag. She gave Coco twenty ten-milligrams, and Coco extended Lillian's term-paper deadline by one week.

It was on the morning of May 31 that Coco took the first fat green capsule, with coffee, as a final effort to shift the stubborn marker on her scale from 118 to 113. Then she went to campus, gave a two-hour-long final examination to her 107 students; stopped off for an end-of-the-year beer at her gay officemate's apartment; came home to make dinner; played with the children before putting them to bed; devised a variation of solitaire with several months' worth of past-due bills; sanded down half of an old rocking chair she had bought at Goodwill; impulsively inspected the children's coloring books and threw away those without empty pages; gathered Mike's baseball cards from around the house, consolidating them into a grocery bag; threw away all the pigeon feathers that Nicky had stored away in the mitten drawer, which, in warm weather, might produce poliomyelitis germs; took a shower; rebleached the already invisible peroxide-blond moustache on her upper lip; finished reading *Some Parts in the Single Life*, by Jimmy Miller, while sitting on the toilet; and then discovered that it was after one A.M. and she still wasn't the least bit tired.

Walking down the hallway, Coco wondered if she might have dropped meth instead of dex, and then opened the bedroom door to see Gavin sleeping soundly in a very immature fetal position on his side of the bed. Perversely, she waited a few minutes to let some hallway nightlight spill into the darkness, but when the glare didn't seem to disturb him, she entered the room and kicked the door shut loudly behind her. Gavin still didn't stir. His sleep seemed like a consummate insult, a logical extension of his daytime insensitivity. Slowly, and involuntarily, Coco felt herself start to shake with tiny ripples of discontent. Fluffs of disappointment fluttered through her body like little lint balls in the Bendix dryer.

Sitting down at her dressing table, she flicked on the small lamp she used for making up, lit a Marlboro, and began to straighten her cosmetics, scraping electric-roller hair clips into the sliding drawer of her carpenter's tool chest, sliding perfume bottles into a line against the mirror, dropping earrings into her jewelry box, and rehanging strings of beads from a coat hook she had pounded into the wall. Next she arranged, in descending order of size, all twenty of the white plastic containers in which she kept creams, astringents, Q-Tips, cotton balls, makeup removers and other essentials. Several months ago Coco had even scooped some Vaseline out of its squat ugly glass jar and finger-pushed it into one of her white plastic traveling containers so that she was totally coordinated cosmetically and prepared to gather her toiletries on a moment's notice to fly away to Paris with a Perfect Lover.

After cleaning the dresser top, she amused herself briefly by reviewing the total effect of her long hair brushed back from her bronze-tanned face in various upsweep styles. After a while, craving more action, she began to run through her repertoire of various poses, manufacturing facial expressions that made her look innocent, then mysterious, then seductive, intelligent, lusty, and finally, mischievous. Midway through her recital, she folded her arms beneath her breasts to produce a stirringly deep line of cleavage and traced her tongue over her lips so that they glistened with Monroe-ish moisture.

But when she looked her most irresistible, Coco felt a palpitating impatience rise up from within her cleavage. She had always believed that her beauty was of such a tentative nature, so unpredictable and so fleetingly dramatic, that she needed a witness— someone else to see and appreciate it so that it could be recorded in reality. To have such incredibly seductive poses go unobserved and unappreciated was terribly provocative. Gavin, still sleeping and totally oblivious to Coco's enormous need for attention, made her so angry that she lost interest in looking beautiful just for herself. Coco tilted the lamp shade upward until Gavin was illuminated by a fierce blade of light and then studied him through the mirror.

The thing about Gavin's physique was that he was very, very long and just too thin. Coco had always felt that his scrawniness was an indictment of her cooking, as well as a hostile threat to anyone with a weight problem, and that his long, narrow, eternally and perversely thin, bony body, stretching from the pillows right down to the foot of their king-size bed, was like a long stretch of undeveloped land near a big city that was badly in need of some subdivision and development. But worst of all, his physical thinness made him look like a sexual lightweight—a man without any magnitude, decisiveness or physical authority.

And, of course, when Gavin stood up, his body extended so high that it made his head seem inordinately small at the top. His head was the head of a short man—decorated with a nice small nose, a small neat mouth, small flat ears, and smallish eyes circled by miniature glasses. Coco always felt that her head looked bigger than Gavin's which upset her traditional view that all parts of a husband were supposed to be bigger than the wife's. And though she sometimes thought that if Gavin's head were delivered to her on a tray, she might say he had a pleasant face, while it remained attached to his long skinny body it bothered her enormously.

"Well, this has gone on just long enough," Coco said in a loud, firm voice.

Through the mirror she watched Gavin open his eyes.

"I want a divorce immediately," Coco said, banging her hairbrush down on the table to startle Gavin so he wouldn't drop back off to sleep again. "I simply cannot stand another day like this. And this time I really mean it."

Automatically Gavin reached back toward the bookcase to find his glasses. He put them on and then propped himself up on the pillow, knowing enough to appear attentive and interested.

"In just three months I'm going to be thirty-two," she announced ominously. "If you remember your Kinsey, you'd know that thirty-five is the absolute sexual peak of a woman's life—a period of incredible passion. I'm just going to have to get a divorce."

After twelve years of rehearsals, Gavin had finally learned all of his lines and cues. He now knew what to say at each appropriate point in the dialogue although Coco, as the star, always staged the scenes, set the tempo for each act, and gave him his cues.

"As soon as the children get out of school, we will have to separate."

"Who? You and the children?" Gavin's eyes were blinking behind his glasses.

"*We,*" she said emphatically, "will have to leave *you.* And it would be best for everyone if we made all the necessary arrangements right now."

"Why do we always have to make 'arrangements' after midnight?" Gavin asked in an aggrieved voice. "Why can't we ever do it in the morning? Or on weekends?"

"I don't really care what time it is, Gavin," Coco said insistently. "I just know something has to be done and it should be done as quickly as possible."

Creating a commotion to fill an emotional vacuum—

which her nature abhorred—made Coco's eyes more hazel than brown. "I simply can't go on living like this, Gavin."

The decision to leave immediately was an important starter-line for one of the Burmans' games, initialed I-L or #7. Coco kept playing with her hair, winding it all into a curl over one shoulder or twisting it into a bun high on her crown.

"All right," said Gavin.

"I work all day, run this incredible crazy establishment . . . blah-blah-blah. And I have absolutely no emotional life at all."

"Well," Gavin said, "since I can't see how or why anything's going to change, maybe you really should leave."

"Not only don't I have any emotional life," Coco said, beginning to accelerate and escalate, "but I also have no sex life."

"I agree with you completely," Gavin said in his usual defensive way. "By my last calculations, we haven't fucked in about six weeks." Then he paused. "Maybe you really should go."

This time his invitation for her to leave hit Coco with the impact of a car accident filmed for a buckle-your-seat-belt commercial. "Go" was not in their regular script and it sounded out of key, especially since Gavin seldom repeated himself.

Coco kept brushing her hair while her heart pounded with an unfamiliar rhythm. Watching herself in the mirror, she finally decided that it was her own hypertension—the ever-warned-about paranoid feeling produced by amphetamines—that was causing her to misinterpret Gavin's tone of voice.

"Where will you all go?" Gavin asked on his own initiative, which was suspiciously out of character.

"Oh," Coco murmured, tilting her head back so

she could observe her husband better, "probably to some island."

"What island?"

Although Coco had kept firmly in mind, for many years, a particular kind of cottage where she planned to flee during her rustic escapes from marriage, she had, in fact, never geographically located the exact stretch of ocean beach where it could be rented.

"Maybe Manhattan?" he suggested nastily.

"Now, listen," she said angrily, delivering Gavin her aren't-you-pedestrian-though look. "I mean a real place on a real island. Near the ocean. A house. This is going to be a permanent separation, Gavin, not just a summer fling. I intend to live on that island all year round."

"That's nice, Coco, very back-to-the-countryish. But tell me, is there a school on your island? I gather some of the kids are interested in continuing their education."

"Of course there's a school." Coco picked up a tube of lipstick and slowly outlined her mouth with a glistening shade of Yardley's honey-beige that evoked a Jean Shrimpton shine. Her immediate allure was so reassuring that Coco decided Gavin sounded hostile simply because he was still sleepy. Nevertheless, she felt compelled to press onward to discover why he was acting so uncooperative when they hadn't had a real fight in almost two weeks and why he was trying to upset her by focusing upon irrelevant particulars rather than discussing divorce in general.

"Anyway, I'll make my own arrangements, Gavin. You don't have to worry your busy little head about any of that. All I hope is that you'll move your ass and get yourself into analysis before you try to start another relationship. Because otherwise the same thing will happen to you all over again. Some woman will feel an initial attraction, decide she wants to live with you, and then . . ." Coco's voice trailed away; it was Gavin's turn to get pissed off about her mentioning his need for therapy again.

Gavin shifted around slightly in the bed, rearranged the lightweight summer blanket over his body, and peered toward the mirror to see Coco's face. "Do you know something," he began with a polite smile, "I don't think you have to worry about my mental condition anymore." His small neat face looked malignantly benign. "In fact, you don't have to worry about anything concerning me anymore. What you should do is just make all the necessary plans to get the hell out of here. I want you to feel free to split even if it's just for the summer. It's clear you've wasted enough time being miserable living with me, and since you're not getting any younger, maybe you really better split now while you've still got some other options."

Gavin's acceptance of her resignation speech was a stunning break with tradition. His words set off a series of shocks that reverberated through Coco's body, making the Island Escape Fantasy fuzzy, like the educational channel on the old TV in the basement.

"What do you mean?" Coco asked.

"What do you mean 'what do I mean?'"

That was enraging—an authentic provocation.

"I take it for granted," Coco said nastily, "that you understand why I want to leave you."

"Well, I sure as hell hope it's for the same reasons you've been bitching about for the last twelve years, because I don't think I'm up to hearing any new complaints right now. I'm tired and I want to get some sleep."

"You're whaaat?" Coco made the word hiss like a blast of steam from the kitchen radiator.

"I'm tired," Gavin repeated.

That was clearly a lie. Gavin was getting more reckless rather than more sleepy. He was willfully pressing her toward a dangerous precipice of rage. Coco whirled around on the little stool. Although she was finally beginning to feel tired, she flipped her hair away from her face and hunched forward to give Gavin a flash of cleavage beneath her blue nightgown.

"You're tired?" she repeated. "You're tired? Well, would you like to know something? That happens to be the exact reason. That's exactly the reason why you're such a failure as a human being. You may be a great lawyer, Gavin. You may be a great success in your career. But you are unquestionably a failure as a human being. That is clearly why your first marriage broke up. That is why you are a two-time loser. *You are always tired.* You are always tired at the wrong times. You have all kinds of energy for everything in the world except for the things that are really important. I mean *really* important. In human terms. And that's the reason why I want to get the hell away from here."

Coco had, indeed, spent a disproportionately large portion of the last twelve years planning, discussing, threatening and fantasizing about leaving Gavin. Her most frequent justification for such a separation was Gavin's sexual shortcomings. Coco had discovered long ago that there was nothing comparable in driving power to a bitter sexual complaint. Orgasm shortages ruled majestically in the realm of grievances and remained the stateliest grudge of all the injustices she had collected over the years. Indeed, Coco used the highly effective low-sexual-profile argument as both a description of Gavin's original sin as well as an explanation for all his subsequent failures.

Suddenly Gavin swung his legs over the side of the bed and sat up. Coco was stunned. Gavin never sat up while they were fighting. Night after night, year after year, he just lay in bed, flat on his back, while she raged and ranted at him, infuriated by the passive resistance of his prone position. But now, all of a sudden, he was sitting up and energetically using a comb of bent fingers to rake paths through his hair.

"Look," Gavin said, "I guess we both have had enough of this. You feel gypped, and so do I. Maybe what we both need is a little time alone to think things out."

Coco felt the world stop and then start to spin in the opposite direction.

Gavin was inviting her to leave. He was actually inviting her *out*.

"Well," she mumbled, "that's funny. It's very funny that all of a sudden you want me to go away, when before you've always begged me *not* to go." She turned around so Gavin couldn't watch while she concentrated on moving a quivering match into contact with her cigarette. "I must say," she continued weakly, gulping a throatful of smoke, "that I'm really a little curious about why, all of a sudden, you want to have a 'little time' alone. Something must be making you feel very independent for a change." The smoke floated up around Coco's eyes. "Maybe you've got yourself a little something going on the side."

"Maybe I do," Gavin said.

And at that moment Coco knew forever that there was another woman in Gavin's life.

Coco stood up carefully, as if she were carrying a tray that might spill, and then walked over and lay down on the bed, flat on her back. She remained

perfectly still, staring up at the ceiling, well aware
that her husband had not moved to make any gesture
of comfort, reassurance or denial. He was still sitting
on the edge of the bed, fingercombing his hair off his
forehead.

"Well, who is she?" Coco asked.

There was a long silence. "You don't know her."

A soft puffy pink organ, frequently featured in
Life-magazine color-photo spreads, shifted into a
lower position in Coco's chest. "How do you know I
don't know her?" Coco asked.

"I just know you don't."

"Well, really, Gavin, you don't really think that I
only know the people who you know I know, do
you?"

He didn't answer.

"I mean, really . . ."

There was another very long silence. Coco listened. There were no background sound effects.
None of the children were crying. No crib was rocking, no bed was creaking, no air-conditioner
hummed, no toilet gurgled. Everything was quiet.
Everything was the same as it had been an hour ago,
except now everything was spoiled. What she had
always liked most about Gavin was that he had divorced his first wife because he found Coco ulti-
mately and infinitely more desirable. That he now
felt attracted to someone else made Coco feel like a
devaluated dollar. Depleted. Depressed. Defini-
tively endangered.

She felt panic begin to picket her.

"So. Are you in love with this . . . girl?" she asked
carefully.

Gavin hunched his shoulders up and down like a
teen-ager unable to recognize his own true emotions.
An unseasonable frost seemed to have frozen his nor-

mal motions and movements. He seemed completely separate and detached from Coco, like a wall painter or carpenter who worked in a house, moving among its inhabitants with intimate ease, but totally ignorant of the essential drama of their lives.

Partially because Coco felt totally imperiled, and partially because she could think of absolutely nothing else to do to show Gavin how much he had hurt her, Coco gave a pitiful little moan, rolled over, and fell out of the bed. She simply went limp, internally gave herself a little push, and dropped down flat onto the floor, banging her head very noisily despite the red carpet tiles. After listening to a shrill ringing in her ears, Coco heard Gavin jump up and begin stumbling around the bed in her direction.

"Coco. What's the matter?" He tried to lift her up, but her head rolled backward. "What happened? What's the matter? Are you all right? God, Coco, what happened?"

He finally lifted her in his arms in an uncinematic, disorderly way that made one of Coco's arms trail behind the rest of her body and hit hard against the radiator as he half-rolled, half pushed her back onto the bed. Freezing in the disorganized position in which he had dropped her, Coco peeked through her lashes and saw Gavin, flushed from having elevated her off the floor, standing unhappy and uncertain high above her. Then he lifted one hand and rubbed confusion across his face with distraught fingers. Instantly Coco recognized the expression that always preceded his undertaking a serious action. It was clear Gavin was trying to decide whether to phone for an ambulance, a doctor or the police.

So that was when Coco started to scream. She opened her mouth, took a deep breath, and began to emit one shrill shriek after another; the more she screamed, the better she felt.

Gavin ran out into the hallway and rushed around closing the children's bedroom doors. When he came back, he tried to cover her mouth with his hand, but Coco bit hard into the fleshy cushion near the bottom of his thumb. As soon as he jerked away, Coco rose up out of the bed and began walking around the room, moaning and groaning, hugging her body with arms crossed in straitjacket style.

"I'm ruined," Coco moaned. "You've ruined me."

It sounded both nineteenth-centuryish as well as contemporary. It felt right to her mouth.

Gavin looked surprised. His head moved back and forth in a mock spectator-at-a-tennis-match motion as he watched her. Then suddenly he jumped off the bed and disappeared down the hall toward the bathroom. After a few minutes he returned with a bunch of dripping towels in his hands.

"You're hysterical, Coco," he said soothing, reassuringly, as he tried to wrap a towel around her head. "You're okay, Coco, honey. You're just a little hysterical. There's nothing wrong. You're okay. You're just hysterical. Now, try to calm down a little."

Coco watched the water dripping down onto the self-adhesive red shag carpet tiles and thought that she just might *really* freak out from the supreme irritation of watching Gavin quietly soaking the rug and probably thinning the glue that held it down on the floor. Indeed, she was so genuinely upset now that she suddenly dropped straight backward onto the floor like the children did into a bank of snow. For a moment she thought she might have actually knocked herself out by falling flat from such a height. The back of her skull banged on the floor, sounding a heavy hollow boom.

"Coco. Coco, are you all right? For God's sake, answer me."

Gavin sounded as if he were crying.

"Listen. I'm sorry, Coco. I'm really sorry. I didn't mean it. I love you. You know I love you. Will you forgive me? Please? Please. I'm sorry, Coco."

And that was when Coco realized he had been sleeping with the girl.

She moved slightly, so that her hair spread out and fanned around her head, before she opened her eyes. She wondered for a moment if she should pretend to be bleeding, since blood wouldn't show on the rug anyway, but decided to go the internal injuries route.

"I'm sick, Gavin," she said in a frail, weak voice. "I'm sick. Please help me. I can't talk now. I'm too sick."

So he pushed her back up on the bed again.

Coco couldn't tell if he was crying or just panting— from running around the room so much and lifting her off the floor twice.

But now, at last, Coco felt genuinely tired, physically and emotionally exhausted. Originally all she had wanted was a little action, a little interaction, but, as usual, Gavin had spoiled it, had misunderstood her needs and made everything go wrong. She lay back weakly against the pillow and, watching her husband move nervously around the room, thought: He's thirty-five, and the only time he cries is if I drive him crazy with my hysteria; that's the only way he knows I'm feeling anything and the only way he ever has any feelings of his own.

The clock on the bookshelf showed three A.M. Coco began to think about Other Men, but she had been without a lover for over two years, including her last pregnancy, and she had not been summoned across a crowded room by a handsome stranger for a

long, long time. Perhaps she was too old. Perhaps sex
and love and passion were already finished for her.
Perhaps everything was finished for her now.

"In the morning," Coco whispered, "you'll have to
call my office. Ask for Claudia Martinez. Tell her that
I'm resigning." Coco felt pale and wan. "Tell them I
just found out that I'm very sick and I have to quit
working."

"Coco. You can't do that." Gavin stopped pacing.
"You told them you would teach two summer
courses. They won't be able to find anyone else now.
It's too late. And how will we have enough money to
pay Mrs. Marshall? You just need a little vacation for a
week or so, honey. When does the summer session
start?"

"You call her up and tell her that," Coco ordered.
"Ask for Claudia Martinez."

Then Coco rolled over on her side. Her stomach
felt upset, the back of her head hurt, and her neck
seemed to be getting stiff. Inside, she felt used,
abused, wounded and betrayed.

Her novel. It was then that she started to think
about writing her novel. Finally, really doing it. It
seemed the only option left. She had always viewed
publication as the only path to personal salvation—an
absolution for wasted time and a ticket for a New
Life automatically hitched to Book Sales. It would
take only one lyrical but slickly constructed novel,
fiercely emblazoned with SELF, to catapult her
to fame, to the distribution of three-quarters of a
million books. Her novel—propped open to display
Coco's enigmatic back-cover smile—on the bedside
tables of three-quarters of a million men would become the national anthem for most matinal fantasies.
There would be: guest appearances on network talk
shows; klieg-lit openings of the filmed version of her

life, starring Ali MacGraw; endless opportunities for writing assignments; and endless offers of romance from incredibly attractive men.

But novels, of course, were hard to write.

Coco closed her eyes and fell asleep instantly.

CHAPTER 3

Coco woke up at 6:30 because she thought she heard Joshua crying, and was quite honestly surprised to discover that the sobs she'd heard were coming from herself. Excited by the authenticity of her grief, she immediately woke Gavin to show him what he'd done. She cried bitterly for ten minutes without wiping away any of the tears that dropped down both sides of her face, irritating her cheeks until they began to itch.

Her weeping was a symbolic trial in which Gavin was subpoenaed, prosecuted and found guilty of total responsibility for her condition. It was so natural and convincing a performance that Gavin lay silently beside her and, without attempting any defense, accepted the verdict of his guilt. He also accepted his punishment because he made no objections to any of Coco's requests when she finally stopped crying and began asking him to do things for her.

First of all he had to get up and go look through the
medicine chest, Coco's jewelry box, and the bottom
of her purse to find one old Librium that she remembered seeing somewhere. He finally found it in an
empty bottle of Senecot anticonstipation pills. Then
he went downstairs and brought up a pot of coffee
with two slices of whole-wheat toast that Coco
promptly pushed off the tray onto the floor because
they had too much butter. Next he delivered Coco's
lavender-colored birth-control-pill dispenser from
the bathroom and watched silently as she emptied all
the remaining pills into the pitcher of Carnation milk
on her tray. That was *that* (except, of course, later in
the afternoon Coco took a pill from the middle of her
next month's dispenser, because the last thing she
needed now was to get pregnant). But Gavin, gullible
and trusting, felt his home sex life was finished and
got the same expression on his face as when the telephone service was cut off because he forgot to pay
the bill.

Sadly, Coco reached over to confiscate Gavin's pillow, tucked it behind her own (a sign of illness in the
family), and leaned back weakly against the foam-
rubber incline, taking tiny sips from her coffeecup
and feeling the same sort of bewilderment that the
children experienced when they were too sick from
the measles to enjoy the comforts and privileges that
accompanied the disease.

"Do you know what I'm going to do, Gavin?" Coco
asked in a half-whisper as soon as the caffeine in the
coffee fortified her self-control.

"What?"

"Nothing."

"What do you mean, nothing?" He stood stub-
bornly near her side of the bed while his distress
shifted into resistance.

"I'm going to do nothing. I'm going to do nothing at all until summer's over and then I'll decide what I'm going to do. The only thing I can do now is rest up so that I can decide what to do later."

"Well, that's sort of the old academic schedule," Gavin remarked in a brisk, businesslike voice. "Finish up at the end of May, start things fresh and new in September. Actually, it's probably best that you don't teach summer session this year." Covertly he was beginning to eye-search the piles of discarded clothing lying around the room to find something to wear so he could officially launch his day.

"That's right," Coco agreed. "I'm just going to stay in bed for three months." She nodded her head slowly. "And you can cope."

"Me? What do you mean? I've got to work." He excavated yesterday's socks from a small hill on the floor. "Mrs. Marshall will take care of the kids."

Coco put the coffeecup gently back into its saucer and watched Gavin reach out to reclaim the tray as it started sliding off the bed. He glared at Coco for not trying to impede the descent of the dishes and then placed the tray safely on top of his bureau. Angrily he walked across the room and sat down on her dressing-table stool. He was holding his underwear, but seemed uncertain about the propriety of dressing during such a disaster.

Coco peeked into the back of the coffee spoon that had slid off the tray onto the blanket and saw that her mascara had smeared into sad, dark circles beneath both eyes. Turning her handicap into an advantage, she looked mournfully at Gavin, who always asked if she was tired when her mascara ran, and sank deeper into the pillows. She sighed heavily and then adopted a calm, practical voice.

"Gavin. I think I'd like to see my calendar notebook."

He lifted her purse off the dressing table and deposited it in his vacant space on the bed. Coco reached over and extracted a purple Flair pen and her pocket-sized red leather notebook.

"I'm going to make a list," she said courageously, in a weak voice, settling back against the double pillow again.

"Of what?" Gavin asked nervously.

"Of what has to be done."

"Oh, God." Gavin got off the stool, pulled on his shorts, and then returned to the bed, where he lay down flat, minus his pillow, and waited.

Coco used her hunched knees as a desk, uncapped the nubby-pointed marker, and opened her carefully organized notebook to Thursday, June 1, 1972.

"It's just too bad today's not Monday," she said.

"Why?"

"Because it's the first. It's better if the first of a month is a Monday. It's more efficient and I think they should always have it that way."

Gavin groaned. "I really don't understand you, Coco. I never really did."

Coco began her list and read each entry aloud as she progressed omitting only #3.

CALL MY OFFICE AND RESIGN—GAVIN

CALL G'S OFFICE, SAY THERE'S ILLNESS IN THE FAMILY. WON'T BE IN TODAY—GAVIN

CALL DR. F. BETWEEN 9:50–9:59 TO START TREATMENT IMMEDIATELY

GET BOOKS FROM PUBLIC LIBRARY—GAVIN

"What books?" Gavin asked.

"I'll have to make you a separate list."

BRING UP CHAISE LOUNGE TO SECOND FLOOR BACK PORCH—GAVIN

"What for, Coco? Nobody ever uses that porch."

"Well, that's where I'm going to be in bed," she said, studying the list. "On the porch."

"But there's no bed out there."

"*That's* why you have to bring up the chaise from the patio."

"Jesus. You're acting like a baby, Coco. What kind of a shit performance is this? What the hell are you carrying on about? First you tell me you want a divorce and then you go nuts because you think I've been cheating on you."

Coco threw Gavin a sidelong glance that resurrected the true psychological enormity of his crime; he returned his gaze to the ceiling.

CALL WOODWARD & LOTHROP, DOWNTOWN BRANCH, TO DELIVER A NEW STROLLER

"Please pass me the Kleenex, Gavin."

INQUIRE ABOUT SUNDIAL SUMMER DAYCAMP FOR CHILDREN OVER FIVE

"How much does that cost?" Gavin inquired tonelessly.

"That's what we have to inquire." Coco sucked on the top of her pen.

CALL CHICAGO BEFORE 6:00 P.M.

"Jesus. What are you going to do *that* for?"

"Because we're going to need some extra money, Gavin. And my mother won't believe it's important unless I call before the night rates start." Coco looked down at the growing List. "You know something? I think I have a very ugly handwriting." She tilted her notebook to the left and tried a backward-slanting style that looked like Good Private School Printing Script.

But all at once the particular and peculiar pleasure she got from making lists evaporated as a searing memory of the past night returned to assault her.

"Maybe that's why you did it," she said irritably. "Maybe you got tired of my handwriting. Maybe my handwriting was not fancy enough for you anymore. Maybe you found yourself a little Cliffie who makes round fat letters."

"You're talking crazy, Coco. Why are you acting like such a nut?"

"You know, my mother always said that I shouldn't marry you because you'd been divorced. Is it raining out?"

"No."

"You know something, Gavin, what's really freaking me out about all this is why you're doing it to me now. In 1972. You had a whole twelve years before now to play around. You had all of the sixties. That's when people had affairs . . . in the sixties. Not now. Not after women's lib. You're probably the only husband in America who's had an affair this year."

No answer.

"Well, let's just finish this," Coco said thoughtfully.

"Finish it! That's a whole day's work right there. What is this? I've got a case to try next Wednesday and I've got a shitload of work to get ready."

CALL DIANA TO FIND OUT GLENDA'S ADDRESS

GET LAWNMOWER FIXED AT HARDWARE ON CO-LUMBIA ROAD—GAVIN

MAIL SUBSCRIPTION BLANK TO *New York Review of Books*—GAVIN

RSVP TO THE BRANDY PARTY

MAIL THE BILLS—GAVIN

BUY BOOK OF AIRMAILS AT POST OFFICE—GAVIN

CHECK FOR BATHING-SUIT SALES

She looked at yesterday's things-to-do list and in-corporated the leftovers into her new one.

TAKE N'S TRICYCLE TO BE FIXED—GAVIN

GET MAIL FROM A.U. OFFICE—GAVIN

Then, cupping her hand in a don't-let-your-deskmate-copy-your-answers style, Coco wrote:

START NOVEL!

Carefully she replaced the cap of the pen, clipped it onto her notebook, and tucked both back inside the secret-center compartment of her purse which served as her office.

"What time is it?"

Gavin looked at the alarm clock. "Twenty to eight."

"The children will wake up soon," Coco said in a sweet, maternal way. "But we still have enough time."

"For what?"

"For you to tell me."

"Tell you what?" His voice was guarded and suspicious.

"Who she is."

Silence.

"I *have* to know, Gavin. I'll have a nervous breakdown if you don't tell me. I mean it. You heard me, I was crying while I was sleeping. This isn't a put-on. This isn't any sixties schtick. You better believe me, Gavin. I'm *very* upset. I mean, I'm really *very* upset. I'm sick. I'm mentally ill from all this. I feel worse now than when I first went to see Dr. Finkelstein and you know how I was then. I mean, how would you feel if I had an affair with you while I was married to another man and then left him to marry you and then started having another affair twelve years and four kids later? Wouldn't you think history was repeating itself? I mean, wouldn't that make you nervous?"

"Well, I did tell you," Gavin said defensively.

Coco cast off the covers and began to moan quietly

so as not to wake the children. "I'm so hot," she whimpered. "It's so hot in here."

"It's not hot, Coco. Just calm down, honey. You're okay. If you just calm down a little, we can talk things over."

"I feel sick," she moaned tragically. "I can't think straight."

She began to shake her head back and forth like her mother did when she heard there were Jewish passengers aboard an airplane that had been skyjacked to Cuba.

Gavin got up and hurried around the foot of the bed toward her.

"What's happening?" she mumbled, twisting from her back onto her stomach.

"Coco. What's the matter? Please don't get hysterical again, honey. That doesn't help anything. Don't start thrashing around, sweetheart. You know I love you."

Coco saw fear imprint itself on his face, so she rolled sideways several more times and clawed at the sheets with crazed, unfamiliar-looking fingers.

"Where is she?"

Gavin kept moving back and forth as she assumed different positions on the bed.

"Where is she?" Coco groaned again.

"Who? Who are you looking for, Coco?"

"You know. Her. Her."

"Stop it, Coco. I don't want anymore of this. The kids are going to hear you."

Immediately, Coco decided to decrease her noise to conserve their privacy. She sat straight up on the bed and crossed her legs in a fashion that made her nightgown hunch up around her waist.

"Your girlfriend. Where is she? Is she here in the house?"

"What are you talking about?" Gavin asked wildly. "The kids are going to wake up in a minute. Why are you acting so crazy, Coco?"

"Call the doctor, Gavin. You'd better call the doctor." Her voice predicted an immediate disaster.

"Honey, which doctor? What doctor do you want?"

Coco flattened out again, rolled over to bury her face in the double layer of pillows, and began to cry. "The doctor I need doesn't make house calls, Gavin. I should probably be in a hospital. I need attendants. I should have known you'd leave me. You kept me when I was young and beautiful. You used me up. You took my good years and now you're going to leave me here to rot in this house with all your kids."

"Coco, I'm not leaving you. You were going to leave me. Don't you remember?"

"How could you do it? How could you?" Then she sat up straight again, stiff and rigid. "Well, you'd better tell me who she is, mister!" Coco's voice changed dramatically. "You goddamn well better tell me who the hell she is. Because if you don't tell me in the next two minutes, I'm going to jump out of that window."

Gavin ran his hand across his face, rumpling his nose and upsetting his glasses. "Look, Coco. I'm sorry. I'm so sorry I want to die. I shouldn't have said anything. I really didn't think it would bother you all this much."

Coco looked at him contemptuously while envisioning the imminent invasion of their children. "Please, Gavin, will you take the kids downstairs this morning without letting them come in here? I don't want them to see me like this."

"Sure, Coco."

"And please make the lunches for Mike and Jessica. You can give both of them peanut-butter-and-

jellies. The lunch bags are on top of the bread-box.
And put potato chips in a Baggie for each of them
and give Mike one of those little grape juices in a
plastic bottle. There's a box of them underneath
where I keep the beer. But you have to put in a straw.
There's a box of them in the cupboard where the
cups and saucers are. Oh, fuck. You'll never find everything."

"Don't kid yourself, Coco," Gavin said in a provocative voice that suggested the duties which derailed
women were really very simple. "I'll take care of it."

Coco's throat tightened in rage. "And I also don't
think I should pick up the car pool this afternoon. I'm
too shaky to drive seven kids in the car."

"Okay, so I'll do it."

Coco waited several seconds. "Well, don't you even
want to know where they live so you can take them
to the right houses?"

"I'll find out, Coco. There's seven hours left for me
to find out before I have to do it."

"Well, you'd better call your office and say you
won't be in today."

"I'm going to do that, too, Coco." Gavin wanted to
be out of the bedroom very badly.

"Shit," Coco moaned, feeling guilty about keeping
Gavin home from work. She was already weary of his
passive accommodations and her own nervous
power. "Well, it won't kill you, since you haven't
taken off one sick day this whole fucking year."

"Go back to sleep," Gavin said. He slammed the
door shut behind him as he left the room.

Coco lay in bed and listened to the sounds of her
children waking up—crying, laughing, yelling, slamming drawers, dressing and fighting. Although she
heard the toilet flush three times, there was little
audible action from the sink faucets. After a while

she heard Gavin, obviously weighted down by the baby, clumping heavily on the stairs, followed by the other three children.

That was when Coco went into the bathroom, checked how many toothbrushes had been carelessly left in the sink, and got into the shower. Unfortunately, the hot water hurt the tender spot on the back of her head, so Coco returned to her disheveled bed and surrendered herself to the enormous and real pains that were now flowing through her system. The pain penetrated every part of her body until even the joints of her fingers ached with the knowledge of Gavin's betrayal.

Oh, no, she swore silently to herself.

I will *not* help him make the lunches. I will *not* put Mike's books in a pile with the biggest one on the bottom so he won't drop the little ones. I will *not* wait at the front door to make sure the carpool driver stops on our side of the street so the kids don't have to cross. I will *not* remind Jessica to take a sweater. I will *not* hold the baby while he drinks his bottle. I will *not* play with Nicky until Mrs. Marshall gets here.

LET GAVIN DO IT.

Nervously Coco got up and poured the last swig of cold coffee into her cup. She was craving the distraction of the morning paper but didn't dare start trouble by asking one of the kids to bring it upstairs. She began to pace around the bedroom, looking up in time to catch her naked body stalk past the closet mirror. She was totally focused on the dislocating, diminishing, devastating idea that Gavin no longer found her totally sufficient, that he no longer believed Coco's failures preferable to the positive attributes of another woman who wasn't Coco. The notion that she was no longer indispensable, unexpendable or uninterchangeable—which had

been the basic premise of their marriage—was terri-
fying.

At 8:52 Coco opened her calendar notebook and
looked up Dr. Finkelstein's telephone number. She
had some difficulty fitting her shaking index finger
into the dialing holes and unexpectedly had to clear
her throat when she first heard Dr. Finkelstein's
Brooklyn voice thunder across the wires.

"Dr. Finkelstein?"

"Yes?"

"This is Coco Burman."

"Yes?"

"I was wondering if I could possibly make an appointment to see you."

"Why not?"

"Actually I was wondering if it could be . . . today?"

"Well, let me see. Hmmm. Yes, you're very fortu-
nate, Mrs. Burman. I have a cancellation at three this
afternoon. Could you come in then?"

"Oh, yes, I'll be there. At three. Thank you, Dr.
Finkelstein." Coco hung up the receiver, half-com-
forted and half-distressed at the thought of seeing
Isadore Finkelstein's face again.

Then she sat down at her dressing table, put the
big hair-blowing cap over her head to blow away any
curls that might result from her shower, and left out
one ear while she direct-dialed Chicago.

"Hello, Mother?"

"Yes. What's the matter, Coco? Are the children all
right? How come you're calling in the middle of the
morning? Is something wrong?"

"No, Mother. Everybody's okay. I just felt like talking to you."

"Well, for goodness' sake, you certainly scared me.
Why didn't you just wait until after six o'clock?"

"Because I felt like talking to you *now*, Mother."

"So what's all that noise?"

"I've got the hair dryer on."

"And there's nothing else the matter?"

"No, Mother."

Realizing that she had embarked upon a long conversation, Coco took the wallet out of her purse and began to clean it. One by one, she unfolded all the little registered-mail receipts, old prescription labels from used-up bottles, several two-cent postage stamps left over from a book of eights, a laundry ticket, the refund receipt for a merchandise pickup from Woodward & Lothrop's for $19.95, and several scraps of paper with phony telephone credit-card numbers which she used only in pay-phones.

"What were you doing, Mother?"

"Oh . . . I was just straightening up the apartment. I've got to get dressed early and go over to the club for lunch. You know, I play Maj on Thursday."

"Oh, right, I forgot." Coco flipped through her seventeen credit cards and turned them around so they all faced in the same direction. Then she looked through her checkbook and tried to remember the amounts of checks she had cashed but forgotten to record.

"Are *you* all right, Coco?"

"Well, I don't know," Coco said ominously, staring at the photograph on her driver's license. After a few seconds she decided that municipal mediocrity made her nose look bigger than it actually was. Quickly she added up the points on her license for illegal turns and then replaced it, along with her car-registration, library and social-security cards, behind the section in the wallet where she kept her checkbook.

"You don't sound too good," Coco's mother persisted.

"Well, actually, Mother, Gavin and I had a fight."

"So?"

"I don't know. I was sort of wondering if maybe I should go away for a while."

"Go away? What are you talking about, Coco?"

Inside the pull-out plastic photograph carrier, Coco found a pediatrician's routine-checkup appointment card for Joshua that she had completely forgotten. Thoughtfully she transferred it to the dollar-bill section to statistically increase her odds for noticing it again.

"Actually, to tell you the truth, Mother, there's a woman here in Washington who's a terrible homewrecker and she's been absolutely pursuing Gavin."

"Coco, I don't understand what you're saying. What do you mean? I simply can't believe that Gavin would ever do anything that might hurt you or the children. Do you mean he's involved with this woman in some . . . way? Are you saying that he's been seeing this other woman?"

"Well, I'm not saying that for sure, Mother. But there is that possibility. And that's why I've been thinking about going away for a little while."

Coco began to scrape bobby pins, paper clips, Kleenex balls, pencils, earrings, receipts, safety pins, chewing-gum wrappers, coins and Clorets out from the bottom of her purse. Everything was covered with crumbs and disintegrated aspirin.

"But this is exactly the time in a marriage when a wife simply cannot leave. Not for a minute, darling. You have to stay right there, Coco. I mean, we do know Gavin has a tendency . . . well, he did get carried away over you when he was married the last time. And women who chase after married men— not you, Coco, darling, but *other* women—who chase

after men who are fathers . . . not just husbands
. . . why, women like that would simply *move* right
in if you even so much as went out to the beauty
shop. I know what those women are like, Coco, and
what they're after is your *home.* So you've got to stay
right there to defend your rights and your property."

"But I'm so upset, Mother." Coco sniffed a few
times to indicate emotional pain and tried to unbend
a creased snapshot of her children dangling their feet
in the stream at Rock Creek Park. "And besides, I
haven't got anyone to talk it over with because
Glenda went to South America with her husband for
six weeks."

"Oh? that's nice. On business?"

"Yah."

"But, honey! You can always call *me.* Collect. Just
call me collect. Even in the daytime. Or I'll come to
Washington, Coco. Let's see . . ."

"Oh, no, Mother." Coco left off cleaning now in
order to concentrate. The long-distance line to Chicago was a narrow tightrope wire. If she didn't ade-
quately establish the fact of crisis, her mother would
simply tell her to stop whining, but if she went too
far, Mrs. Silverman could appear within two hours at
National Airport. "It would be awful if Gavin found
out you knew about it, Mother. That would embar-
rass him so much he might do *anything.*"

"Oh, the poor children!" Mrs. Silverman had begun to cry.

"I think I should probably go see a psychiatrist,
Mother." Coco launched her offensive so prema-
turely that she even caught herself off guard. "I
mean, just enough times to find out the best way to
handle this situation so it won't disturb the children."

"A psychiatrist!" Now Mrs. Silverman's voice was
strained by shock. "Oh, now I'm sure you're not tell-

ing me everything, Coco. I've been feeling that right along."

"Oh, Mother." Coco unzipped her plastic cosmetic bag and looked inside. The cap from her tube of eyeshadow had come off and everything was stuck together with globs of Midnight Forest Green. She plucked several tissues out of her sateen-covered purse-size Kleenex holder and began cleaning up. "You really are terribly provincial about psychiatrists, Mother. It doesn't mean there's anything *wrong* with you if you go to one. It's just a way to avoid getting sick. It's like a psychological DPT. For God's sake, Mother, it's a form of *preventive* medicine nowadays."

Because she had emptied out her entire cosmetic bag, Coco was rewarded by finding a new eyelash-curler rubber refill she had forgotten. Instantly she located her slant-edged tweezer and began extracting the old rubber cushion from the curler so that she could insert a fresh new one which would produce a much stronger crease in her lashes.

"I just can't believe any of that's necessary," Mrs. Silverman said.

"Mother. Do you realize how I feel? I'm so humiliated I could die. Don't you know anything about mental health? About preventive mental health?"

"But it's very expensive, Coco. How can you afford it?"

"Well, that's one of the things I'm calling about. Don't I have any of my old Israeli war bonds left?"

"Oh, Coco. You know you used them all up before you got married."

Coco made a little crying noise while she tried using a nail file to squeeze the buoyant rubber refill into the curved ridge where it technically belonged.

"Otherwise I think maybe I should just get a divorce, Mother."

"Oh, now you're talking crazy hysterical talk," Mrs. Silverman said hysterically. "I'm going to hang up and call Daddy at the office and have him call you right back. No marriage is easy, Coco. The best thing is to stay married to your first husband, because a second one is just as bad. And listen. If Daddy's out playing golf, he'll call you early tonight. Just don't do anything until we talk to you again. I told you not to marry a divorced man. They're like alcoholics."

Coco expelled another sob and then hung up the receiver feeling very hopeful about receiving some financial assistance. After she finally finished fixing her eyelash curler, she wiped off her lipstick, Lash-on, Blush-on and mascara, turned off the hair dryer and began to hang up the week's accumulation of clothing heaped around the bedroom. When most of the surfaces were relatively clean, Coco tiptoed down to the second floor to retrieve her briefcase and rushed back to her room to begin grading the first of her 107 blue books. At two o'clock she got dressed, gathered up the furnishings that belonged in her purse, tiptoed out of the house and walked downtown to her psychiatrist's office.

CHAPTER 4

Because she was afraid of self-operating elevators, Coco walked up the three long flights to Dr. Finkelstein's office. The chipped and peeling green-painted walls of the stairwell were depressingly familiar and she felt as if she were going backward in life as she ascended the steps. On the fourth floor she pushed open the fire doors and entered the waiting room like an aging alumna returning to the student union for a homecoming weekend. But beyond the oasis of leatherette furniture Coco could see that Dr. Finkelstein's door was expectantly ajar, so she hurried gratefully toward his office without doing a wait.

"Good afternoon," Dr. Finkelstein said discreetly from his swivel desk chair.

Coco smiled, closed the door, and marched daintily through the Danish-walnut environment to the yellow square in the center of the imported area rug with the Mondrian design much favored by area shrinks. From that position she could first sit, and then lie, down on the couch without seeing Dr. Finkelstein's face again. Once safe in her customary position—flat on her back—her head on a pillow protectively covered with a fresh paper doily, Coco spoke to the ceiling.

"Well, here I am again."

"Yes. So I see."

She listened to the sound of Dr. Finkelstein's chair scraping as he moved away from his rolltop desk—an old-fashioned accent amidst his modern furniture— to the invisible armchair located behind the couch where Coco lay.

"Well, I bet you thought you'd never see me again," Coco said flirtatiously to the doctor via the Amazon River cracking its way across the ceiling.

"*You* thought that, Mrs. Burman," Dr. Finkelstein corrected her. "I didn't. Unfortunately, I never arrived at such an optimistic prognosis. I, of course, thought there was still a great deal more work to be done."

That was silencing. For a man who had barely escaped being a proctologist—his second specialty— Dr. Finkelstein had a very smug attitude.

"Well . . . anyway," Coco continued, magnanimously forgiving Dr. Finkelstein his limitations once again, "you'll never believe what's happening to me now."

"Mrs. Burman, I would believe *anything* that you told me happened to you."

Coco began to feel sorry for herself. Now that she was back in Dr. Finkelstein's office—like an insecure Ph.D. doing postgraduate work, she felt oppressed by his Dr. Marcus Welby rendition of Sigmund Freud. Upset, yet convinced that she needed psycho-

logical support to sustain her through the shoals of
Gavin's love affair and the ordeal of writing an important novel, Coco decided to ignore Dr. Finkelstein's negligible sensitivities and simply utilize his
technical skills.

"As a matter of fact, doctor, if it weren't for what
happened last night, I would probably never have
come back here again."

"Oh? What, exactly, happened?" Dr. Finkelstein
asked. Lacking any sense of humor or imagination,
he disliked vagueness and kept up an insistent demand for details.

"Well, last night Gavin told me that he's been having an affair and it sort of sounded a little bit like
maybe he was falling in love. Oh, I don't know. I can
hardly believe it. And besides that, he won't even tell
me who she is. And if he won't tell me who she is, I
know I will probably go stark raving mad. Like in
Gaslight. Because if he thinks I'm going to go around
town not knowing if I'm sitting next to his girlfriend
at a dinner party or not, he's crazy." Coco began to
cry. "But it's also going to drive *me* crazy and I won't
be able to do anything all summer except try to find
out who she is and then I won't be able to write my
book, which is what I've decided to do."

"The fact you feel badly about Gavin having an
affair would seem to substantiate my theory that you
really do care about him . . . despite the fact you
feel compelled to deny that possibility year after
year."

Coco cried louder. Dr. Finkelstein's name and syn-
tax had always bothered her, undermining any hope
that his mysterious healing arts could override his
cultural and chauvinistic handicaps.

"Oh, God, why did this have to happen?" Coco was

weeping steadily now. "Everything was going along just fine. It was almost perfect."

"Had you stopped having all those screaming fights and threatening to divorce him?"

"No."

Pause.

"So why do you say things were just fine?"

Pause. "Because we were used to all that. It was . . . part of our relationship."

"In other words, the same old stuff was still going on?"

"Yes. But everything was really okay, Dr. Finkelstein. Until this happened."

"So, in actuality, we're back where we started from," Dr. Finkelstein grumbled. "And things are still haaaaappening to you." He elongated the word indefinitely. "Things are still haaaaappening to you and you don't know why. You, of course, are still not accountable for yourself or your own destiny. You, of course, are still not responsible for what haaaaappens. Do you still believe it is *fate*, Mrs. Burman, that causes these things to haaaaappen to you?"

"But it's true, Dr. Finkelstein. Nothing's any different between me and Gavin now than it ever was. So how can it be my fault if some girl latches onto him right at this moment? How can I be to blame?"

"And it just haaaaappens that men fall in love with you. . . ."

"But they don't anymore," Coco sobbed. "Honestly, I haven't cheated on Gavin since the last time I saw you."

"Me?" Dr. Finkelstein squealed.

"I don't mean with *you*, Dr. Finkelstein, I just meant—"

"Don't you see, Mrs. Burman, that you are persisting in the same old pattern? Like, it just haaappened that you got married before you *meant* to get married."

"But that's true. That was in 1960. Girls still *had* to get married back then. You know, I had to get married so I wouldn't waste all my time being afraid that I wouldn't get married. I mean, you know how it used to be. I told you that before I got married, I never finished one whole Russian novel, not one, because I was so anxious I couldn't remember anyone's name. I mean, you know I was so anxiety-ridden that I couldn't memorize the Great Vowel Shift. And there were only five vowels. On account of my anxiety."

Dr. Finkelstein didn't respond, but continued with his own rap. "It just haaaappens that you have had ten different jobs in ten years, that you've lived in a dozen different houses, that your maids quit every few weeks, that you have children you didn't *mean* to have . . ."

"Nicky was the druggist's fault, Dr. Finkelstein. You remember that. He gave me the wrong size diaphragm. You remember. I told you how I was really a seventy but my gynecologist made a sloppy zero that looked like a five."

"That a four-year-old girl is still wetting the bed . . ."

"No. No, she's five and a half now, and she's stopping. I meant to tell you. I mean, I couldn't very well drop you a postcard to say that Jessica has definitely slowed down in the enuresis department, but I really wanted to let you know that she's gotten much better. In fact, she hasn't done it in several weeks now."

"Ahhh, Mrs. Burman. It is hard to believe that such things as happen to you could haaaappen to anyone. Unless, of course, the person *wanted* them to happen."

Coco munched on her bottom lip. "Do you really think I want Jessica to wet her bed, Dr. Finkelstein? Is that what you really think?"

"I'm not sure what I think, Mrs. Burman, because I haven't been thinking about it much during the last few years."

"Well, I didn't expect you to think about it when I wasn't coming here, but you should think about it now," Coco said in a firm voice she never could have used before her consciousness had been raised. "Because this is obviously a case for some crisis intervention. I've come back here for crisis intervention because I'm terribly upset about this crisis I'm having. Believe me, doctor, I wouldn't start in on this all over again if I wasn't really *very upset.* I mean, I've got a hundred and seven lousy final examinations to read before next Tuesday."

Dr. Finkelstein didn't answer. He made no sound at all. Coco captured a small but satisfying piece of dry flaky skin off her bottom lip, pulverized it between her teeth, and decided that Dr. Finkelstein was in a bad mood because it was Thursday and he had had a long week. A long profitable week. Coco should have known better than to take a Thursday appointment. It was just more bad luck to have a reunion with her shrink when he was so tired that his inflections, right from the start, had been unguardedly Brooklynesque.

Silence.

She decided to wait him out. She twisted her wrist, sneaked a look at her watch over the tip of her left nipple, and wondered if poor Dr. Finkelstein was bitter because he never got to see anything but laid-out-flattened boobs. Thoughtfully Coco crossed her ankles so that the better pedicured toes on her right foot were exposed on top and then leaned slightly to one side so that her left breast ganged up on her right breast producing, for Dr. Finkelstein, what had to be an attractive line of cleavage in the scooped neckline of her navy-blue cotton sundress.

But by 3:18, convinced that crisis-intervention did not entitle a doctor to the reprieves of classical analytic silence, Coco began to feel angry about the money and time Dr. Finkelstein was wasting. She was also distressed at having reverted to the pre-lib-ploy of cleavage production to amuse and cajole Dr. Finkelstein out of his sulk. Coco's regressive show-of-tits tactic, simply because she felt nervous and uptight, clearly undermined her militant commitment to the sexual revolution. A post-lib lady succumbing to such a pre-lib number clearly demonstrated that her prerevolutionary habits had not been completely purged.

Instantly Coco shifted back into a flat position, magically withdrawing her offer.

"Well," she prompted impatiently, "what do you think I should do?"

"About what?" Dr. Finkelstein asked in an uninterested tone of voice.

"About Gavin's having an affair. About his doing this now when the issues are clearly different, when it's no longer a question of getting laid anymore. Now is the time when all decent men are getting involved in the real complexities of family living. No one's cruising around picking up women these days. That's all finished. That shit is old-fashioned. It's obsolete and irrelevant because that's not where it's at anymore. And the fact that Gavin's having an affair *now* . . . I mean, it's like buying a Model T Ford. It's just a counterrevolutionary hostile thing to do. It's just a dirty male-chauvinist effort to discredit the entire women's-liberation movement and everything it stands for. Maybe you haven't noticed lately but no-body talks about men screwing their secretaries any-more. The real question now is how secretaries can stop being exploited by managerial chauvinists so they don't do all the shit-work in the office. And that's why I don't know what to do about Gavin's affair."

"Well, what do *you* think you should do?"

Coco dug her fingernails into the palm of her hand. "Dr. Finkelstein, you are giving me my old kind of headache that's just over the left eye and no place else. If all I'm going to get from you is a headache—I don't need to come back here, you know. I can get headaches at home. For free. I mean, coming back here after two years is like getting sent back to kin-dergarten after high school. I mean, I was finished, remember?"

Silence.

"Wasn't I?"

"Well. You stopped coming, Mrs. Burman."

"Yes, but not until after five years, Dr. Finkelstein. Five long years."

"That's true."

"Actually, Dr. Finkelstein," Coco said, noticing that she had stopped crying during the time she felt most angry at him, "if I could just get Gavin to tell me who this girl is, what her name is, and what she does, then I wouldn't really care anymore, and I could stop thinking about it and get down to work. Since I won't be teaching any summer-session sections"—she said the last three words very slowly, so as not to make a slip and say "sex-ion" like she usually did—"I'm free to just concentrate on my novel. I'm planning to finish the whole book this summer. And then, after I'm finished with it, I can decide what to do. That's really why I called you up this morning. I think if we discuss what I should do—while I'm writing my novel

—then when it's finished I'll know what I should do after that. And, Dr. Finkelstein, this time I'm really going to try to remember everything that you say each session. That is, if you'll let me come back again. I mean, I won't forget everything you say the minute I walk out of the office anymore."

"Hmmmmmmmmm."

"But what we really have to figure out is why Gavin chose this time, this particular time in my life, when I really felt on top of things, to have an affair. It certainly sounds hostile to me. And the other thing that's flipping me out is why anyone would want to have an affair with Gavin anyway. I mean, anyone who would want to sleep with him must be either very hard up or have some ulterior motive—like wanting to marry him or something. And I think that's what's making me upset. I think if we discussed that, I'd be able to get a grip on myself."

"I seem to remember that you had an affair with your husband, Mrs. Burman," Dr. Finkelstein said in his cunning voice.

"You mean before we got married?"

"Yes."

"Well, yes, but I was only twenty then."

"Well, maybe that's how old his new girlfriend is."

"What?" And then Coco started to cry again. "Oh, God. Twenty? These damn young girls . . . these hippies . . . what do they know about anything except how to make bread? What do they know?"

"And remember, Mrs. Burman, you married Gavin *after* you had your affair. He left his wife and married you."

"Well, for God's sake, Dr. Finkelstein, I know that," Coco panted. "Don't you think I see the pattern? Can't I see the handwriting on the wall? Why do you think I'm so nervous?"

Dr. Finkelstein cleared his throat.

"If you can remember, Mrs. Burman, at one point we agreed that there must have been some reason you chose Gavin for a husband. Try to remember. If you recall, we tried very hard to find out how your marriage *happened* to you. And maybe if we clarified that again, right now—today—it would throw a little light on why you feel so anxious about the possibility that someone else might want to marry him."

Coco stared up at the ceiling and felt her mind go blank and aimless. Since she couldn't think of the right answer, she decided to take the offensive.

"Listen, Dr. Finkelstein. To be honest with you, I'm getting the feeling that you're a little hostile toward me. And since I can probably guess the reason, maybe I should explain to you why I stopped coming here. I mean, I really did feel guilty about it and I wanted to write you a long letter to explain, but it was so complicated I couldn't have gotten it all down on paper."

"Uh-huh."

"You see, let's see, well, I guess it was exactly two years ago this very month. It was June, wasn't it, when I quit coming? Because I remember it was about two months after I joined the Columbia Road Local Women's Liberation Consciousness Raising Group. I mean, I joined it in March and by June I was pretty converted."

"I see."

"And, well, during a couple of the sessions, I mean the consciousness-raising sessions, we discussed psychiatry and how it was one of the methods used to keep women oppressed. We decided that when psychiatrists try to make a female patient feel better, what they're actually doing is trying to make her adapt and adjust to her own exploited condition. And if the female condition—historically as well as currently—is exploitative, then psychiatrists are in collusion with our whole paternalistic culture."

"I see," said Dr. Finkelstein.

"I mean, if you found an enslaved race of people in some far-off continent, you wouldn't start giving them therapy to make them feel happily adjusted to their slavery, would you, doctor? Wouldn't you really join with them in their struggle for liberation? And also you have only to look at all the new novels that have been coming out, like *Up the Sandbox* and *Walking Papers.* Did you read *Up the Sandbox*, doctor?"

"Mrs. Burman. Are you sure you want to discuss women's liberation rather than your own problems?" Dr. Finkelstein asked in a neutral voice.

"But see"—one of Coco's knees jerked upward in exasperation, just as if she'd been given a Babinsky test—"that's just what I'm trying to show you. And I'm not trying to be a smart-ass now. But that's exactly the point. Maybe my problems aren't *peculiar* to me. Maybe all women like me have *exactly* the same problems. Maybe we're *not* all neurotic, although maybe some of us are, but maybe we've gotten to be this way because of cultural and societal and political reasons. So maybe we're not really *crazy* if we feel rebellious."

"Ummmmmmmm."

Coco had long ago decided that Dr. Finkelstein's intellectual limitations should not, theoretically, hamper his technical therapeutic services. But she bitterly resented his slowness when she had to pay for the time it took to further his education.

"Oh, I don't know," she said impatiently. "Haven't you read any of the literature? I mean, didn't you even see Germaine Greer on the *Dick Cavett Show?*

If you don't keep up with the news, please don't act like I'm paranoid if I mention society. And don't forget that the reason men oppress women is because they're oppressed, too, by the alienating kinds of jobs they have which obviously screw them up and also fuck up their other relationships. I mean, that would seem to be true, wouldn't it?"

"You clearly believe what you're saying," Dr. Finkelstein conceded.

Suddenly Coco began to cry again. "Jesus, I'm sorry. I didn't mean to lecture you, Dr. Finkelstein. You really did help me a lot when I was coming here, but I simply wanted to tell you why I quit two years ago."

"Yes, Mrs. Burman. But now you're back."

"Yes, I know, Dr. Finkelstein, but that's because I flipped out over a particular thing. I'm having a crisis and I need some intervention. Because I have really been functioning fairly well since I last saw you. At least, up until now. I haven't been hysterical very often until last night when Gavin told me"—Coco's sobs began picking up momentum—"that he was having an affair. And that didn't seem fair to me because, well, I'm not having one and, after all, that's how we got married—from an adulterous affair. I mean, he was the adulterer, I wasn't, and I don't have anybody in love with me now, and there's no reason I shouldn't if he does, except that if you had four kids and four sections of freshman English and a big house and a billion-zillion things to do, you wouldn't have the time either. And also I really feel extra badly because feminism really has become very important to me and helped me put men into some kind of perspective that I never had before. You know, I used to gear my whole life around men, Dr. Finkelstein. Either Gavin or some other man on the side. And I used to dress up for them and be amusing for them and wait for them and look for them and want to be with them all the time. But now I understand how I got that way and how distortive it was and how it took away my own dignity. Now I feel more at peace with myself than I ever did before. Now I don't need a man to define who I am and I don't have to make myself be who they want me to be. But now that Gavin has done this, has started whoring around, it's put me back. . . . It's like I'm being held back a grade. I finally got over men being the most important things in my life and now Gavin has started all this sex-love business again, so I'm back in the same old bag. It's the whole bit all over. I mean, now I'm going to regress back to where I spend all my time thinking about men so that my own life gets fucked up. And I just haven't been liberated long enough to have made something of myself in the meantime. I mean, that damn American University is still only paying me $7,490 after seven years of teaching! I mean, is that equality? Is that job opportunities for women for you?"

Coco breathed deeply and looked over toward the Aztec Indian Kleenex box by the empty chair where patients who actually got promoted (instead of dropping out) could sit in an upright position. But then it occurred to Coco that graduating patients probably didn't have to cry very much anymore, so it was clearly very hostile of Dr. Finkelstein to locate the fucking Kleenex where it wasn't even needed.

Dr. Finkelstein didn't make any response.

Surreptitiously Coco turned her head a little. Dr. Finkelstein's eyelids were lowered. He was either looking at his notebook or sleeping.

"Dr. Finkelstein?"

"Yes?"

"What I'm really afraid of . . . well, I know I always sort of act a little bit crazy, but this time I'm afraid that I might really flip out. Like that time I was involved with Jeffrey. That corporate executive in natural gas? Remember Jeffrey?"

"I'm afraid it's time, Mrs. Burman."

Coco checked her watch. It was 3:49.

"We'll have to stop now," Dr. Finkelstein said. "We can continue on Monday. I have eight o'clock free all this month on Monday, Wednesday and Friday. Will that be all right?"

"Oh, yes, thank you, Dr. Finkelstein."

Coco got up and wiggled her thighs a little to release the crotch of her panties which had crept up between her buttocks. Then, noticing Dr. Finkelstein watching her curiously, she said good-bye and marched across the office and out through the doorway.

CHAPTER 5

Coco took a taxi home because she was tired, frustrated, hungry and convinced that taxis functioned as semicolons between parts of the day and she very much wanted to put a punctuation mark after her highly unsatisfactory return to therapy. When she reached home, she let herself inside very quietly, stood in the hallway long enough to ascertain the whereabouts of Gavin and the children, and then glided up the staircase to her bedroom without being caught. But the moment she flung herself down on the bed, the telephone on her dressing table started to ring and she had to get up to answer it.

"Hello."

"Coco?"

"Oh, Daddy. Hi." She waited a second to see if Gavin would pick up another extension, but there was no tell-tale click. "How are you, Daddy?"

"Fine, sugar. But how are you?"

"Oh, just fair." And then Coco began to cry, sound-lessly releasing soft sweet strokes of tears that slid down her cheeks like warm puffs of baby breath when Joshua put his mouth near her face.

"What's happening, sugar?"

Somewhere along the North Shore of Lake Michigan, Morrie Silverman was looking out of a glass building at a Great Lake that he viewed as his own Little Pond while preparing to tackle his daughter's problems with speed and efficiency.

"Oh, Daddy, nothing, really. I'm just sort of feeling uptight. You know, Gavin and I are sort of having some problems."

"Yes. That's what Mother said. But what the hell's really going on up there?" Mr. Silverman didn't like to wait for taxis, waiters, information, airplanes, ex-planations, salesclerks, answers, operators or break-fast. "Has . . . Gavin been seeing someone else, honey?"

"Yes. Yes he has, Daddy."

"Hell. Well, what do you want to do about it?" Mr. Silverman, the most successful prize-fight promoter in Chicago, had no patience for the indiscretions of anyone outside his immediate family—which did not include in-laws.

"I don't know yet, Daddy."

"Son-of-a-gun." Mr. Silverman paused incredu-lously for a moment. "Well, is it serious?"

"I don't think so, Daddy. But I do know he's been—"

"All right, sugarplum," he interrupted, clearly not wanting to hear the details. The Silvermans had never totally accepted Gavin because he had been married once before—to a shiska. "I think what we should do is wait a few days to see what develops. If he's ready to behave himself and act decently, then you should let him. But if he's going to keep it up, he'd better pack his stuff and get out of there, because it won't do you or the kids any good having a man around who can't keep his pecker in his pants."

Coco smiled at herself in the mirror as salty tears washed her face.

"What you've got to do is keep a cool head on your shoulders, sugarplum. Check out the situation so you've got a bead on it, and then we'll talk again in a couple of days to see whether or not he intends to shape up."

"All right, Daddy."

"How are the children?"

"Oh, they're fine, Daddy. We bought Mikey a two-wheeler a couple of weeks ago."

"You don't let him ride in the streets around there, do you, honey?"

"No. He just rides on the sidewalk or over at the park."

"You know, I think maybe you should send them all out here for a couple weeks. Maybe not the baby, just the big ones."

"Well, I think I better wait to see what's going to happen, Daddy. Anyway, I told the university that I couldn't teach there this summer."

"Why's that?"

"Oh, I don't know. I just feel too uptight and done in. I'm terribly tired and I think I'd rather hang around the house this summer and get things straightened away with Gavin and everything. You know?"

"Sure, sugarplum. But are you going to keep the schwartza?"

"Oh, Daddy. Please. Please don't call her that."

"Well? Are you going to?"

"Yes."

"So how are you going to pay for her? And what's this Mother said that you wanted to go to a psychiatrist? What's the matter with you? Are you nuts or something? You know how I feel about psychiatrists."

"Yes, I know, Daddy."

"Please, sugarplum, don't start in with all that crap. I'll just send you out a check to help you get back on your feet. How's that?"

"Oh, that *would* be nice, Daddy."

"But don't you spend it on any psychiatrist. You hear me, Coco?"

"Okay, Daddy."

"You buy yourself a couple new dresses or something. Or take the kids out to a nice restaurant for dinner a couple nights and give yourself a vacation from cooking."

"I will, Daddy. Okay. Thank you. Have you been feeling all right?"

"Sure. Why shouldn't I? But you take care of yourself, sugar, and make sure you're eating enough."

"Okay, Daddy. And tell Mother not to worry."

"We'll be talking to you soon. Kiss the kids for me."

Click.

Coco changed tactics that night because while she was in the bathroom waiting for Nicky to put his entire naval fleet through their war maneuvers (after reading the terrible bathtub tragedy in *Rabbit, Run*, Coco never left any child alone in the tub) she had time to put on makeup. Then, later on, when Mike came into her bedroom to talk, she hid behind her closet door and wiggled into her favorite white T-shirt dress. (Coco's 11:00 M-W-F had read *Oedipus* during spring semester which made her super-wary of seducing her eldest son.) So on the basis of having had time to repair herself while getting the kids to bed, Coco decided to lay some sugar on Gavin instead of vinegar. She paid Mike a quarter to read Jessica and Nicky two chapters out of *Babar* (unfortunately, they were each in different parts of the book) and feeling potentially sexy, hurried back downstairs where Gavin was watching the network news.

Coco set up an elaborate stage in the dining room for her evening performance. She arranged fake flowers in a vase on the table, put out her best orange linen napkins, liberated one of the last bottles of white wine from the broom closet, splurged on glass goblets (which couldn't be put in the dishwasher), supervised the box of Uncle Ben's wild rice absorbing water on the stove and several times finger-tasted the chicken Kiev that Mrs. Marshall had boned, seasoned and baked. Finally Coco tossed a self-consciously stylized salad, with three kinds of lettuce (excluding boycotted iceberg) and then, feeling supercompetent, summoned Gavin into her supper-club theater.

While serving the food, Coco mentally reviewed her menu of conversation topics. After Gavin had punctured his chicken so that the tarragon-flavored sweet butter blurted out over his shirt, Coco gently provided him with a damp paper towel from the kitchen. Then she sat down and began to chat disarmingly. Like a guerrilla directing enemy attention away from a strategic site about to be sabotaged, Coco asked Gavin about several of his current cases, particularly the class action being brought by the D.C. 10,000—who were suing the police department for brutality during the May Day demonstration.

After passing Gavin some oven-hot butterfly rolls, Coco mentioned that the City Council was considering the enactment of a curfew for anyone under sixteen. With *Youth Wants to Know* ingenuity, Coco asked if such a regulation might be unconstitutional. Since Gavin's great passion was constitutional law, Coco felt she had scored several points by having found a constitutional issue in the Metro Section of the *Washington Post*.

Over salad and their third glass of wine, Coco casually mentioned various sorts of summer vacations, one with the children and one without, probably during the later part of August. Gavin strained to seem pleased and contributed two exotic vacation-spot suggestions which were fairly imaginative but which made him look sick, since he hated to travel. For dessert, Coco produced some instant Jell-O Chocolate Whip which she casually called mousse and served in small earthenware pudding cups.

Gavin, impressed by the friendly conversation and eager to believe in Coco's miraculous resurrection as a self-controlled, self-restrained wife, smiled happily. At frequent intervals he sent Coco loving looks down the long table above the tops of the candles, the now-empty wine bottle and the tall fake flowers. Partially drunk, he was able to convince himself that Coco somehow—for some reason—had, during the afternoon away from home, forgiven him his indiscretion, forsaken her hysteria, forgotten her excessive outrage at his semiconfessed peccadillo and come to understand how, in many ways, she was responsible for pushing him into adultery.

After finishing his second cup of coffee, Gavin leaned back, peered through the dim light and said, "Tonight we're going to go to bed early." He cleared his throat. "I don't think we slept more than two or three hours last night."

Coco finished her last glass of *blanc de blanc,* smiled in a manner which made her eyes glisten, and

chose an appropriate opener against her now defused and disarmed enemy.

"I saw Dr. Finkelstein today," she announced casually.

Gavin's head jerked up as his eyes went on alert.
Dr. Finkelstein meant trouble to him either in the
original or in translation.

"Already? He saw you already?"

"Yes. He had a cancellation this afternoon."

"Oh. So that's where you were."

It was strange that this was the remark which triggered her anger. Coco sipped a little empty air from
the bottom of her wine goblet and felt her lips
tighten with rage. "Oh? Were you wondering where
I was, Gavin?" An edge of ice crept into her voice.
"Did you feel a little uncomfortable stuck at home
while I was off wandering around in the big outside
world?"

Gavin set his small features into a miniature wall of
resistance. "Oh, so we're going to get into it now,
huh? I was feeling pretty good since that was the first
decent dinner you've fixed in months, and now we're
going to have to hear all about it again, huh?"

"Well, what did you expect, darling?" Coco murmured. "The car key and my Diner's Club card to
charge your hotel bill?"

Gavin pushed his chair away from the table.
"Look. Don't start in again. I can't stand any more
hysteria. I mean it, Coco. I can't take any more of
that. It makes me sick to my stomach. That talk
doesn't go anywhere and it doesn't settle anything.
It's fucking counterproductive."

"Well, what did you think, Gavin?" Coco asked
again in the same flat voice as before. "Did you think
it was all right for ipsy-bipsy to go fucking around
while I worked full time with a hundred and seven

freshmen—freshmen shipped here from Long Island
—who—"

Gavin stood up, blew out the candles, and walked
quickly out of the dining room.

Coco piled the leftover food onto the serving platter, pushed it into the middle of the table where
Happy couldn't reach it, and then ran into the den.
Gavin was lying down on the couch, so Coco folded
herself into the green corduroy armchair near the
television set.

"Dr. Finkelstein thought if you made a clean
breast of things, if you told me everything I want to
know, it would help me get over it quicker."

"You're a fucking liar," Gavin said without looking
up. "No decent psychiatrist would ever say anything
like that."

"How would you know, Gavin? You're too good to
go to a shrink, aren't you?" Coco pulled hard on her
cigarette, happy now that the enemy had been engaged and the battle begun. "You're the only man in
the world who leaves a perfectly fine first wife to
marry someone else without ever going to see a
shrink to find out why you did it."

"Oh, keep quiet," Gavin began. "Just forget it."

"Forget what, Gavin? Forget that you've got a girlfriend?" She paused. "Actually, maybe I could forget
it if you would just tell me how it was."

"How what was?"

The ten-o'clock anchormen were trying vainly to
capture Coco's attention with a come-on series of
international crises.

"It," she said.

"It?"

"I mean, with her."

"Oh, Coco. Please. I'm not going to talk about that.
If I tell you anything, you get hysterical and, besides,

there's no reason to talk about it. It's all over. It's done. I wouldn't have even mentioned it if it was still going on." Gavin pulled the big pillow from beneath his head and placed it on his stomach as he began watching the news.

Coco went into the kitchen, made herself a gin-and-tonic, and then returned to the television room.

"Really, Gavin, I wish I *could* stop thinking about it," she said melodramatically, standing near the couch and half-watching to see what the late movie would be. "If you just tell me everything, once and for all, then I'll be satisfied. I promise I won't talk or ask about it ever again." She smiled alluringly, although she couldn't tell if Gavin was looking at her or the television. "I mean, maybe if you and Ann had been able to talk about *me*, your marriage wouldn't have broken up."

Coco returned to the green corduroy chair, sat down with her legs tucked neatly beneath her, and began again. "You know, I really don't like to feel like a dentist extracting teeth, one detail at a time. That really freaks me out. I mean, all day today I've been wondering what restaurants you went to or if you ever bought her a present or if she wore a nightgown or if she's prettier than me or how old she is. All that kind of stuff. That's the kind of stuff I want to know, Gavin."

"Look," Gavin said, drumming time on the pillow with his fingertips, "I know what I said hurt you, honey, but I've promised that I'll never see her again. Trust me now. I never gave a damn about her and I swear I'll never touch another woman ever again. But you've got to knock off the hysteria or you're going to drive me out of my mind—not to mention out of the house!" Then he turned to study the credits for *Splendor in the Grass* over the tops of his shoes which protruded several inches past the end of the couch.

"All I really want to know is how I failed you, Gavin." Coco smiled with sincerity and love. "I just want to know when it all started, so that I'll know where I was coming from then. Even Dr. Finkelstein says it's healthy for me to want to know. Just tell me the times. I don't mean the exact number of times. Just the dates . . . approximately."

"Look," Gavin said in a hard voice, "I'm not going to talk about it anymore. Now knock it off because I want to watch this movie. I never saw it before."

"Listen, you son-of-a-bitch," Coco hissed. "You're going to tell me tonight or I'm going to call David Kaplan tomorrow morning and start the filthiest divorce this city has ever seen. I'll ruin you and I'll ruin your precious little law firm and I'll tear your fucking world down on your head."

There was silence. For a while both of them watched Natalie Wood suffering the persecutions of a small, bigoted town. That was when Coco began to consider the public implications of Gavin's extramarital lovelife.

"You know, Gavin, the more I think about it, the more I'm positive that everyone in Washington must know about you and her. I must be the laughingstock of the city. Me. The big women's-lib lady. I've got a husband who's fucking some hippie all over town."

"Oh, Coco. Nobody knows. I can assure you of that."

In the mystical blue light of the television, Gavin looked a little desperate.

"How do you know nobody knows? How do you know who's seen you? How do you know she's not going around town telling everybody?"

"I can assure you that's not the case."

Coco's blood ran as hot as fuel heated for a missile launch. "But how can you defend her?" she asked pitifully, walking around the room now, wild with rage and self-pity. "Why should you think she has any integrity? Why shouldn't she talk? She's got nothing to lose. She's in love with you, isn't she?"

Silence.

"Well? Is she in love with you or isn't she?"

Gavin shrugged his bony shoulders in a particularly provocative way that made Coco advance threateningly toward the sofa.

"Well, you must be very happy now that you've ruined my life." She decided against throwing her drink in his face because she was too upset to make a fresh one. "I just know that all my friends know," she said in a weepy voice. "I'll bet you made me lose all my friends."

"Well, what if somebody else does know?" Gavin asked very rationally. "We know plenty of things about other people."

"That's not the point, Gavin. It's awful knowing other people know something about me that they don't think I know. It makes me feel pathetic. I mean, if they think I don't know, they must all feel sorry for me. But if I know that they know that I know, then I won't feel so bad."

Coco paused thoughtfully as she considered her public relations. Then deciding that the only way to re-establish any social equilibrium was to let out the word that she too knew about Gavin's affair, she lifted her heavily weighted purse off the floor, took out her calendar notebook and opened it to the address/telephone numbers section which was her Dictionary of Permanent Friends.

Just last year Coco had relegated all temporary relationships, medical personnel, Movement offices, neighbors, business establishments, friends of the children, small appliance repair shops and babysitters to the beatup old tablet in the kitchen so that she could keep the addresses/telephone numbers section of her calendar notebook uncontaminated. Now it was exclusively used only for those people who remained eternally important to her—either as friends or as enemies. These eighty-six names (and constantly changing addresses) constituted the select audience for whom Coco played out her life and, unspeakably weak as it was, everything which she did was to please, provoke, annoy or challenge this small group of people whose opinions mattered desperately to her and with whom she lived in constant league or competition.

"My reputation is ruined," she said flatly. "You know second wives are terribly vulnerable just because we're all second choices to start with—we're just second-best second-class citizens. But if you have a mistress, how do you think I look? Well I'll tell you how I look, like a fat Jewish mother! Why should I even try to stay thin if you can make me look fat just by screwing somebody else?"

Gavin smiled. "You're out-of-it, Coco. You know you've never been skinnier."

"Really, Gavin, being fat is not just physical. What other people think doesn't matter. If a person thinks she's fat then she feels fat." Coco tore a sheet out of her clean-paper section, fumbled blindly through her purse until she captured a pen, and then began to work on a list of FRIENDS WHO SHOULD HEAR IT FROM ME. "Right here in the middle of Washington," she mumbled, "so everybody I know can laugh at me! I can't believe this."

Suddenly it occurred to Coco that Gavin—just like Richard Messinger in *Such Good Friends*—might

very well have been sleeping with one of Coco's Pre-
Lib Friends of Permanent Interest or even a C.R.
Sister rather than a passing-fancy-type person whose
name would only appear—if at all—in the kitchen
tablet. Coco's hand shook as she deposited that horror in her bank of suspicions.

"Why did you do this to me, Gavin?" she asked
solemnly, with genuine curiosity.

"Because you don't love me."

A shock of surprise shot upward through her body.
Coco looked over at Gavin and for the first time felt
sorry about the campaign she was waging. She sometimes suspected that her instinct for malice was
somewhat overdeveloped and that she was perhaps
too hard on her husband, although she could hardly
say that she loved him at a time such as this. She was
much too hurt to talk about love—to bring up such an
intimate and sensitive subject at a time like this. Quietly she sank back into the green armchair to watch
the movie.

An hour later, just as Natalie Wood waved goodbye
to Warren Beatty, Coco started to feel a little romantic and decided that it was best for Gavin to deposit
his sperm in her bank at home rather than carry it
around all over town like so much loose change in the
bottom of his pocket. Resolutely, with a seductive
motion, she unraveled herself from the chair and
walked over to the couch.

Gavin raised his eyes from the television, visibly
startled by Coco leaning over him, and involuntarily
lifted one arm above his face in a gesture of self-
protection.

"Oh, Gavin," Coco said achingly, "I wasn't going to
hit you."

And at that moment, stricken by his defensive motion, Coco silently conceded that she had a lot of

feeling for her husband who was, after all, probably
her best friend—even better than Glenda. And
though he failed her frequently, Coco still felt it
would be sort of nice to ball a little right there on the
couch in their gently air-cooled TV room, with the
test pattern blinking on the telly, because practice
had made him perfect in all the secondary sex skills.
Ever since they met, Gavin had been supercoopera-
tive about sex and did everything he possibly could to
please Coco. Indeed, he never kissed her on the
mouth in the morning because she believed her af-
ter-sleep breath was a major source of pollution and
had decided long ago that the politest thing she could
do, if she consented to a pre-breakfast quickie, was
press her lips tightly together so no bad smell could
seep out.

But besides his cooperativeness about bad breath,
Gavin was a great and artistic crotch man. And here
again he was in secret league with Coco because,
embarrassingly enough (indeed, she never even
admitted it during the most passionately intimate
Columbia Road Local Consciousness Raising Group
sessions), Coco was and always would be a vaginal
orgasm person. Now that the entire American Left
had swallowed the there-is-no-vaginal-orgasm propaganda and diplomatically refused to recognize any
but the clitoral kind, Coco felt politically discredited
and sexually reactionary. Because there was no doubt
that she got her orgasms deep within the hallowed
halls of her vagina—wonderful multiple vaginal orgasms—optimally six in a row. And though Coco un-
derwent vigorous, rigorous self-criticism, there was
no arguing her way out of those thunderous contractions deep inside her, no matter how unfashionable
they had become.

So Gavin politely and sweetly bypassed the now

well-acclaimed clit and was digging marvelously
away with several (she had, after all, had four kicking,
squalling babies) fingers inside of her. Coco had once
read a remarkable article in the *Washington Post*
about a man standing trial for pulling out a woman's
womb, doing just what Gavin was doing right now,
although if Coco remembered correctly, the newspaper had called it mutual masturbation. The man,
luckily, got a suspended sentence because the judge
said it was in the heat of passion. And right now, Coco
could clearly understand such a Gallic ruling, because right then Gavin was beating time and batting
away at the marvelous walls of the Hollow Tunnel
that ran right up the center of her. And it really felt
terrific.

And that was how Coco came, or at least one of the
two possible ways. Because while those fingers were
thumping madly, she simply began tripping to some
upbeat feeling that moved ponderously along until
the pleasure burst out into rather glorious contractions. 1-2-3-4-5-6-getting weaker-7-oh-8-ah-yes.

And next it was Gavin's turn and though sometimes he went in for some grotesque gymnastics—
junior-high-school positions that made Coco feel positively ridiculous with one ankle hooked over the top
of the dresser while she concentrated (hurry up,
please) on not falling (hurry up, please, it must be
time)—tonight Gavin went missionary instead of na-
tive and simply plunked down flat on top of her,
probably because the couch was rather narrow.

And that was when Coco got bored. Because even
though Gavin was as good a screw as anyone else she
knew, married intercourse was terribly repetitious
once you got the swing of it—which, of course,
helped to explain the Great Clit Hit of the 1970's.
Because what every woman knew was that balling

guys with sizes Sm., Med., Med. L., or even L., when you were married to it, was quite dull, regardless of the position. And since the celestial manufacturer offered no warranty, no little postcard to mail back, postage guaranteed, when the crazy, mixed-up initial passion was over and routine domestic screwing could no longer trigger the contraction mechanism inside the vagina that worked like the delicate timer in the dishwasher that caused the soap dispenser to open and release the Cascade automatic detergent at precisely the perfect moment—a wife was stuck. Because at least with a dishwasher—if you had a Sears Roebuck repair-insurance contract—you had a chance for a replacement whereas once you were legally married, the family penis was yours to keep whether or not it worked satisfactorily.

So Gavin began thrashing around, and Coco assumed that it felt good to him, since he got a happy look on his face. But she couldn't feel worked up about what was going on, and that was what originally caused the creation of her Perfect Lover, who, of course, had an X-L that just grew and grew so that it could hardly get in, and Coco could just lie flat on her back and explode internally without any physical effort, because the combination of illegitimacy and an X-L was endsville. . . .

CHAPTER 6

On the third Sunday of June, Coco woke up unusually early, while the house was still silent, and lay in bed flooded with a sense of aimlessness. Sundays always made Coco feel the same as when she put a carbon paper in backward, typed a clean page of copy, and then discovered that the duplicate was blank. Lately, all her Sundays had felt like the shakingly empty second sheet of a weekend. Inevitably her first thought was that somewhere, soon, Mrs. Marshall in her pink-and-rose-print dress would be lifting her voice in praise of the glory of God in the Baptist storefront church where she sang in the choir. That vision triggered both metaphysical and domestic anxieties.

Invariably, Coco spoiled Sundays by trying to over-achieve because she had consolidated all her maternal guilt into weekends and had become obsessive about producing happy adventures for the entire family all day long. Instead of simply deciding to be patient and interested, she would arrange complicated excursions—to the zoo, the Phillips Art Gallery or the lobby exhibit at the National Geographic Building—followed by ice cream at Griffith's out in Silver Spring or hamburgers at the junior Hot Shoppe in Georgetown, where the balloon man also sold nickel packs of marijuana.

These tedious Sunday odysseys were always such emotional or physical disasters that this morning Coco didn't know if she had enough strength to travel at all. Feeling depressed, she put on her bathrobe and walked into the boys' bedroom. It was almost eight o'clock, but they were still sleeping. Coco tucked Josh's blanket back on top of him, recovered the wandering mate of one blue tennis shoe, gently lifted Mike's soiled undershorts off the floor, unhitched Nicky's sunsuit from the railing of his topdeck bedpost to throw in the hamper, retrieved Josh's pacifier from where it was wedged between the mattress and the bars of his crib and then stepped down, barefoot, on a metal Hot Wheels car hidden by a hump in the rug. Too wounded to muffle her cry of pain, Coco looked up expectantly, only to discover that she hadn't disturbed the boys at all and that they were so spiteful they simply wouldn't wake up when she needed to love them.

To divert herself, Coco ran downstairs for the morning papers and carried them back up to her bedroom. Quickly she skimmed the front page headlines and then fished out the prize. For twelve years Coco had been studying the *Post*'s book review section as if it were a racing form to check out long shots, dark horses, fast starters and late comers. But the reviews (good or bad) of any new woman novelist

sent Coco into a frenzy because, with growing
frequency, the lead sentence—used simply as a
self-starter by some semi-articulate male assistant
professor of American Lit. at George Washington
University—would contain one of Coco Burman's favorite insights.

Sooner or later all of Coco's best ideas jumped out
at her from the book review page, showing the growing popularity of her own privately copyrighted ex-
periences. Her personal past was being plagiarized
and published (as major plots, or even worse, minor
episodes) in other women's novels. By now almost all
the meaningful events of Coco's life had been used
up by much younger women in well-edited novels
neatly welded together by the insertion of an in-
teruterine coil, an abortion in Mexico, a nasty divorce
or a Tom Wolfish title—copping the corner of the
market Coco coveted. All across America beautiful
young blondes, like Cynthia Buchanan, were stealing
Coco's unique perceptions plus her prospective sym-
bols, settings and even NAMES OF CHARS. And when,
late at night, she saw her rival sisters doing guest
spots on the Dick Cavett show—despite her commitment to the women's movement—she would feel
sibling, rather than sisterly, feelings in her isometri-
cally-exercised breast.

But today, luckily, the book review dealt with an
ecology study, so Coco politely reconstructed the
Post for Gavin. Now the Sunday feeling of the morning was lodged in her throat like an irretrievable bit
of apple peel or peanut skin. She turned over so her
weight shifted the mattress; Gavin moaned slightly
and Coco, seizing the opportunity to pretend she
thought he was awake, began talking loudly.

"You know, Gavin, it's really your fault that I never
wrote my novel. You always sabotaged it."

"Oh, sure," Gavin grumbled, too groggy to know how early it was. "And it's my fault if it snows in the winter."

"You never think you do anything wrong, do you?" Coco inquired, feeling vindicated for waking him up because he had never once looked out into the porch where she had been spending her days trying to track down a major theme.

"How the hell is it my fault if you don't do something?" Gavin asked, opening his eyes wider. "I mean, you have to *try* to do things. Things don't just happen by themselves."

And suddenly, without making any romantic overtures, Gavin sat up, dropped the long anchors of his legs overboard, and began eyeing the piles of discarded clothes on the floor near his side of the bed. Since Coco was quite compulsive about keeping used clothing in His and Hers piles, Gavin quickly spotted a prospective outfit, jumped up, sprang into a pair of blue jeans and prepared for departure.

Coco felt the hammer of anger. "You know, Ann was really the smart one," she began slowly. "I felt like such a hot shit getting you away from her, but she was really the winner. She took off like a bat out of hell and made a real name for herself the minute you sprang her loose."

"Shut up, Coco."

"So tell me, Gavin. Does your new girlfriend have a nice body? Better than mine?"

"I told you I'm not going to talk about that anymore."

"Why not?"

"Because I don't want to and I don't have to." He was edging toward the door.

"Dr. Finkelstein says if you provoke me by continuing not to talk, I might go off my rocker. I'm probably going crazy bit by bit every day anyway, but if you keep on baiting me, I'm really going to crack."

Gavin kicked his foot against the door and whirled around. "Listen, you nut. Where do you get off persecuting me because I balled some broad two or three times?"

"I'll bet . . . two or three times."

"Well, you haven't been an angel these twelve years either."

"Oh, I can assure you that I've never committed *adultery*," Coco lied emphatically. "That I can assure you."

"Bullshit. I didn't fall off a tree yesterday," Gavin said, moving threateningly in her direction. "I always knew when you had something going on the side."

"You never knew anything about me," Coco said with authentic despair.

"Screw you, Coco." Gavin turned away, as if he were seriously prepared to quit fighting.

"Why the hell don't you stop lying to me, Gavin? Why don't you tell me who she is?"

"How do you know it's just *one* woman?" Gavin asked maliciously. "Why not more than one? Maybe I've got a harem."

"Oh, come on, Gavin. Face it. There's not enough of you to spread around that thin."

"That's what you think, baby."

"I guess *I* should know, Gavin."

"You don't know anything except how to whine and bitch and complain all the time. Don't you hear the baby crying? What kind of mother are you, anyhow?"

"I know I'm a better mother than you're a father."

"Tell that to the kids."

"Well, where did you plan to take them today? Or

do you have a very, very, very important brief to write to help the oppressed fight injustice?"

Gavin walked toward Coco's dressing table and looked at himself in the mirror. "Well, maybe we should go to the zoo," he said in a suddenly conciliatory voice.

"We went to the zoo last Sunday."

"Yah. But we didn't go down to see the bears or the seals."

"Really, Gavin. Can't you come up with something better than the zoo every Sunday?"

"For Christ's sake, Coco. Joshua is getting hysterical. Why don't you go change his diaper? He's probably going to get that rash again."

"And how would you know if he got a rash?"

Gavin marched over to the bed. "Get up, Coco. Get up and shut up or I'm going to walk out of this crazy house and never come back."

"You haven't got the balls to do that, Gavin."

"You want to bet?" he jeered. Then his expression softened. "What's made you so hard, Coco?" he asked, looking down at her rather tenderly. "What made you so bitter and hard?"

"Frustration," Coco answered promptly. "Sexual and creative frustration."

"Well, I'm not to blame for both of them. And maybe if you stopped weeping and wailing, you could write something and then you *would* feel better."

"Well, why don't you take the kids to the zoo by yourself today, then? If you gave me some free time to do some work, maybe I would feel better."

"Okay. Fine. I'll take them myself, but get up now and dress them at least."

"Sure, sport." Coco climbed out of bed in a fashion that whirled her nightgown high up over her body.

But when she turned her back on her husband to dig for underpants in her cluttered dresser drawer, she heard him sneaking out of the room behind her.

Actually none of them went to the zoo that day. The children wanted to play in the backyard and, by the time Coco got downstairs, Gavin had slumped off into his usual Sunday passivity and was reading the *Washington Post* at the kitchen table. Silently Coco joined him and, after a short time, the coffee, the cigarettes and *The New York Times* took the edge off her anger. Around ten, Coco mixed up a huge batch of eggs and bacon, enough so that no one would need lunch, and fed everyone breakfast. Afterward the children disappeared again, so Coco finished reading the newspapers.

"Jesus, the kids are being great today," Gavin said once, glancing at the clock.

"Yah, they really are," Coco agreed, feeling more relaxed than usual.

The morning and early afternoon drifted past in low profile; even interruptions to take care of the baby or break up a sibling wrestling match were low-key. Around three, Coco went up to the corner grocery to buy frozen pizzas for dinner. She walked slowly even though the heat hung only halfheartedly over the city, brushing—rather than banging—against her. Actually, she felt rather peaceful by the time she returned home.

"Guess what?" Gavin asked in a testing voice, camouflaged in nonchalance, when she entered the kitchen.

"What?" Coco put her bag of groceries on the highchair tray and sat down at the kitchen table again.

"Suede Bellock just called from New York. He's doing a story about radical law firms around the country and he's coming down here for a week or so. He's been out to Portland, California, Chicago and down to New Orleans, but he wants to wrap up the story here in Washington."

Coco felt instant fluster, so she stood up and began to unpack the groceries.

"He's coming in on Thursday and I invited him to stay with us," Gavin concluded.

Coco returned to the highchair and extracted a box of elbow macaroni from the bag. Since she always forgot to cook macaroni or make Jell-O, she left those kinds of boxes out on the counter as menu memos. Then she fussed about in the canned-goods cupboard long enough to regain some composure so she could come on negative and sound natural.

"Well, that will certainly make for a little more commotion around here . . . and a little more cooking."

Gavin shrugged and opened *The New York Times* Book Review section.

"He says his new book is coming out in September and he thinks it's going to make a lot of bread. But he has to keep doing magazine articles until he starts getting the royalties."

Coco began to fill the percolator with water, procuring another few minutes of face-averted safety as she stared out through the finger-smudged window above the sink. Mike was oiling his two-wheeler bike on the patio. His slim hard body was tense with concentration.

"Where are the other kids?" Coco asked.

"Jessica went over to the Baumgartners' and Nicky's upstairs. Jesus, you know Josh is taking a hell of a long nap. Maybe we should wake him so he won't stay up too late tonight."

"I'll go get him," Coco said, pouring coffee directly

into the percolator basket without benefit of a table-
spoon. Commingling with her excitement about seeing Suede again was a slight sense of deprivation
since a house guest would certainly cramp her
nightly campaign to bully Gavin into disclosing his
secret lovelife. She could hardly carry on like a far-
out Broadway production of *Who's Afraid of Virginia Woolf?* with Suede there. A week-long visitor
would put the lid on both her fishing expedition and
her well-coordinated nervous breakdown.

Still . . . Suede . . . What   a   lovely   retalia-
tion. . . .

After plugging in the coffeepot, Coco went into the
TV room instead of upstairs. Nicky was lying on
the floor constructing one of his cowboy-and-Indian
battlegrounds on the fake-brick linoleum tile, re-
arranging the positions of his troops with great preci-
sion. He would pick up one of the hundreds of small
plastic figures—all of whose miniature faces he could
distinguish—and patiently try to stand it up on its
bumpy plastic bottom.

"How's it going, Nick?"

"Dood."

He had a terrible lisp, compounded by a confusion
of consonants. Coco lay down on the couch and
turned so she could watch the ambushes being laid
behind plastic cactus plants.

"Who's winning?"

"Nobody."

Nicky's straight black hair covered his eyebrows
and Coco was reminded of the massive clean-up effort that all the children needed.

"Want to take a bath, Nick?"

"No."

"I'll take one with you."

"Don't talk, Mudder."

Coco closed her eyes and listened to the sweet scrapings of Nicky's cowboys and Indians preparing for battle around the den. Then she began to think about Suede and those confused years before she had engaged Dr. Finkelstein or started her Ph.D. or conceived Mike one night in an unendurably hot little apartment on Capitol Hill where the FM played *Tristan and Isolde* and her future stretched like an empty desert ahead of her. She hadn't seen Suede for . . . well, it was before Joshua was born . . . almost three years?

She and Gavin had gone to New York for a weekend and Suede had invited them over for drinks. She remembered experiencing her old kind of raunchy feelings for Suede as they walked inside the remodeled brownstone and up a flight of stairs to his fashionable apartment with his telltale-titled books lined up like billboard advertisements for himself. His college-days flat on Ellis Avenue on the South Side of Chicago had hardly been chic. It had been a very long cold windy walk from the campus, but it was there—in that ugly-furnished, out-of-the-way flat— that Coco and Suede became and remained lovers until he introduced her to his friend Gavin. And when Coco married Gavin for a variety of reasons, among which was the fact that Gavin was really the first man to actually propose to her, Suede was wildly jealous. (Really, Dr. Finkelstein, that was why, really. How long could a nice Jewish girl from Chicago sleep with three or four graduate students—even sequentially—right in her own hometown without legalizing one of them? And Gavin *wasn't* on the rebound, Dr. Finkelstein. You don't seem to understand that I left Suede for him and he left Ann for *me.*)

But during the first five bitter years of their mar-

riage, after they'd moved to Washington, Coco had
frequently taken the bus to New York. There, in a
diligent but also desultory way, she had resumed old
friendships with college roommates who had done
the brave thing and stayed single to make it in the
Big Apple. She had also reignited her old affair with
Suede Bellock who still made fierce passionate love
to her if she appeared at his apartment on a rainy
Saturday afternoon because she couldn't find Bloom-
ingdale's and decided to seek out love rather than
seasonal sales at some different department store.

And though her erratic erotic affairs—during the
years when Kennedy clamor and glamour ignited
occasional high spirits—were distributed among five
or six gentlemen, it was Suede who most clearly dom-
inated the memories of that fading time when they
were all in their early twenties. That was when
Suede had been drafted into the army (no draft resistance then) and stationed at Fort Bragg. Every
weekend for over a year, he visited the Burmans in
Washington, sleeping on the ratty old sofa in their
bedbugged, furnished apartment and wandering
around Capitol Hill with a little stenographic notebook that he used as a journal. But after his discharge,
he moved back to New York to begin writing good
strong journalism about the civil-rights movement
and finally scored with a novel *Making Out,* while
Coco retreated into successively bigger apartments,
poorly spaced pregnancies, and dull coursework at
the drab, dour Catholic University.

After Mike was born, Coco only visited New York a
few times a year—and always with Gavin. They usually stayed at the Chelsea and perhaps Coco was even
pregnant with Jessica by then, since in the sixties it
was socially unacceptable to have only one child.

Coco always remained strictly monogamous when she was pregnant, because she had once read a magazine article about a Welsh woman who bore fraternal twins fathered by two different men. That story had put the fear of any affair into her—thus spoiling her safest period.

Within two years after Jessica's birth, Coco was pregnant again. (She didn't get an abortion because she'd had three in college and hated each of them and also because she felt it would be an insult to Mike and Jessica). So she continued teaching freshman composition at American University, and Nicky was born and had colic, and Coco didn't sleep for a year and was too tired for love, let alone sex. Once she took a vacation alone in Puerto Rico and had a very good, intensely glamorous five-day affair, but she still went dutifully home again—to teach outlining to Long Island freshmen, to do a little more research on her dissertation, and to make dinner parties twice a month.

And then, drugged by demands and diapers, spaced out and done in, she decided she might just as well have one more baby. So one sweet spring she simply dispensed with her diaphragm while dreaming about an eventual book-jacket boasting that the finest female writer to emerge in a decade was raising not one, not two, not three, but four little children, plus a poodle. Because, in those pre-lib days, three children were the expected number for young professionals and four was such an easy one-upper. So then there was Josh—the cutest, the fattest, the giggliest baby of all.

Indeed, during the rush and flurry of those days that turned into years, she had little time to think about other men much anymore, until now, when

Gavin had revived the old battle of the sexes so that her blood stirred once again to the clarion call of competitive sex and struggle.

"Mudder, Joshua is cwying."

Coco jumped up guiltily and ran upstairs.

CHAPTER 7

---

*C*oco slept badly Wednesday night, vaguely aware, even while still asleep, that she was moaning and thrashing about the bed. She woke up headachy Thursday morning to discover: that Gavin had retreated during the night to relocate on the living-room couch; that she was getting a monstrous pimple on her lower-left cheek (thirty-year-old acne?); that the baby looked splotchy and seemed inordinately cranky; that Nicky had lost or thrown away one of his flip-flops, so he had no shoes to wear to the park; that Mrs. Marshall wanted to take off Monday (July 3) as well as Tuesday, the fourth, so she could go visit her sister in North Carolina; that there wasn't any Captain Crunch or pancake syrup in the reserve cupboard; and that Gavin had a suspicious expression on his face when he slammed out of the house to go to work. Coco drank a cup of instant coffee that kept curdling a lukewarm skin on its surface, and felt harassed, hyped up and half-hysterical.

But once upstairs out on her porch again, Coco reappraised all her possessions, still safe in their predictable places, smiled gratefully, unzipped her dress and let it slide down the length of her body to crumple on the floor. Without exposing herself, she surveyed the backyard to see what the children were doing, glanced across the alley toward the fifth-floor-center apartment balcony to check if the handsome-from-a-distance man who frequently watched her was there (he wasn't), adjusted the top of her bikini, rubbed some QT lotion on the front of her body, wiped her hands with a spit-dampened Kleenex so there wouldn't be any telltale yellow-stained palms to reveal the secret of her speedy tan, and then lit a cigarette.

A sun-tinged breeze whispered through the screens and rippled Coco's supply of papers beneath the chaise. At that moment the manifold carbons seemed to offer a much faster, happier catharsis than Dr. Finkelstein. Feeling the stir of potential success and sexual allure, she got down on the hot wooden floor and commenced her daily quota of fifty sit-ups. Back on the chaise, she took the hand mirror out of her makeup kit only to be assaulted by a view of her pimple, which she had forgotten, growing bigger. She fingered it tenderly, seeking the secret source of its pollution, and then decided to compensate for her skin problem by starting to take care of business earlier than usual.

The sun was hot. She would have liked a G & T but had forgotten to bring any ice cubes upstairs, so she poured a shot of gin into one of the tumblers and drank it straight. Then she took out her calendar notebook.

CALL REVEREND PARKS AT QUINCY STREET
CHURCH—ASK ABOUT USING HALL OVER JULY 4TH
WEEKEND

CALL UNIVERSITIES—SEE IF THEY RENT DORMI-
TORY SPACE

TYPE AND MAIL LIST OF HOSPITALITY HOUSES TO
OFFICE

Petulantly Coco crossed out Thursday, wrote in
"Monday, June 26" at the top of the page, added GO
TO DRUGSTORE—BUY FLIP-FLOPS FOR NICKY, and re-
turned the notebook to her purse.

It was almost 11:30 when the gin struck and Coco
began to feel high, tan, thin, artistic and committed.
Power and promise surged through her. Instantly she
felt convinced that she really *could* produce a brilliant novel, that before long she really *would* deliver
a book that would produce total self-fulfillment—at
least for as long as a newborn baby did. And it was
quite clear that one published novel would eternally
immunize her from the hurts which other people
tried to inflict upon her. Now all of her vital life
energy would be channeled into beautiful prose and
sensitive perceptions rather than the emotionally violent, self-destructive behavior that Dr. Finkelstein
warned against. Instead of tearing her life apart,
Coco would engage in rapier-sharp analysis and poetic flights of fancy.

Suffused with Determination To Write The Con-
clusive Thing, Coco inserted a paper into the typewriter, flipped ON, and waited for something like *The
Sound and the Fury* to appear on her roller like teletype bulletins materializing off an AP wire-service
machine. Slowly two paragraphs emerged. Coco
stopped typing, read the words, tore out the paper
and crumpled it up into a tight angry ball. The
phrases that filtered through the typewriter were an

enormous aesthetic distance from what she had anticipated. Disappointed by what had arrived—a garbled message teletyped from her unconscious—she sank back on the chaise.

It was obvious that Coco was blocking because all across the nation Didions, Goulds, Kaufmans, Jongs and Roiphes were selling their novels to the movies. That pressure—plus the fact that in just a few hours Mrs. Marshall's voice would rise up the stairwell announcing her departure—was too much for Coco. The realization that *Take Heaven By Storm* was nothing more than a collection of contemporary clichés plagued her. Coco's book was turning out to be a series of poorly constructed sentences in a string of underdeveloped paragraphs that took off like a posse in hopeless pursuit of a still unformulated theme.

And it was not like she was ignorant of literary structure. Indeed she had a B.A. and an M.A. and half a Ph.D. with eighteen months still remaining of the original eighty-four in which to finish her dissertation. She had taught English composition for seven very long years—endlessly discussing outlines, paragraph structure, organization, topic sentences and the vivid use of detail. But she simply couldn't organize her own life into a well-wrought novel.

Every day now, the structural problems of writing fiction overwhelmed her so that invariably she began typing in a mindless sort of way, letting things occur on paper the way they did in her life—haphazard, accidental and redundant—except that printed in pica they seemed, worst of all, unlikely. Ever since she had first recognized this problem, Coco had dedicated half of her REVIEW HOUR to thinking seriously about FORM and only last week had written out a list of guidelines:

RETHINK ENTIRE DIRECTION OF BOOK

TRY TO FIND AN OBJECTIVE (get an IMPORTANT pt. to make)

FIX CHARS. SO THEY CARRY MORE SYMBOLISM

REVISE OLD SCENES OR THINK OF NEW ONES TO DEVELOP MINOR CHARS.

DO OTHER CHARS. SEEM SCRAWNY NEXT TO GWENSANDRA?

WHAT STYLE IS THIS BOOK BEING WRITTEN IN?

WHAT ARE THE PHILOSOPHIC IMPLICATIONS OF VARIOUS PATTERNS OF PROSE?

Coco reread the list in her notebook and felt like a messy drawer full of lingerie that badly needed straightening. Hating herself for lacking a fixed identity, she decided that her role-playing nature excluded the possibility of implanting a structure in anything she created. It was logically impossible for someone who had a multiple-choice personality to have a single coherent point of view on paper. And the saddest part of all was that she wasn't even overly ambitious. She didn't even aspire to the heavyweight intellectual division of serious American authors.

All Coco wanted was to make the minor literary leagues, to recycle some of her own leftover life (like converting slightly green Saran-wrapped roast beef into hash) and show how a sensitive American woman, reared in and ruined by the inverted values of the 1950's, could never find happiness. Theoretically, *Take Heaven by Storm* was to be a riotously funny mock-epic of an American girl on a hunt for happiness, working her way through battalions of men—every age, color, size and kind—while accumulating college credits, cute clothes, groovy memories, job experience, airline ticket receipts, souvenirs and Wisdom. But for some reason the scenes of Gwensandra Rappaport husband-hunting, which were to have an up-to-date-upbeat Tom Jones

quality, sounded terribly *Candy*- ish and Coco hated
Terry Southern.

Torn between fears of formlessness vs. infinite pos-
sibilities, Coco started typing again. But at four
o'clock, instead of rereading and revising the ten
pages she'd written, she went downstairs an hour
earlier than usual. After changing her clothes, she
began picking up the toys and clutter that reaccumu-
lated during Mrs. Marshall's brief bed-making tour
on the third floor. Hustling around in a six-o'clock
style—although it was only five—Coco tried to trick
the children into a premature dinner, which was her
only chance to appear put-together when Suede arrived. Coco always tried to outfox her own existence
when ex-lovers or in-laws visited. Even now, in her
post-lib days, she used pre-lib ploys to camouflage her
oppression in front of judgmental visitors and spies.
Coco firmly believed that exposing the horrors and
errors of her domestic days and ways was just as rude
as the crazy exhibitionist up in the park whipping his
penis out of his pants for no practical purpose at all.

But right after Mrs. Marshall left, Coco nonchalantly asked Jessica to watch Joshua, while she cooked
dinner, and the request produced a hysterically shrill
refusal. It was at the peak of Jessica's shrieks that
Coco heard the front door open.

Coco wasn't ready. The house didn't look right, the
children weren't behaving, and her heart, unexpectedly, began to pitch about wildly inside her chest.
Stooping to scoop up a heavy, wet Pamper lying
crumpled on the floor, she tossed it toward the trash
basket, missed and then, inhaling urine, moved into
the hallway.

Gavin came forward to side-swipe her face with a
kiss. Then everything blurred because Suede was
standing close beside her and for one moment—with

Ultra Man roaring on the television set in the background—Coco felt an instinctive, almost forgotten quickening in her core as Suede's shoulder grazed her breasts.

Ahhhh, her body whispered.

Coco blushed as she realized that after so many years Suede could still stir the same eternal moan in the center of her being.

"Hey!" He hugged her close while printing a friendly kiss on her cheek.

"How are you, Suede?" she asked, smiling and moving back a few inches so she could see him better.

"Good," Suede grinned. "How've you been, Coco?"

His voice was perfect. He always spoke in professionally tender tones so that social and pillow talk sounded the same. Everything about him was smooth, but his voice was especially reassuring. He had a perfect anchorman tone—a compromise between intimacy and authority—so that when the three of them were together they could all pretend the past hadn't happened and thus preserve the triangular friendship they still treasured. In the denial of those distant days of illicit passions, which had buried loyalty in a grave of desire, they were conspirators. Only Suede could pull off a heist like that one. He was that good, Suede, that professional.

"What a great house," he said happily.

Standing in the center of the hallway with his legs spread sea-captain-wide and one hand absently rubbing a caressive palm across the white-shirted mounds of his chest, Suede was clearly speculating about his creature comforts in this new environment.

Coco lifted her hands to her face and swept back the damp strands of hair clinging to her cheeks.

"It's really a bit too big," she complained proudly, smelling the warm odor that rose from beneath her raised arms.

Suede looked even handsomer and tougher than Jean Paul Belmondo, who had played the film version of America's most famous antihero—the underground American (only a slight exaggeration of himself) that Suede had created—to catapult himself onto the bestseller lists and the cover of *Time* magazine last year. Actually Suede seemed more like the movie version of himself than when Coco had last seen him. Now the topography of his face showed that his favorite expressions had permanently cleaved themselves into deep crags and nicely etched lines around his feverishly dark eyes. His heavy black hair was long over his neck and his gentle, but terribly knowing, smile was less frequent than Coco remembered, making the occasional flash of hard white teeth more rewarding when it appeared.

Suddenly Jessica and Nicky came tearing through the hallway, bumping into the little red wagon parked near the radiator, before chasing each other back toward the kitchen.

"God, this place is a zoo," Coco laughed nervously. "Jessica, why aren't you watching Josh?" Since her anger at her daughter was so intense she could only approximate a please-don't-eat-the-daisies-ish tone, she smiled brightly so that it would all seem like some madcap sit-com.

"Jesus!" Suede laughed, pulling his knapsack out of the way as Nicky reappeared driving his tricycle in a furiously fast U-turn toward the kitchen again.

"But wait until you see this one," Gavin said suddenly, turning to walk down the hall.

Coco stood her ground, paralyzed by the sense of pure luscious yearning that spilled through her body.

Oh, it had been a long, long time. Suede was like some forgotten Thanksgiving holiday treat which, after a year-long abstinence, returns with unbearable sweetness and pleasure.

Coco felt a soft surgary ache for love like the gentle pain caused by a school-made Mother's Day card or a homemade paste-lumpy Valentine.

"You look fantastic, Coco," Suede said quietly, methodically inspecting the shape of her body and then her hair and her face and even her bare feet below the cuffs of her tight white jeans.

Coco stood perfectly still, feeling rewarded and fulfilled.

"Here's the baby," Gavin said, reappearing with Joshua in his arms. "This is Josh."

"Hey, he's cute," Suede agreed awkwardly. "You know, you guys are getting to be a legend in New York. Nobody there is having any kids anymore."

"Oh, God, he's just filthy," Coco groaned, stretching out her arms as Josh flung his weight forward toward her. "I'm going to give him a bath in the kitchen sink. You guys go upstairs until I get this riot under control down here. And, Gavin, please tell Jessica to come downstairs if she's up there."

Gavin picked up Suede's duffel bag.

"I'll show you where your room is. Coco, ask Nicky to bring us up some ice cubes, will you?"

The men started up the stairs and Coco waited for a moment to watch them. Suede's shirt was pulled taut against the thick, wide set of his shoulders and his narrow, but cupped, buttocks rounded out the seat of his chino pants.

"Oh, God, something's burning."

She whirled around, arms full of Joshua, ran back

into the kitchen, and began stirring some of the
steaming pots on the stove with a hand that shook
pleasantly from anticipation rather than impatience.
Finally she called the children to the table and demanded that they eat spaghetti that she had cooked
with six-day-old hamburger. She insisted that the
sauce did not smell, while Mike gave her a dirty look
and talked about ptomaine poisoning, Ralph Nader
and the fair labeling of hot dogs. Afterward she let
the children run through the sprinkler in the backyard so she wouldn't have to bathe them and finally
took everyone upstairs, purchasing an extra hour of
time by letting them lie in her bed and watch television before going to sleep.

Back downstairs, she set the dining-room table,
called the men and served them Chicken Kiev.
Gavin and Suede ate happily and talked about the
different political cases Gavin had handled over the
past three years since he had set up his four-man
radical legal-defense firm. Coco sat at the foot of the
table, letting her food grow cold, while she began to
feel tragically sorry for herself. Not only did Suede's
presence prevent her from quarreling with Gavin,
but Suede was already getting a take on the shabby
state of her marriage. To be married, in Suede's eyes,
was bad enough, but a miserable marriage was nothing less than moral turpitude. At the same time,
things were too shaky between Coco and Gavin to
allow her to capture any freebie feels off Suede.
Gavin had co-opted and intimidated her by having a
real, live affair, so that Coco was afraid even to flirt.
Feeling isolated and aimless since she was unable to
make either love or war at the dinner table, she continued administering glass after glass of Chablis Côte
de Plume to her mouth.

Occasionally Suede would smile at her as he passed

a serving platter and then his dark handsome face would lighten and brighten, reminding Coco of lost options. His ancient affection only made her feel sadder, because the easy reprieve of a quick sexual encounter—to rebalance domestic power—seemed unlikely. She was in no position to antagonize her husband or right his wrong in an old-style reversal-of-the-Double-Double-Standard. All of a sudden her standing in the Amateur Betrayal Division had become irrelevant, because Gavin had secretly, sneakily, turned pro.

So when she reached a point of drunken euphoria, tarnished only by a touch of nausea, Coco served the Jello-O pudding disguised as mousse and left the dining room, without speaking, to go sit outside on the patio.

It was cool and rather windy. June's soft blowy nights always apologized for its hot humid days. Coco took several deep breaths of fresh air and then circled the cookie-and-cracker-crumb-coated stroller, climbed over several generations of overturned tricycles, stepped around endless coils of unwound garden hose, discarded like the cast-off skin of a serpent after the children's sprinkle-bath, kicked several toys across the uneven bricks and sat down in a low-slung canvas chair.

Along the back edge of the yard, chrysanthemums were wilting before their formal blooming season and tulips swayed, crushed and broken, like dead horsemen still strapped in their saddles. The azalea bushes were shriveled, starving for water, while holes that Nicky and Jessica had dug in the dirt were filled with biologically rich stagnant water. A few foolhardy dandelions crept across the hard trodden dirt beneath the swings, apparently undaunted by endless attacks of lethal feet. Meanwhile, because all the trash cans near the back gate had lost their hats, garbage flowered forth in profuse abundance and its daily spillage made the surrounding topsoil so rich that in this area only grass, weeds and wildflowers blossomed, unaffected by children or neglect. A sweet stench of decay wafted through the yard.

Coco lit a cigarette and wondered what could be done to improve the sanitation. Often, late at night, she saw rats, the size of cats, stroll across the patio. Gavin did not mind debris or filth. Mrs. Marshall did not consider the backyard part of her domain and Coco felt defeated by the decadent condition of her private wilderness area. Blowing several slow smoke rings, she looked up at the neat, tidy, well-swept sky. The moon was like a 3-way bulb—clean, shiny, and bright in the center of the celestial chandelier that dangled stars like pendants over the unkempt, unplanned, unsanitary and unsafe Burman patio.

Coco sighed and thought about what Dr. Finkelstein called her proclivity for disorder. She never totally understood what he meant when he talked about Order and Disorder, but now she genuinely felt that there was a psychological message waiting to be uncoded and deciphered right in her very own backyard.

After a while the telephone in the kitchen began to ring. Through the doorway Coco watched Gavin pick up the receiver and then settle down on a chair. A few minutes later, a patch of light fell on the ground as Suede pushed open the back door and came down the stairs. He leapfrogged over the juvenile hurdles, dragged a chair closer to Coco's, and sat down. Then he let the silence grow and wrap itself around them while he studied her face in the moonlight.

In deference to past pleasures and indecencies,

Suede implicitly acknowledged the fact that they had been lovers. What had been, still was, and he would never betray the past by either ignoring or altering it. Simply and silently he acknowledged that what they had shared affected the present and Coco always appreciated his casual allusions to distant days and nights—his unstrained and gentle remembrances.

"What's up, babes?"

Coco shrugged and looked toward him helplessly. The moonlight softened his battered nose and blurred the deep, jagged clefts in his face. It was just like Edgar Allan Poe had said. Irregularity and imperfection were the height of beauty. Suede was still one of the most handsome men Coco had ever known. His large body was comfortably relaxed, yet still sexually challenging, and now that he was sitting close beside her again, Coco heard the same internal sigh and felt the same old yearning for love within her once more. It was Suede's professionalized brand of passion—without immaturities or romanticisms to promote any portion out of proportion—that allowed him to incorporate so much, so smoothly into his life.

"Why didn't you stay and have coffee with us?" he asked.

Coco felt self-pity quiver her bottom lip. She shrugged her shoulders, brimming with undifferentiated emotions.

"Jesus. You still look so fantastic, Coco. You really are smashing. You never change." He took her hand. "Are you going to have any more kids?"

Coco smiled gratefully, shook her head, and tasted the salty preview of tears in her mouth.

"Gavin told me you quit your job at the university. How come?"

She let two small tears drop. "Well, I wanted to

start writing my novel, Suede. I'm really working hard for a change. Really hard. I know I'm going to make it good this time. I know it."

"Shit, Coco, are you still shticking around with that writing crap? Forget it," he said with genuine disgust. "Writing sucks. You can bust your ass trying to do a good book and even if you finally score, it never really pays off. Jesus . . . a woman with four kids . . ."

"Oh please don't start in on *that*, Suede. I don't want to hear it from you."

His antagonism was instantaneous. "Well. It just can't happen, babes. Anyway, it hasn't yet."

"Are you kidding?" Coco squeaked. "Haven't you read—?"

"I've read 'em all," he nodded knowingly.

But his interest in convincing Coco was slight since he had never viewed her seriously as a writer. For a decade he had been totally oblivious of the fact that his literary successes and professional paternalism were devastating to Coco.

"I don't want Gavin to know about my book, though, Suede. I feel uptight when he knows what I'm working on."

"That's funny."

Suede's fingers encircled Coco's wrist so she transferred her cigarette to the other hand and locked her fingers through his.

"Look, I'm not going to say anything about it to anyone," Suede promised, "but I just feel bad because you seem so sad." He was pumping gently for information. "I've got a good rep for keeping my mouth shut, you know."

Coco smiled appreciatively.

"Well, as a matter of fact, Gavin and I are at war," she said, looking toward the kitchen where Gavin was still speaking on the telephone. She had originally decided it would be wrong to confide in Suede, but now that Gavin was using him as a buffer to run interference, she felt justified in trying to enlist him as an ally. Although they had always kept their friendship loyalties straight, even when there were sexual betrayals, Coco felt a little high-schoolish and guilty about ratting on her husband.

"A big war?"

"Pretty big. Gavin's got a girlfriend."

"Oh, come on, Coco!" Suede laughed. "You're kidding."

"No. Really."

"Hell. I would seriously doubt that. Whoever told you must have been bullshitting for some reason."

"I don't think so; Gavin told me."

Suede slumped back in his chair, injured by the sudden damage done to one of his own neat verities —the Burman marriage secure among the rocky marital shoals.

"Why?" he mumbled. "Why would he?"

But now the back door ripped open, suddenly spilling light like water onto the patio, and Gavin thundered down the wooden stairs.

"You know, it's really great to be here again," Suede said, rising suddenly to stride along the brick wall that enclosed the patio.

Gavin looked at Coco suspiciously because their friend had moved too quickly, and spoken too formally, breaking the normal rhythm of their trio.

Coco felt a surge of anger at Gavin for having forced her to enlist support from a mercenary for lack of loyalists at home. She lit another cigarette, threw the match on the ground, and hated Gavin harder than ever.

"It's good to get back to Washington," Suede offered the awkward silence.

But then the first irreparable silence of their long friendship fell upon them. Suede smoked. Coco smoked. Gavin looked up at the sky. A conclave of alleycats was howling. Suspicious sounds darted out of the neighbors' windows.

"Well, maybe we should all crash," Suede said, again with terrible timing.

"Yah."

The three of them rose to their feet as if leaving a theater at the end of a movie and walked single-file back into the house. Coco went directly to her bedroom and left Gavin to find towels, if there were any clean ones, to give their guest. Anyway, she knew Suede could take care of himself.

CHAPTER 8

Coco pulled the telephone toward the chaise by the cord of its receiver so that it squiggled across the floor like a black rat caught by the tail. Then she stretched out flat again and watched a branch of the backyard tree (dying, said the lady next door, from American elm disease) scratch, sick but still green, against the screen. During the past few weeks she had been having difficulty remembering Gavin's office number, which hadn't changed in four years. Now when she phoned him she had to rev herself up by silently repeating the whole series of digits from the very beginning each time she dialed one number. Coco began mumbling her little numerical incantation.

"Burman, Berry, Conover and Katz."

"Gavin, please."

Click. Switch. Coco envisioned long limber fingers milking the rubber teats of the switchboard as she continued straightening out her legs so they wouldn't flip over into the comfortable position which caused the insides to get browner than the fronts.

"Hello." It was Gavin's professionally expectant voice.

Coco was momentarily struck silent with anger.

"It's just me, Gavin," she said nastily. "Not *her.*"

Silence. Then a short, bitter laugh.

"*She* wouldn't be calling you so early in the day, would she, Gavin? *She* probably sleeps till the middle of the afternoon."

Now he emitted an injured silence.

"Well?" Coco intoned.

"What've you been doing, Coco?" Gavin asked to change the unmentioned subject.

"Nothing."

Coco had a way of saying "nothing" that notified Gavin she spent her days prostrate and paralyzed on the porch, suffering incessantly from the pain he had caused her and unable to read, let alone write, a book.

"You know we're invited to a cocktail party at the Brandys' tonight, from five to seven?" she asked challengingly.

"Well . . . do you feel like going?" Gavin knew that any social excursion was contingent upon the state of Coco's mental health.

"I guess so. We could take Suede along."

"Sure. I'm going to see him for lunch, so I can ask him. But I've got an appointment at six o'clock that will probably take twenty minutes or so. Why don't you drive over there and we'll catch a cab and meet you around six-thirty?"

"I guess that's all right," Coco said poutingly,

pleased at the prospect of going to the party alone, but using the same opportunity to sound neglected.

"Who's going to take care of the kids?" Gavin asked, ignoring her implicit accusation.

"Mrs. Marshall said she'd stay. Time and a half."

"Actually, it might be a decent party," Gavin mumbled encouragingly.

Coco made her voice sound both brittle and threatening. "Well, it's good for me to get out of here for a couple of hours once in a while. This is not a normal existence."

She hung up, pulled the coffee table closer to the chaise, and removed the jar of pencils so they wouldn't bounce while she typed. That afternoon Coco finished the chapter in which Gwensandra Rappaport dropped out of graduate school, joined Delta Airlines, and graduated as valedictorian of her stewardess class.

Going upstairs at five o'clock to dress—rather than descending into the first-floor inferno—had the same effect on Coco's metabolism as popping an upper. Locked into the bathroom alone—without anyone sailing boats or splashing water or trying to see her pubic hair if she took advantage of her lifeguard duty to use the toilet—Coco stripped off her bikini. She turned on the skimpy shower which sprayed only tired, tepid water, weakened by its climb to the third floor in rusty lead pipes, and scrubbed her body abrasively before establishing herself in front of the medicine-chest mirror where she wiped away the steam with brisk, businesslike flicks of her hand before beginning to prepare for the party.

Coco had always believed that she possessed a beauty which could only be appreciated by a properly imaginative person. Such a viewer, however, was very hard to find nowadays since no one really

looked at anyone else anymore. Everyone seemed to
have lost the fine art of seeking quintessential qualities of character revealed in a stranger's expression.
Nevertheless, Coco continued to live her life like the
star of a low-budget European movie, playing her
existence into an invisible camera which she envisioned suspended six feet in front of her, eternally
recording each of her theatrically poignant scenes.
Compulsively Coco still strained to meet the high
standards demanded by the director of her eternally
unreleased film. Daily she rehearsed the soulful expressions which revealed the texture and complexity
of her nature and silently practiced dialogues for encounters which would never occur.

She carefully glued on nighttime-density false eyelashes, perfumed the cleavage between her breasts,
swatted some bath powder toward her already pun-
gent crotch, and adopted a complicated expression
that could be decoded only by the particular Perfect
Lover whom she eternally hunted. The message she
sent simply notified him that they had finally found
each other. Although it was highly unlikely her P.L.
would finally materialize at a Georgetown cocktail
party, it was important to remember that Coco
didn't belong there either, so there was no reason he
shouldn't make a surprise appearance.

She stared into the mirror and arranged her face
into a particularly desperate expression that suggested several dramatic explanations for her presence at so-prosaic-a-party. Silently she signaled a
need for help and if, as Coco expected, her predes-
tined P.L. had seen and liked Jeanne Moreau in *The
Beautiful and The Damned,* he would instinctively
know his part and immediately come forward to
comfort her.

Pleased with the rehearsal, Coco returned to her

bedroom and stopped to study the one small invitation tucked into the frame of her dressing table mirror.

COCKTAIL PARTY
WHEN: 5–7 Friday, June 23
WHERE: Sherry and Matt Brandy
      3601 Q Street N.W.
RSVP: 265–8097

Murmuring the address to herself, Coco put on a long white dress cut like a T-shirt, sprayed her arms with lemon-scented cologne, and ran downstairs to kiss the children good-bye. Deeply inhaling each of their different smells, while trying not to let them get fingerprints on her dress, she promised them lots of all-day fun on Saturday and then ran outside and down the block toward the fire hydrant that was her permanent parking place. Coco got into the driver's seat, opened her window, listed slightly to the left like a carjock so that her hair would blow in the early-evening air, and wondered if Mrs. Marshall had remembered to take in the milk and if Mike had replaced the wooden plank under the warped back gate after the milk delivery so that Happy couldn't get out.

Once on Connecticut Avenue, Coco made a conscientious effort—at all the stop signs and stop lights —to pull up evenly with cars in the next lane so restless commuters could wonder who she was. Although driving through Georgetown bore no resemblance to traffic conditions in *Play It as It Lays,* Coco identified with Maria (Pronounced Ma-rhy-ah) Wyeth who went speeding through southern California at ninety miles an hour on the Freeway, while falling apart and flipping out psychologically.

Deprived of drama during urban rushhour congestion, Coco's sense of discontent became even more bloated. Turning, so she could see herself in the rearview mirror, she saw that the expression in her familiar tawny brown eyes was so terribly worried and concerned, her sense of quivering dissolution grew even greater.

The only parking place she could find in the smug, narrow Georgetown streets was four blocks past the Brandys' house. Coco was hot, smudged and messy-feeling by the time she reached their front door. She entered the narrow, classically decorated living room that opened onto a patio at the rear, and stood inside long enough to observe the early guests, leaning toward each other in small intimate clusters. Coco felt a thrill of opportunity—a chill of the hunt—spill through her.

But then Sherry Brandy, who was standing near the French doors, trim and hard beneath a silk striped hostess gown, the late-afternoon sun frosting her streaked blond hair, looked up and spied Coco.

Coco sucked in her stomach, distended her chest, and engineered a smile.

"Coco." Sherry floated into the long dim tunnel of her living room. "I'm so glad . . . where in the world is Gavin . . . oh, sure . . . lots of people will be late. I want everyone to stay forever. . . ."

"He's bringing our house guest," Coco murmured. "Suede Bellock. You know . . . he wrote *Making Out.*"

Coco moved through the French doors with Sherry Brandy holding her arm.

"How lovely," Sherry whispered. "That's lovely. I just love National Book Award winners. And he's so handsome."

Coco made a quick survey for celebrities, acquaintances, enemies, competitors, superstars, Gavin's mistress, losers, winners and, of course, her own Perfect Lover. Perhaps he was here, at this very moment, standing with his back to Coco at the bar where the bartender, imprisoned behind a long white-linen-covered table, was stirring requests. Perhaps in a brief moment Coco's P.L. would turn . . . some enchanted evening . . . see Coco . . . freeze . . . stunned . . . incredulous that his Co-Star in Life stood in the doorway . . . at the Brandys' of all places. . . .

Cool and reserved, long light-colored hair curling softly over a white silk shirt collar, he would move negligently past the other guests like an adventurous explorer, his steel-gray eyes impervious to the beautiful people watching him, exploiting the absurdities of the party, only to assert his own superiority. Only her P.L. knew how to simultaneously use and reject an alien environment, rape atmosphere so as to seize and sculpt time and space into an ornate, artistic frame for himself and his destiny. Walking as if on water he would stretch out a tanned hand to claim Coco, as she waited in the doorway, still virgin to authentic passion, submissive in surrender to his sexual authority.

"Wouldn't you like a drink?" Sherry asked. "The bar is over there."

Coco smiled and moved forward toward the regal rental bartender. But Coco's P.L. was not standing at the bar or anywhere else in the patio. The guests were only second-stringers—like herself—legislative assistants from Capitol Hill, contributing editors for small liberal publications, lawyers, attachés from Latin American consulates, and local television news commentators who would never make the networks. It hardly seemed worthwhile for Coco to conduct any business here—to run any tests, play any scenes, launch any flares.

Disappointed, she grasped her gin and tonic and looked around to find some snug harbor or at least a cocktail party comfort station. Floating forward on an unpremeditated course, she navigated toward a small group of strangers and anchored herself along its edge. Two young women, apparently executive-branch summer interns, were speaking of congressional subcommittees considering various legislation with show-stopping fluency. Totally overshadowed, Coco stood silent as the talk shifted into a rap about George McGovern's staff which included a large assortment of their friends named Boo and Pooh and Foo-foo.

Coco sipped her drink and then suddenly, unexpectedly, felt a cramp of terror constrict her body, triggered by the possibility that one of these girls might be Gavin's mistress. Perhaps one of these creatures with center-parted long blond hair stroking her cheeks had a thing for Jewish intellectuals. Perhaps the blondest girl (if blondness was relative) was the one who met Gavin for lunch before they discreetly taxied over to the Hilton.

The patio was becoming more crowded. Eventually several people Coco knew arrived and she joined them. Then she stood in the early-evening shadows, waiting for Gavin to appear, picturing Suede gliding into the patio and beginning to circulate, casing the faces, picking himself a girl—some winner—whom he would quickly corner and begin to hustle, softly, steadily. . . .

But Coco had finished three drinks before Suede and Gavin arrived. When she saw them standing in the doorway, she moved forward eagerly and thus was totally unprepared for the rebuff of their combined disinterest. Suede grinned, as she walked toward them, but then looked away—skeptical but expectant—to see if he would be recognized, approached and admired. Coco instantly remembered Suede's compulsion to use parties as scouring pads, so she quickly shifted her needs toward Gavin.

But he, too, seemed suddenly remote and distracted. By the time she reached him, he was gazing out to the far corner of the patio toward the trellis of pink roses.

"Hi," Coco said very softly, her voice muted by gin and disappointment.

"Hi." Gavin smiled and gave her a vague embrace.

"Want anything from the bar?" Suede asked, impatient to take off to collect some drinks and tribute.

Then Sherry materialized beside them, smiling and delighted by the prize of a surprise celebrity and a possible flirtation. Excitedly she introduced herself, greeted Gavin, took Suede's arm, introduced herself, and then moved off to pass Suede around from guest to guest like a canapé.

"Let's get a drink," Coco said, straining to capture Gavin's attention.

"Haven't you had one yet?" he asked with brief interest.

"Two."

Coco smiled, feeling the lie float out of her mouth into the rose-scented air. But Gavin was still staring far beyond her, and Coco felt totally deprived and disconnected, as if her connection to her husband had been cut like a telephone wire.

"Well, hello, Gavin."

A large cumbersome girl in an Indian dress suddenly appeared next to Coco. She had a round, flat face featuring fat lips that were smiling toward Gavin.

"Surprised?" she giggled, obviously happy to see him.

"Hi, Sylvia," Gavin said, flushing as he reached out to shake hands. His face seemed to contract and tighten. "This is my wife, Coco. Coco, this is Sylvia Brydan, a client of mine."

"Hello," Coco said politely, for she had heard Sylvia Brydan's name at some Northwest Area Theoretical Council meeting.

The girl made a swift grimace of acknowledgment toward Coco and then turned back to Gavin. "So how's the brief going?"

Gavin began what sounded to Coco like a law-review cram course.

"Sylvia's one of the plaintiffs in the Channel Eight case that I'm handling," he explained, suddenly pompous and solemn. "A group of female employees from the station are challenging the federal license renewal on grounds of discriminatory hiring and promotion practices."

"Yes," Coco said, pausing long enough to radiate extreme annoyance toward Gavin. "I know. It was in the newspaper."

Apparently he was still enough in touch with her signals to receive the message, because Gavin became perceptibly more uncomfortable, tightened his thin narrow lips and sank into a sullen silence.

Coco turned with scientific curiosity toward the young woman who was emanating such amazing amounts of unwarranted self-confidence. Sylvia Brydan seemed totally uninhibited by the condition of her complexion, which was still flirting with adolescent acne, by the twenty pounds of excess fat around her hips and buttocks, or the undeniable fact that she had a most extraordinarily commonplace face. Her loose cotton dress had small round mirrors

and yellow elephants embroidered around the neckline and, as she shifted her weight from one dirty
white sandal to the other, Coco saw she had enormous breasts that were spilling and flopping about
inside her tentlike dress.

"Maybe I should get us some drinks," Gavin finally
suggested.

"I guess I'd like a gin-and-tonic," Sylvia announced.

"I'll get three," Gavin said, moving off into the
crowd.

Then Coco, feeling petite, composed and sophisti-
cated, smiled at Sylvia. "I knew you worked with the
D.C. Coalition, but I didn't know you were into television," she said in a mature, generous tone of voice.

"I don't work at Channel Eight," Sylvia answered.
"I just organized the women employees over there.
The D.C. Coalition sent me in to help them get their
shit together."

"Oh," Coco said. Eternally intimidated by the mys-
teries of organizing, she couldn't think of a rejoinder.

The girl shifted her eyes and looked away.

After a few minutes Coco asked if a court date had
been set yet. She was condescendingly informed, in
monosyllabic prose, that there would be a hearing—
not a trial.

But when Gavin returned, juggling three glasses,
the girl erased her lackadaisical, surly expression and
smiled eagerly—way, way, way up high—at Gavin
while he distributed the drinks.

"Suede Bellock's coming over to meet you," he
informed Sylvia. "He's doing an article for *Esquire* on
different women's-liberation cases being brought
into courts around the country, so he wants to talk
with you. There's a couple of other cases similar to
ours in New York and California."

Coco felt a great surge of anger pulse through her. Not only did Gavin have a secret lovelife, but even his legal activities had become private and exclusive. Her husband and his unattractive client were apparently bound together by ties much stronger than sex or marriage, and their closeness seemed offensive and affronting to Coco. Upset, she mentally exempted herself from the scene and instead went into a movie pose. She froze for a still—stomach taut, chest out, hair ruffling romantically in the warm breeze, lips and eyes glazed with mystery—ready for her P.L., who might be arriving late, delayed by a deadline or a congressional committee meeting.

But it was Suede who bounded toward them, glistening in his own excitement. He skidded into place, cigarette dangling from his mouth, layer upon layer of thick straight hair following the handsome curve of his head, and his eyes dark with expectation. Instantly Coco felt herself brighten, cheered by his enthusiasm. Suede always responded to parties, cluing into the scene, cuing in on the people, absorbing through osmosis the dominant feelings, feeding his mood on unfamiliar faces and places. His ability to extract highs from even the most ordinary occasions was a heavy contributor to his sensuality and another magnet which drew women to him.

But the moment Gavin introduced them, Suede began to ask Sylvia questions about the license challenge and then—right then—right before Coco's jealous and disbelieving eyes, he began to turn on to Sylvia, unperturbed by the heavy lethargic fat that smothered her youthfulness and padded the enormous breasts undulating beneath her dress.

Haughty, heavy, and humorless, Sylvia began to explain the case. Eventually the conversation shifted to changes in federal and state laws that affected

women and then Sylvia really lit up. Each time one of
the men made a declaratory statement, he would
direct it toward Sylvia. While awaiting her response,
he would study her face, check to see if both her
breasts were still there, and then turn away, seemingly educated and refreshed by the encounter.

Totally ignored, Coco stood her ground, feeling
her body begin to dissolve from the gin that she still
sipped delicately through a straw. For a while she
amused herself trying to spot other guests who might
be watching her discomfort, but when she conceded
she wasn't attracting any notice, she returned to the
trio's discussion. Slowly the minutes were becoming
blurred and unchartable as she felt herself dissolving.
Occasionally she marshaled her senses, hastening
back to the present, but each time her perceptions
were progressively more detached and tangential.

After a while the fervent discussion tapered off and
turned to dinner talk. Coco protested that she didn't
feel like going out to a restaurant, but the arrange-
ment-making drowned out her resistance, so she
obediently followed Gavin inside the house to say her
good-byes and thank-yous. After half an hour of aimless walking, she finally remembered where the car
was parked. She moved silently beside Gavin, radiat-
ing unhappiness and complaining that she felt she
had forgotten something back at the party, although
her little beaded purse still dangled from her wrist
and she hadn't brought a jacket. Gavin seemed impatient with her confusion and, since he didn't seem to
like her very much anymore, Coco kept quiet while a
childish sadness dripped through her body.

Gavin drove. Coco sat in the front but turned her
head slightly so she could see out of the corner of her
eye into the back seat where Sylvia was slouched
close to Suede, despite the thick, heavy heat in the

car. Her head was bent awkwardly near Suede's shoulder, while the rest of her generous body spread across the seat. The long colorless wings of her hair drooped like curtains over her eyes and her enormous breasts, which sprawled loosely to each side, shimmied with each motion of the car.

CHAPTER 9

Coco followed the others into the small recently discovered Cuban restaurant, feeling as if she and Gavin were on a double-date with Suede and Sylvia (Most Popular Couple) and tagging along in a desperate effort to get in with the Popular Crowd.

I'm not going to know what to talk about when we sit down, Coco thought, staring straight ahead at the back of Gavin's blue striped sport jacket as they conga-lined behind the manager through a maze of tables in the authentically dark, non-air-conditioned room. They shuffled into hard, straight-back chairs and Coco stared at a large fan churning near the kitchen doorway, feeling as if the entire universe was temporarily dwarfed into a square white linen world with four sharp corners—over any of which an other-directed sailor might fall.

"They have pretty good food here," she said sud-

denly, attempting to establish some friendship to offset her acute ache of loneliness.

It was hard to feel cozily alienated from Gavin
when they were in the company of a suddenly happy
couple who were manufacturing a mutual sexual attraction which they guarded protectively as if it were
a small energetic child they were baby-sitting. Gavin
grunted agreement and Coco felt a spasm of neglect
race through her. She lowered her head and studied
the wine-stain map on the tablecloth, featuring one
huge pink continent (Australia? Africa?) until the
waiter appeared, looking forlorn and foreign, to take
their orders.

Coco was trying desperately hard to save the cube
of her alcoholic numbness that was quickly melting
from the heat and the fact that the Cuban restaurant
had no liquor license. Gavin was talking rapidly, obviously attempting to appear brilliant, witty, sophisti-
cated and impervious to the developing sexuality at
the table. Suede was conspicuously content: watching Sylvia possessively, touching her presump-
tuously, and passing her bread with parental relish.
Sylvia had nestled quickly into the orbit of Suede's
attention and was now expressing total sympathy
with all his New Left clichés. Only twice, when she
thought she could do so without detection, did she
attempt to inspect and evaluate Coco's face.

"Are you tired, Gavin?" Coco asked in a domestic
tone of voice.

She leaned forward, hoping to appropriate some
marital intimacy that would offset the distracting excitement developing along the north and east sides
of the map and wondered if the vulgar availability
that Sylvia advertised reminded Gavin of his mistress. A sharp icepick of emotion pierced her body.

Gavin smiled a grimace of controlled exasperation

and said he felt great. Coco made a quick inspection
of his face and realized that he was trying to hear
what Sylvia and Suede were saying.

She ate more bread. She drank. She smoked. She
listened. She waited. She hated everyone. And then
suddenly, Sylvia, who had begun noisily guzzling
gazpacho out of a large spoon, turned directly toward Coco.

"You're sort of into women's-liberation stuff a little,
aren't you?" she asked.

Self-consciously, as a sisterly afterthought, she
stretched her broad thick lips into a smile. Her teeth
were very straight and white, making her face look
less gross and hefty, more generous—more soft and
accessible. With that single smile Sylvia somehow
translated her heaviness into a lushness that brought
her up from the farm team to which Coco had originally assigned her into the major leagues of threatening women.

"Yes," Coco answered stiffly, while her alcoholic
high lost altitude like a helium balloon brought home
from the zoo. "I'm in the Columbia Road Consciousness Raising Local and the Northwest Area Theoretical Council."

"Uh-huh," Sylvia said with belittling approval.

Coco felt totally deflated. Her far-out membership,
which in PTA circles was equivalent to a CP card,
was no longer sufficient. Somehow Sylvia had simultaneously infiltrated the ranks of the men and upped
the ante by endowing her feminist activities with
great political value—an alchemization Coco had
tirelessly pursued but never achieved. She waited
tensely for the next attack in the unannounced intra-
mural scrimmage.

"Are you into the July Fourth march at all?"

"Oh, yes," Coco said. She felt so grateful that her

anxiety turned into recklessness. "I'm co-chair of the
Citywide Coalition Housing and Accommodations
Committee."

It sounded ridiculous.

Gavin looked at her with authentic surprise, while
Suede smirked in a way that was only a trifle more
churlish than cruel.

Coco shifted in her chair, futilely trying to release
the dress, which was glued to her thighs with sweat,
and to erase the impression she had just made.

"Yah," Sylvia said, stuffing a thickly buttered piece
of bread into her mouth. "I guess that's where I saw
your name. I'm on the National Steering Committee."

The waiter appeared carrying four platters which
he rhythmically swung down in front of them. Coco
stared at the dark meat bobbing in brown gravy and
realized she had totally and permanently discredited
herself. The irony of being put down by a newfound
sister for not being heavy enough into the movement
was a total denial of everything women's liberation
represented. And at the same time Sylvia was belittling Coco, she was simultaneously elevating her
feminist activities so they sounded respectably radical enough for both Gavin and Suede.

"I guess I'm supposed to march with the Steering
Committee next Tuesday," Coco said, pathetically
grappling for composure by trying to appropriate
some aura of purpose and prestige. "Or at least that's
what Helen Blumenthal told me."

Then she tossed her head back, as if to sling her
hair away from her face, produced a proud profile
and unleashed one of her outlandishly Hollywood
hard-on hold-it smiles. Coco's pantomime signaled a
magnanimous forgiveness of Sylvia's trespasses by as-

signing them to an understandably inferiority complex.

The men decoded Coco's message. Suede's eyes touched Coco accusingly before sweeping away to survey the room. His face was stained with hot anger, and though Coco invariably felt cheered at discovering someone else's discomfort corresponded to her own, she realized that she had gone too far. Sylvia had totally ignored Coco's prize performance and now began to tell Suede and Gavin how she was organizing and planning the tactics for challenging any Democratic state delegations that had less than fifty percent women in Miami at the National Convention.

Coco listened in stupefaction as Sylvia snapped a sound of legitimacy into the challenge tactic, as if she were representing chicanos or blacks rather than women—people who were clearly, rather than debatably, oppressed.

"So what's the status of the Channel Eight suit?" Coco asked irritably, to interrupt Sylvia's monologue.

Everyone turned to look at her.

"I mean, you know . . . Gavin never fills me in on any of his work." Coco picked up the last piece of meat from her dish with her fingers and stuck it in her mouth as she spoke. "You know how it is," she said, winking Female Complaint #10 toward Sylvia. "He probably doesn't think I'd be *interested* or that I could *understand.*"

That caused a devastating silence.

Suede looked away as if Coco had belched or cut wind at the table, while Gavin turned red with anger. But instead of falling into line, Sylvia transparently shifted over into the men's camp to get on the winning side.

"Jesus, Coco," Gavin groaned, swallowing a harsher curse.

"Well, why haven't you told me anything about it?" Coco persisted. "You know I'm interested in equal opportunities for women."

"I know," Gavin said reluctantly to appease Coco without really conceding any ground, "but don't come on about it now. Like *this.*"

So Coco turned back to Sylvia. "And how long have *you* been working in the movement?" she asked.

"Since I dropped out of Bennington last year," Sylvia answered.

But even from behind the tan screen of her hair, she seemed overly interested in the static between the Burmans. She was watching them like an anthropologist out in the field observing the strange customs of some exotic couple, victims of a decadent and divisive social order.

Then, gracelessly, she began to explain about her involvement in women's liberation, scattering clues to her identity like a Homecoming Queen throwing rose petals from the back seat of an open convertible.

Coco's irritation shifted into outrage. She began stamping out the butt of her Marlboro into the greasy gravy left at the bottom of her heavy white porcelain dinner dish. Involuntarily she remembered reading a theory that new mothers who compulsively tap their babies' backs to bring up burps are really suppressing murderous beating impulses. Coco wondered if her quick abbreviated jabs at the dinner dish were restrained slaps at Sylvia for being an aggressive opportunist. To hear an unpleasantly self-assured young girl talk abstractly about the female condition as if it were her own offshore oil strike, a natural resource for her own private development, was intolerable to Coco. Sylvia was shamelessly using Coco's problem as her own solution.

Frantic, Coco smiled toward Suede, trying to enlist his support, but then she saw he was incapacitated by a total body/mind hard-on. Sylvia's delivery of all the ideas which had achingly emerged from thousands of consciousness-raising sessions had become the biggest come-on and turn-on of all. Totally stymied, Coco administered several fast swallows of espresso into her soiled-tasting mouth.

It was all too much for her. Slowly, insidiously, the poor little Cuban restaurant melted into a stage drop, an inviting, irresistible setting for another love fantasy. Obliterating the unpleasant realities at the table, Coco put down the miniature coffee cup and sent her favorite film up to the projectionist's box in the rear of her head. This was the one in which The Ultimate Man—her P.L.—turned up at Rehoboth Beach, Delaware, the summer spa for Washington housewives and children too young for day camp. Politely Coco sent a farewell smile to her dinner companions, who were still discussing methods of translating their psychological needs into various political programs, and left for the beach.

But this time something was causing some serious static that interfered with the reception of her fantasy flick. All her life Coco had created carefully detailed, list-accompanied fantasies—no misty tremulous dreams for her. When she lay awake in bed, resenting the sleeping body of her husband beside her, she would carefully pack imaginary trunks to take to a deserted beach hide-away, remembering refills for her favorite Papermate pen (no country store could be expected to stock such esoteric items), extra boxes of inspirational Manifold Carbons, large bulky sweaters to wear with skinny muslin pants on

rainy days, op-art plastic manuscript folios to protect
her papers at the shore, all her spices so she wouldn't
need to replace them from scratch, and matching
striped swimsuits for the children. Coco had always
accepted the responsibilities of her fantasies. But this
time, despite all her advance work, the proper film
did not appear on the screen of her mind. Nor did
her X-L P.L. turn up at the appropriate moment
outside the carmel-corn corner candy store. Coco
was drawing a great big fat zero.

A jarring shuffling of chairs and a noisy inspection
of the bill interrupted her. She looked across at
Gavin, but he was still ignoring her.

"Let's get going," he said. "It's got to be cooler
outside."

He looked at Coco like a lab tech studying an
X-ray.

So Coco stood up and walked away from the table
ahead of the others so she could wait alone in the
street for a few moments, embracing the cool fresh
breeze that blew debris along the sidewalk.

Then they all drove back to the Burmans' house.

CHAPTER 10

Once upstairs in the second-floor living room, Coco sat down in the blue chair that was a flattering background color for her, and watched the scene develop. Gavin had extravagantly sent Mrs. Marshall home in a taxi and then enthusiastically led everyone upstairs, made drinks, and began pacing around the room acting the charming, now-barefoot, host. As an act of good faith, he began his conversation by asking Suede about his new novel. This was the first introduction of a nonpolitical subject and a polite, though begrudging, acknowledgment of Suede's commercial acclaim.

"So when's your book coming out?"

Year after year, Gavin had increasing difficulty dealing with Suede's success. They had both left college as equals—indeed, with Gavin holding a slight edge of intelligence over Suede—but now it was

Suede who was famous, photographed, promoted and pursued. The bylaws of their unmentionable, but eternal, competition demanded that Gavin verbally acknowledge his defeat in the pop culture race while claiming a serious lead in the social-contribution heat. A favorable Supreme Court decision was of higher rank than a National Book Award on the original Achievement Scale they had both agreed upon back in their undergraduate days.

"In September," Suede said dismissingly, trying to minimize what was profitable about the path he had chosen.

"Do you think the movies will buy it?"

It had been established long ago that Gavin must fathom all the depths of his repressed jealousy in exchange for Suede's concession that Gavin's work was more valuable (though less visible and sexy) than fiction-writing.

"Jesus, I hope so. I'm broke. And writing articles is a ball-busting way to make a little bread."

"They'll probably offer you half a million for this one—after *Making Out,*" Gavin said magnanimously.

In accordance with their original contract, Suede now had to acknowledge his deficiency in the arena of radical politics, which he entered only as a journalistically detached observer and commentator.

"But I'm really going to bust my ass writing this radical-law piece. People just don't know anything about these test cases and class actions."

"Great," Gavin conceded, placated and satisfied.

Now he could return to the subject of the *Esquire* article that dealt with his professional, political and personal obsession—the need for radical law firms to combat social and political inequities through the court system. He quickly ran through his customary

lecture on the hideous composition of the Supreme
Court, the endless instances of police brutality, the
possible outcome and consequences of the Democratic National Convention, and the need for revolu-
tionary reforms throughout the society.

"The country's falling apart," he said ominously,
eating cashews from a can he had succeeded in pry-
ing only half-open. "This fucking war is ruining the
country."

Suede, who had unknowingly chosen Gavin's favorite chair, thus causing the endless pilgrimage up
and down the room, listened good-naturedly because
Gavin had been decent about the novel and even
extravagant in mentioning possible movie sales.

Sylvia was visibly excited by the situation although
oblivious of its subtleties. She had started out seated
on the couch, but after several drinks, heady from
the rarefied atmosphere produced by a nationally
known novelist exchanging antiestablishment pro-
nouncements with her very own lawyer, she slipped
down onto the floor and deposited hunks of her body
across the rug as well as up the side of the couch. The
skirt of her dress was stretched so tight that when she
bent her knees the dark foliage of her crotch appeared, and each time she turned to flick her cigarette toward the ashtray on her left, her enormous
breasts swung, independent of each other, from side
to side. Occasionally she stuck two or three fingers
into her glass to fish out a lime slice to suck while
asking Gavin *Meet the Press* type questions about The
Law, smiling promiscuously toward Suede, and ignoring anything Coco said.

"Would you like another drink?" Gavin asked
when he passed near Coco's chair.

And because the puzzling phenomenon of Sylvia—
apparently hiding some great sexual magnet beneath

the pillowy pads of her hips and some intellectual bonanza behind the muslin-colored drapes of her hair—affected Coco adversely, she nodded her head.

The giggling sound of gin rushing out of the bottle into her glass pleased her so much that when Gavin left the ice tray etching its shape into the coffee table, she didn't even complain. As soon as he recommenced his odyssey around the room, she put the ice cubes in the bucket, and after Suede made a round-trip visit to the toilet, she sat down on the rug beside his chair and commenced a flashy flirtation with him to reestablish her own sexual and domestic territory. Her fatigue was frosted with a thick layer of alcohol and jealousy.

"So what's up with you and Ms. Brydan," she asked in an accusative, suggestive, stagy whisper.

"My dick," Suede answered, squinting through the smoke of his cigarette.

"Terrific," Coco countered, feeling that her foreign policy was in total disarray. "You know, I'm counting on you to put me in touch with a good publisher in the fall."

She smiled and, as an accompaniment to her request, expanded her chest isometrically by blowing out imaginary candles on an invisible birthday cake.

Suede seemed to appreciate Coco's physical gesture more than her assumption of his literary assistance. He stamped out the butt of his cigarette, pushed a fresh one out of the package, struck a match, crunched up his blue eyes to avoid the first blast of smoke and slashed a very white smile across his tanned face.

"Well, it better not be anymore of that clit-lit stuff. One more prom-queen book and I'm going to barf."

Coco considered Suede's attack on the women writers she worshiped sacrilegious, but her need for an ally made her traitorous, and so she decided to mobilize Suede with an attack on Sylvia's feminist fanaticism.

"Yes, that's gotten a little out of hand, hasn't it?" she agreed, selling out her sisterhood.

But Suede looked at her suspiciously. "Didn't Gavin say that you were into all that shit too?" He blew a fascinating stream of smoke out from between clenched lips that held his cigarette like an erotic erection. "I wouldn't be surprised if some of your . . . other troubles"—he blinked euphemistically— "were a result of all that same crap." He looked over toward Sylvia, who was talking softly to Gavin across the room. "It brings out the worst in women. Not to mention books."

That was a bit heavy for Coco. Suede going gaga over Sylvia, while putting down the women's-liberation movement, seemed inequitable to Coco. But since, at the moment, her personal peril was paramount, she caught her hair at the nape of her neck, twisted it around into a Mary McCarthy-type bun and said, "Well, let's just say my novel deals with realities."

Generously Suede decided to let that pass. He inspected Coco's body admiringly several times, taking a third tour of her legs as a show of forgiveness, bent over, lowered his voice and said, "You know, nobody else ever got it up for me as fast as you did." Then he grinned and raised his voice. "Hey . . . I've got a whole lid of grass in my room. How about turning on?"

Sylvia rose to her knees. "Wow! Why did you hold out so long? I thought none of you smoked or something." Her voice moved like a caress across the room.

"Well, you can't smoke pot in here," Gavin said. "It gives me hay fever."

Sylvia laughed disbelievingly.

"No. It's true," Coco said. "He gets hay fever and asthma from both kinds of grass. But we can go sit outside on the back porch."

She looked toward Gavin anxiously, but he seemed relieved as he picked up a book and sprawled out on the living-room couch. So Coco led Sylvia and Suede out to her porch, which looked very different and strange at night. She flicked on the yellow antibug bulb on the brick housewall, watched Sylvia confiscate the chaise, and then sat down on the floor.

The sky was very dark and the moon kept swimming in and out of the clouds. Suede rolled several joints so that soon the strong sweet smell of marijuana lilted through the porch. They all took long burning gulps of smoke into their lungs. When the cigarettes finally grew pinched and empty, Suede gathered the butts together, flicked off the light and stretched out flat near Coco, with his head propped against the wall close to hers.

Right away Sylvia began to move around restlessly on the chaise, and finally she too got down on the floor on the other side of Suede. Coco saw a flash of Sylvia's fleshy buttocks and then watched one of Suede's hands reach out to casually collect a little of her stray fat in his fingers. He seemed totally engrossed by the bright promise of burying himself in the rolling prairies of her flesh.

Why doesn't anyone want me like that? Coco thought, beginning to feel gusts of suspension engulf her.

"How you doing, babes?" Suede asked, trying to include Coco in his honeymoon expansiveness.

But his good intentions seemed scorched by the

hot night and the sexual transactions and negotiations going on between him and Sylvia. Crammed against the wall, with the lower half of Sylvia's inert body imprisoning his legs, he was helpless.

A filmed preview of Suede and Sylvia making love filtered through Coco's mind. Their physical desire—the uninvited friend of her uninvited guests—was a reproach to Coco. She closed her eyes and felt her legs become weightless appendages to her body, immutably there, but somehow severed and disconnected.

"I'm getting high," she said aloud, tortured by the nearness of a passion that excluded and eluded her.

"Wow. It's nice out here," Sylvia said. She was now lounging even more impudently beside Suede, her legs relaxed like two fat arrows pointing at the target toward which Suede's large presumptuous hand was slowly sliding. "That's good dope."

"Aren't you thirsty?"

Coco exhaled her own funny, non-meaning words and felt a warm liquid sensation flood the lower part of her body. She wondered if her post-lib libido was geared toward orgiastic orgasms, and involuntarily she shuddered as several pleasant waves of desire rippled through her. She felt fanciful and turned on because she lay near a man who had once rummaged around inside her.

"What did you say?" Coco mumbled in response to no one, her mouth dry and her head heavy. "Huh?"

From a great billowy distance, through blankets and pillows of space, noisy memories were clamoring. Then the sound came closer until it seemed to have occurred much earlier. Coco stretched out flatter on the floor and suddenly realized Suede had tucked his free hand into the soft pocket between her thighs and was scratching against the silk crotch of her panties.

Reason and disbelief stirred within her. It was impossible that he was fingering both Coco and Sylvia at the same time, diddling both of them, under the cover of darkness. Still, Coco's lower body began to feel damp and loose, as if all her insides were listing downward. A block of real time intruded upon her confusion. Flooded with uncertainty as to what was happening, Coco moved, straightened the long skirt that had somehow crawled up her body, and rose to her feet.

"Hey, where you going?" Suede asked hoarsely.

Coco gripped the screen-door knob, feeling sad and separate.

"Coco." Gavin was calling to her from the third floor.

She ran through the guest room and down the hallway to the stairs.

"What?" she called weakly.

"I think the baby wants a bottle."

"Just put in his pacifier."

She could hardly speak. She started slowly up the stairs and after a long while reached her bedroom. Then she lay down on the bed, closed her eyes, and waited for another billow of time to enfold her.

"I think the baby's getting sick," Gavin said, coming into the bedroom.

He planted himself near Coco, looming above her like a palm tree with his little coconut head waving up on top.

Coco tried to anchor her runaway thoughts to Gavin's voice. His practicality offered to reestablish reality for her. Since he wasn't part of the sexual flurries and storms that had raged on the porch, he was still uncontaminated and safe.

"I hope not," Coco said after a long silence.

"I think he's got a stomachache."

Flat on her back, she looked up high at her husband.

"I've got a stomachache in my heart," she whispered.

Gavin looked down at her quizzically from the isolating height of his own preoccupations. Coco watched his small, neat features reshape themselves into a speculative expression.

She struggled for self-control. "I don't know what's the matter with me," she said, brinking on tears. "Everything seems to be going wrong."

Gavin's narrow forehead corrugated into a frown.

"Oh, I know you're tired of hearing me complain all the time."

Coco felt swollen with discontent.

Gavin bent the length of his body in half and sat down beside her. He leaned over and placed an outstretched arm on each side of her body.

"Look, honey, I know you're upset. Things have been sorta rough for a while."

Coco raised herself a little so that she could nestle her head into the hollow between Gavin's neck and shoulder, still trying to extract a percentage of him.

"But you think all my problems and troubles are inconsequential—next to what you think about," Coco said, feeling spatially dislocated.

"That's not true," Gavin answered. But his words came out too quickly, like "that's all right" when the kids broke a glass—impatience and insincerity humming behind the disclaimer.

"You just don't understand what it's like for me," Coco continued. "I'm not like you. I'm different. Men and women are different. I can't think about the world when I'm hurting inside. It's not that I don't care about Vietnam. I do. But when I feel so miserable, I can't think about faraway things. It's like blotting out a building by holding up just one finger in front of your eyes. My problems are blocking out the rest of the world for me. No wonder Jane Austen never mentioned the French Revolution."

Gavin's steadfast kindness consisted of silence. He began stroking the top of her head with soft, thoughtless fingers.

Coco felt weak with bewilderment. "I know what you think. You think that I'm silly and selfish. But all you ever do is evaporate before I can get to use any of you. And it was that way even before you fell in love with your girlfriend. Don't you think I feel bad enough without Suede seeing how things are going around here and without that freaky witch watching us fall apart?"

"Who cares about that?" Gavin shrugged.

Coco's spirits were fading. "Well, if you don't care about anything that matters to me, you should get the hell out of my life."

"That's not what I meant," Gavin protested.

"Fuck you," Coco groaned.

He moved away with a wrenching motion that shattered her.

"Why don't you go to sleep?" he said angrily. "I'm going downstairs."

Coco watched him turn his back on her, retreating into his own urgent agenda of responsibilities and purpose.

"Please don't go," Coco said suddenly, pathetically. She rolled across the tangled sheets of the messy bed—a poetic and graphic symbol for her own disorganization—and saw her husband stop, flick off the overhead light, and return to lie down beside her. Complacently he pulled her toward him, placed his hand inside the top of her dress, and captured one of her breasts.

Disgust flooded through Coco's body while her flesh tightened involuntarily under Gavin's probing fingers. He made the curve of his palm a proper size to fit her breast into the cup of his fingers. Then he examined the nipple until it grew hard and springy. Coco thought she might survive this encounter if she activated one of her pre-fab pre-lib fantasies, but she was too upset.

"Gavin," she said determinedly, "I want to talk."

Her body was rigid and a familiar objectless rage had begun to assert itself within her.

"What do you want to talk for?"

He rolled closer to kiss her and the pressure of his lips made her feel seasick and queasy.

"What do you think of that girl? Sylvia? Suede really seems to like her, doesn't he?"

"Ssssh."

She felt the moist warmth of his sound upon her skin and her throat felt prickly.

"Please, Gavin, answer me."

"What do you want to know?" he mumbled.

She turned her head so that the side of her face touched a rough exposure of uncovered mattress. Her arm was stretched out along the wall. At the end, her hand held a cup of darkness.

"I have to talk," she said finally. "I feel sort of nervous."

"What are you nervous about?"

She felt his body flatten out against her own.

"I don't know. It's probably because they came over."

"Relax, Coco. Quit thinking for a little while and take a vacation."

"Listen," she said wildly, desperate to divert him without knowing what to say or how to say it.

Gavin didn't answer. He began to caress her stomach, mechanically extending each stroke downward. His breathing became louder as his rummagings quickened. He began to roll her skirt upward and to push her panties down the length of her legs.

"Please just tell me what you think of her? Isn't she a nut? Far-out?"

"Oh, she's all right," Gavin mumbled.

"Oh, it's one of those days, huh?" Coco asked flatly. "It's one of those days when everybody's okay by you. Even Hitler."

"Look, I don't want to fight," Gavin said.

"Well, how do you think I feel," Coco asked, "with them screwing around on my porch right now, right here in my own house?"

"Look. What do you care? Don't pay attention."

Coco escaped from Gavin's arm. Gratitude for his attention faded with his lack of agreement about Sylvia. "You know, there's certainly not much point in talking to each other if you're in one of your Christian moods of understanding. No matter what anybody says or does, you'll find a good reason to understand their motives. But I'll tell you one thing. I think that Sylvia is crazy."

"Ssssh. Don't talk so loud."

"I can assure you that they're not listening to us."

Gavin took Coco's hand and placed it upon himself, silently reproaching her for her lack of interest.

Coco's body felt nearsighted, unable to focus upon the instructions implicit in Gavin's movements. She remembered how he had ignored her at the Brandys' and betrayed her at the restaurant. She felt her own private brand of rebellion move through her as he crawled upon her, covering her limbs with his own.

Internally Coco collapsed in exasperation. Gavin's touch felt like the assaults of a relentless mosquito that she couldn't evade or escape in the darkness. Her body became only an extension of her anger.

And then, suddenly, Gavin rolled away from her toward his own side of the bed.

Totally discredited, Coco's eyes filled with tears at the unexpected demise of his desire and she began to cry.

He put his arm beneath her neck.

"Now, what the hell's the matter?" he asked, with disinterest printed upon each word. "You know, fighting all the time gets to be one hell of a bore."

"Oh, it's not that you don't like fighting, Gavin, it's that you don't like the *idea* of *you* fighting."

Gavin locked his arms around her again. "Can you tell me when the hell I ever said I was a better son-of-a-bitch than anyone else? What's started you off on that kick?"

"Oh, God. You think you're Jesus Christ, that's all." Coco pulled away and rolled over to stuff her face in the pillow. Her words were muffled messages sent out into the darkness. "You spend every minute of your life acting good, defending good, thinking good, talking good—except when you're fucking around with your little girlfriend."

"You know something, Coco. I'm beginning to think you're not really jealous."

Coco groaned.

Gavin remained silent, demonstrating his equanimity and appropriating great judiciousness unto himself.

Coco looked toward the window and for a moment the city outside beckoned her with noises that mixed escape with decision. But inside her body a riot of conflicting feelings—hurt, revenge, jealousy, bereavement—were churning about so she couldn't translate the dialect of her own emotions.

Suddenly Gavin switched tactics and crouched above her again, emanating anticipation.

Coco felt detached and distant as he worked, solitarily, through his own excitement. She measured progress only by the tempo of his movements, letting the thudding rhythm of his passion wash over her. Finally, her numbed body received his lurching conclusion and she lay silently beneath him until he moved away.

CHAPTER 11

*S*un was streaming through the windows when Coco opened her eyes. She twisted around so as to avoid the reproachful light and recapture her unconsciousness, but a musty odor of sex rose from the crossly wrinkled sheets and a spurt of dark memories raced through her.

"Gavin. Wake up."

She began to shake him frantically. It seemed as if a full-blown nuclear attack of hysteria was upon her and she needed some deterrent—heavy hardware or at least a defense shelter—to protect herself from the approaching holocaust.

"What time is it?" Gavin moaned.

"It must be late. Look at the sunshine."

He unlocked himself slowly but purposefully to the day, rubbing sleep out of his barely opened eyes. Then he sat up, fully intact and invulnerable, to feel

around on the radiator for his glasses so he could read
the alarm clock.

"Jesus Christ, Coco," he groaned. "It's only seven
o'clock. It's Saturday, for Christ's sake. I'm tired: I
don't want to get up yet."

"Oh, I didn't know it was so early," Coco apologized. "I'm sorry, Gavin. Go back to sleep. Sleep late
today," she advised virtuously, "and I'll make you a
good breakfast when you get up."

Then Coco got out of bed and pulled on a pair of
jeans and a denim shirt that had been crumpled up
on top of the dresser. Troops of self-disgust, fear, and
frustration were marching through the lowlands of
her soul. Etchings of Bosch-like images from the past
night were on display in her head. The dark sexuality
with which she had coexisted on the back porch and
the sad scramblings later in her own bed were war-
ring for attention like jealously demanding siblings.

"Shit," Coco said, feeling sick.

She looked in on the children, who were still sleeping, and then ran down the stairs. Suede's door was
firmly shut and for the first time it occurred to Coco
that Sylvia might still be in there, sleeping on the
narrow guest bed with Suede. Coco paused on the
landing to consider the contingencies of that possibility, but finding it too much to handle, ran quickly
down the last flight of stairs. The heat in the rear of
the house was a silent, motionless presence that em-
braced her the moment she entered the kitchen. For
a brief second Coco felt anchored by the humidity
and moored by morning duties. Automatically she
moved toward the coffeepot to empty out yesterday's grounds (for divorce?).

And that was when she heard the first hurried
sounds from the guest room above the kitchen.

On, no, Coco thought weakly. They're both up

there. She could hear them padding around. How awful. How hideous. They were going to hang around all day. They were going to liberate Coco's house for their own Saturday headquarters. How rude. How wrong of Sylvia to have stayed and of Suede to have let her. Now Coco would spend a hurried, harried and harassed day trying to look cool while they both spied on her. They would watch Coco cook, clear, clean, care, carry and cope, so that later on they could inform on her, testify, in front of the world, as to her failures as a woman, a wife, a mother, a hostess, a housekeeper, a cook, a social-activities leader, a chauffeur, a sports-and-nature guide—the weekend cruise director.

Coco made a fresh pot of coffee and then sat down at the table, certain, in her acute state of dissolution, that a mouse or a roach would suddenly dart out from some dark corner to scoot across the linoleum floor.

—I'm feeling sort of flimsy this morning—she thought. Things seem sort of temporary. I'm never going to smoke grass again. Ever.—

Upstairs she could hear suspicious creaking noises in the guest room. Impulsively Coco stood up, walked to the refrigerator, opened the door and took stock of her supplies. If she could get the breakfast together before the children came downstairs, she had a chance of stalemating the first half of her Saturday.

Resolution and weakness were strolling around companionably inside her body. She pulled the breakfast table away from the wall, squeezed in two extra dining-room chairs, and then began scurrying back and forth between the cupboards and the table, setting out her best dishes. Photographs of a *Better Homes and Gardens* bruncheon danced through her head as she trotted through the first round of chores.

Half an hour later, back upstairs again, she went
into action like a speeded-up twenty-millimeter film.
She washed, dressed, shushed the children and
brought them down to the kitchen. But she had fed
only half of them half of their breakfast when Sylvia
suddenly appeared in the doorway.

"Good morning," Sylvia said brightly, like a forty-
watt bulb trying to shine.

She was wearing what looked like a pair of Suede's
Bermuda shorts, which were several sizes too small
for her, and one of his white BVD shirts. Her lower
fat wobbled as she came through the doorway, while
her upper appendages swung and swayed.

"Oh, hello," Coco said.

"Who's dat?" Nicky shouted.

"I'm Sylvia."

"What are you doing here?" Jessica asked coldly.

Mike just sat stoically, staring at the two huge
breasts dangling near the table.

"Can I do anything to help you?" Sylvia asked.

Die, Coco thought.

Then she smiled and shook her head.

Sylvia sat down on one of the dining-room chairs to
watch the four Burman children eat their frosted
Pop Tarts with a critical granola gleam in her eye.

"Good morning!"

Suede walked into the kitchen wearing his macho
like a tennis sweater over his clothes and a perfect
expression of constraint and conspiracy on his face.
He sat down at the table next to Sylvia, sent her an
Eyes-Only Memo Re: Sex, and finger-combed his
thick dark hair in the way that used to knock out
coeds at the C. Shop in Chicago.

"That was some outa-sight grass," he said, smiling
at Coco with careless charm. "How's chances for
some coffee?"

Coco felt an involuntary shiver of approval for Suede—as a sex object—shimmy through her body even as her Raised Consciousness voted him the Most Pernicious Pig of All the Male Chauvinists. His early-morning nonchalance clearly confirmed her suspicions that he had finger-fucked both Sylvia and her at the same time last night and his audacious adulterous camaraderie showed he felt no guilt about it because he recognized no trespass. Suede was still diddling his way through the world's women, occasionally two at a time, with the same sick compulsion that had driven Coco to alphabetically read her way through the Chicago Public Library, drawer by drawer, of the card catalog.

"Sure," Coco said flatly without moving to serve him, "the coffee's ready."

Instantly Sylvia jumped to her feet to fetch the creamer and sugar bowl from the counter, eagerly entering into a unilateral competition to serve Suede his breakfast.

When Gavin came downstairs, looking totally disheveled, an hour later, he was struck dumb at the sight of Sylvia and Suede drinking coffee in the kitchen.

"Good morning," he said after a lengthy awkward pause. "What's for breakfast?"

Coco stood motionless, leaning against the air-conditioner, so the movie studio still photographer could catch her—hair blowing and shirt flattening against her back—as she reported from on-the-scene back to her team of anchormen:

Things aren't going right; I have on underarm deodorant, vaginal deodorant, foot deodorant—sent to Occupant free in the mail—Binaca still burning the roof of my mouth, and I can actually smell myself sweating. Also, there is a definite taste and smell of decay from my gums. Stim-u-dents do not prevent decay. They only move it around. Weak gums come from bad nerves rather than from not brushing and Dental Floss doesn't do the trick. Bad body odors come from internal corruption and external tension.

Then Coco moved off-camera and began frying eggs.

There were several perfectly hideous discussions. One began with Sylvia, speaking as a national official of the women's liberation movement, summarizing the problems of motherhood. After a congested run of child-care requests—Nicky wanting help to get his sunsuit off so he could go number two, Jessica begging to invite Sarah over, Mike wanting Gavin to walk him to the filling station to fill his bike tires, Joshua needing a clean diaper and an extra bottle— Sylvia looked up from the table where the three adults still sat smoking and skimming through the newspaper and said:

"No wonder American women can't break out of their bag. Four kids can monopolize one adult full time for fifteen years."

And though Coco agreed—thoroughly, heartily, and bitterly—she could not allow her condition to be diagnosed by a woman who sat perfectly still while Coco met all the juvenile demands, never once offering to help or even clearing away her own breakfast dishes, although it was almost noon and time for lunch.

"Well, it's always been that way," Coco said, "and besides, weekends are a little more desperate than weekdays."

"But it's time that women see an alternative to nuclear families," Sylvia insisted.

"Yah. There should be a better way," Suede agreed sympathetically.

Gavin politically kept quiet while reading the editorial page.

"You know, the average workweek for a housewife with kids is between eighty and one hundred hours," Sylvia continued educationally. "Think of the waste and the duplication—the loss of creative potential—simply because each woman is chained inside her own little house, doing everything alone, while right next door another lady is doing exactly the same things. In an age of mass production, that's a pretty weird trip. And, anyway, the country needs those women to work and build and organize. The feminist revolution will have to precede any takeover by the workers."

Coco finished feeding Josh his bottle and then got up to put him in his playpen in the TV room, hoping he'd fall asleep.

"So what's your solution, Sylvia?" she asked when she returned to the kitchen, trying to sound like a neophyte in order to goad her on.

"Communes, of course, as an opener." Sylvia spoke like a recording—not even bothering to inject enthusiasm or emotion. "Or city-block collective day-care centers. If everyone on your street put their children together for the day and another group prepared food for everyone, that would free up seventy-five percent of the women." Sylvia kept one hand fastened possessively on Suede's thigh.

Gavin sat a bit apart from the others looking at the newspapers stacked in front of him.

Coco's anger had opened a three-ring circus of wild feelings in the coliseum of her chest.

"And why all of a sudden are women going to start doing things for each other?" she asked. "How come they haven't gotten together before now?"

"Well, in most primitive societies they do. It's only

capitalism that divides women. Once American women find out that it's best to organize on a local level, they will."

Sylvia helped herself to another slice of Sara Lee coffeecake and wiped some extra frosting off the side of the container with her finger. Although Coco's only satisfaction was watching Sylvia overeat, she still felt uneasy because the Sara Lee was out on the table in its tinfoil box instead of having been transferred to a cake dish.

"Well, I don't think helping people out seems to be a very common human habit."

The moment she said it, Coco thought she had been too obvious. But none of the adults sitting at the table took her criticism personally.

"Of course, I see going far beyond communal child care and community cooking," Sylvia said. "Eventually people will simply exist in groups, either living or work collectives, and share everything—including each other—with everyone else."

"Terrific," Coco mumbled, carrying a stack of egg-smeared dishes to the sink and hoping that one of the many sausages Sylvia had eaten contained a small unnoticed bit of fatal-on-the-spot—according to Mrs. Silverman—pink trichinosis. Sylvia deserved to die. She viewed herself not as Coco's equal, but as her superior.

"What did you say?" Sylvia asked.

There was a silken thread of hostility audible in her voice now as she sat in her fat overblown certitude, hanging onto Suede's knee, awaiting the arrival of a social revolution.

"I mean, do you think everyone is going to give up marriage?" Coco asked.

"Oh, yes," Sylvia said enthusiastically. "Just look at the divorce rate right now. It's almost eighty percent in some social and economic classes. It's happening anyway. People just aren't monogamous," she laughed seductively.

Coco felt gooseflesh crawl over her body, but then she heard a thin wail from Joshua wanting to get out of his playpen.

"Well, how come most people spend their whole lives looking for the one right person?" she asked.

Sylvia stared at Coco.

"It's other things that cause all the trouble," Coco concluded obliquely.

"Listen," Suede interrupted good-naturedly, "the only difference between you two chicks is that Sylvia's generation thinks men are the problem and Coco's generation thought men were the solution."

Stunned, Coco couldn't regroup fast enough to reply. All she could do was hate the smugness and superciliousness of Sylvia Brydan, who certainly was no sister of Coco Burman's if she couldn't even help clean up the fucking kitchen.

After another hour of Sylvia's inanities, Coco wanted to stand up on top of the table and start screaming. She felt an overwhelming urge to deliver an impassioned speech denouncing Gavin as a passive parent as well as an adulterer. She wanted pity and sympathy and drama to blanket her, and only the fear that Gavin might meet her wail of pain with countercharges deterred her.

A few minutes later Sylvia suggested that she and Suede go out in the patio to play with the children and they both sheepishly disappeared through the back door.

Gavin moved in close to Coco as soon as they were alone.

"Listen, this little visit is fucking up my day. I'd been planning to work all afternoon over at my of-

fice. But as long as Sylvia's here, I think I'm going to
pull out the brief I'm writing for their license challenge and do some work on it with her. I was going to
hold it off for a week or so, but I might as well kill two
birds . . ."

Coco shrugged, feeling instantly exiled by Gavin's
sudden, energetic determination to work. His bright
commitment reinfected her with a need to return to
her novel. Even her own disorganized efforts at
working on a book-without-a-theme seemed better
than a long lethargic day in the kitchen waiting to
make the next meal, waiting to unbutton the next
pair of pants, waiting to untie, unknot or undo another child.

Feeling abandoned, Coco unconsciously moved toward the cookie jar and transferred an Oreo cookie
into her mouth.

Eat . . . eat, she thought. Stuff it in . . . fill up
your little vacuum.

"And what do you think I'm supposed to do?" she
asked Gavin as the white inner frosting began to
dissolve in her mouth, softening her anger.

Gavin examined her face, decided that she had
only issued the challenge automatically, without any
battle plan, and retreated back into his own invisible
docket of legal cases. "Listen, later on I'll take the
kids out for a while. I have to pick up some papers at
my office, so I'll take them over there and you can
have a rest."

Then, remembering some affection for her, he
moved toward the sink, where she was standing,
looped his arm around her shoulders and, in a rush of
apology, pulled her against him. Although Coco desperately wanted his nearness and attention, wanted
to rebalance the emotional scale by which they
weighed their marriage, she pulled back, dissatisfied

with the quality of his attention and determined to disdain anything short of total engagement.

So Gavin turned toward the back door and walked outside to summon Sylvia. Within a few minutes he led her silently back through the kitchen and disappeared. Seconds later, forsaking the baseball game he had been playing with Mike, Suede returned to the kitchen and sat down at the table to watch Coco wash the dishes.

"You know, if McGovern wins the nomination, I'm going to work on his campaign," Coco said. "I bet if I really worked my ass off and he won, I could get a job in the government. Actually, maybe I could be undersecretary of transportation in charge of elementary-school carpools."

Coco was pushing a sponge in and out of the water, clenching it dry with an angry fist, and then benevolently letting it fill itself up again.

"What's wrong with you, Coco?" Suede asked. "If you're upset because Gavin's got a girlfriend, why don't you just split? Get out. You can make it on your own."

Coco looked through the window above the sink and slowly strangled her sponge with murderous fingers.

"Listen, I've got to go to the grocery store," she said suddenly.

Suede looked surprised that she would voluntarily sacrifice an opportunity for a soul talk with him, but he played it cool, since he knew his customer.

"Say. I meant to tell you. I bumped into Ann last week in East Hampton."

Coco froze into a Masters and Johnson preorgasmic state which could dissolve into despair or crescendo into ecstasy depending upon the next moment's move.

"Oh?" she cued him.

"Yah. She was out there staying at some arty-farty commune. But she looked great."

Coco lifted the aluminum strainer out of the sink and thumped its debris into the garbage can. Suede had always liked to provoke Coco by mentioning her predecessor and then watching her reaction. But over the years Coco had finally devised a who?-oh-yes-how-*is*-she? tone of voice with which to respond while she steeled herself for the news.

"She said she's coming down to Washington for that women's march on July Fourth. She's covering it for *The New York Times Magazine*."

"Oh," Coco said, feeling faint.

Painfully she could remember night-long conversations with Suede in the Billings Hospital Cafeteria on the University of Chicago campus discussing Ann, Ann and Gavin, Gavin and Coco, Coco and Suede, or Suede and Gavin. They talked endlessly, in delicious detail, unraveling and retangling the incestuous knots that bound them together while they smoked and drank coffee and Coco got high on nicotine, caffeine and the sweet-sour taste of Ann's name on her lips.

"Have you seen any of her articles lately?" Suede asked.

Coco smiled at his lapse into obviousness, replaced the strainer, and wiped her hands on a paper towel.

"They'd be hard to miss," she said, cleverly cloaking her bitter jealousy behind an honest admission of envy. "Well, listen, I've got to run out to the store. I'll be back in half an hour or so. If Josh wakes up, just call Gavin."

When Coco came home from a long car ride and a quick stop at the grocery, she walked into the front hall, placed her packages on the radiator, and then heard the sounds of ultimate betrayal drifting out of the TV room. Standing in front of the hall mirror, she watched her face grow soft with sadness as she listened to Gavin, Suede and Sylvia producing genuinely happy laughter which filtered into the hall, announcing that gaiety had happened without Coco, that happiness had occurred in her absence, that Coco was not only excluded, but forgotten. Slowly she walked toward the den and stationed herself in the doorway, smitten by embarrassment as a cramp of loneliness moved through her body.

Everyone said hello.

Coco forced an aching smile to her lips and waited while the silence became heavy and emphatic. Stricken by a consummate sense of desolation, she looked toward Gavin, who lay on the couch.

Move, she begged him silently, pitifully. Sit up a little straighter because I'm home again. A lady . . . your wife . . . just entered the room. It's not necessary to sit up completely or stand, but just move a little. Shift your body around.

Gavin remained motionless. "Did you buy stuff for dinner?"

"Yes. I'm going to make chili," Coco answered, printing loneliness on each word like the brief messages stamped on heart-shaped Valentine candies.

She took a swipe at a strand of hair that drooped disconsolately across her forehead and continued sending silent distress signals toward Gavin, commanding him to at least lift his head off the dirty pillow that Happy dragged around the house like a rabbit. Her anger toward her husband entered active combat with her enormous need for him.

Suede and Sylvia were sitting in the two chairs near the television set and Suede was watching the

Burmans' domestic pantomime of pain with a raw smile that Coco couldn't quite interpret. His expression wavered between curiosity and sympathy as he observed the estrangement being acted out before him. Occasionally a glint of opportunity flickered like a sick neon bulb in his eyes.

Exhausted, Coco leaned against the door frame without entering the room. Originally wounded by the alliance they had formed in her absence, her sense of injury now festered with rejection.

"Well, I guess I'll start dinner," she said, tonally indicating her general displeasure with all of them.

Suede stirred uncomfortably. Sylvia looked stupid. Only Gavin remained untouched and untouchable, a reserve of indifference greater than Coco's emotional demands.

Finally he responded. "Need any help?" He used his small-talk tone of voice which was emphatically and qualitatively different from his important-discussion voice.

"I don't know." Coco shrugged and began backing out through the doorway while they watched her. Her motions were harsh and self-consciously tired. The distance seemed elongated by her sense of humiliation and the intensity of all her unspecified but urgent needs and desires.

"Just yell if you want any help."

Gavin's promise of deferred assistance floated into the hallway. One of his baffling habits was to act concerned while he remained essentially unhampered by any of the unspoken requests Coco made of him. Anyway she knew he was paying only superficial attention to her. He was busy performing for Sylvia and Suede—showing off his intelligence like a scrapbook of clippings. Hurrying out to the hallway, Coco grabbed the grocery bags and fled into the kitchen.

She began drinking gin mixed with grapefruit juice about five o'clock while browning hamburger for some chili con carne. When she wasn't stirring the meat, she sat near the back door and let her mind follow the teasing path of the gin through her system as she watched a collection of Mike's friends playing basketball.

"Coco, honey"—Gavin walked into the kitchen, startling her—"why don't you go take a nap upstairs? I'll give everyone supper."

"Did you and Sylvia finish your brief?" she asked sarcastically, wanting to get into the cliquishness issue.

"No. It's going to take a lot more work," Gavin said. "But we did get some of the background stuff finished."

"That's good," she said nastily.

"Go ahead, Coco," Gavin insisted. "It's too hot to start drinking so early."

He donned a summer-weight look of sympathy.

Coco shrugged.

"Sueeede."

Sylvia's voice came floating into the backyard, from the guest-room window, full of invitation.

"Sueeeede," she wailed, so much a stranger to subterfuge that anyone could complete the predicate of her call. At the terrible witching hour of five, when resourceless women are afflicted by acute anxiety attacks, women like Sylvia used sex for self-definition until the dinner hour. "Sueeeeede."

Coco shivered despite the fact her air-conditioner produced more rasping noises than cool air. Quickly she gave Gavin some cooking instructions and then went into the hall. Suede was still slumped in his chair in the den, obviously struggling against the temptation to run upstairs and knock off a quickie. Coco waved in his general direction and then ran up to the second floor. Hurrying into the living room, she slammed the door and flopped down on the couch. Leaning over to turn on the transistor radio Mike had left on the floor, she listened to "Bye-Bye Miss American Pie" considering if she wanted to run through a number with her Perfect Lover at (a) some secluded seashore shack, (b) Orly Airport (c) or on an archeological dig site in Greece.

But she fell asleep before making her multiple-choice decision.

CHAPTER 12

She woke up because Gavin was shaking her.

"Listen, Coco. Go sleep upstairs so you'll be able to hear the kids if they cry. I'm going to drive Sylvia home."

Coco opened her eyes and saw Gavin's face high above her. "What?"

"I said I have to drive Sylvia home because Suede got drunk and fell asleep and we can't wake him up. And Sylvia wants to get back."

"Back where?"

"Home."

Gavin straightened up, wrinkled his nose to readjust his glasses and peered disapprovingly down at his wife.

Coco brushed her hair away from her face and sat up straight on the couch, carefully placing her feet on the floor.

"What's the matter? Are the taxis on strike?" she asked.

Gavin's body jerked as if she had struck him. He turned and then Coco saw Sylvia standing near the telephone table a few feet from the couch looking frightened.

"Yah. We could call a cab," Gavin said very slowly.

"I don't have any money," Sylvia whispered with equal amounts of apology and pride.

"Charity begins at home," Coco said menacingly, trying to re-orient herself.

So Gavin walked over to the telephone and began to dial.

"What time is it?" Coco asked.

"It's almost ten-thirty," Sylvia said. "You slept through supper, three baths and four bedtimes. We did it all for you."

"It feels like three in the morning," Coco complained, but basically she felt rested and relaxed apart from the blade of suspicion that poked through the edges of her mood. "God, I've been sleeping since five. And everyone survived beautifully. That's good news."

Gavin turned back toward them, holding the telephone receiver like a gun. "It'll take fifteen minutes."

Sylvia retrieved her Mexican fabric purse off the floor, hooked it over her shoulder, and then walked nervously toward the door.

"I guess Suede will just have to sleep it off," she said apologetically. "I think he drank too much. Listen, thanks a lot for all the meals and drinks and everything."

Coco felt bored by Sylvia and impatient to be rid of her.

"Sure. No trouble."

"I'll turn on the outside light," Gavin said, gesturing so Sylvia would precede him through the doorway.

As soon as they went downstairs, Suede appeared in the living room.

"How do you feel?" he asked.

"Okay. I was really tired." It seemed difficult to look at him directly. "You know, Sylvia was trying to wake you up to take her home."

"I was aware of that." Suede smiled. "But since I don't have a car, I thought I'd cool her out. It won't kill her to take a cab. Jesus, I've had enough of that chick for a long while."

Coco flushed and smiled.

"You know something," Suede said thoughtfully, "you really are a beautiful woman, Coco. You knock me out, you're so beautiful."

"Thanks." Coco felt enormously restored by the compliment since the day had drained away most of her reserve ego supports.

"Anyway, I think I'm going to crash. Do you have any blankets?" Suede asked.

Coco elevated herself off the couch and walked down the hall to the big linen closet off the landing. She opened the door, climbed on top of the box she used as a stepladder to reach the top shelf, and grabbed several blankets. Then she slid down, lost her balance, and felt Suede's arms reach from behind to catch her. Coco sank into a whirlpool of sensation that made it difficult to extract herself from his arms. For a few frantic moments she allowed him to hold her in the mothball-scented closet, pressing herself against his hardness to taste his forbidden strength.

"Don't," she whispered in a hot breath against the side of his face as a sudden powersurge of desire shot through her.

Suede looked stubborn for a moment but then shrugged, released her and twisted his body to resettle his tight chinos. Coco slid past him, moved shyly back into the hallway, and then walked down the three stairs to the landing.

And that was when she saw Gavin standing in the hall foyer with Sylvia, fondling her shoulder and talking softly and comfortingly to her, his mouth close to her face.

Pain, anger, love and terror throbbed through her body as she realized that Sylvia was Gavin's girlfriend—not Suede's.

Vaguely she sensed Suede moving closer to stand behind her on the darkened landing. Then he too was looking downstairs as Gavin stroked Sylvia's hair once again with infinite tenderness just before a car horn blasted its signal outside. Gavin kissed Sylvia quickly and then watched her run out through the front doorway.

"Wow, that's out of sight," Suede murmured in a stunned whisper.

Coco shivered.

"Hey. Don't do that," Suede ordered softly, putting his hands on Coco's shoulders. "Take it easy. Just cool it out for now. We'll talk later."

Gavin waited near the door until the taxi roared off, turned to switch off the outside light, and then began running up the stairs two at a time. When he first realized Coco and Suede were standing on the landing, he stopped, stared up at the two of them for a moment, and then grabbed hold of the banister. A few seconds later he remobilized his body and continued coming up the stairs.

Suddenly there was a great deal of movement and confusion. Suede picked up the blankets off the floor, turned into his room, and began saying good night.

Gavin, totally confused, looked as if he might try to shake hands with him. Coco paused to turn off the light in the linen closet before running up to the third floor. Gavin followed her reluctantly, tapping out an anxious rhythm with his fingers on the banister. Coco had flung herself across the bed and buried her face in the pillows before Gavin entered the room, cautiously shutting the door behind him.

"Well. So that's her," Coco said in a cold murderous voice.

"What?" Gavin asked mildly, still standing near the door.

"So that's her," Coco repeated.

"Who?"

"So Sylvia's your girlfriend . . . huh?"

"Are you kidding, Coco? Are you crazy?"

This time, with the image of the girl bright in her mind, Coco experienced a jealousy capable of catapulting her into homicide.

And at that moment Gavin realized Coco had seen him kiss Sylvia.

Sitting down on the bed beside her, he stroked her face with a love-cupped hand.

"Look, Coco, maybe it is worse for you to go around dragging up candidates than if I tell you the truth. The famous leading lady in that quickie little affair I had was a woman from Baltimore who works for the *Sun*. She's forty, lonesome, bad-looking and will sleep with anybody who will take her to bed. That was my mistress, as you call it. I slept with her three times."

Coco looked at him carefully. "You're a fucking liar."

"She comes to Washington to cover social events that have political connections and her name is Catherine. Now, are you satisfied?"

"Catherine what?"

"What difference does it make? What are you going to do? Call her up?"

Coco closed her eyes. "Then why were you making love to Sylvia downstairs in the hall?" Her voice sounded unfamiliar and husky. "Why didn't you tell me she was one of the plaintiffs in that lawsuit? Why didn't you tell me about her, that you knew her and see her all the time and that you really like her?"

Gavin began to undress, turning his back on Coco until he had pulled on pajamas. "Because you've been acting so crazy. Because you've been acting completely nuts. You knew I was handling that case. You just weren't interested."

Coco pivoted around on her elbow so she could see how unattractive Gavin looked, long and shriveled in his pajamas, moving forlorn and frightened around the bedroom.

"So why were you touching her?"

"Because she was upset."

"About what?"

"About something that happened with Suede."

"How do you know?"

"Because that's what she told me. That's what she was so upset about."

"When did she tell you all of that?"

"While you were sleeping on the couch."

"Bullshit, you motherfucking liar. That's the same kind of shit you used to lay on Ann."

"You're sick, Coco," Gavin said with a look of ugly contempt. "You're a selfish, self-centered, self-pitying, selfish bitch."

"Get out of here," Coco said very quietly, sitting up. "Get out of this room."

He started toward the door.

"Where the hell are you going?" she asked.

"I'll go sleep in Jessica's bed."

Coco started to cry. "I hope she pees all over you, Gavin. I hope she pees in your face. You're a mess of a father and a crud of a husband. I wish you would die."

"Look, let's go have some coffee and talk for a while," he said, obviously terrified.

So Coco stood up, twisted her rage into a heavy rope of self-control, and followed him downstairs.

They sat at the table in the kitchen and Coco was certain Gavin could hear her heart thumping, so violently was it pumping blood.

"Do you want some coffee?" Gavin asked.

"All right. Instant's okay."

He got up, found a huge three-quart pot, and moved toward the sink. He was so tall that he dwarfed and distorted Coco's kitchen appliances.

"I certainly hope you're not going to fill that all the way up to the top," she said flatly.

"Nope."

But she heard sloshing sounds as he spilled some water back into the sink.

Those are the things I always hated about him, Coco thought. Those are the things that make him revolting. If I were with *him* (her nameless Perfect Lover) up in a cabin in Vermont and it was late at night or early in the morning (he would be wearing a red-and-black checkered lumberjacket), he would know exactly how much water to boil for two cups of instant coffee before we made love in front of the fireplace.

"You know something, Gavin?" Coco reached out for her cigarettes. "I really do feel better now that I know."

"Know what?"

"That it's Sylvia."

"Sylvia?"

"Please. Let's not have any more of that, Gavin. We've lost a month of our lives from just that kind of shit. I simply want to say that I really do feel better now that I know it's her. Not that she can ever walk in this house again . . . and I'll tell that to Suede also,—I'm not afraid—because she's such a disrupter, a real dyed-in-the-wool destroyer. I'm going to tell Suede that we've always had a rule house guests can't bring dates in here to sleep with them because of the kids. Especially Mike. I don't want Mike to see some guy's line-up of girls over a week. But, anyway, I'm sure Suede's not going to want to do her again, because he saw you, too, and it was perfectly clear what was going on. But besides all of that, Sylvia and I aren't the same kind of people. Now, are you going to let it all boil away, Gavin? I mean, can't you even stay connected with something for three short minutes?"

Gavin got up, looking reproved, and began hunting for coffeecups before turning off the burner.

"They're up in the corner cupboard, Gavin. Right where they've been for the last five years."

Gavin ignored the reprimand. Having conceded, during the past month, that his preoccupation was really a hostile act, he didn't dare get angry now.

"So at least I won't ever see her again," Coco said. "That much I know. And I certainly doubt that Suede will either, now that he's seen what a sick chick she is —sleeping here with him at our house while she's having an affair with you. I mean, after fucking you literally, and fucking me figuratively, coming here to fuck our friend is a bit much. We don't use cream, remember, Gavin? And any sick creep who would want to come around under those conditions is really pathetic—I mean, even if she wasn't your girlfriend, she couldn't come here again, since she obviously has such hostile, jealous feelings toward me and keeps

trying to put me down. Thank you, Gavin. I bet it's
too cold to drink now. And, of course, she was just
insanely jealous because of the children, especially
Joshua. Not that she even knows how to hold a baby,
let alone talk to a child. She treated Mike as if he was
two years old instead of seven. I mean, you don't
have to have any experience—just some sensitivity.
And, anyway, I really thought she was a perfectly
vulgar opportunist from the very first minute I saw
her and the way she talks as if she not only made up
the idea of women's liberation but that she was the
goddamn queen of it and the rest of us—especially
me—are the drones who do the fucking committee
work which I know, goddamn well, is a lot more
time-consuming than just being on the National
Steering Committee—and acting like she's such a big
mucky-muck in charge of Delegation Challenge Tactics, which happens to be pure bullshit, because last
week several women who are actually executive of-
ficers of the D.C. Women's Political Caucus were
talking and they said that they were *both* going down
to Miami. But, anyway, Gavin, I really do feel bad
you never told me about that license-challenge case,
but then, I guess you couldn't have, because that
might have jeopardized your nasty, pathetic little
love affair."

"Oh, Coco. You never listen to anything I say about
my work."

Gavin had finished his cup of coffee and decided to
use that inopportune opportunity to look up at the
clock.

Coco could feel adrenaline streaming through her
veins and she wondered briefly if a person could
O.D. on their own secretions.

"But apart from all that," she continued, "I must
say you showed abominable taste getting involved

with someone who's so coarse and gross and vulgar. Not to mention *fat* and pathetic. She's obviously just latched onto a women's-lib-line as a crutch because she's so personally ghastly. I mean, if a man has a mistress, she should at least be better-looking than his wife—not just bigger."

(That hurt, but Coco *had* to get Sylvia's tits out on the table.)

"And the fact that she would so willfully and flagrantly come into my home—my home, with my children—is, well, it's just too much for me. It's a real mind-fuck."

Wasted by frustration and enraged because Gavin just sat silently at the table taking it all in, polite and passive as always, made Coco think that her head was going to explode. Instead, two drops of tears splashed down on the table next to Coco's untouched coffeecup.

"But to have to listen to her tell me—tell *me*—about the plight of the housewife, the problems of raising kids in nuclear families, the hardships caused by the demise of the extended family in an industrialized society, about all the things in *my* life that I know about, just blew my mind. But even worse than that is that when Sylvia-baby says it, when poopsie makes her pronunciamentos, you listen and Suede listens and everyone listens because when she says it, it's not nagging. Oh, no, if Ms. Tits says it, she's not whining. She's not hysterical. If Big Boobs says it, then it's official. Then she's a goddamn motherfucking sociologist, a fucking political scientist, a fucking radical activist. Oh, no, her shit doesn't stink. But I'll tell you something else, Gavin, she doesn't really know what the fuck she's talking about. She's just talking because she happens to be hysterical. That's right. All that talk is just hysteria, Gavin, in a little different vocabulary than the one I use. All that feminist talk is just a cover-up for the fact that she's fat and ugly and doesn't have a man and wants one so badly she'd even try to steal you. You, Gavin. Can you dig that? And when I say exactly the same stuff she says, exactly the same, that it's hard raising kids in the middle of a city all alone without any family around, and that working full time and giving, I mean really giving myself"—uncomfortably she remembered the pills she had taken from Lillian Greenberg in exchange for a later deadline—"to my students and then coming home . . . Right, Mrs. Marshall does clean the house and take care of Nicky and Josh during the day, but after all, I'm not home, so how can I? And then making supper and bathing the kids and putting them to bed every night, all the while feeling guilty because I'm not with them more and still not wanting to get buried here in the house, which God knows would be perfectly easy, because that's exactly what most of the women in my consciousness-raising group do—I mean stay home all day—and never feeling that anyone else in the world, especially *you*, understands the pressure and the tension and the constant worry I feel. I mean, even when I'm haranguing up at the lectern about D. H. Lawrence blah-blah-blah, I'm hoping that Joshua doesn't climb up the stairs and fall down or that Nicky isn't too lonesome because Mrs. Marshall doesn't talk to him enough. But what really kills me, what really knocks me out, is how when Sylvia says the same exact things I've been saying for the last twelve years, you listen as if someone just discovered America. Just because a professional *libber* is saying it, that makes it interesting and politically relevant and important."

Coco's mouth was so tired from talking that her cheeks began to ache.

"You forgot one little thing in that little speech of yours, Coco."

"What?"

"Me."

Gavin got up and walked out of the kitchen.

And then Coco felt palpitating, pulsating, shaking, quaking anger drain through her. Her resolution to stay loose and keep cool evaporated. The heat of her rage was irresistible and she rose to her feet, coffee mug in hand, to rush through the kitchen doorway into the hall.

Gavin was beginning to walk up the stairs when Coco took aim and flung the ceramic cup. It hit him on the side of the head so that his glasses went flying off his face. The cup cracked and broke against the wall. Some coffee ran down over Gavin's shirt as he lifted his hand to his forehead where he had been struck. For a moment Coco thought he was going to come after her with a violent response, but instead he fumbled around for his glasses, picked them up, and then walked back down the stairs, into the television room. He slammed the door shut with a great deal of finality.

So Coco went up to bed alone.

The next morning Suede and Gavin left early for Gavin's office to spend the day going through his files for the *Esquire* article. Coco's Sunday was like an anesthetized operation—complicated but painless. At 9:30, when she put the children to bed, she lay awake in her room planning how to deliver her story about Gavin and Sylvia to Dr. Finkelstein.

She fell asleep without hearing the men come home.

CHAPTER 13

She must have known what was going to happen because she woke up earlier than usual which gave her time to take a shower, perfume her body and shave her legs. (She had given up on armpits in tribute to the more radical feminists.) Since Gavin had slept in the den again, Coco hurried to feed and exile the children into the yard so she could confront her husband in private. But just as she finished fixing a buffet of Captain Crunch, Quisp, Quake and Lucky Charms, she heard Gavin sneak out of the house, slamming the door with a cold hard fury.

Stunned by his escape, Coco went upstairs to dress and then waited in the front hall for the ritual changing of the guard. As soon as Mrs. Marshall appeared, Coco squeezed her hand like a runner in a relay race and ran outside to jump in her car and speed downtown.

Ten minutes later, lying on Dr. Finkelstein's sofa, weeping copiously while trying to infuse her narrative with a correct description of her emotions, Coco realized she had been in a state of shock for almost thirty-six hours. When Dr. Finkelstein asked what had gone on between her and Gavin on Sunday, Coco calmly explained that Gavin had been away at his office. When Dr. Finkelstein asked what had transpired Sunday night, Coco reported she had fallen asleep before he returned.

Dr. Finkelstein seemed more than mildly surprised. Indeed, for the first time, he seemed actually concerned about Coco's condition.

"Do you mean to tell me that you saw Gavin making love with this hippie girl and all you did was say she couldn't come over to your house anymore?"

"Well, I did throw a cup of coffee at him."

"But it was cold coffee, wasn't it, Mrs. Burman? It took Gavin so long to fix it—it must have been *cold* coffee."

"Yes. Yes, it was."

"And are you telling me you didn't bring up the subject of his girlfriend all day long on Sunday?"

"I didn't get a chance to, Dr. Finkelstein. I was taking care of the children and I was very tired."

"And this morning, Mrs. Burman. Didn't you see your husband this morning."

"No, because he slept in the den and I was still in the kitchen feeding the kids when he sneaked out of the house."

"Goodness," Dr. Finkelstein mumbled. "This is certainly an unusual reaction formation for you. You have broken dishes and bottles and windows and bones with much less provocation than this; I'm terribly surprised at how well you are restraining yourself. Have you taken any tranquilizers?"

"No."

"I think I'll give you a few sample packages to take home."

He rose to his feet and crossed the room to unlock his closet, which housed thousands of free pharmaceutical goodies. Coco had once estimated that there were probably ten thousand uppers per square inch stashed away on those narrow shelves.

The doctor returned to his chair. "As long as you continue to restrain yourself, we can leave well enough alone. But should you begin acting out, getting violent—as has been your habit in the past—I want you to take one of these pills every four hours. And if I may be so bold, I would suggest that when you do get angry—as I suspect you will—and want to punish your husband for his infidelity, since we have not achieved the necessary clarification about your true feelings for him or your marriage, that you do *nothing* or, at least, as little as possible. In fact, tactically speaking, I might suggest the silent treatment rather than some others which might come to mind such as murder or arson. Do you understand my meaning, Mrs. Burman?"

"Yes, Doctor." Coco rolled herself up off the couch, checked her watch, adjusted her skirt, pushed her shoulder bag into position and reached out for the samples. "I suppose that it just hasn't really hit me yet."

"Well, when it does," Dr. Finkelstein said ominously, "take the first pill immediately and if things should get out of hand, feel free to call me. Even at home."

Coco smiled gratefully. For the first time, without any threat of overkill, Coco had gotten a real reaction out of Dr. Finkelstein. Feeling terribly mature, she left his office and hurried home.

The house was silent. Coco walked upstairs and slipped quietly into the guest room which was shadowy with the shades drawn. Inhaling the unfamiliar smell of a stranger's sleep, she tiptoed across the rug in exaggerated motions of quiet, unlatched the screen door and stepped out onto the porch. Slipping off her dress, she picked up a swatch of typed papers and lay down on the chaise.

Within seconds Suede appeared in the doorway wearing only his Jockey shorts and a raffish smile. He let the screen strike against his back to silence its slam and then stepped barefoot onto the hot wooden floor. Leaning back against the wall, he inspected Coco very slowly, but with obvious appreciation. A long period of silent, seductive activity passed between them before he spoke.

"So this is where you're doing it, huh?"

Coco nodded, feeling the old antagonism and heat that preceded Suede's sexual desire.

"Where's Gavin?" he asked.

"At work."

"You had something of a hassle down there in the kitchen Saturday night, didn't you?"

Coco shrugged.

Suede surveyed the treetops.

"It was nice of you to let me stay here," he said awkwardly. "I mean, since things are . . . a little tense right now. But maybe I should take a hotel room for the rest of the time. I'm on expense account."

"Oh, don't be silly, Suede. Actually, things are much better if there's someone else around."

Distraught as she was, Coco still felt humiliated that Suede had seen and heard the despair and disrepair of her marriage. Even when her children were their naughtiest, she wanted them to look clean.

"Well, I wanta tell you that that Sylvia is really something else. That's a pretty ballsy thing she did coming into the house that way. You know, she never ever said a word to me about Gavin. Except that she thought he was handling the TV-station case very well."

Coco smiled and shrugged again. "I still haven't had a chance to relate to any of it," she said. "I had to sleep fast the last few nights."

Suede studied her face, trying hard to decide whether or not to believe her.

"But what do *you* do, Coco? Who keeps *you* happy?"

Coco shrugged again. "I keep busy with my novel."

She was pleased with the way she delivered the line. It simultaneously opened the door for sympathy and promoted her into the realm of serious writers. Then she looked dramatically out through the branches of her elm tree, toward the high-rise across the alley, hoping Suede would accept her as a writer, an equal in his world, as well as a sex object. Recognition by a professional was important to her.

Suede put his hand on the knob of the screen door and opened it invitingly.

"Why don't you just come back inside here with me? For old times' sake? You look like you could use a little loving."

Coco took a deep breath.

Still psychologically dismembered from having witnessed Gavin's love scene Saturday night, she still hadn't had time to explore her emotions or choose a preferred reality. Yet she had waited so long for both love and revenge that when Suede motioned to her, deliberately summoned her across the narrow porch after such a lengthy wait, she felt exhilarated. Now she would finally be rewarded for the vigil she had kept. Although she didn't feel particularly sexy, the pleasure of having extracted Suede's love or desire was overwhelmingly pleasant. Now he could simultaneously make love to Coco, do penance for his mistaken infatuation with Sylvia and punish Gavin for *his* adultery.

Coco got up and glanced down through the green branches into the yard. Mrs. Marshall was outside with the children and things seemed quiet and happy. Coco turned around and looked guiltily toward her neighbor's window. There didn't seem to be anyone watching, so she walked toward the door and let Suede press close against her as he pushed her gently back into the shadows of the guest room.

Then he arranged her on the bed, that was still damp from the heavy sleep of his body, and stretched out beside her.

The hands that soon began to move over her were still familiar; good lovers leave indelible memory traces. Coco softened beneath his disarmingly aimless touch as he examined her flesh, eventually sliding his fingers under the wired bra of her bikini to play with her breasts. After a while, he returned his hands to touch her face and neck again.

It was all pleasantly introductory, interesting and promising. Suede's penis, rubbing against Coco's stomach as he shifted about, felt huge—hard and thick, cupped inside his Jockey shorts like a restless horse waiting for the trackgate to open. Coco lay motionless, paralyzed with the image of a thoroughbred horse bucking to slip out of its stall and start the race.

Suede's leisurely R-and-D technique hadn't changed over the years. For long minutes his fingers encircled her arm or kneaded her thigh. He still had the executive-styled control that a man with an X-L developed in his lovemaking. Suede did not have to squander himself trying to excite a woman and so he could be formidably decisive about program and timing. He would simply continue his methodical examination of Coco's body until he decided to enter it because his staff could do the job alone without any advanceman's assistance. He could afford to be arbitrary, because he had sufficient capability.

Then suddenly he shifted. "I've wanted to do this from the minute I saw you standing in the hallway."

And that was all he said.

Coco felt faint beneath the descent of his heavy body as his knees pried her legs apart. The combination of a Sanforized X-L plus the singularity of the attached man's intentions left no need for fancy positions or wild thrusts. Both Suede and Coco were content concentrating on the thick flab of flesh between their legs that he generously inserted to share with her. The solidness of the connection paralyzed Coco with pleasure. She barely moved, feeling the passion of his body as she received it, until slowly she turned liquid with pleasure and surprise, fell in love with the continuity and constancy of his understated, almost indifferent, penetration. It was incredible.

And then suddenly, surprisingly, it was over.

Instantly he began to withdraw, retreating back into his own satisfaction, severing Coco's reality and shattering the wonderful pressure of his flesh. Cradling his head against her breast, Coco silently mourned the loss of both union and promise. For a long while they lay in silence, Coco trying to contract her body so as to feel the memory of his penetration.

"Fantastic," Suede whispered against her cheek.

"Ummmmm," Coco purred thoughtfully.

He lifted himself up, collapsed flat on his back, and

lay silently beside her, reserved and somewhat evasive.

But now a new wave of desire plunged through Coco. She burrowed into Suede's chest and hid her face between his head and shoulder. Her thighs clenched from emptiness and her hands moved down between Suede's legs, enclosing the soft, slightly damp equipment lying in repose. She juggled the handful of softness away from his thighs.

"They'll get stuck to your legs," she warned, "if you don't be careful."

"I am careful," he said, but he had obviously lost interest in the subject of sex.

Coco looked at him. He seemed more handsome now because his eyes had darkened with desire and Coco felt more loving because—having satisfied him —she was now entitled to touch the cleft in his chin and to scrape her fingertips against the rubble of beard along his cheek. With one hand she began memorizing his face and with the other searching for pressure points that might ignite and rustle the soft animal sunk head-down into its dangling nest.

Coco turned her head to attain an aerial view of their nude bodies. She surveyed the angle of her breasts, which had a tendency to disappear when she was flat on her back (a failure offset only by the fact that her stomach also withdrew), and gazed between Suede's legs.

Acknowledging that any resumption of sexual activity appeared unlikely, she mentally shifted her perspective into a higher, more celestial position. Over the years, Coco had developed an ability to exempt herself from a scene so she could look down from a great height and watch herself in the center of her environment. This way she experienced the delight of inclusion with a margin of safety for error or repair.

"How come you're so serious all of a sudden?" she pouted.

He didn't answer. Now that he was finished, he was perfectly relaxed and self-sufficient.

"Well, you don't have to act so . . . arrogant," Coco complained. "Men always get so damn arrogant after they come."

"What are you talking about? What do you mean, arrogant? And how many men are you talking about? Two digits? Three digits?"

"Oh, I don't know. As soon as a guy feels satisfied he's just done."

She felt his arm stiffen beneath her neck.

"Well, what do you want me to do?" he asked angrily.

"Nothing," Coco answered, hurt and embarrassed.

His voice seemed to be filtered from a great distance. "Didn't you come?"

"That isn't what I'm talking about," Coco hissed angrily.

Then she sat up and bent over to reclaim her bikini from the floor. Quickly she replaced the two pieces of fabric over the untanned areas where they belonged —like Nicky sticking adhesive geometric forms into their proper places in his Shape and Space book.

"I really should know better by now," Coco mumbled. "I've had enough conditioning to know what to expect."

"What in the hell are you talking about?" Suede asked again, hooking his arms beneath his head. His hair was rumpled, and he looked as if he might have become available again if the mood hadn't changed.

Coco stared out toward the porch but remained seated on the edge of the bed.

"I'm talking about the sloppiness of my human relationships," she said softly.

"Hey. Why you so upset now, Coco?" Suede reached out and cupped Coco's right buttock in his hand.

Unhappily she felt some extra flesh escape his grasp, but despite her overflow, she felt somewhat soothed by his caress.

"I'm not really sore," she said in a conciliatory voice. "It's just that I'm late getting started this morning."

"Late?" His voice squeaked in an adolescent way. "Starting what?"

Mentally Coco began to revamp her schedule so as to reallocate some time for balling Suede. Although there was a sense of presumptuous prematurity about the idea, she decided to cross out the original time chart in her notebook and draw up a new one, allocating an hour for Love after Gavin left for work on Tues. and Thurs. and starting after 10:00 on M-W-F. Then she spotted Suede's duffel bag propped up in the corner of the room and suffered several painful minutes wondering how long he would stay in Washington and whether it was really practical to redo her schedule for what might be only a short-term fling.

"How long do you think you'll be here?" she asked cautiously.

"I don't know yet."

Coco stood up.

"Actually, it depends on my appointments today and tomorrow," Suede added quickly. "By tomorrow I'll be able to tell how many other people I have to see before I can finish."

"Well, try to remember to let me know," Coco said nonchalantly.

"Yah, sure. I'm going over to the Hill again this morning and I'll have a better sense of what still needs doing after I talk to a couple of people."

Coco moved toward the door.

"By the way," Suede continued awkwardly, "I probably won't be back until late tonight. I made some other arrangements a few days ago."

Coco unlatched the door and felt jealousy bite into her already overworked soul while she wondered if her new lover had a date with her husband's mistress.

"Well, there's a front-door key downstairs in that wicker basket on the chest in the front hall. It's on a strip of blue leather. Just take it."

"Great. Thanks. Hey . . ." His tone was demanding enough for Coco to turn around. "I appreciate all your hospitality," he said with his favorite roguish smile.

But now Coco found herself incapable of looking at him any longer, so she let herself out onto the porch and splashed down on the chaise feeling emotionally as well as physically miserable. Still haunted by the hangover of adolescent loneliness and sexual frustration, Coco had little tolerance for non-orgasmic sex which only inflamed her appetite for more monumental passions. She firmly believed that only through a crash program of sexual excesses could she ever recoup her past love-losses. But she was well into her third five-year plan without much success and it didn't seem as if Suede was going to become her private relief program.

After a while Suede came out on the porch dressed in a clean white shirt, laundry-pressed khaki pants and a striped summer blazer.

"My. Don't you look nice," Coco said.

Her sense of a sexual debt put an edginess into her

voice and she thought about Daisy Buchanan, who sounded like money rather than an overdue bill.

"Look, I've got to get going," Suede said, "but I didn't want to leave without saying something."

"What?"

"Well, I didn't know exactly *what.* I just wanted to say *something.*"

"Oh, come on, Suede." Coco felt her patience evaporate. "A National Book Award winner like you? Can't you come up with a clever exit line? Philip Roth or Saul Bellow or Malamud could come up with something just like that," Coco said, snapping her fingers. "Can't you say something about Jewish mamas never being satisfied? Make believe you're Herzog. He'd say something good. And then I could make a rejoinder. Go ahead. Say something immortal. You know . . . one heavy charge against All Of Us. You don't even have to limit yourself to Jewish ladies. Say something about All Of Us. You know how. Freak out like you did in that shitty story of yours in *Playboy* last year. Go on. Say something clever and successful."

He was laughing. He leaned against the wall and laughed very loudly, touching his chest again with happy hands that loved his own body.

Coco clutched several pages of her manuscript against her bare midriff and stared at him. Beneath the sharp-edged papers, her breasts sagged while her anger rose.

"I mean, if you really are one of the gang, a bright light in American Jewish fiction, sock it to me. For a guy who writes about messing up ladies' brand-new pink-striped Pepperell sheets, you should at least be able to get off a good exit line."

He sobered up a little, insulted.

"You know, you do look like Moses Herzog, Suede.

Tell me how it feels after you fuck a married lady and have an appointment to get to and don't know how to weasel your way out of the house? All you need is one good put-down so you can split."

Now he looked totally somber and insulted.

"Okay." He mashed his cigarette out against the brick wall and moved toward the door. "I'll see you tomorrow."

"Pretty good. But not too original."

And then he was gone.

Coco slumped back in the chaise.

I just committed adultery with a schmuck, Coco thought.

She sat up straight, put on her sunglasses, a luxury she seldom permitted herself, and tried to read yesterday's ten pages. But her eyes wandered over the words, spotting too many adjectives, while her mind recited a liturgy of laments.

Gavin doesn't love me. He loves Sylvia Brydan. Brydan. Bride. He's going to divorce me and make her his bride. He was touching her face and her hair. He watches her mouth when she speaks. He nods his head every time she says something. He really loves her.

I mustn't think about anything, Coco thought. I must make my mind perfectly blank and keep it empty. Otherwise I'm going to crack up.

My book is terrible. It is obvious, amateurish and self-centered.

Also, I neglect my children. They are growing up without sufficient maternal attention or supervision.

Her mind was darting about, touching base with every guilt that she had ever gilded and saved.

She wondered if perhaps she should relax her work schedule a little for the day—given such trying circumstances. Perhaps what she needed most now was the comfort that could only be derived from a female friend. Coco reached over to the coffee table and picked up the address book which listed her Real Friends. Nervously she flipped through the pages, hoping that a perfect possibility would leap up from the K's or the S's, a miraculous replacement for Glenda, who wouldn't return until August 15. Evoking past encounters as a test of compatibility, Coco slowly eliminated the names of all her B-squad girlfriends one by one.

The best A would certainly not be able to find a baby-sitter on such short notice, even though she certainly would have been instinctively indignant about Gavin's adultery. A long-unseen G would undoubtedly overstay her visit, since she had a Latin live-in, which would necessitate Coco making messy excuses to get rid of her. L would undoubtedly be funny, but she would only be looking for things to gossip about with her other girlfriends and, besides, she never responded quickly enough. F was too thin and threatening. J was too competitive; she'd be secretly glad. D was too dumb to be any help or comfort.

I want Glenda, Coco thought. No one else. Just my best girlfriend.

Coco closed the address book and felt very lonely.

Although she stayed out on the porch all afternoon, she didn't work. Instead she napped fitfully several times and spent the rest of her hours picturing Gavin and Sylvia as lovers, with occasional splices of Suede and Sylvia going at it.

Gavin called at 6:30 to say he couldn't come home for dinner because he had an ACLU meeting. Coco didn't believe him, but she didn't go berserk since she knew that Sylvia was with Suede. After dinner, Coco played Monopoly with the children before they went to bed. She fell asleep while watching the ten o'clock news without hearing either Gavin or Suede come home.

In the middle of the night she awoke aware that Gavin wasn't in bed. Turning on the light, she got up, put on a cotton bathrobe and dug around the closet to find her bedroom slippers. She never walked barefoot through the house when it was dark because she feared stepping on bugs, mice or unexpected piles of Happy's doo-doo. Then she went downstairs to the den. Gavin was sleeping on the couch.

For a moment Coco felt a hard homicidal feeling sweep through her. Briefly she considered waking and shaking him by his lean, bony shoulders until he saw the silliness of his infatuation, the indignity he was perpetrating upon his wife, the fact that he was doing the same thing to Coco that he had done to Ann. But instead she shut the door and went back upstairs, still so stung by betrayal that she was glad to be sleeping alone again.

On Tuesday she woke up firmly committed to giving Gavin the silent treatment. When she encountered him on the staircase, she adopted a mysterious expression and hurried past him without speaking.

Dr. Finkelstein was right, Coco thought. After twelve years of throwing tantrums, she could make more points being silent.

Wednesday was also a quiet day although, for a few hours after her therapy session, Coco got into a heavy jealousy trip and sat at the counter in People's Drugstore exploring her pain. The poignant memory of Gavin brushing Sylvia's hair away from her face and kissing her good-bye ran through Coco's cerebral theatre several times as she drank iced-coffees and watched the waitresses serving up breakfast orders. The idea of Gavin caring for someone else produced involuntary Technicolor film clips of her husband bequeathing his affection upon Sylvia in various places and situations. Gavin's affection (a commodity of uncertain value) had suddenly—like wooden Coca-Cola cases, old church pews, and Tiffany lampshades—become quite chic.

So that now—oh, yes, now, for the first time—Coco could understand what the first Mrs. Burman experienced when Gavin split or how even the queen of the Western world, Jackie Onassis, had to pay her dues—a *second* time—when she received telescopic photos of Ari at a Parisian restaurant with the fantastic Maria Callas. Now Coco could relate to the plastically beautiful Joan Kennedy, summering comfortably, when news of Chappaquiddick trickled through her ears and into her bloodstream like poison running through King Hamlet's body. And then there was Eleanor Roosevelt, the Great Lady, used as a front for Lucy Rutherford, and Princess Margaret watching her consort consorting with her own ladies-in-waiting and Mrs. Profumo seeing Christine Keeler's picture on top of her breakfast tray every morning and even Liz Taylor, who finally got hers after she did in Debbie and Sybil, when Dickie took a tumble for the *slim, thin* Florinda Bolkan. And then there was Simone Signoret ducking photographers when Yves Montand was putting it to Marilyn Monroe and Princess Saroya bopping through airports while the new queen presented heirs to the Shah and Dory Previn singing her heart out while Mia Farrow gave birth to twin baby boys. That was a good one—that was really putting the old knife in.

Because now for the first time, Coco could really dig Medea and Clytemnestra and Marianne Faithfull and the coach's wife in *The Last Picture Show* and Simone de Beauvoir and Lady Bird Johnson and, oh, dear, how many more?

CHAPTER 14

*C*oco came home from Dr. Finkelstein's office Friday morning with her heart pounding in panic because ten minutes before the end of the hour he had coolly and cold-heartedly announced he was going on vacation for the entire month of July. Coco objected strenuously and Dr. Finkelstein apologized for not having warned her sooner, but said he had told all his regular patients in May and had simply forgotten Coco didn't know when she resumed therapy on the first of June. He said he was certain she would get along fine, that she should work hard on her novel and not feel compelled to act out all of her emotional impulses. He said he was trusting her not to escalate her estrangement from Gavin. Then he handed her a $360 bill for June, politely opened the door, and said good-bye.

Coco ran all the way home. Several times tears of

betrayal rose to her eyes. The leadership of the D.C. Women's Liberation Coalition was right. Psychiatry was just another put-on, another put-down for women—another commercial endeavor mining money from miserable wives by plying their pain.

The early-morning heat made her sweat as she ran and one of her leather sandals rubbed uncomfortably against the back of her foot. For a moment she thought of removing her shoes, but the city felt unfriendly that morning and she feared calling attention to herself. Instead of being fortified by a joust with psychological factuality, Coco felt totally demolished, demoralized and endangered as she ran home through the streets.

She let herself in quietly through the front door. The house was silent because on Fridays the park fire hydrants were turned into sprinklers for the children and Mrs. Marshall always rescheduled her work so that the kids could play in the water during the morning.

Coco kicked off her sandals in the front hall, ran up the carpeted stairs, and opened the door to the guest room. It was hot and stuffy inside. Suede was still asleep, sprawled on his back across the bed. His thighs were spread apart so that the fly of his Jockey shorts spread open invitingly over the dark hair of his groin.

Coco's excitement was instantaneous and of embarrassing proportions.

She slipped out of her dress and lay down carefully on top of Suede, following the outline of his body with her own. Nestling her torso against his, she let her arms and legs follow the sleeping form of his limbs.

He never opened his eyes, but the unformed flesh between his legs immediately began to unleash the silhouette hidden within it. His hands moved slowly down her back, pressing her harder and more firmly against him.

They never spoke.

Coco's head was pressed against his chest and she felt herself vaporized between the pressure f his hands and the firmness of his body.

Finally he began to enter her from beneath and Coco dissolved with pleasure as Suede's X-L blundered blindly about, nearsightedly bumping into bikini crotch, clit and thigh before partially penetrating her. Her hand, reaching downward to guide him, discovered surplus inches being wasted in space. Caught in a pitch of wild excitement, Coco maneuvered the slippery sightless instrument into proper position, squatted slightly to swallow it and then flattened down on top of Suede again. She hitched upward and sank down in three rocking motions that released a mighty, monumental orgasm and when the pounding inside her stopped, she listened to the chorus of their gasps diminish in unison.

Coco felt seared by love.

"Now, that's how I like to get waked up in the morning." Suede's voice restated the satisfaction of his body.

Coco was drowning in a rich romantic sensuality.

"You've got a great body, babes, and I like the way you help put out your own little fire."

He reexamined her buttocks, kneading the flesh until mini-contractions vibrated like a dim echo through her body again.

Coco lifted her head high enough so that she could see the handsomeness of Suede's face.

"And I'm still half-sleeping," he said cozily. "You know, I never could understand how come you're such a swinger in the sack when you're so screwed up about everything else."

Coco received his compliment with a magnanimous smile, pleased because he was beginning to realize that her portfolio of powers was diversified.

"Oh, I'm starting to like you very much again, Suede. Like I used to back in Chicago. Remember?" Coco whispered.

Suddenly she wanted to explain very slowly and logically how life had not allowed her to do everything she had intended to do. She wanted to explain that she was the product of all the things that had happened as well as certain things which had *not* occurred. Together she and Suede might share the total vision of everything she meant to be and do.

But instead he let one arm relax so he could snare his wristwatch from the floor beside the bed.

"Jesus." His breath was musty with sleep. "I'm going to have to get my shit together. I've got an appointment at twelve."

Coco winced. After dispensing with his sexual business and making an allowance for recovery time, Suede was rebounding back into his work routine with all the enthusiasm of a man who had jogged several miles to put himself in shape for a strenuous day.

"Do you have to get up right now?" Coco whispered against his shoulder. Lying on her side, she injected one evenly tanned leg between his thighs and then half-rolled her body across him.

"Yup. One of the editors at *Esquire* arranged for this luncheon meeting a couple of weeks ago. I couldn't interview anyone from the Justice Department until I had gotten enough background material."

Coco twisted slightly so that all her protuberances

bit into Suede's body. She pressed her pelvic bone like a sweet reminder against his thigh and slipped one hand over his chest, enveloping the mound of muscle beneath one handsome brown nipple. Then she closed her eyes and swam through a second great tidal wave of desire.

"Okay, babes." Suede swung himself off the bed. He retrieved his shorts from the floor, charmingly looked into the crotch for skid marks, and then put them on again.

Coco felt instantly embarrassed at not having offered Suede some laundry services, but she felt too shy now to say anything about it. Instead she reached down to untangle the sheet so she could pull it up over her body.

"What's on for tonight?" he asked casually. He was rummaging around on the top of the bureau, shuffling through coins and keys he had unloaded from his pockets the night before.

Coco pressed her head into the pillow, unwilling to hear the sound of such practical activity. She let her thoughts float away and wondered if her children were cool, running through the sprinklers, splashing in the spray. She couldn't understand why Suede was striding around the room taking care of business rather than taking care of her, discarding the possibility of making passionate love all day. She wondered if all men used work to sublimate their sex drives.

"Nothing special," Coco said after a long while. "You must have gotten home pretty late last night. I didn't hear you come in."

"Yah." He heard her implicit accusation of infidelity but didn't bother to respond. "Hey, is there any coffee downstairs?"

"Probably. There's an electric pot right next to the sink."

"Jesus," Suede groaned. "Don't you think you can get your butt out of bed and fix me something for breakfast? You must of fed your old man bacon this morning, because I smelled it all the way up here."

"That was for the children," Coco said defensively.

She was beginning to feel persecuted, but her estrangement from Gavin made it risky to display any discontent toward Suede. When there was trouble in the family it was best not to quarrel with friends. Unfortunately, she felt sticky and sweaty and could smell the unfamiliar, but still fishy, odor of Suede's sperm on her skin.

"So where *did* you go last night?" she finally asked, forced into making a formal inquiry since her jealousies subsided if she didn't refuel them with fresh information.

"I saw Sylvia," he answered offhandedly. "We had a date."

Suede was too cool to be either hypocritically silent or even a trifle apologetic. He was rustling around in his duffel bag searching for something and sending out earnest directives for Coco to get up and assist him in his departure.

Coco shriveled up in silence and wished she could retreat one hour in time and simply twitch her bottom at Suede while cutting through his bedroom on her way to the porch. She wished she could have ignored him with the chill indifference of a happily married woman or at least held out against his advances long enough so that his needs would have accumulated and taken longer to satisfy. She also wished she'd never have to see him again.

"Come on, babes. Speed it up a little, can you?"

Coco extended one hand from beneath the sheet

to grab her bikini bottom, pulled it under the covers, and then hoisted it up her legs. But the bra was so far out in the middle of the rug that she had to get up to recover it. Keeping her back toward Suede, she quickly shook her breasts into the wired cups. Then she brushed the hair away from her face and turned to confront him for the first time since meeting his eyes amidst the hard rocking of their lovemaking.

"Hey. You look good." Suede smiled with happy surprise. He was still bare-chested, wearing only trousers. "I put some roses in your cheeks this morning." Silently chalking up several invisible points, he collected his shaving equipment off the bureau. "Give me ten minutes for a shower, will you? Maybe you can throw some eggs in a pan while I get cleaned up."

Coco stared at him, preparing a pithy put-down. But then she heard the front door open and the sounds of her children spilling into the house.

Hurrying into the hallway, she ran downstairs, smiling expectantly.

They grabbed at her from all levels—around the calves of her legs, her hips, her waist. The baby stretched upward to pull her hand down toward him and Coco tried to gather them all together inside her arms, refreshing herself against their cool skin and still-damp hair.

"I'm going to start up on the third floor today," Mrs. Marshall said authoritatively. "Whereabouts is the house guest?"

"He's on the second floor," Coco said. Jessica had gotten on top of the hall chest, thrown her arms around the back of Coco's neck, and boosted herself into piggyback position. "I think he's taking a shower."

"They should go out back," Mrs. Marshall advised as she started up the stairs.

Coco began to move toward the kitchen, towing and carrying her children.

"I'll make you a picnic," Coco said. "Crackers with peanut butter and pink Hawaiian punch with ice cubes. Okay? You didn't eat at the park, did you?"

"No," they shouted again and again.

Energized by love and attention, they hurtled through the kitchen and out the back door. Coco carried the baby down to his playpen that was parked on the patio and then came back inside.

"Mom, I'm going to call up and see if Stevie's home," Mike announced, slamming into the kitchen.

"Okay, honey."

Through the windows she could hear the hum of Mrs. Marshall vacuuming and the children fighting as they reclaimed their toys and reestablished territorial rights in the yard, gleeful after their sprinkle time and excited about the promised picnic. Quickly Coco brushed a variety of crumbs off the kitchen table into her cupped hand, scattered them in the sink, and set a place mat for Suede. Then she cracked three eggs into a mixing bowl, ransacked the spice shelf, and blessed her omelet with a touch of curry. At the same time, she softened the butter for English muffins and filled a small jar with marmalade.

Finally Suede ambled into the kitchen with a puckish stride that sent a whimper through Coco's body. Fully dressed, he looked even more seductive than he did in his self-composed nakedness.

Coco lowered her head, turned off the burner and slid the omelet onto a dish.

"Sit there," she said, nodding as she poured two cups of coffee.

Suede paused to look through the back door at the

jumble of children around the swing set. "Jesus. Can you believe all of those are really yours?" he asked.

Coco flushed. "Well, they're running around," she explained apologetically. "When they run around, it looks like there's more of them than there actually are."

Suede shrugged and sat down at the table.

"You know, this is something else—this establishment you run here—plus all the fucking around that goes on, on the side. You and Gavin each do your own thing—go through all your own changes—but all the while you're raising these great kids."

He began to eat his eggs very seriously.

Coco sat down across from him and poured cream into her coffee as a special treat.

"That's nice of you to say," she smiled. "But there's a strong possibility that the shit we're laying on them doesn't do them too much good."

She studied the various bruises on the familiar wooden tabletop and held back her tears of guilt. Suede looked sympathetic for a few seconds, ate several forkfuls of eggs, and then reached over to touch Coco's hand softly with his own. "You're a good chick . . . whoops"—he laughed in compliance with his own self-correction—"lady . . . woman."

Mentally Coco readjusted her page quota for the day up to fourteen, looked at the clock, and then got up to bring the Ritz-cracker box and peanut-butter jar to the table. She began spreading sandwiches.

"So what are you doing tonight? Are you going to be back for dinner?"

"Well, I don't know how long my interviews will last. I'll call you this afternoon, though, and let you know. I'm not too hip on eating dinner with Gavin . . . you know. . . . Except that he's gotten to be such a swinger himself, he probably wouldn't mind, even if he knew. Or would he?"

"Who cares?" Coco wondered what Suede meant by "swinger," and if he had secretly found out a lot of gossip over the last few days from Sylvia. He surely must have pumped her for information.

"Those were good eggs." He lit a cigarette and squinted seductively through the smoke. "I'm kind of sorry I've got this appointment now," he said, his voice thick with suggestiveness.

Coco looked at him with a Masters-and-Johnson challenge in her eyes.

He stared back at her, somewhat unnerved. "You've still got some complaints, babes?"

Coco smiled again, this time beautifully. "No. Not at all."

"Okay."

He stood up, unhooked his striped summer sport jacket from the back of the chair and slipped it on. Then he brushed a kiss on the top of Coco's head and hurried out of the kitchen.

Coco listened to his footsteps and smiled when she deduced from the lapse of time between the kitchen and front door that he had stopped to inspect himself in the hall mirror.

When she finished making the picnic she carried it outside and served it to the children. But even after they had eaten, she loitered on the patio, collecting their lost Jell-O molds and cooky cutters so they could bake sand pastries. Coco's sense of moral jeopardy was so extreme that the innocence of her children seemed to offer a spiritual sanctuary. She ran her hands through the sand (careful not to connect with any feline feces deposited by neighborhood alley cats who used the Burman sandbox as a public outdoor kitty-litter facility), scooping out small buried toys until she felt some hot water splash on her arm.

"Nicky! What are you doing?" Coco asked indignantly.

Although Jessica wet her bed, Nicky continued peeing in such improbable places as the fishbowl (three goldfish died within ten minutes) wall sockets (which short-circuited four houses on the block) and decorative hotel or restaurant fountains.

"He always pees in there to make the sand wetter," Jessica said, running over to rat on her brother. "That's why it stinks."

"Go in the house, Nicky, and use the toilet."

"I don't want to walk all the way upthairs. And it thtinkth from cats alwedy."

"Go ahead," Coco said firmly, picking up Joshua to move him away from the urine-damp section of sand.

"Anyway, I'm done," Nicky said with finality, edging the leg of his sunsuit back into place.

Coco frowned, covered the wet spot with dirty but dry handfuls of sand, and then hurried back inside the kitchen to score some downers. High on the window ledge above the sink, behind the curtains where the children could neither reach nor see, were her medicines. She took down the dark green bottle into which she had transferred Dr. Finkelstein's twelve Stelazines, peered through the smoky glass, shook the jar to see how many remained and then thumbed off the cover to pop two powder-blue capsules into her mouth.

But it took an hour before she felt composed enough to go upstairs to work. Once on the porch she lay down on the chaise, opened a new pack of Marlboros, and took out her calendar notebook. It had been exactly thirty days since she had commenced her daily exile to the porch, but subtracting weekends, only twenty-four full working days. According to her plan—10 pages x 24 days—she should now have 240 pages or eighty percent of her manuscript completed. But despite the fact she had faithfully written ten pages each day, in the unavoidable and wrenching process of editing, she invariably lost half of her daily output so that now she was left with only 122 finished pages. And it was the end of the month—a Friday, the 30th of June.

Coco studied her calendar intently. If she didn't finish a first full draft by the end of July it would be impossible to sustain her self-confidence or continue paying Mrs. Marshall's salary. That left only thirty-one days, minus four weekends. And tomorrow was the beginning of the Fourth of July holiday. Mrs. Marshall would be gone for the next four days and Coco would have trouble salvaging the week.

She put out her cigarette and shivered in the hot sunshine, regretting June and dreading July. Indeed, the damage done to June 30th was already irreparable. Just because Dr. Finkelstein had FORGOTTEN to warn her of his trip to Europe, Coco had spent the morning channeling her separation anxieties into sexual activities so that now more than half her work day was lost and she was suffering a paralyzing sense of defeat. Once again she had let the men in her life —husbands, psychiatrists, lovers—wipe her out emotionally and impede her productive, creative activities. *Take Heaven By Storm* lay neglected while Coco wasted her time worrying about a bunch of pricks.

A little spaced from the tranquilizers, Coco let her mind begin to wander. In a rather scientific manner she wondered if the curly little Y genes which turned boys into girls had a special trait (inscribed in invisible ink) which caused congenital female self-destructiveness. Doris Lessing said that women are willing

to give up their work for a man but that no man
would forsake his art for a woman. That made Coco
wonder if she could somehow translate her affair
with Suede into something a trifle less casual, into
something more immature and . . . compulsive. If
balling Suede was going to interfere with her work,
she should at least get a real thing going, so that it
made sense politically and served as proper repara-
tions for Gavin's infidelity. She wanted to be certain
that screwing Suede, right in the house, was equal to
Gavin making it with Sylvia or even Catherine from
Baltimore—if there was such a person.

GET TO WORK, her post-libby self shouted.

Coco straightened up guiltily. She would not lie
down. It didn't matter that this was the time of day
when she usually turned over to tan her back so that
her frontside wouldn't be browner than the rest of
her. She had to GET TO WORK.

But perhaps she should use this last day of June to
look through her old manuscripts, packed away with
the winter clothes in the trunk down the basement,
to find some ideas or excerpts she could possibly incorporate into her novel. That would clearly save
some writing time. But poking through old fiction,
looking for usable phrases or paragraphs or passages
from other rough drafts, could become distracting
and time-consuming. Although cutting out ready-
made scenes and stapling them onto a manuscript in-
progress produced a good consolidating high—like
dropping off dirty shirts at the laundry right when
the clean ones were ready, or cutting up leftover
hotdogs into the next day's baked beans, or using the
hard end of a Cheddar cheese in a pot of macaroni—
it always took more time than expected and usually
made more of a mess than an improvement—like
defrosting the refrigerator.

Coco wished she had an almond Hershey bar. She tried to imagine how she would look if she cut off her hair and wore it short and curly like a boy. She wondered if the kids were being so quiet because they were playing with the garden hose under the back porch. For a moment she thought that she heard the sound of Dr. Finkelstein's voice calling to her, but she didn't answer. She wondered, quite rationally, if she might be going insane, while a small transistor in her brain repeated . . . tomorrow is the first of July.

She began to envision the weekend, seeing how the children would try to consume her. Railing inwardly for their inevitable misbehavior, she decided to check out the *Post*'s Amusement Page to see if there would be any Walt Disney movies in town. Detesting the approaching, encroaching trivia that would devour her time and mind, she felt an enormous desire to devote herself to a new, great work of art which was waiting to spring, perfectly constructed, out of the typewriter. Emotionally she began to pant with a commitment to work every waking moment until the book was finished, to remain impervious to anyone or anything which might attempt to detour her.

But a rush of despair gushed through her as she looked toward the neatly stacked manuscript on the coffee table which fell so short of her dream. Recklessly she wondered if she should start over again. With thirty more days—if she did some moonlighting on weekends—she could start anew—fresh from the beginning—banishing forever all equivocations and ambiguities. She would only record Truths from now on. No more gossiping about herself under the guise of an unruly heroine, tainted and poisoned by Coco's own self-contempt. She closed her eyes and experienced several passionate moments of firm determination to outline a truly great and ambitious book.

Take Heaven By Storm wasn't nearly *heavy* enough. It wasn't even dirty enough to become controversial or notorious. If Clifford Irving had risked all, why couldn't Coco? She needed something totally different, dramatic, dynamic. New versions and visions of her novel came spinning through her head and suddenly the self-hating character of Gwensandra Rappaport began to take on new proportions.

Coco pulled the chaise into stern Upright Position. Now she knew what she should do.

She would simply write the story about what was happening to her now—right this minute. Her book would be THE novel about the Women's Liberation Movement. Gwensandra Rappaport would be a young married woman struggling toward her own consciousness, fighting all forms of chauvinistic oppression, by identifying with the new women's movement. Then there would be a character like Sylvia Brydan who would crawl out of the woodwork to run around organizing and making little statistical speeches about how thirty-one percent of all working women are secretaries or filing clerks, fifteen percent waitresses or domestics, fifteen percent factory workers. By packaging the problem and marketing the Movement, the Sylvia Brydan-type character would gain Gwensandra's confidence and infiltrate the Rappaport home. Then, under the guise of sisterhood, she would rip off Gwensandra's husband. And why? Because a Sylvia Brydan could not survive one single day or night without a man! She could not tolerate her own independence! She was compelled to share her liberated body with legions of dirty male chauvinist pigs.

Coco would create a character like Captain Ahab.

Sylvia would become a monumental American literary figure—a compulsive, man-chasing, power-humping, home-wrecking, family-shattering movement-scattering monomaniac. And *Take Heaven By Storm* would be transformed into The Great American Novel—the female version of *Moby Dick*—*The Big White Knobby Dick*.

Coco would NOT appear on the Dick Cavette show; she would be invited to Cambridge, Radcliffe, Sarah Lawrence. She would give lectures, listen to aspiring young female writers, advise them to keep working, keep writing . . .

CHAPTER 15

*I*t was late afternoon when Gavin suddenly kicked open the screen door and walked out onto the porch. He looked around briefly, surprised by the clutter of papers stacked on the floor along both sides of the chaise, but then dismissed her stash of office supplies with a blink of erasure behind his glasses.

"Come inside, Coco," he said in a high-school principal tone of voice, "I want to talk to you."

Coco looked up at him from Semi-Recline and felt the same kind of fright that overcame her when she lost her wallet.

"What's the matter?" she whispered.

Her heart lurched in her chest, while she automatically recapped her purple Flair.

"Something's come up," he said.

A nasty remark flitted through her mind, but it dissolved as she watched her husband's familiar backside disappear into the guest room. The wooden floor planks were burning hot beneath her bare feet as she stood up to follow him inside.

"Sit down," Gavin ordered.

Obediently Coco moved toward the bed, creased her body at the center, as if her waist were a dotted line, and placed herself on the edge of the mattress, where she had perched, hooked on Suede's X-L, in an upright, uptight position.

He's found out about us, she thought. He knows we were fucking around right here in the house while he was out earning a living and the kids were playing unsupervised in the backyard. The man from the apartment across the alley must have seen us through the window and telephoned Gavin at his office.

Gavin's face looked spray-set with resolution; his features were frosted with a newly manufactured brand of determination.

"I'm through, Coco. I'm leaving today." His voice was cold and matter-of-fact.

"Leaving?"

"I'm moving out. I'm through."

"What do you mean?"

"I mean I don't love you anymore, Coco. I haven't loved you for a long time."

Her tongue stuck to the roof of her mouth, hiding from speech.

"Oh, Gavin, it's because you've got a girlfriend," Coco finally said in a weak but accusative voice. "That's why you want to leave."

"Maybe I do have a girlfriend. But that's not why I'm moving out. I'd rather live alone the rest of my life than spend another night in the same house with you."

Coco began to cry. Slowly she became aware that

Gavin showed no sign of concern about her tears. There was no expression on his face at all. He was totally impervious to her. Out to lunch. He simply didn't care. He didn't care at all.

"And what do you expect me to do?" Coco asked between gulping sobs. "What's supposed to happen to me? What am I supposed to do now? Raise the kids by myself? Take care of the kids and grow old while you whored around with every hippie cunt you can find?"

"Shut up," he said, banging his hand down on top of the bureau so that Suede's shaving kit jumped several inches into the air. "I'm sick of your hysteria. I'm sick of your kvetching. This is what you've been aiming for all these years. You wanted to destroy us. To kill off my love. And you did. You won. And now I'm going upstairs to pack my stuff."

Coco succumbed to an uncontrollable torrent of tears that interfered with her speech processes. "Oh, yah," she said, finally regaining control. "And where are you going to go? Are you going to move in with Sylvia?"

"No," Gavin shouted, "I've got a room. I rented it this morning."

"Without telling me?" Coco shrieked in rage.

His audacity brought her to her feet. She whacked the side of his head so hard that his glasses flew off his face, but he was suddenly in possession of an enormous new strength that allowed him to grab her arms and keep them spread apart, safely away from him. His fingers bit into her wrists with a vengeance that verged on brutality and for a brief moment Coco felt physical fear infiltrate her other emotions.

"And what are you going to tell the kids?" Coco shrieked. "Are you going to tell them you're leaving them to go fuck Sylvia?"

"No," Gavin shouted. "I'm going to tell them the truth, that I don't love you anymore and that I'm leaving so that they'll never hear you shrieking at me ever again."

"Well, I'll tell them the real truth," Coco screamed.

She brought her knee up and out toward Gavin's groin, but he was still maintaining his distance, holding her away with stiffened arms.

"And I'll tell them the truth about how you ran out on your first wife, too."

"You never knew the truth, Coco. You don't know the truth about anything."

"You fucking hypocrite," she screamed, ducking her head while trying to land a knee into him. "You ugly fucking hypocrite. You set me up. You planned this."

Her face was wet and hot. But suddenly he released her arms with a violent thrust and Coco fell back against the wall, liquid and limp. Weakened, she could only sneer while he bent over and began to fumble around on the carpet for his glasses.

"Don't come near me," he hissed. "If you come near me now, I swear I'll beat the living shit out of you." His fingers connected with the glasses, which were lodged against the baseboard, and he examined them before putting them back on. Then he looked at her, pale with rage and revulsion. "Don't come upstairs," he warned. "I need one hour to pack my stuff and if you come near me, I'll ruin that pretty face of yours forever."

Coco slid along the wall until she slumped back onto the bed from where she watched Gavin walk out of the room. Then she sat perfectly still with hands clasped, fingers clutching at each other. Fury and rage, now swollen to painful proportions, were locked inside her body. It seemed as if the anger inside would have to rupture, erupt and rip open her flesh, ejaculating inner organs in an explosion of skin, bone and blood. But then, sitting still, she slowly realized that there could be no climax now. Her rage had reached a pinnacle of purity, dazzling in its perfection, but permanently petrified because the enemy was sneaking away, escaping like a group of guerrillas into the hills, refusing to meet and do battle.

"No way," Coco suddenly said outloud. "There's no way."

The words felt right on her parched lips, although she didn't know what they meant other than the fact that Gavin's performance had felt intolerable to her.

So it has come to this, she thought formally, still uncertain of the antecedent of "it."

Very slowly she stood up and walked back out to the porch. She reclaimed her Marlboros from the table, lit a cigarette and clutched hot smoke into her lungs. Out in the hallway she could hear Joshua crying as Mrs. Marshall carried him upstairs for his nap. Now Mrs. Marshall would see Gavin packing. But since he was always taking trips, she would probably think he was just going away on business.

That's what I'll tell her, Coco decided inside a newly constructed defense shelter in the cellar of her brain that hadn't existed fifteen minutes ago.

That's funny, Coco thought. Why don't I want Mrs. Marshall to know?

Next Coco became aware of a fluttering in her chest that felt like a fetal foot or elbow kicking in the womb, demanding internal attention. Her body stiffened as she heeded the strange little knock. Was that sensation a twitch in her lung? Did cancer start with a dull thud like *that* in some unspecified interior region? Was that suddenly sensate section that she had never noticed before her left lung? The flut-

tering intensified. Coco stamped out her cigarette
and expelled all the smoke she could dredge up. Her
breath made a soft swishing sound, a blowing
whewww, through the air.

Then she turned, ran out to the hallway and took
the stairs two at a time.

Gavin was stationed in front of his closet pulling
shirts off their hangers and parachuting them into his
big black suitcase. Joshua's bedroom door was closed
but Coco could hear the crib rocking in a steady,
masturbatory motion.

"Where are you going to go, Gavin?" Coco asked in
a subdued voice.

"I told you. I'm leaving."

"Yes, I know. But where will you be?"

"Not anywhere I can be reached."

Coco emitted a shrill whimper of hysteria. "But
what if I *need* you?"

He laughed.

The strange fist of emotion, bagged in her chest,
began shadow-boxing her heart again.

"Listen, Gavin. There are four little kids here.
You're not just going to walk out on us."

"Oh, yah. Who says I'm not?"

Now he was pulling down the winter sweaters
Coco had wadded up on the shelf above his clothes
rack, throwing them into the suitcase on top of the
short-sleeve drip-drys. He was packing with a year-
round-run-away-pappy kind of abandon.

"Well, I'm going to call Dave Kaplan," Coco said,
feigning a decision-made-with-reluctance tone of
voice.

"What for? You going to file for divorce? Or are you
going to get an injunction to stop me from leaving?"
Gavin snorted out the words without turning around
or decreasing the tempo of his packing. "You know

something? I finally believe it now, Coco. I really believe you're crazy. You really are just plain schizy."

Coco sat down at her dressing table.

Why am I shaking? she wondered, looking into the mirror with medical, rather than cosmetic, interest. What's the matter with my chest? Idly she considered the possibility she might be having a heart attack. She felt much sicker than she had the night Gavin confessed his love affair. But then, of course, everything had still seemed conversational—debatable and negotiable. Now everything was different. Now she was confronting a vacuum, an enormous gaping crater in the center of her universe. She had been transformed into a colonial army fighting a sneaky band of rebels who disappeared after surprise attacks that left injured women and children in their wake. The Burmans' civil war had turned into a revolution and Coco was definitely on the imperial royalist side.

Gavin began dragging the suitcase toward his dresser. He started at the top, opening each drawer, and began dumping handfuls of unmatched socks, faded-pink Jockey shorts, torn T-shirts and mateless pajama halves into the yawning suitcase.

Coco watched in frozen horror.

He was going. He was really going. He was leaving her alone. She was going to be alone.

"Please, Gavin," she said firmly. "Please. Stop it now."

He didn't even look up.

Coco experienced an unexpected resurgence of anger.

"Is somebody going to pick you up with a ladder? Can't you talk to me for a second? I mean, isn't this just a little bit too fast? Too unilateral? I mean, isn't this just a little bit too much?"

He looked around the room, but everything else belonged to Coco.

"You know, I don't believe this," Coco said. "It's really too incredible."

Gavin, standing straight and solitary, looked at her with distilled contempt.

"For Christ's sake, Coco, how long did you think I was going to take all that shit? Isn't twelve years long enough? What do I get out of staying here any longer? You cut off my balls in front of the kids, you don't want to fuck, you hate my guts, you yell and scream . . ."

Coco felt awed by the new egocentricity that was emanating from her husband as he delivered his speech.

"And this morning, I just suddenly realized that I don't want to see you anymore and I sure as hell don't want to live here anymore. I'll call up toward the end of next week to talk to the children and then I'll take them out and explain everything to them. I talked to a lawyer this morning, but I want to see him before I tell the kids, so I'll know where things stand. He'll draw up all the custody and separation papers next week and we can get the divorce started right away."

"I don't believe you," Coco whispered. "You can't just leave. You can't just leave me here alone with the children." Then amazement fired her imagination. "Listen! Why don't you stay here and I'll go. If it's just me you can't stand, then I'll go. I'll get out. Put your stuff back in the drawers and I'll pack."

"No, thanks."

"Well, how come I automatically win the kids and the responsibilities? How come when I win, I lose? How come when I got you away from Ann she became a success and I became a piece of shit? How come?"

Gavin issued a short snort of laughter. Then he bent over to push the excess clothing down farther into his suitcase, without displaying the slightest interest in compromise or justice.

"I'm not reconsidering or renegotiating anything. I don't think there's any reason for us to talk to each other again or see each other anymore."

"Gavin," said Coco. "Gavin, what are you saying?"

Now he was trying to force the top of the suitcase into line so he could snap the lock.

"You better believe it, Coco, because I'm not kidding. This ball game is over. No more fun and games."

Coco thought she heard prison doors clang when the Samsonite clicked.

"Games," she shrieked. "Games? You must be totally insane, Gavin. You turn on and off like some lobotomy case." She was crying now while she yelled. "I was right about you not having normal feelings. You don't feel anything at all. You're the crazy one. You're just out of it."

"Sorry."

"Well, I'm going to sue you for adultery," Coco screamed. "I'm going to roll you for every penny you have."

"There aren't too many pennies, Coco, but you can have whatever you need that I can afford."

"And who are you going to live with? Answer me that, why don't you? And tell me something else, Gavin. Is this how you did it to Ann? When you came to take me to Indiana to elope? Is this how you left her?"

"I'm not answering any more questions, Coco. You don't seem to understand. You're dead. You're finished, done, gone." He put his thumb up to his teeth and snapped the nail in a vulgar motion toward Coco's face. Then he yanked the suitcase off the floor. His face was scarlet. "And if you make a scene now in front of the kids, I'll see to it that you pay for it the rest of your life."

The fact that threats kept tumbling out of Gavin's mouth seemed to validate his intentions more than the packed suitcase.

Coco got off her small dressing-table stool. For a moment she thought she might attack him, lunge forward and begin tearing at his body. But instead she walked over to the bed and lay down flat on her stomach with her face turned into the pillows.

He didn't say another word. Coco heard him open the bedroom door and then close it. She listened to him clump and clatter down the uncarpeted stairs and eventually slam the front door with great finality.

CHAPTER 16

*C*oco stayed in her room until Mrs. Marshall yelled up the stairwell that she was leaving. Then, dazed and numb, she went downstairs, paid Mrs. Marshall her week's salary, wished her a good trip and went into the kitchen to begin cooking dinner. Shortly after six she sat down at the table with her children and pretended to eat. Jessica asked where Gavin was and Coco said he had to go to New York for a few days to try a case. Mike commented in a nasty voice that Gavin had promised to take him along the next time he went to New York. Then Jessica went into a monologue about some geographically misplaced cities that distracted everyone. Within a few minutes the talk shifted to the Fourth of July fireworks.

After dinner, Coco watched the children watch television. When Nicky grew restless she lay down on the floor to help him build a cowboy fortress and kept

Josh busy with his blocks on the other side of her legs so he wouldn't grab any of the Indians. After *The Brady Bunch* and *The Partridge Family,* she marshaled Josh, Nicky and Jessica upstairs and put them to bed. Mike stayed behind to watch *The Odd Couple* and *Love American Style.* Convinced that ABC had maliciously rescheduled every family show they owned to torture the Burmans on the first night of their orphanhood, Coco snuck down to the living room, made herself a double gin with tonic, and carried it back to her bedroom.

After putting on a pair of white bell bottoms and a tight-ribbed shirt without a bra, she sat down at her dressing table. The supersophisticated, semicorrupt sensation of drinking alcohol in her bedroom gave Coco a guilty sense of wickedness. Her only worry was that Mike might come in and discover she was actually having a drink off livingroom limits. To cover the clink of her ice cubes, she rattled her can of hair spray so that the tin mystery inside produced a camouflaging noise. With the spray can in one hand and her drink in the other, Coco studied her face in the mirror to see if there were any visible signs of her psychological deterioration.

Coco could not remember ever being so frightened before. The tremulous shaking and quaking in her hands, knees and thighs felt like the first serious symptom of some deadly disease. For several hours she had been recalling a childhood campfireside ghoststory about a man in Texas who died from fear when he found a rattlesnake wrapped around him in his sleeping bag. Coco was now prepared to believe in fear as a scientifically acceptable Cause of Death. The terror that had pierced her body was so perilously pointed and sharp that if she negligently let it lacerate her consciousness, severing her precarious rope to sanity and rupturing her life-support system of self-control, she would die.

"You're okay," Coco said to herself, smiling kindly at her face in the mirror. "You're okay," she intoned in the same voice she used for the children when they fell and scraped their knees on the sidewalk.

Medicinally she administered a little more gin to her mouth, which periodically had been going bone-dry over the past few hours.

—Why don't you put on a little makeup—her pre-lib consciousness suggested. —Put a touch of Yardley's London Gold on your lips.—

Coco's fingers clawed some cosmetics closer to the edge of the dressing table so she could begin decorating her face. But the paints and powders couldn't disguise her expression. Within half a day, Coco's feisty look had changed to one of fear. But, of course, why not? Coco was no longer a reckless young wife and mother, charmingly chafing at the bit, constantly contemplating Capri or Corfu. Now she had joined the ranks of x-ed-out women—ex-maidens, ex-prom-queens, ex-wives—the realm of the formerly. Now she was a desperado—an unemployed, over-aged, unwed mother of four children with no expectations.

Frantically Coco began gluing on her best night-time-length Revlon double-fringe lashes. (Why hadn't Gavin phoned yet? Why hadn't he called to apologize or to tell her to meet him downtown at a bar so he could give her a deadly serious lecture about reformation rather than repentance before he would come home again?) The surgical glue smeared along the nylon spine of the lashes was so clumpy that the ends kept popping up. Impatiently Coco tore them off and tossed them down on her dressing table where they began to curl up and wilt like black widow spiders.

But without false lashes Coco felt naked and un-prepared. Immediately she experienced an urge to apply eyeliner to make up for her lash deficiency. Was making-up now going to be like another long career of counting course credits? Was an unmarried woman who omitted her lashes now required to use both liner and shadow? Was making-up now going to become a crisis like choosing nine credits of social science or three quarters of a foreign language to meet a B. A. requirement?

Call me up, Gavin, you dirty son-of-a-bitch, she ordered.

The phone remained sullenly silent.

Please come back now, Suede, she requested more politely. Now we will have enough time and space to get this little affair of ours institutionalized. Coco felt an extraordinary desire to enroll Suede as a Perma-nent Life-Long Lover right away. But then her pre-lib counselor sent out a special-delivery message. Since Coco didn't look her ethnic best this evening, it might be advisable to present herself as a wild adul-terous housewife rather than a déclassé divorcée.

Coco colored her lips, painfully aware that her beautification ritual was no longer a gratuitous act but a very serious preparation—like studying for final exams. Making up was no longer a frivolous glossary to her charms, but rather an essential introduction to the text. Just like Gavin said, no more fun and games. No longer would she dare to identify or inspect her imperfections. From now on everything was deadly serious. A single woman had to deny any flaw or failure, any fears or fat.

And then, suddenly, involuntarily, an unsum-moned parade of single women began to march through Coco's head. One by one, all her female acquaintances—whose singleness was their singu-

larly most outstanding characteristic—appeared in
review before Coco's eyes, smiling bravely as they
moved desperately through life. The stage was always a small apartment where Mennen's foot powder was never exposed in the bathroom, where there
were no telltale whiskers stuck to the sink faucets, no
damp towels balled up in the tub, no extra-firm
toothbrush parked in the soap dish, no ties lassoed
around doorknobs, no coats draped over chairbacks,
no shirts dripping over the banister, no vacant shoes
parked under the sofa, no newspapers drooling
across the floor.

Coco could see a woman—whose name had long
ago been relegated to the Burmans' kitchen telephone directory—eating dinner alone, unwilling to
sit down on one of her two ice-cream soda chairs at
her round butcher-block kitchen table that never got
dirty and, instead, ate standing up at the counter
next to the breadbox, the way Coco did when Gavin
was out of town. Did single ladies live on sandwich-
thin slices of white bread, scooping peanut butter out
of a miniature-sized Skippy jar with a stiff but trembling forefinger? Did they eat thick slices of onion on
buttered bread and rain garlic salt on their vegetables with impunity? Did they peek through the
mailbox every time the bell rang, wait for best sellers
to arrive at the Discount Bookstore, check the week's
late late night movies first thing Sunday morning
when the television guide fell out of the paper and
cry when they came home alone after a party?

Oh, no. Please, no. But perhaps in these post-lib
days, ad-libbing was easier. Maybe ladies-in-waiting
were better off now. Optimistically Coco saw a vision
of brussels sprouts defrosting picturesquely next to
the colorful ingredients for a hollandaise sauce beneath a sunny kitchen window. Perhaps the single

life had become more graceful. Perhaps single ladies spent glorious weekend afternoons walking along the C & O Canal, biking out to Seneca, attending piano concerts at the Phillips Gallery, playing tennis on private courts with arch architects from Georgetown. Perhaps single ladies, nowadays, became D.C. Democratic-party delegates to national political conventions, housed attractive university professor protestors in town for peace demonstrations, and went shopping for lingerie at Saks Fifth Avenue in Chevy Chase on Monday nights before 9:30.

But then Coco remembered *Maiden* and suddenly saw herself haunting and hunting in the swinging singles bars—Luv, Clyde's, the Crazy Horse. Was there a maximum age limit? Would the maître d' check her ID—card her?—to ascertain if she were over thirty? And what about those beastly ski weekends for singles? Would she have to buy all that expensive equipment to sustain the inevitable humiliation of singing college songs on a chartered Trailways bus bound for the pathetic Poconos? Was she going to spend the rest of her nights polishing her nails, her shoes, her silver, her dining-room table, and her teeth?

But then again, perhaps Coco would suddenly be swept up in a series of elegant Georgetown dinner parties and become the toast of the capital, the woman most sought after by America's political establishment, pursued by Maxine Cheshire and other gossip columnists, while trying to slip away for a weekend with . . . who? Widowed congressmen? Lecherous Supreme Court justices? Philandering journalists? Egomaniacal anchormen?

—I have made a mistake—she said to the frightened face in her mirror.

—Well, so be it—answered her Raised Consciousness.

—So be it? Was that like "And So It Goes?"—

"I'm going to bed now, Ma," Mike shouted.

Coco jumped up and ran into the hall to kiss Mike good night. Then she continued on downstairs to the living room. She adjusted the air-conditioner, emptied the ashtrays, rearranged a spray of dead flowers in her favorite vase, tilted several lamp shades so as to avoid direct lighting, and prayed: Dear Lord, please send Suede back here right now.

She made herself another drink, picked a small percentage of lint off the carpet, and resolved not to go near the telephone. "I will not start calling people," she said out loud. After one phone call the entire city would know she was trying to track down her husband, that she was the injured-and-deserted party, that after all her bitching about Gavin for so many years, she was the terrified and hysterical, leftover wife. Only Glenda could understand what had happened and she was gone.

Coco pulled her chair closer to the front window and stared down into the street while she gulped fresh icy gin from her glass. I have not yet determined my position or posture, she thought. My future can be destroyed by a few badly handled phone calls to the wrong people. Besides, I do not want to keep the line tied up when Suede might be trying to call. It's almost eleven. Also, Gavin might be trying to get through.

But the phone hadn't rung for hours. The last call had been for Mike.

Across the street Coco saw one of her neighbors sitting outside on the stoop. The woman was tall, slim and crowned with an enormous Afro that seemed to diminish the size of her body. Coco knew that the

woman had three sons and no husband on the premises. She had always known that fact unconsciously,
as an irrelevant piece of gossip. But tonight, as Coco
sat alone in her house with her sleeping children,
hearing for the first time in years the sounds of her
own existence, she suddenly realized that solitude
was not a tangential consideration. Suddenly she was
aware of the harsh irregular sounds of her own heavy
breathing, the pout of her lips when she released a
cigarette, and the slightly perceptible noise of the
alcohol sliding down her gullet. The sounds of her
body made her feel extraordinarily solitary and suddenly she was curious about the black woman whom
she had seen coming and going for the past four years
out of the apartment across the street.

The woman lived without a man. She came and
went a great deal, often looking tired, but seemingly
eager about her life. There were always lots of visitors—relatives and friends and boyfriends—who
came over and disappeared into her basement apartment or horsed around with the kids outside on the
front stoop or played ball with them in the street and
fished change out of their pockets when the Good
Humor truck came by. But Coco had never paid that
woman tribute (they waved to each other or said
hello but never spoke), so that now, as the woman sat
alone on her front stoop, drinking a bottle of soda
pop, probably tired from having just put her sons to
sleep, Coco felt admiration for her because the
woman had brought a transistor radio outside to set
on the top stair and as she sat there, sipping the soda,
she tapped one leg back and forth against the gray-
brick stoop while listening to the music.

Coco felt humble because the woman had enough
spirit in her solitude to want to hear a little sound.
Coco wondered if she was waiting for a man to join

her; the expectation of a friend could explain the
radio. But that idea felt fearsome and wrong. Coco
wanted to believe that no one was coming to visit and
that the woman was playing the transistor radio just
for herself. And if, somehow, that were true, it was a
clue to something, a partial answer to the enormous
question that was developing within Coco's soul.

—Please don't be waiting for anyone,—Coco
urged through the window, silently but persuasively.
—Just be playing the radio for yourself. Even if someone's coming by later, when you're back inside, even
though you have to work every morning, year after
year, and take care of your boys alone, and have such
small windows in your basement flat, sing to yourself,
so I won't be afraid. —

—Why should that black woman have to make it
alone?—a more rigorous voice roared through Coco's
head. —Just because she's black and supposed to be
stronger and not as middle-class as you? Maybe she
has even more needs than you do because she is
poor. —

—Impossible. —

But then Coco remembered two other moments.

She and Gavin had taken a train to Chicago the day
before Christmas of 1960 and as they walked through
Union Station, Coco remembered thinking about
how Scott Fitzgerald had done midwestern train de-
pots so well, so long ago, that there wasn't much left
that needed doing on that subject in American literature anymore. Outside it was snowing and there
were no taxis. Since they had splurged on a sleeper
from Washington, they had had the privacy and opportunity to quarrel constantly across half of the
country. Coco had lain flat on her back all night,
tucked beneath her husband's berth, hating the
lump in the middle of the mattress that was him.

When they finally reached Chicago, the tiniest details seemed pristine and precious because she hadn't slept enough. She felt like running away from Gavin and rushing back to the South Side of Chicago, to Hyde Park and the university they had left only one year before but which still remained perfectly intact in her mind, permanently idealized by the heady feelings she had felt when she lived there.

But, instead, they had just walked around the dirty train station, looking at magazines, drinking coffee twice, finally holding hands because they felt so alienated by their inexplicable anger, and that was when Coco saw a group of porters standing next to a freight car unloading a big crate. (Why am I remembering this, Coco wondered, alarmed at the possible significance of such a long-buried image surfacing, full-blown and insistent, on this particular night.) But the memory continued, replaying the scene of her witnessing something dreadful happening before comprehending what it was, feeling something fearsome go wrong with the environment without understanding why.

Because then a lady, whom Coco had seen on the train sitting alone in an open-doored compartment, came to stand nearby and then she too was watching as the men struggled with the box and suddenly Coco knew there was a casket inside the wooden crate and that the woman's husband was inside and that it was the day before Christmas and Coco had simply forgotten that people went on dying, while she went on struggling to live. So she had stood there helplessly, holding Gavin's hand, watching another porter roll up a flat wagon and help to get the box on top of it. Then one thin black porter began to push the wagon and the woman ran along beside it, sort of hopping like a bird, watching the crate with the casket inside and trying to keep up with the wagon as it separated the crowds of people. But the whole time the woman looked confused because her husband couldn't help her with her two little satchels plus a handbag and because he was causing all this trouble, causing her to hop alongside the flat wagon rolling along next to the train tracks, making her hop across the slippery wet pavement without any help because he had become a problem instead of a solution.

"Shit," Coco said outloud. She got up, went to the bar, reconsidered, scooped two ice cubes out of the bucket and then hurried back to her chair.

The black woman was still sitting on her stoop. The soda bottle was empty now, tucked safely in a corner of the stairs. The radio was still playing and the woman was still leaning back against the dirty gray-brick wall, staring into space, maybe waiting for a breath of cool air and yes, yes, she was still listening to the music. Coco could see her foot marking time.

—Thank you—Coco whispered, fearing the fear that was coming up strong now in her chest.

Where is Suede? she moaned silently, confronting the truth of her terror from a lateral perspective. Was he still doing research at the Library of Congress? But the L.C. closed at ten. Maybe he was in some congressional office rapping with a legislative assistant or having drinks in a bar? Or was he over at a restaurant with some friend whom Coco didn't even know existed? Or had he picked up a girl at the Senate cafeteria during lunch time, some summer intern from Nebraska, a pale-haired creature with luminous gray eyes and a flat hipless body in love-and-peace patched dungarees that slid down over a concave tummy while her soft round breasts undulated in a faded tie-dyed shirt?

Or was he with Sylvia?

—Come back now, Suede. I need you. I need somebody very badly—her heart blurted.

But she kept staring out of the window, because
now she was remembering another morning, more
than ten years before, when she and Gavin had lived
in a rodent-infested apartment building right behind
the Supreme Court. Since she didn't have a job, Coco
made a ritual of watching the justices come to work
in the mornings, after Gavin had left, when she had
nothing to do. Was she pregnant with Michael then?
No. Not pregnant. Just out of work, with nothing to
do. So she had spent long hours feeling messy and
grouchy, peculiarly morningish all day long, because
the day never developed for her. She dreaded Gavin
coming home for dinner from that mysterious organized world outside the apartment where there was
work to do and coffee breaks and lunchtime and a
sense of morning, afternoon, evening—a sensate pro-
gression of time that somehow evaded her when she
was locked alone inside the apartment, feeling totally
aimless.

So that morning, she had been sitting on the radiator, drinking coffee and looking out the ugly crooked
bay window, when she saw a cat stalking something
in slow motion. Shortly a little robin, too sick or hurt
to fly, appeared on the sidewalk in front of the apartment. Nearby the crippled robin's mate was hopping
along the curb, hopping and chirping and launching
quickly aborted flights that caused great wing shud-
ders, trying to distract the cat, doing everything a
little bird could do to save its mate. But nothing mattered. Because very soon there was a fluttering of fur
and feathers, and then the cat had the robin in its
mouth, and the bird's mate was still hopping up and
down on the curb, chirping and squeaking, while the
cat killed the robin and it was all over.

Coco walked to the telephone, paused, and then dialed Gavin's office number. There was no answer. She pulled the telephone directory out of the closet, looked up Sylvia's number, dialed and let the phone ring ten times. Then she made herself another drink and went back to the window. The woman across the street had disappeared.

But suddenly a taxi, that was moving slowly down the street, stopped in front of the Burman house. With an explosion of relief, Coco watched Suede climb out of the back seat and reach through the open window to pay the driver.

Now . . . now Coco was safe. She was safe. She wouldn't spend the night alone. Wildly she ran down the stairs and through the hallway toward the dark hulking shadow outside the front door. The moment Suede walked inside, she lurched violently against him.

Startled, he recoiled, reflexively jerking away from her.

"Hi," she said breathlessly and then, seeing his alarm, instantly began to explain. "Gavin's gone. He went out of town. He's going to be gone most of the week. We're alone."

She pressed up against him again, making her body hard and insistent, pulling in her stomach so that the bone of her pelvis dug into the softness of his groin.

Suede folded his arms around her automatically but without any enthusiasm. Coco didn't even care. Her gratitude for the nearness of his body, blurring the boundaries of her own consciousness and reducing her panic by offering external definition, voiced over his coldness. Her pain couldn't be infinite if it didn't extend indefinitely into space.

"How about a drink?" he asked, holding her back

as if to study her face but simultaneously separating their bodies.

—Be very careful—the director of Coco's cerebral civil-defense shelter cautioned.

"Were you at the library," she asked, "or doing interviews?"

"Both." He was being wary. He draped one arm around her shoulder, but it was more to control her enthusiasm than to excite it. "Tell you what," Suede said, "I'll make us some drinks if you rustle me up a sandwich and bring it upstairs."

His voice was silvered with skepticism, suspicion and caution.

What was he afraid of, Coco wondered. Was he afraid of her because she was afraid? What had changed or was different about her now that he had sensed so swiftly? Had she overwhelmed him by exposing her excitement? Had she seemed assaultive rather than seductive? Or was he simply still tired from their morning romp?

"Sure. I'll make some sandwiches," Coco said, turning toward the kitchen.

And that was when she felt the sting of his hand on her bottom—an encouraging smack on the buttocks with which coaches sent second-string players into a ballgame—a go-to-it-fella-you're-finally-off-the-bench-so-let's-see-you-show-your-stuff sort of pat. And that was when Coco realized Suede's aloofness had increased in direct proportion to her need for him.

He started up the stairs. "And dig up your peace pipe, honey, so we can smoke some of that dope I brought."

"Oh, you still have some?" Coco murmured, pleased at the prospect of a prop for their passion. Then she ran back to the kitchen.

But standing alone in the huge shadowy room, watchful and anxious lest a mouse suddenly scurry out of nowhere, like some neurotic dread slipping loose from her unconscious to slither in a dark flash past the corner of her eye, she felt her composure slip away again. With shaking hands she began to hunt through the cupboards for some forgotten delicacies —some leftover provisions from an imitative Georgetown French-style dinner party which reflected the value she attached to her guests. Compulsively she knocked over cans of Campbell's soups and Del Monte kernel corn, hunting for value-laden buried treasures—olives or kippers or capers or pate paste.

Why, Coco wondered, never pausing now in her hurried, harried hunt, am I doing this when there's a perfectly fine Hebrew National salami in the Frigidaire? Down on her knees, beneath the oven, kneeling like a supplicant in front of an open tabernacle, half-drunk from vodka and the backwash of her violent emotions, she reached far back behind the paper plates and paper toweling for a can of anchovies (could they spoil?) and a tall thin jar of artichoke hearts that she'd long ago forgotten. Finally clutching her newly excavated treasures, Coco rose unsteadily to her feet.

She felt feverish and disoriented, on the edge of an uncontrollable episode of screams.

Don't do it—post-libby warned. —You're okay. Hang on. Hang in there.

But standing at the bread board, her fingers peeling icy slices off a miniature frozen pumpernickel bread that she had chopped loose from the glacial wall of the freezer in an antic arctic expedition to find some buried treasure, her soul called out for Dr. Finkelstein. She wanted him to know she wasn't

pretending and that now she really was feeling
hysterically in need of psychiatric—if not spiritual—
support.

Still, it was with efficiency that she inserted a can of
stuffed olives into the can opener—an electric Sun-
beam Pandora that instantly released a horrid frieze
of tragic women culled and collated from flicks and
literature who began to sway through Coco's head in
a Dantesque congo line. Coco saw Mrs. Stone freaking out in Rome as her next-gigolo-lover urinated
beneath her window and then the gorgeous Ann
Bancroft having a breakdown in the major appliance
department of a major London department store in
The Pumpkin Eater. The memory of Peter Finch's
audacious adultery while his wife was having a hys-
terectomy made Coco shiver as she laid out some
cheese just as Edith Vanocur suggested in the *Post*'s
Food Section and arranged the little anchovies exactly like poor, heartbreaking Ramona who had tried
so hard to trap Moses Herzog with her curried
shrimp.

Oh, no, not me, Coco insisted. I am above such
devious devices, such dirty deceptions. But hadn't
Neil Klugman loved Brenda Patemkin a little bit
more because of that extra refrigerator down in her
basement filled to overflowing with fresh summer
fruit—ripe as Brenda's breasts? And what *was* the
Magic Mountain but a Big Swiss Tit?

Coco's hand faltered as she tried to twist the tight
cover off a jar of capers and it was then a parade of
betrayed actresses began running across the stage of
her mind. Coco saw several of Ingmar Bergman's
beautiful but betrayed heroines grieving in guttural
Swedish and next little Giuletta Massina cringing
tragically as Anthony Quinn strode away from her in
La Strada and then Shelley Winters sinking beneath

the water so Montgomery Clift could make it with
Liz Taylor in a real *American Tragedy*. Was Coco
Burman going to forsake her own glorious destiny to
stand at the bread board in the kitchen cutting
canapés for a supercautious gentleman who was lol-
ling around upstairs in the livingroom waiting to be
served and then serviced?

Wouldn't it be better to take her children and
follow the circuitous path of Lowry's Consul through
the labyrinth of Cuernavaca, pursuing Death rather
than expire from spiritual starvation while slicing
green olives very carefully in order to keep the
slippery pimiento safely intact? Still—and she was
working more quickly now—what was wrong with
making a little late-night dinner look appetizing?
What did it matter if the Columbia Road W.L.G.R.
Local struck her name from their membership list or
if Kate Millet and Germaine Greer conspired to off
her? What did it matter if Joyce Carol Oates or Joan
Didion or Sylvia Plath (in sheer spirit form from her
deep sad grave) or Doris Lessing or Grace Paley or
Anais Nin (oh, how she would shudder) or Allison
Lurie or Lois Gould or Toni Morrison or Sandra
Hochman or Maxine Kumin or Sue Kaufman, who
certainly got there first with *The Diary of a Mad
Housewife*, or Edna O'Brien or Alix Kate Schulman
vetoed Coco's name if it were ever put in nomination
for membership in that Mighty Living Tradition?
And wouldn't they have Just Cause if it were *known*
that Coco made zesty little hors d'oeuvres as an
aphrodisiacal offering before the main (inter) course
—the main entre (nous)—so pathetic and paltry a
spirit was she?

Could there possibly be any other self-respecting
Serious American Female Writer who would stoop to
such depths? Could there possibly be any other au-

thentic artist who could be so insecure, so identity-
less, so frightened, so hysterical as to concentrate on
getting the pâté right to the edge of the rims of the
little garlic rounds, so that some slobby man would
consent to spend the night with her? Was Coco re-
verting to type—trying to demonstrate that she had
time for details just like Mrs. Sophie Silverman
(whom Coco was firmly exiling from her mind, re-
pressing, dismissing, disregarding) doing up a Youth
Aliyah or B'nai Brith luncheon? What was the meaning of all this—all these party favors and sexual favors? Was it so she wouldn't have to work, to think, to
be?

Shouldn't Coco right away this very night—instead
of balling Suede—reread dear dead Warren Miller's
The Way We Live Now and simply translate it, trans-
pose it into female key, take that tragic hero and try,
with the grace of God, to create his counterpart, the
flipside-female version of that very man. Is that not
what Coco should do?

It was with a heavy tray that Coco went back up
the stairs.

But when she was finally seated in a spaced-not-to-
scare-Suede location on the couch, with the elegant
platter centered on the coffee table, companionably
close to the highball glasses and airmail envelope
filled with dry hash-laced marijuana, the children
(please dear God) fast asleep upstairs safe in their
beds (would she now have to install a latch lock on
the livingroom door so there would be sufficient
warning if someone was going to burst in?), Coco felt
an almost uncontrollable groundswell of sensual love
for Suede—for his handsome, indolent, self-assured
body, legs outstretched in penis-swollen khaki trousers, offering Coco total oblivion and escape from her
soulful sadness. For wasn't physical passion the best

alternative to psychic pain, indeed, the payoff for the
hideous fear that had enveloped her during the long
hours of waiting for Suede's return so she could pur-
chase mindless oblivion in exchange for her body.

But she had to wait a long time. It was almost one
o'clock before Suede could unwind and adjust to the
freedom which alarmed him more than the danger
of discovery. After all, hadn't he gotten laid even
while there was still a blood-daddy, a support-provid-
ing husband, a perfect foil, living on the premises?
There was certainly no reason for him to be ecstatic
about Gavin's strange, unexpected absence. Why
should he be happy about becoming eligible, available, vulnerable—a target just because someone else
took a walk? He'd have to be crazy.

But, finally, after Suede had downed three
Scotches, eaten a huge submarine on half a loaf of
warm (yes, she had turned on the oven in that
breathless, airless tomb of a kitchen) French bread,
sloshing a tomato so that it squirted on the carpet
(Coco made no move to wipe it up, thereby guaran-
teeing an eternal red spot right next to the couch), he
finally began to relax a little. He turned on the stereo,
rolled some joints and began smoking. But his
creased, handsome face still looked rather elusive
and when he spoke he was careful not to sound
promising about anything.

Oh, dear, Coco thought. She had almost forgotten
that terrible novel by the lady who started the Pussy-
cat Society. What was the name of that book. . . .
I Was Never a Princess? That was a whole other terror
trip, but Coco had time to think about it because she
had to act cool even after she too had smoked a joint
that made the tops of her thighs begin to melt into
liquid sensuality. And though she was getting stoned,
feeling herself drifting away from caution and sub-

terfuge, she remained uncomfortably conscious of
the subtle loss of power that she had suffered.

No longer was she dallying in seventeenth-century
opulence with an adulterous lover. Instead, she was
engaged in a serious, self-conscious eighteenth-cen-
tury episode best expressed in rhymed couplets so
uptight and constipated was the experience. She was
now forced into trying harder, like a second-class car-
rental corporation (notice the hearts of artichokes
wilting and drying up like her own heart upon the
platter), while she maneuvered her way through the
shoals of singledom. Even with momentary reprieves
of drug-induced somnolence, she was still aware of
every limp word and gesture that yesterday would
have seemed sweetly insignificant and that now
sounded serious, portentous, ominous and threatening.

For despite the drinks and the joints, Coco was
being nagged by concern over the lastability of her
foot, underarm and vaginal deodorants, the danger
that a sudden heaviness in her stomach might possibly (God forbid) create gas, and a growing compulsion to test the quality of her breath by blowing into a
cupped hand, and sniffing the odor before it escaped
through the cracks between her fingers, so she would
know whether to run to the bathroom and squirt
some Binaca on her tongue.

Outside, the larger world, too, was full of threats.
Outside a civil war raged between the government
and the people, between bedeviled federal agencies
and civil rights marchers, draft-card burners, ecology
supporters, early feminists and gay activists. Presi-
dential peace candidates with armies of young long-
haired supporters were striding across the country.
The battle lines were clearly drawn.

Suede will stay here with me, Coco promised her-

self. He'll hang in until I get my bearings. When
Gavin hears Suede's still living here, he'll get jealous
and come back home. In the meantime, it won't look
too bad because Suede was staying here before Gavin
split, so it will look pretty kosher, not that little Sarah's mother would approve. (But what if some of the
neighbors hadn't noticed Suede around before they
hear Gavin is gone? Would they think Coco had simply kicked Gavin out to move in her lover? Would
they stop letting their children come over to the
Burmans' so that her children would lose not only
their father but also their friends? Oh, please, dear
God, don't do that, Coco telegraphed heaven.)

CHAPTER 17

*B*ut when Coco's anxieties became intolerably acute, she pushed the coffee table away from the couch to give herself more operating space and reached behind Suede for some matches. Then, instead of retreating back to her own turf, she went through an elaborate charade suggesting that accidental proximity had unexpectedly triggered irresistible passion. Slumped over, with a portentous moan of unsolicited surrender, Coco leaned against Suede's shoulder and eased one hand down onto the khaki crease which was really a firmly packed bunch of genitals—his earth-moving equipment.

And now, because she was out of it, drunk, drugged, stoned, spaced and sleepy, she felt totally uninhibited—justified in the laying on of hands. Now she was no longer responsible, no longer psychologically accountable, legally treacherous or socially suspicious. Drunk, she could not possibly be a threat to any man's individual freedoms or civil liberties. Now she was home free . . . oleoleolsome-freedom.

"Uhmmmmmmm," she said, and that meant: It's all off the record now, deep background only, no strings, ties, credits, debits . . . nothing. She pressed against Suede until he finally flattened out his body and then she rolled halfway on top of him, partially to anchor herself on the narrow couch, that was floating unmoored around the universe, and partially to press home her points.

Slowly Suede's mound began to stir, moving and spreading beneath the fabric of his trousers. Coco could feel the thickening, hardening process beneath her hand, but she couldn't capture or enclose the still-undefined shape. Heady, high and unhampered, she succumbed to her urge to liberate that living object uncomfortably bunched up inside the jockey shorts waiting to lurch free instead of remaining imprisoned in the crowded, congested, odoriferous crotch.

"Let's go into your room," Coco whispered against the side of Suede's face.

The children would never ever stumble into the guest room and Coco needed that security because now she was tripping through a valley of sensual desire. Messages emanating from her mind were being instantaneously translated into flesh. The very center of her consciousness was sinking down into the dark murky regions of her lower body, that inferno which was straining and salivating for penetration—yearning and aching to be opened, pried, parted, divided, entered and filled.

"Come on," Coco moaned again.

One of Suede's hands was moving in a small monotonous motion on her thigh and involuntarily her attention shifted toward that area. Would he move his hand? Were his fingers, ever so slowly, moving a little, a trifle, higher—more inward toward the opening of her emptiness? And now—if she were truly liberated—if she were really ready to practice the preachings of the Women's Liberation Local Columbia Road Consciousness Raising Group, she would be able to ask him please to please her.

But she couldn't. And it was becoming clear that eventually the local would have to set up an information bureau to hand down guidelines, or a public-relations department to issue policy statements to the press, because no individual citizen was ready to accept personal responsibility for making public-pubic statements on her own behalf. So Suede, being a cock-jock, just kept rubbing her thigh until she wondered if he could feel the flesh quiver beneath his hand.

"Okay," Suede said suddenly, "get up. Let's go."

Coco rose to her feet feeling sweet bloated sensations swimming through her pelvis and down into her thighs. Sexuality, like a full bladder, was gently pressuring and stirring all her inner organs, creating the same delicious sensation as a cultivated fingernail wedging its way between two teeth into a fleshy mound of gum, triggering pleasant nerve spasms for the practiced masochist.

"Wow," Coco said, shaking her hair back from her face.

She reached out toward Suede, but her hand didn't connect because he was farther in front of her than she had judged. All sense of time and space was out of kilter. Coco stumbled along, feeling the hallway carpet undulate beneath her. Her heart began to flutter when she reached the stairs leading up to her children so she ran through Suede's doorway and fell down upon the bed. Coco was going to have to learn how to refine her body language so that men wouldn't misconstrue her dishonorable intentions for honorable ones. Somehow she must reassure Suede that there were no conditions attached in tiny print to their physical contact.

But then Coco heard Suede begin to laugh and suddenly her body went on alert. Was there danger in that laughter? Was something wrong? She opened her eyes. Next to the bed, Suede was undressing, unbuttoning his shirt and unzipping his fly. Finally Coco could see the bald pink head of his X-L pushing its way out of the slit in his shorts—like the wigless head of Jessica's Barbie doll.

"Hey, suck this a little while, honey," he said.

Coco felt a sense of wariness and worry flood through her. Why did he want to do *that*? Was she going to lose her chance of feeling that X-L thumping, humping, pumping its hardness into her softness, defining her interior through the rude act of intrusion. Was she going to lose all that delicious clarification.

"Listen," she began, "why don't you . . . ?"

But then, because he was standing beside the bed right near her face, Suede just pushed his huge swollen organ into her mouth and Coco smelled the homey, buttery odor of an object kept under wraps all day, sticky and sweet—not the rancid, sourish smell that rose from behind, but the cozy, rumpled odor of sweat turning sweet from lack of ventilation, like the warm uriny odor of baby pajamas first thing in the morning, no longer wet and sour but transcendingly, subtly sweet.

Okay, okay, Coco thought, and let her tongue ripple along the vein beneath the shaft, that long inside-out seam that sewed up his penis like the thick rolled hemming on a football jersey. But when the vein began wiggling under her tongue, she felt worried because only Suede, pressed between her legs, could release the response waiting inside—like the art form lurking in an unsculptured rock needing a chisel to liberate it.

So Coco tongued the wet rubbery object out of her mouth and finally Suede groaned and lay down on the bed next to her.

Quickly Coco reached down, like a helpful Girl Scout, to direct the myopic, one-eyed creature in the proper direction (why should the darkness down there bother the blind?), and then lay back to finally feel the thick insertion between the soft, inchoate, inner walls of her being.

For hours they made love, punctuating their passion either with orgasms or sleep.

It was growing light outside when Coco got herself together and finally slipped out of bed. She gathered her clothes and then walked naked upstairs to her own bedroom. The sex had left her physically satisfied and psychologically fortified. She climbed into bed, nude beneath the sheets, and slept until the baby woke her up a little before seven o'clock.

CHAPTER 18

Coco was sitting next to Joshua's high chair, absorbed in feeding him his cereal. She was catching the slosh-over, that seeped and squished out of his mouth, on the edge of a spoon that she scraped over his puckered chin back up to his lips again.

Open, fill, wait. Squish, slosh, scoop and scrape. Then she would try slipping some of the sweet rejected mess back into his mouth. Clenching a wad of crumpled buttered raisin toast, Josh used his fist to push Coco's spoon away from his mouth. Then he would scratch off a layer of crumbs on his bottom teeth and trail a batter of toast and cereal across his face and over the high-chair tray.

Scrape the spoon to scoop the slosh. A fat fist filled with floppy toast moved near Coco's face and she flashed out her tongue to lick Josh's plump sticky fingers. Sometimes her babies made her mouth ache

so much from love that she had to grab and gnaw at
something like a yellow lead pencil so as not to
munch on some baby flesh.

"Want eggies, Joshie?" She wiped her hands on the
sides of her blue jeans and stood up.

"Good morning." Suede barreled through the
kitchen doorway dressed in fresh chinos, white shirt,
and a seersucker sport jacket.

Coco smiled, flushed and pirouetted toward the
Frigidaire.

"Do you know whether the shuttles leave on the
hour or half-hour from here?" he asked.

Hands trembling, Coco lost her grip on the
Frigidaire door. It swung out combatively and
cracked Happy on the side of his head. There was a
sharp yelp from the dog at the same time Josh's milk
glass hit the floor with a plop.

"On the hour," Coco said, bending over to look for
the eggs and hide for a moment. "Why?"

"Well, I want to get back to New York before
noon."

The hands of the electric daisy clock near the sink
swished away another minute and Coco heard a
crack as her heart started to break.

"Today?" Shut door, walk toward stove, don't faint.
Why wasn't there enough air in the kitchen this
morning? Why wasn't there enough oxygen? Suede
was using up all the oxygen needed by her family.

"Yah. This morning."

It was only 7:30.

"Oh. Would you like a glass of orange juice?"

"Sure. Is there any coffee?"

"It's perking. Is there something you have to do
back in New York?"

"Well, as long as I've finished up here, I want to get
back so I can start writing."

She looked up then because the pain, though localized, was very intense.

Suede walked past the high chair and paused to study Joshua for a moment.

"How about some eggs?" Coco asked, remembering Herzog's Ramona again.

Coco's chest had constricted so she could neither draw nor expel air without concentrating.

"Yah, I could use a couple of eggs. You-know-what gives me an appetite."

He was sitting at the table quietly awaiting the appearance of some food. He didn't even look up when Joshua began kicking his shoes against the tin legs of the high chair and pushing his stomach against the tray to show he wanted out.

Coco walked over to liberate her baby and place him on the floor. Immediately Happy left his station near the stove and trotted over to lick Josh's hands and face. The baby sat stoically, like a midget Buddha, watching Coco move around the kitchen while Happy lapped congealed cereal from various baby crevices.

"You know, Gavin's going to be gone four or five days," Coco said, too embarrassed to turn around.

She stood at the stove sliding a lump of butter from one side of the frying pan to the other, chasing it back and forth with flicks of her wrist while it squirmed, heated up and slowly liquefied.

Suede struck a match. "Yah, you told me yesterday."

Coco could smell sulfur infiltrate the oxygen which was already too sheer and thin for her needs. The more desolate she felt, the more her chest constricted. Her breath became more shallow every moment.

Coco cracked four eggs while she measured her

intake of air. She had once read an article about hy-
perventilation. Was it in some *Reader's Digest* at the
pediatrician's office? Or at the obstetrician's? Or was
it in a *Woman's Day* at the Safeway checkout
counter? The location didn't matter, except that she
couldn't recall the remedy. If you were short of
breath, you were supposed to . . . breathe into a
bag (was it a paper bag or a plastic one?) so that you
could recycle the pure oxygen (or was it nitrogen?)
that your system expelled. What about using a sandwich Baggie? What about a 10 gallon trashcan Baggie
so she could crawl inside and die?

—Just be calm—Coco's post-liberated raised consciousness said to her heart, her lungs and her lower
digestive system whose functional development had
already been stunted by stress.

The trouble is simply that right now you feel like
you're in love, when all you're really experiencing is
a desperate sense of neediness. Consequently, you're
fixating on the only man who's around because he
happens to be just a few feet away, with the bottom
half of his body hidden below the table and his X-L
tucked inside those tight chinos that—obliterating
what you're really interested in. So you are misread-
ing and misinterpreting symptoms that you think are
love but which, very clearly, are only sexual needs.
Needs. It's nothing to worry about, the post-lib voice
reassured her with post-grad authority. —It's a simple displacement of a physiological sensation. It's like
acupuncture that attacks a distant—but relevant—
region.

—But I do like that guy—Coco's pre-lib libido insisted. —He's very handsome and flashy and he does
some fancy things in the sack. —

—Forget it—said her post-lib super-duper ego.
He's just a classic seducer type, a lightweight. See

how his shirt pulls into horizontal creases across his
back? That's what's causing the minor contractions
you're feeling in your upper thighs, uterus and groin.
It's not him. It's just you—so cut it out.

Coco melted, scrambled, salted, set, poured, and
served. She moved around the kitchen, skirting the
baby, avoiding the dog and feeling exactly the same
as when she was locked inside a jet coming down for
a landing, upright and uptight in an unyielding seat
without a steering wheel, anxiously awaiting a decent touchdown procured at the expense of a reckless bargain with God that if He let the landing gear
descend it would be all right with Coco if the jet slid
off the runway. But then, of course, after the high of
coming down safely, flushed with the thrill of rebirth,
Coco always reneged on the runway accident.

So it was only fair that now, caught in a fever of
panic, the celestial control tower radioed her to remain in an eternal holding pattern over National,
fated to flirt forever with the tip of the Washington
Monument which always tried to prick the bellies of
passing passenger planes.Now she was last in line to
receive landing clearance and was left in a suspended state of horror at the cocktail hour of air
traffic—destined to remain forever on the lookout for
high-rises, weather, private planes, flocks of swallows
and confused pilots from other commercial airlines.
Perhaps Coco would never be able to land and would
never be able to catch her breath ever again. Perhaps she would have to keep an Eastern Airline barf
bag in her purse (like the two tired, crumpled Tam-
pax she carried) in case of emergency.

She served Suede his food and when he began
eating she sat down across the table from him and
pulled Joshua up on her lap. Instantly he reached out,
grabbed a paper napkin, and stuffed it in his mouth

so that Coco had to start extracting small wet paper
balls from between his clenched lips. Under the guise
of rescue work, she clung to her baby, inhaling the
warm smell of sweet dried urine, cereal, powder and
semisour milk.

—I'm hanging on, Joshie—she thought, retrieving
the last piece of napkin with the tip of her finger.
—I'm hanging on to you. —

Trying to anatomize her panic, Coco decided it
was the same kind of fear she would feel if she were
to open her closet door in the middle of the night and
see a man standing inside. Or if she saw a truck pitch-
ing down the middle of a black highway on the
wrong side of the meridian directly toward her car.
Or if she slipped on a patch of ice in the center of a
busy intersection. Or if she didn't see one of her
children in a crowded kiddy pool when she made a
head count. Coco was paralyzed at the apex of panic,
petrified at the peak of a scream when every nerve
freaked out—like an alley cat caught by the head-
lights of a speeding car—frozen and unable to run in
either direction.

—Beg him—her lungs cried from within the vise of
her chest. —Beg him to stay just one more day. Then
we'll relax and inflate so you can breathe again. —

—Help—panted her diaphragm—Give me air. —

"Why don't you spend the weekend?" Coco asked,
hiding her face against Josh's head.

Beneath the sheer black curls, she could see small
brown splotches of cradlecap on his scalp. When was
the last time she had rubbed cotton balls soaked in
warm olive oil onto his sweet, still-soft scalp? Only
newborn infants were supposed to have cradlecap,
not year-old toddlers. Oh, yes, Coco was a negligent
mother. A terrible mother. Dr. Spock should only
know.

"I've got to start writing this article, babes."

"Can't you work upstairs?" Coco asked pitifully, humbled and humiliated by the enormity of her need and the gargantuan terrors that were piling through her system, hyping her up to a crazed pitch.

Never before had she felt so dependent, so imperiled, so endangered. Never before had she been forced to beg for help from an unrelenting man who had control over her survival. Perhaps she had been lucky before not having to plead like this with someone over whom she had neither claim nor clout. For at this moment, it seemed that Suede Bellock was the only human being in the world who could alleviate—not obliterate—just *lessen* her panic a little. Coco felt stung by her own powerlessness. All she was asking for was the comfort of Suede's physical presence—like one of those technical advisors Kennedy had sent to Vietnam to assist the Saigon military simply by being there.

"Baby," Suede said with a little conciliatory smile, "I can barely work in my own pad, let alone anyplace else."

Work, Coco thought. Work. The Great Escape and ultimate apology for crumping out. It was like sending a note to God. "Please excuse Suede's absence from Life today. He had to work so he couldn't attend any scheduled events. He will try to make up whatever he missed. Sincerely, His Mother."

"But you *have* been working," she insisted, holding onto Joshua who was banging a spoon against the table. All at once Coco saw herself and her baby through Suede's eyes—a disorderly, noisy, messy madonna and child caught in a sticky, icky situation.

And then, suddenly, unexpectedly, Coco gave it up.

Oh, go, she thought, just go. Like an addict unable

to score, she was momentarily high on her own deprivation. Go. Though I'd give up almost anything to keep you here, I really don't like you one little bit.

Suede finished his eggs and pushed the dish away.

To where did men think the dishes they pushed into the center of the table disappeared? Did they believe in secret hatchways? Tunnels to the center of the earth?

And it was at that very same moment Coco suddenly realized that Suede was going to leave without mentioning anything about the future. He was not going to say anything about their next encounter, about coming back to Washington to see her or about Coco coming to New York to visit him. While the wild impulsive pre-lib coach in Coco's brain frantically urged her to correct his oversight, to remind him of the proprieties of sin, her post-lib prompter cautioned her to be silent, to be discreet for the sake of the new vulnerable Coco, a creature who had to be cautious and careful.

Now there was a new Coco Burman, who, at some future time of greater need, might want the illusion of a reunion with Suede. A direct confrontation at the present time must be sacrificed for the sake of some long-range planning. Salvation—a day or night in Suede's bed in Manhattan—must not be jeopardized or precluded by a struggle for justice now.

Observe. Conserve. Preserve. Talk softly to the big stick. Use caution and make passes with care. All of Coco's careless, reckless lawless days were over. The casual consumer had become a hoarder. The seller had become a buyer.

Suede pushed his chair away from the table.

There are other men around, Coco thought, breathless with misery. There had always been so many, others who wanted her long ago or even now after so many years. Let Suede go. Let him disappear. She could call someone else. She wouldn't be alone.

"Well," he began, looking a trifle awkward since he wasn't a total fool. "Thanks for everything. I hope you get things straightened out the way you want."

What did that mean? Had he guessed? Probably. People could smell hysteria miles away.

Now the dangers of accidentally exposing herself as the victim of a desertion ripped through her, slowing her already labored breath. Isn't this what you wanted, Coco, baby? pre-libby queried. Didn't you choose this path of pain, this superhighway of fear Ms. Masochist?

Gavin, Coco called silently. Gavin, she screamed, without making a sound.

Then Michael walked into the kitchen.

"Good morning," he said, folding himself into a chair and smiling at Suede with his naturally nice manners.

The man remained oblivious to the boy's charm.

Coco smiled. Michael. Oh, Mikey.

"What's for breakfast?" Mike asked.

"Want some eggs, honey?"

"Are there any pancakes?"

Coco's son wanted pancakes. Her seven-year-old son, her oldest child, wanted pancakes. Coco hated making pancakes, hated pushing all the messy ingredients into the narrow neck of an empty bottle—as prescribed in the Shaking Method—because later, after negligently letting the residue harden for hours, cleaning the bottle was impossible.

Oh, but do it. Do it for Mikey. He doesn't even know what has happened. He has no inkling that his father is gone and that his life has been spoiled. He doesn't know what lies ahead. All he wants are a few pancakes swimming in a lake of sweet syrup.

My children don't have a father, Coco thought. My children don't have a father anymore. Still, she shouldn't tell them that because any minute now the phone would ring and she'd have to rush around to find a baby-sitter so she could meet Gavin some-where—at Schwartz's drugstore for breakfast?—to engage in a stormy reconciliation leading to a truer, more lasting relationship.

—Go on—she commanded her body. Don't sit still. Don't look pathetic. Don't look weak. Get up. Make pancakes.

"Okay," Coco said. "I'll make some. But first go help get the kids dressed so they'll be ready to eat. And here, honey, take Josh upstairs with you so he won't be under my feet."

Mike stood up, respectful, honest, sincere and growing handsome. He reached out high above the table to grasp Joshua, flexing his arms to lift the baby from such an awkward angle (he ain't heavy, he's my brother) and something in Coco—was it her soul?—died for a moment and then was resurrected, no sanctified, so that she could stand up, finished now with needing, diverted by the prospect of providing, and smiling because she had two wonderful young sons whose arms were wrapped about each other.

Only Suede, foreigner to feeling, noticed nothing, felt nothing, erased both fact and fantasy with his earth-moving insensitivity.

"Well," Suede said again. Although eager to move out and avoid any further confrontations, he was briefly uncertain how to proceed. "Those were good eggs."

Walking across the room, Coco stretched up to-ward the cupboard above the stove where she kept

the box of pancake mix, and then bent down to find
an empty orange-juice bottle beneath the sink, twice
exposing the width of her hips and buttocks in the
tight Levi's which revealed, rather than girdled, her
backside.

Forget it, she said to herself. Forget him. Crack
eggs, pour milk, stir batter. The fry pan's still dirty
from the eggs. Wash it. Okay. Think of all the things
to do later. Think of all the things to clean, scrape,
scour, shine, tighten, repair, refinish, rescrew, fix,
sew, glue, paint. Coco felt a growing desire for order.
Later . . . later she could steel-wool all the pots and
pans, polish the once shiney copper-bottomed wed-
ding-gift Revere Ware. Later she could separate the
tea and soup spoons, hang up the spatula so that it
wouldn't jam the utensil drawer and even replace
the long nail on which to hang potholders that had
fallen out of the wall.

"Well, I guess I should take off," Suede said with a
fake tone of reluctance.

Walking up behind Coco, he put both hands on her
shoulders.

Coco wanted to whirl about and slap his face.

"Have a good flight," she mumbled, hoping the
shuttle would crash.

I shall not cry in front of a stranger, she thought
biblically. But then, what right had she to cry in front
of a friend? Which was right? Or had a woman—
wronged—no right to cry?

"How about a little good-bye kiss?"

Gross. Vulgar. Don't think about what went on last
night, what she had done. Coco turned, lowered her
eyes as his face flashed toward her, and felt his mouth
on her forehead.

"You can let yourself out, can't you?" she asked,
turning back to the stove.

"Sure. And listen. Thanks for everything."

Then he was gone.

Coco waited a few minutes before lifting the frying pan off the burner. The butter had burned brown. She could hear a clamor upstairs in the bedrooms. Her heart was thudding, slowing down and then speeding up. Her hands were shaking. She turned off the burner, walked into the hall, opened the front door, and looked out to watch Suede weaving down the street, swaying beneath the weight of his duffel bag but still swaggering with freedom. And that was when she saw a post-office card hooked over the doorknob—instant announcement that a special-delivery mailman had made an unsuccessful attempt to deliver a package.

"Oh, no, that's too much," Coco said outloud. Not an unsuccessful attempt to deliver mail now—not now, not when she'd been home all night and awake before seven. Hadn't the mailman rung? Was the doorbell out of order? Didn't he knock? But then, why hadn't Happy barked? What was it that the mailman was trying to bring her? The card, punched-out like a doughnut to hook over a doorknob, specified that her item could be picked up at the Irving Street Post Office. But wasn't this the first day of a holiday weekend? Could the post office possibly be open on Saturday or Sunday or Monday of the Fourth of July weekend? Had Gavin sent her something? A gift? A bomb?

"Shit," Coco cursed, close to tears. "This is really too much."

And then she heard the children starting to come down the stairs, helping and hindering each other en route, hurrying to claim Coco as their Cracker Jack prize for the weekend. Coco came indoors, hustled

them into the den and turned on the TV to a roaring
rerun of *I Love Lucy*.

"I'm going to make the pancakes now," she announced, but she paused for a moment to watch Lucille Ball bat her enormous 20-inch TV eyelashes at
the Burman children. Wondering how Lucy's new
marriage was working out, Coco walked back to the
kitchen, made pancakes, called the children, fed and
banished them, cleared the table, stacked the dishes
and then sat down to decide, in a reasonable manner,
to make peace with her kitchen.

It was quite clear that without a maid or a husband
Coco could hardly exile herself to the second floor.
She would obviously have to reconcile herself to cen-
trality, domesticity, accessibility, distractions, noise
and the constant temptation of food. There could be
no avoiding it. Coco would be constantly confronted
with jumbled drawers and chaotic cupboards, non-
graduated pots and pans, patches of spotted
or cruddy linoleum, crusted utensils, disorganized
pegboards, splattered clock faces, greasy bulbs,
finger-spotted walls, crumb-stuffed seams in the
tabletop, dirty drip marks on the chairs and food-
splattered radiators. Coco could smell the foul water
collected under the crisper in her refrigerator. The
kitchen contained a thousand indictments.

But she sat stoically on the chair next to the wall
telephone near the little wicker basket, holding a
notepad for messages, several unmailed warranty
postcards and a list of emergency numbers. The
Washington Post (still totally intact and untouched
by human hands) was at the far end of the table.
Behind her, a row of greasy-finger-printed cook-
books marched across the top of the kitchen radiator
within easy reach to look up some no-man-in-the-

house tunafish-casserole or salad-stuffed-tomato reci-
pes. But suddenly the shadow of Ann Carradine
floated through the kitchen, stinging Coco with
guilty fear.

Was this what Ann had felt like thirteen years ago
—in May of 1959—when Gavin had packed his suitcase and left their Lake Shore Drive apartment to
move in with Coco on inferior Woodlawn? Was this
how Ann had felt and, if so, was this Coco's punishment—neatly worked out by the galactic chairwoman of the Intercontinental Women's Liberation
Movement? Or was this the revenge of the Bursar at
the University of Chicago to whom Coco still owed
$329 in library fines? Was it, perhaps, the punish-
ment arranged by Mr. and Mrs. Morrie Silverman of
Chicago. Or Mr. and Mrs. Courtney Carradine of
California? Was this the retribution for what Coco
had done to Ann? Had Coco made Ann's heart hammer and her lungs heave? Did Ann's body sweat and
her ears ring and her stomach rebel?

Probably not. Because while some people are
losers, Ann had not only survived, she had flourished;
she had triumphed. She had never rung up Coco's
apartment in the middle of the night or appeared at
the door to demand a confrontation or asked for any
alimony or threatened Gavin or tried to seduce him
back or carried on in any publicly inappropriate
manner. But maybe Ann had always known she
could make it alone—so cool and California was she,
so tough and self-sufficient. Still, perhaps just that
first night alone—forced to remain in Chicago for
several more weeks until graduation—perhaps then
Ann had felt the same kind of panic Coco was feeling
now. Perhaps that first night Ann hadn't known she
would become a journalist, a well-known New York

radical-chic type who would run with the Beautiful People and always be smiling out at the world from some Editor's Notes.

—Don't think about Ann—Coco's pre-lib Chicago counselor advised.

CHAPTER 19

*C*oco drew a laborious breath and looked around
the copper-tone coordinated kitchen with the sad
dingy white ruffled curtains and thought—Well, here
I am. —She should never have become such a snob
about kitchens. If she were really a great writer, the
fact she had to sit at a cup-scarred table with crumbs
in its seams should not adversely affect her output or
her talent. Perhaps there was even a new variety of
discipline to be achieved in such surroundings. With
a surge of optimism she retrieved her shoulderbag
purse and reached into the pocket—which functioned as her office—and extracted her little notebook with a new Paper Mate cartridge pen clipped to
its cover. But suddenly Coco felt acutely cramped;
the three-by-five-inch sheets looked too small, too
confining and restrictive.

Coco's life was different now. She must prepare

herself for a period of expansion. Remembering a sketchpad that was down in the cellar, she impulsively sprang up from the chair and ran downstairs to the basement, clapping her hands on the stairs to warn rodents of her approach so they could hide. —It's here somewhere—she thought, moving slowly through the piles of boxes, crippled suitcases filled with outgrown clothing, torn screens, retired training pots, broken appliances, sleds, skates, skis and shovels until she saw the sketchpad that she had used when she took still-life classes at the YWCA. Perfect. Coco squinched her eyes tight so as to miss the exodus of insects that would be dislodged, swatted the drawing pad against the wall several times to knock off dust, roaches, plaster dust or centipedes, and then carried it back to the kitchen.

Spread open, the pad covered the entire tabletop. This was psychologically reassuring but impractical, since Coco couldn't reach the far page and also because the edges molested the children's vitamin bottles. So she folded it back in half and still felt pleased by its extraordinary expanse of space. Now she could make different lists simultaneously on one page— lists of new clothes she would need, people she should invite for dinner, organizations to support, ideas for articles to write, new telephone numbers for new people who would enter her life, and all the social engagements that would ensure from her new (what?) Condition. On a single page Coco could list everything that needed doing, plus have plenty of extra space to doodle, set down a coffee cup and keep an ashtray—right there next to what she wrote.

Since she was experiencing some dull cramps in her stomach, Coco poured a little cream into her coffee and then attacked the sketchbook.

CALL U; MAKE APPOINTMENT WITH DR. FOLLY TO
   REINSTATE ME FOR FALL. ASK FOR *extra* FRESH-
   MAN COMP.
FINISH PH.D. DISSERTATION IMMEDIATELY
CALL EDITORS OF ALL CITY MAGS
CALL WOMEN'S LIB. OFFICE
CALL DEMOCRATIC CENTRAL COMMITTEE. GET AC-
   TIVE. RUN FOR D.C. NATIONAL COMMITTEEWOMAN
   IN 1976.
FIND MIKE'S BASEBALL MITT
TRANQUILIZERS???
SCORE SOME DOPE
MAKE APPT. WITH DERMATOLOGIST
CALL LISA MEYER AT THE FREE FARM. LIVE AT FARM
   WITH CHILDREN?
CALL PARK SERVICE RE: 4TH OF JULY FIREWORKS
CALL GAVIN'S OFFICE
CALL SYLVIA; HANG UP
FIND OUT WHERE GAVIN IS LIVING
CALL SUEDE TO SEE IF HE GOT HOME SAFELY
ORDER GIN FROM WOODLEY'S.

Coco lit a cigarette and wrote: QUIT SMOKING
Now that she was a Parent without a Partner she
would have to be doubly careful about not getting
lung cancer, since she had become totally responsible for not turning her children into orphans, social
misfits, stutterers, drug addicts, psychopaths, under-
or overachievers, criminals, perverts, kleptomaniacs
or slow readers. She simply couldn't afford a premature death if she had to avert each of these disasters
four times over.
DRUGSTORE—GET SENECOT ANTI-CONSTIPATION
PILLS TODAY!!!
She finished her coffee, toyed with the unfamiliar

residue of cream on her tongue, recapped her pen and sat motionless.

"I am scared shitless," she said to the clock, which was apparently suffering from a stroke that had left it paralyzed at 9:21.

—Gavin isn't going to call me. Nobody's going to call me. I'm so terrified I can't breathe. —

—That's only anxiety—the post-lib cheerleader explained in an educational tone of voice. —That's all it is—an attack of anxiety. —

But where had it come from, so full-blown and with such devastating psychosomatic accompaniments?

OF WHAT AM I AFRAID? Coco printed in fat squat letters, filling the hoops of the O and the D.

I AM AFRAID OF . . . She paused, groped, and wrote a colon: FAILURE. That was good. Strong. But what kind of failure? She wrote (1) ENGINE FAILURE (2) HEART FAILURE (3) SOCIAL FAILURE. All morning long Coco had unconsciously been listening for the sound of a jet airliner, waiting for landing clearance at National, losing one of its engines right over the Burmans' house and diving straight down into her roof. She and the children plus a hundred and seven strangers would die instantly. The *Washington Post* would innocently assume that Mr. Gavin Burman, husband of the dead housewife and father of the four dead tots, was also lost in the holocaust. Then Gavin could take off with Sylvia for Samoa and live happily ever after.

Jessica came into the kitchen. "I don't want to watch television anymore."

"You have to, Jessica," Coco said firmly. "It's compulsory until twelve."

"But I'm tired of television."

"Well, go play in the backyard."

"I don't want to."

Coco felt her will wilting as she realized Jessica's stubborn streak was in ascendance.

"Can I invite Sarah over to play?"

"We'll see."

Jessica looked at Coco with pure hatred and then turned around, wiggled her butt in an obscene gesture at her mother, and disappeared.

—I shouldn't let her get away with that—Coco thought, lighting another cigarette. —But she's too strong for me, too together for me to handle. And now Gavin isn't here anymore to back me up against her. Now it's just going to be me and Jessica battling it out for the next twelve years until she splits and goes off to raise horses and organic tomatoes in Vermont without so much as a good-bye or a thank-you or a P.O. box number.

And even worse, how could Coco manage to raise the boys all alone, especially now when there were rumors that the country was planning to change over to the metric system within ten years. How would she cope with the kids when the anxiety lodged in her diaphragm impeded her breath? (Was that really the right word? Did they really use the same word for the breathing organ as they did for female contraceptives?) And if she could never catch her breath again how could she possibly play shortstop in the spring or save several of her children from drowning in different depths of an Olympic pool simultaneously or, even worse, bend over upside-down to center a pass so that the world came spinning up at her from between the triangle of her legs, making the football go crooked and making Mike mad?

And how could she ever assemble tricycles from Sears, which arrived in sixty-three pieces, for Nicky or Joshua in Christmases to come or move the spare

tire in the trunk of the car to make room for five
suitcases or turn over her king-size mattress when
one side got bumpy or smelly from baby pee? And
how would she ever fix the bathroom door when the
knob fell off? Would she have to Band-Aid all the
suspicious locks into their sockets again? And what if
she were inside the bathroom when the handle fell
off and Josh was loose in the house hunting for some
Mr. Clean to drink and die from? How could she
manage all alone now that she was developing emphysema, now that her veins were constricting
throughout her body, slowing down her circulation
while making her blood pressure rise. There was
probably a birth-control-pills-plus-bad-circulation
clot forming right now and casually traveling around
looking for a direct route to her broken heart or
addled brain.

"Mom, can I invite Sarah over now?"

Jessica had suddenly reappeared in the doorway,
her thin little chest pumping from the short run to
the kitchen and her shy lyrical face contracted with
the urge to make a non-negotiable demand.

"Later," Coco said. "Just watch television for a little longer. I have to make some telephone calls."

"But when?"

"Later. After lunch."

Jessica's blue eyes, dark beneath the shadow cast
by her extravagant lashes, evaluated Coco's sincerity
and waited to see what her mother was really going
to do.

Impulsively, to prove her virtue, Coco lifted the
receiver and dialed the mentally indelible number
of the D.C. government. Then, even though Jessica
departed, reassured, Coco decided to use the
unexpected Saturday-morning connection with the

Public Health Department to launch her semi-
monthly complaint.

"Rat Control."

"Yes, sir. I want to request that our alley be baited."

"Have you seen any rats in your backyard, lady?"
the man asked.

"Yes. Oh, yes," Coco said enthusiastically.

"Well, we don't take care of rats on private property," the man said with finality. "You'll have to find a
private exterminator."

Coco envisioned the man getting ready to slam
down his receiver. "But they came in from the alley,"
she protested.

"Yah. I know, lady. But we don't take care of rats
on private property."

"But they're back in the alley now. They just went
back out to the alley."

"Well, then, that's different. Okay. What's your address? We'll bait the alley, if they're really in the
alley, but not if they're in your backyard."

Coco provided her address while she uncapped
her pen and wrote CALL NADER'S OFFICE. She no
longer had any doubt that the D.C. city government
had actively contributed to her psychological deterioration. If city officials were crazy, what did they
think would happen to concerned citizens? And
women were most vulnerable. Government workers
never feared ladies who didn't have rich, powerful,
Republican husbands in reserve. Coco lit another cigarette.

Now that she was single again she could no longer
make veiled threats of male intervention if the
Health Department harassed her. She could no
longer pretend she had a joint checking account
when Garfinckle's stopped her from charging because her balance was too high. Now she no longer

had any backup for emergencies, no one to interpret federal economic policy or explain what was bad about property taxes that sounded graduated, no one who might hear the alarm clock on Monday morning if she didn't, no one to chase a mouse or kill a giant water bug or provide an extra key when she locked hers inside the car, now there was no man to leave a residue of change in pants and jacket pockets for the newspaper boy so he didn't have to make two trips. Now Coco had no man to deal with insurance claims, tuition loans, plane reservations, indignant creditors, obscene callers, nasty neighbors or incompetent repairmen. Now there was no channel-changing, prescription-fetching, garbage-disposing, fuse-changing, vomit-cleaning, noctural-infant-high-fever colleague, skipped-a-monthly-period conspirator, tight-space car-parker, no Office or Business Telephone Number to Call in Case of Emergency When Mother Cannot Be Located.

Tears filled Coco's eyes.

Nicky came into the kitchen and climbed up on a chair. "I want to go to der park, Mama. Take me to der park."

"A little later on," Coco murmured.

Nicky was almost three. He shouldn't be lisping. It was obviously psychological. And Coco had never even mentioned it to Dr. Finkelstein. During none of those thousands of dollars of hours had Coco ever informed her psychiatrist that her middle son lisped. All Coco cared about was herself. Thus becoming the unwed mother of four defenseless, neglected children was poetic justice. Now she would have to learn how to pay attention to them and their needs. Guilt struck.

"Okay, Nicky. We'll go to the park. I'll even make us a picnic lunch to take along," she offered recklessly. It was almost eleven o'clock. "At twelve we'll take a picnic and go to the park."

"Yah, yah, yah, yah." Nicky jumped up from the chair, victorious and important. "We're douging to have a picanic with-th Mama in der park," he yelped, running through the dining room toward the den.

Immediately Jessica flashed through the doorway again. "You told me Sarah could come over. That's what you told me. You promised."

Coco felt weak. "All right. I'll call her mother and see if she can come on the picnic with us."

"Right now," Jessica demanded, stationing herself permanently at Coco's side. "Call her right this minute."

"Okay. I'll dial the number and you ask Sarah to ask her mother," Coco compromised, wilting at the thought of Mrs. Baumgartner's voice. Clara Baumgartner—Diligent Mother, Dedicated Wife, Super Square—dismissible unless someone felt totally insecure and vulnerable. Coco looked up Sarah's number in her second-class telephone directory.

Soon all the neighbors would know that Gavin was gone. All the neat nuclear families would be enriched by the Burmans' breakup—reconfirmed, fortified and strengthened by the Burmans' failure. Instantly the Burman children would be treated differently—like deprived and underprivileged inner-city kids at summer camps on scholarships.

Now Mike and Jessica and Nicky and Josh would join the ranks of weekend refugees traveling like gypsies in accord with some court visitation order so that they wouldn't be at home—was it on Wednesday nights and Sundays?—if their friends called up. Was that the end result of all this? Did all the years of togetherness end in dispersal and division, lessening and weakening, reduction and loss, shoving and schlepping? Would there soon be several half-brothers and sisters—Gavin's second family, not Coco's—so no one would know who belonged with whom? And unlike the Auchinclosses, the Burman children would look like the Jukes and the Kallikaks of Upper Appalachia—a postnuclear-family mess.

"Sarah's mother says okay," Jessica reports jubilantly into Coco's ear.

—Well, what did you expect?—Coco thought bitterly observing Jessica's surprise. —Was there ever a moment's doubt? Why should Mrs. Baumgartner say no? Why shouldn't she take a cool nap, a guiltless little sleep, while Coco assumed responsibility for Sarah's life and limb, a fifth responsibility that she needed like a hole in the head?—

So Jessica ran off to announce her separate victory and Coco was suddenly seized by a spill of fantasies which flushed through her head like Drano bringing up foul bubbles in the kitchen sink.

—You've got to get an apartment, an L-shaped apartment—a strange voice said. —You've got to live in a high-rise building with a doorman, a sauna, a swimming pool equipped with four life guards and an army of teen-age baby-sitters on the premises. —

—But we'd need four bedrooms—Coco countered.

—And I would like a study. —

—Well, then, move out to a commune in West Virginia. Find a place that has attractive divorced or widowed middle-aged professionals whose children are old enough to baby-sit while you work in the fields all day planting lovely green beans and fresh dill in your marvelous make-believe army fatigue suit from Saks Fifth Avenue.—

—But they'll probably want me to do all the cooking—Coco argued. —I might end up cooking and cleaning for eight or nine men with twenty ravenous teen-aged kids. Even with nonexclusive sex and nice nature walks, I'm not sure I want to cook that often.—

Coco began to think about a box of chocolate-covered doughnuts in the breadbox. Its plastic window was temptingly soiled by frosting that had melted a little bit from the heat.

—Dear Lord, please don't let me start eating now, Coco prayed. She knew she would never be able to stop after just *one* chocolate-covered doughnut. There would be two. Or two and a half. And an equal number of glasses of milk to make it come out even.

—Please, God, I don't want to whine or nag, but I simply cannot afford to gain weight right now.—

She got up and poured another cup of coffee. If she began eating now, she would never stop until her stomach protruded farther than her boobs. And constipated as she was, three doughnuts could remain intact inside her body for five or six days.

See? That's what was wrong with sitting in the kitchen, she thought angrily.

Coco got up, took a doughnut out of the breadbox, put it back, got it out again and devoured the whole thing in three bites.

—This is the end—she thought wildly, walking away from the counter toward the table and then back again toward the breadbox.—The living end. The dead end. I will now begin eating myself to death. And it's starting with sweets. I don't even like sweets.— Coco sat down and then got up again, went to the cupboard, pulled out the giant-size box of Captain Crunch, tilted it toward her face and swallowed three sticky mouthfuls directly out of the box.

—Somebody stop me—she pleaded, remembering the Chicago killer who wrote a similar message with lipstick on bathroom mirrors after murdering young women. Somebody help me. Somebody help me stop. I will weigh 130 within minutes and then my life will be finished, over, done for.

Coco opened the Frigidaire door and then closed it. Strong waves of food guilt were drumming through her as she experienced incredibly strong hunger pangs.

It was too late. If only she could go back five minutes in time. If only she could vomit. She could never redeem the day after eating a doughnut and Captain Crunch. She opened the back door and hurried onto the porch. Fat. She would be fat. She was already fat. It was too late. Now there would be no men, no love, no security, no marital status, no quality of life. Just fat. Her and her fat. She stuck two fingers deep into her throat and leaned over the porch railing. Several houses away, the hippies who lived in the YES commune were watching her from their back veranda. So what? Let them think she was tripping on acid. She had to vomit up all those carbohydrates. They were the very worst kind of calories. But she couldn't. She was so totally distraught now that she couldn't even make herself vomit.

Coco went back into the kitchen.

Gavin was trying to destroy her. Coco walked over to the silverware drawer, opened it, took the wedding band off her hand and threw it into the jumble of utensils, most of which were supposed to stand erectly magnetized on the knife holder. The ring settled down next to a potato peeler that had a piece of red apple skin stuck in it.

—Everything's dirty—Coco thought, staring into the drawer. Funky, Filthy, Nasty. Dirty. And it was all Gavin's fault. His departure, like his presence, caused a waste of precious time. Just like today . . . it was always the same. For a breath-rewarding moment Coco hated Gavin with a liberating rush of loathing. Yes. Yes, she was glad, happy he hadn't phoned. She was delighted and thrilled that he had moved out of the house so that now she could get herself together, at last. She would finally organize all the loose ends of her life.

Now she could get things tidied up. Now she could move all her winter clothes into Gavin's hall closet. Mentally she called dibs on his big bureau and silently repossessed the three small chest drawers that she had lent him on indefinite loan five years ago but which would be perfect for her pantyhose (all of which had snags) and her knee-highs. Now she could rearrange all her sweaters and put Gavin's ultra-intensity reading lamp on her side of the bed. (But how could there be a His or Hers side of the bed if there was only one occupant? How could there be sides in a demilitarized zone? Which was Coco's side of the bed if she slept alone?) Now she could throw out all the old pill bottles with Gavin's name on the prescription label and gain at least two more shelves in the medicine cabinet. Great. And then she could get rid of all his books, thereby liberating space for her Histories of Literary Criticism so they wouldn't have to hide in double layers behind her various Literary theories, surveys and anthologies.

And this very day she would move all his classical records to the left side of the shelf in the livingroom so she could push all the hard-rock albums closer to the stereo and not bump her knee on the fireplace poker when she tried to reach her records. For a moment she considered filling out a change-of-address card at the post office, when she went to claim her unsuccessful-attempt-to-deliver-the-mail package, redirecting Gavin's mail to his office and thereby eternally uncluttering the front-hall chest. But then she reconsidered and decided it was much more politic to inspect all the return addresses on Gavin's letters or even hold his mail as bait to get him home.

Oh, yes, Coco thought, smiling now as she lit another cigarette and poured a fresh cup of coffee. Now she would actually save a lot of time. Now there would be plenty of time to write at night. Now she could speed up the novel and still be free to do some free-lance articles as well as complete the research for her Ph.D. dissertation on *A Causal Explanation for the Paucity of Female Prose Writers in Eighteenth Century England* since there wouldn't be any more of those terribly long, awkward holiday phone calls from Gavin's relatives in Los Angeles or any more shopping expeditions for Bar-Mitzvah gifts for all his nephews; in Gavin's family Bar Mitzvahs were really fund raisers. And now there would be no more stopping at the laundry to pick up his shirts or drop off spaghetti-spotted ties. Now there would be no more delays at the supermarket in the fancy delicatessen section which she had been previously forced to review and audit every week for the past twelve years. Now she could just bypass all of Gavin's favorite salamis and smokefish and jars of gefilte fish and gehactah leber. Now she could march right past all those kosher horrors in the same way she bypassed the cat-food and kitty-litter section (which was at least five yards long) and (since Joshua's graduation from strained infant food) the Gerber section, which eliminated almost twenty yards of decision-making shelves, thus speeding her up and over to the soups and sandwich spreads with a fresh burst of energy.

Indeed, now everything would be simplified.

Of course, there was always the danger that Coco might now find herself putting out in totally new and different ways—like waiting for Suede to come home or anguishing over that platter of sandwich spreads or feeling too groggy in the morning from gin, grass and sex to be able to work effectively. And, of course, now she'd have to remember to go to the hardware to make an extra set of house and car keys to leave with Maryanne, her nextdoor neighbor. Now she'd have to buy some new underwear and more deodorants and have her teeth cleaned and attend more cultural events and political rallies and . . .

Oh, God. Why was Coco's best friend in South America? Her shrink in Europe? Her lover on the shuttle and her husband in hiding?

Feeling consummately confused, Coco was experiencing her panic both psychologically and physically. Impulsively she picked up the telephone and dialed Maryanne's number. Good. Nice, dependable Maryanne was always home and always answered after just one ring.

"Hi," Coco said, but her voice sounded so weak that she cleared her throat and started over again. "Hi," she said, trying to inject a lilt of brave independence. "Guess what?"

Suddenly her position came into focus. The official line would be that Coco Burman had kicked Gavin Burman out of the house because he was a dirty male chauvinist pig who did not respect her as a woman, a mother, a wife, a novelist, a graduate student—indeed, a candidate for the doctoral degree—or as a potential leader of the new women's-liberation movement in which, some day, she hoped to achieve active national leadership alongside Gloria Steinem, Bella Abzug, Shirley Chisholm and Betty Friedan.

"We've split," Coco announced lightly, laughingly.

"Who is this?" Maryanne asked.

Irritated, Coco identified herself. "Listen, Gavin's moved out—lock, stock and barrel."

"Where'd he go?" Maryanne asked.

"How should I know? I don't care. I'm free. I'm finally free."

Coco wrote down FREE three times in an indented vertical line on her sketchpad.

"Well, how do you feel?" Maryanne asked cautiously.

"Swell. Fantastic."

Gradually it was becoming clear to Coco that she would have to develop a varied first strike capability and alter her story depending on her audience. To the Columbia Road Women's Liberation Local she would present her current marital status as a premeditated response to sexual inequities within her marriage. But for Maryanne, a semilapsed member of the local but a mainstay of the Columbia Road Consciousness Raising (C.R.C.R.) Group, there was less need for political analysis and more emphasis on personal problems.

"Actually, it feels a *little* bit funny," Coco amended. "It's been a long time since I've been alone. Freedom feels a little scary at first, you know."

"Sure," Maryanne agreed supportively.

"But I just had to do it. After twelve years, I knew I was either going to flip out from living with him or just go it alone."

Silence.

Coco cautioned herself against overplaying her hand. Her credibility—like her virginity years ago—was now her most priceless possession. In the eyes of the public, she had to establish and maintain herself as a credible source of information or else eternally suffer the fate of all victims—whose basic stories were created by others—scorn. She had obviously made a tactical mistake phoning Maryanne before she had her official line formulated.

"Well, if you feel like doing something with the kids over the weekend, give me a call," Coco said. "Maybe we could go watch the fireworks on the Mall together or something."

"Sure," Maryanne said kindly, "or just stop by over here. Anytime."

"Bye-bye."

Now Coco was completely hysterical. She was becoming convinced that anxiety could shrink her blood vessels just as fear of impotence could deflate a penis. Her scanty knowledge of biology might now prove fatal. Wasn't the blood supposed to carry oxygen through the body via veins and out through the capillaries? Why had she believed all the sexist propaganda about girls having no affinity for science? Why didn't she know how her own body worked? This was ridiculous.

Folding her arms on the table, Coco laid her face down into the dark cavelike enclosure created by her elbows. Of course her constipation was not helping her respiratory system one little bit. That much she knew. Her future was short but clear. She would begin eating compulsively and simultaneously stop passing any waste whatsoever so all that food, all those carbohydrates, all those chocolate-covered doughnuts would stay in her stomach for weeks consolidating, compounding, solidifying and even multiplying like amoebae.

She would get rolls of fat on her back and shoulders just like her mother and three aunts in Chicago. Oh, God, she would have those moving, vibrating, shaking appendages of fat that followed the indentations of elastic bra straps and which jiggled during Mah-Jongg games. Now Coco wouldn't be able to wiggle into her sheaths. Her zippers wouldn't zip. Rolls of fat around her midriff would fold over and wrinkle when she sat down. All of her belts would be permanently pleated—by the pressure of bulging hips. Her thighs would wiggle when she played tennis. Her buttocks would shake when she walked. Soon she would not even be able to attend PTA meetings in fear of embarrassing the children. She would get hemorrhoids again—like when she had Nicky.

Coco began crying quietly, so the children wouldn't hear, and dabbing the tears so she would leave no incriminating streaks on her face. Oh, no, she didn't want to die from bloodclots, emphysema, hemorrhoids or heartbreak when the children were home alone with her. They wouldn't know what to do. Jessica would get hysterical, pee all over the floor, continue wetting her pants for the rest of her life. Nicky would run outside to find a policeman, dart across the street from between two parked cars, and be buried beside his mother. Josh would simply starve to death—no milkee, no bottee, no eggies, no yum-yum. Coco put out her cigarette. She still was unable to capture a full deep breath, but the shortness didn't seem as acute as it had a little earlier.

Now the tape already inserted in the deck of her mind was playing fast forward, rushing ahead to some future encounter with Gavin when she would be able to read her indictment against him. Almost unconsciously, she kept planning speeches in her mind to deliver to him at the first opportunity. Most of the speeches concerned the fact that he wasn't going to have a telephone in his new apartment. Her frustration and rage on this issue supplied fuel for several elaborate dialogues.

"What happens if one of the kids gets sick, Gavin? What if someone has to go to the hospital? What if I die?"

"You can call me at the office in the morning."

"Well, if I'm dead, *I* can't call you anywhere. But what do you think Mike should do?"

"He wouldn't know you're dead if he was sleeping."

"But he'd know in the morning."

"Well, then he could call me at the office."

"I'm going to kill you Gavin."

Click.

Coco's heart raced.

Or #2:

"If you don't have a phone at your apartment, you will not be allowed to call up here at the house."

"Why not?"

"Because life isn't a one-way street."

"What does that mean?"

"That means it's not fair for you to have the option of calling here anytime of the day or night that you want, if we can never call you at any time."

"That's right."

Click.

Most of the scenarios she planned dealt in one way or another with injustice, but before she could develop a complete catalog of accusations, a new horror struck Coco. It was Saturday! Later on it would become Saturday night and she didn't have anything to do. Vaguely she had thought she and Suede would go carousing around Georgetown. But now he was gone and she had nothing to do on her first solo Saturday night. Also it was the start of a weekend, a holiday weekend—the supreme endurance test. Can a real American woman survive without a real man, without *any* man, for a long weekend? when everyone is *required* to have fun?

Of course she could go to a bar and pick someone

up, but how could she possibly be promiscuous in her current condition? Even if she stopped eating right now, even if she fasted for three days, she was not in shape to start sleeping around. She was too small-breasted to be promiscuous if she weighed over 120. If a woman was fat, she should at least have huge mobile breasts—the only consolation for other flaws such as acne on the ass, appendix scars and white stretch marks lacing tanned skin. Boobs that simply slid away in Position #1 did not contribute to a free mind for a free love life style.

A chilling shiver slipped down the skin of her arms as Coco remembered a long-forgotten conversation concerning whether or not a woman should sneak out of bed after initiating a new love affair to redo her face in the towel-shielded light of a strange bathroom to avert the danger of her new lover waking up first in the dawn's cruel light to catch a glimpse of a makeup-smeared, baggy-eyed, frizzy-haired old witch who had magically sneaked into his bed during the night while he was sleeping as if in some Shake-spearean comedy to replace the beautiful Jewish American Princess with whom he had retired.

—Oh, Lord—Coco moaned. —I am afraid. —

—Now get a grip on yourself—Dr. Finkelstein cautioned from Western Europe someplace where he was touring with his wife and 2.5 manageable children in a Volkswagen bus. —Don't bolt. —

CHAPTER 20

"*I* won't," Coco said in a perfectly audible voice. "I won't flip out."

—Why don't you start making the sandwiches— her helpful post-lib lobby suggested.

Slowly Coco pushed her chair away from the table, stood up, and went over to the breadbox—Make sandwiches—she ordered herself—Make sandwiches and do not taste anything. Do not lick off a single knife. Do not get one drop of mayonnaise or one dab of peanut butter on your fingertips. Do not put one potato chip between your lips or you will die slowly of interminable terminal lung cancer at Sibley Memorial Hospital starting tomorrow. Do not finger-swipe any excess filling protruding over the edges of a squishy sandwich when you squeeze the bread together. —

—Now. Sandwiches: Mike loves bologna, Jessica

peanut butter and jelly, white bread and mayonnaise for Nicky with nothing else on it. Buttered toast for Josh—not too dark. Set toaster back to L. Barbecue potato chips wrapped in individual Baggies so they won't fight. Start opening, unwrapping, spreading, scraping, slicing, covering, wrapping, closing. We can stop at Seven-Eleven for Slurpies. Put in cookies. Fruit: one plum, one apple (yellow for Jessica), one bag of watermelon balls (scooped out like Mrs. Silverman does it) for Mike and Josh. Look under the sink for big brown grocery bag. Do not notice any roaches rushing Maypole fashion around the pipes. Please, dear Lord, do not let me see a mouse. Stand up. Stand up fast. Grip the chrome edge of the counter so you don't faint and scare your children.

Don't bolt. Don't faint.

Please, Gavin, please call up right now. —

Coco ran back to her chair to sit down, sick and dizzy, in her little executive suite next to the telephone. The dog was scratching at the screen of the back door. Coco reached out her hand and then stopped. —Was it really the dog? Was it really Happy? —Perhaps it was a rat scratching at the door this time. Maybe Coco would turn the knob and see a huge black rat wag its tail and walk right in. Wasn't the scratching just a little too loud? Maybe the rats had watched Happy to learn how to do it, how to get inside. Certainly lots of rats learned lots more complicated tricks than that in laboratories across the country. If they could master ringing a bell for food pellets, they should certainly be able to learn that scratching on a screen would gain them entry into a gloriously dirty, crumb-filled kitchen. Rats weren't stupid.

Coco opened the door a crack, barricading it with a

braced foot, peeked through the slit like the bouncer in a speakeasy, recognized Happy and let him inside.

Then she reached over and dialed Gavin's office number.

"Hello."

"Is Gavin there?" Coco asked, surprised that anyone had answered on a Saturday.

"Who's calling please?"

"Who's this?" Coco asked in a cold, commanding voice.

"Susan."

"Susan who?"

The world was suddenly over-populated by Other Women—secretaries and stenographers, temps and temptresses, hookers and hippies, careerists and communards—slim, beautiful, unattached creatures available daily for sin during lunch hours or all day on Saturdays.

"Who is *this?*" Susan asked irritably, usurping all authority.

"This is Mrs. Burman," Coco choked.

Any minute now someone was going to storm into the Burman house, probably gaining entry by scratching on the back door in order to rip Coco's *Mrs.* off her epaulettes. And then—then—who would she be? Just Coco? Like Vera or Viva or Hildegarde or other first-namers-only? What would Coco Burman do without her *Mrs.*? Would she become the first lady to go around town calling herself Mzzzz, like a German messerschmidt about to bomb London?

"Look. I want to speak with Gavin Burman."

"I'm sorry. He's not in."

An old *Saturday Evening Post* cartoon, of a gorgeous blond sitting on the boss's lap while informing the wife via telephone her husband wasn't available, popped into Coco's head.

"Where is he?"

"I think he's out of town. He said he couldn't be reached before Wednesday."

Coco's rage and terror united to create fresh hysteria. For a brief moment she believed that Gavin was right there in the office and that she should get dressed and hurry over there to catch him in the act of not accepting her call. But then an even more threatening idea occurred to her. Maybe Gavin really wasn't at his office. Maybe he really hadn't rented a room somewhere. Maybe he had run away with Sylvia. Maybe they had just taken off—for the weekend or forever.

Confronted by a stubborn silence on the wire, Coco committed a last feeble old-style act of pre-lib vengeance and hung up the telephone without saying good-bye.

Incredible. Amazing. Coco's total loss of power was symbolized by the fact her name meant absolutely nothing anymore over the telephone. Her name now was only a noise, a sound—not a status report. The next thing she knew, she would begin receiving telegrams demanding she return all her charge and credit cards. Obviously American Express knew that a lady without a *Mrs.* wasn't good for heavy bills. Of course they would call in all her cards. There was probably a federal regulation stating that deserted mothers are not eligible . . .

Terrified, Coco picked up the telephone and dialed Sylvia's number. There was still no answer. Then she called the D.C. Women's Political Caucus office. After many rings someone who had never heard of Sylvia Brydan answered, but that was only a small consolation to Coco.

Where had Sylvia and Gavin gone? To Rehoboth Beach to weekend in one of those marvelously atmo-

spheric A-shaped cottages on the Delaware shore?
Did Sylvia have a car? Or did they just rush over to
the Hilton? But no, Gavin was too smart for that.
Coco could get out the Yellow Pages and begin phoning every hotel in the metropolitan area. But they
were probably registered under false names. Should
she call the police and report Gavin missing? But
then what would happen if they found him—them?
Anyway, they were probably in that furnished room
Gavin had rented somewhere on top of a soiled,
secondhand mattress making metaphysical love.

Slippery with perspiration, Coco's elbow, cocked
on the edge of the table, suddenly slipped from beneath her so that she almost fell off the chair, jarring
both her body and soul. It seemed as if the kitchen
were bobbing up and down like a cork upon the
water and it took a long time before she heard a
narrow electronic voice repeating, "Your telephone
is off the hook. Your telephone is off the hook."

Coco stood up, replaced the receiver, took the two
last Stelazine from their windowsill perch and
downed them with cold coffee. Dr. Finkelstein had
not even been professional enough to provide her
with a prescription for more tranquilizers while he
was cavorting through Europe.

A little before one o'clock, Coco started the troop
movement out of the house. First she carried Josh's
stroller in from the patio, rolled it through the house,
and carried it down the front stairs, spitefully lifting
it completely off the ground rather than bumping it
down the steps so that the unwieldy weight could
further aggravate her temper. Next Mike helped her
carry Nick's trike outside. Then she helped Mike balance his two-wheeler on the thin curbing alongside
the stairs, stopping it from speeding out of control
down onto the sidewalk. The red wagon was easy,

because it was parked in the front hall (Coco had promised to pay Jessica and Sarah a dime apiece if they pulled it to the park), but then Happy escaped through the open door and Coco had to chase him across the street and carry him back into the house. By the time all their vehicles were strewn across the sidewalk, Coco had a skinned shin, a smear of grease on her denim shirt, a bruised elbow and raw rage pumping through her shrunken veins.

—Dear Dr. Finkelstein . . . Coco paused on the top stair to address a mental letter to her doctor—I do not have the strength. I simply do not have the physical or emotional strength to do this. We haven't even left yet, we haven't even embarked, and I am already exhausted and impatient and totally obsessed with the idea of pulling all that shit right back up the stairs when we come home, when everybody will be hot and tired and Josh will be crying and Nicky will be carrying on while I schlep all the bikes and trikes and tykes back up where I started from.

"Can we take Happy with us?" Jessica asked, puckering up her face to squeeze out a few tears when she received the expected negative.

"No," Coco said angrily, foreseeing a long hot search for the dog's collar, which would be separated from the leash because Josh liked to unhook them and invariably left one part *under* some chair and the other part *under* something else. It had taken Coco four infants to learn to look for car keys or coin purses *under* places rather than *on* top of things.

Right on schedule Jessica burst into tired tears and slouched down on the top step near the front door.

Coco recalled several recent child-beating stories in the *Washington Post.*

"Jessica," she said calmly, "if you carry on now, if you cry one more minute, I am going to slap you and send you to your room and take Sarah home." (Wasn't Coco just like Mrs. Silverman—yelling at her kids right in front of their friends—no holds barred?) "Now, Mike, please carry Josh downstairs and put him in the stroller," Coco panted.

She wiped her face with a dramatic sweep of her hand, a throw-away gesture for any invisible drama critic who might be watching Coco's far-off-Broadway production of *This Is My Life*, pulled Jessica to her feet with two fierce fingers dug into her shoulder, and gave her a sturdy push down the stairs. "Get going, missy. I mean it. March."

Then Coco began a series of round trips between the house and the sidewalk, loading the rear basket of Joshua's stroller with paper diapers, his bottle, her wallet, his suntan lotion, her keys, Kleenex and a spray can of bug repellent. Loading the bags of sandwiches in a place where they wouldn't get squashed took almost five minutes. By that time, Josh was screaming ferociously and stiffening his legs until he was about to tumble out of the stroller. Finally, just after she slammed the door shut, Coco heard the phone start ringing in the kitchen and for one glorious moment she *knew* that it was Gavin calling to apologize, to recant, to restate his love and to say he was returning home.

So she began to run—first down to the stroller to get her keys and then back up the stairs to unlock the door and then, finally, through the long hallway toward the kitchen. She had only heard five or six rings but there was an ominous extra second of silence just before she lifted the receiver so that she half-expected, no, knew that the dial tone would leap up in her ear. Still, she remained frozen—as if playing a big Disappointment Scene for her movie—holding the telephone with a stunned expression on her face until Jessica ran into the kitchen.

"Mamaaa. Nicky hit Sarah and Sarah wants to go home," Jessica reported in a frantic voice.

"Okay. Come on," Coco said, backing Jessica into the hall. "I'll see what's happening."

"I think Nicky should go see that counselor you know because he's three and he still talks baby talk and he's always hitting my girlfriends."

"Keep quiet, Jessica," Coco ordered, stepping outside. "Where's Mike?"

"He's waiting up at the corner," Jessica answered, delicately edging away from her mother's wrath.

Coco slammed the door shut again and started down the stairs.

"Sarah, honey, would you like to push the stroller? You can if you want to."

"I think I want to go home," Sarah said with freckled-faced flatness.

"Oh, don't go," Jessica pleaded, urgently clenching her fists. "Oh, Mama, please tell her not to go. Please."

"Come on, Sarah," Coco said gaily. "Nicky's sorry and you can push Josh. We're going to have a lot of fun."

Quickly Coco got Nicky onto his trike, gave the back bumper a firm push with her foot to start him up the hill, and then began to maneuver the girls into position.

—Get them going—she thought. —Put them into motion and everything will be okay. Dear Lord, if I'm going to do this, please let me do it without every one of my nutty kids doing his own number right now when I don't have the strength for it. Also, that phone-call bit was unnecessary so we'll be even-steven if you make the kids behave.—

Up the block she could see Mike, sitting straight and patient on his bike, waiting for them and that was when Coco's spirits lifted and flew out of her body for a moment, winging toward her son—up at the corner—loving his young strength and decency.

Her breath was coming in short, shallow strokes, as if she had been running for miles, but she continued to hop and skip along the sidewalk, trying to stay close behind Nicky's trike so she could shoe him forward when his little legs failed in their fight against the incline. Her chest ached and there were occasional shots of pain from her shoulders that moved down under the arms toward her chest when she looked backward to check on the girls pushing the stroller.

"Come on, Mudder," Nicky yelled.

It was hot and the air was heavy. Very heavy.

Coco ran forward again, planted her foot on the tricycle bumper, and skipped a few steps to propel Nicky forward again. And that was when she felt the first stinging moment of authentic remorse and grief for her marriage. As if she were approaching a funeral home, Coco experienced a stabbing sorrow, a desperate desire to return her life to its previous form, a yearning to have her marriage restored, in any way, under any conditions, so that Gavin would walk beside her once again. Now that she had driven him away, banished him forever, she wanted her old life returned unharmed, like the time she found her wallet at the lost-and-found in the basement of the Giant supermarket with not a penny missing.

—I'm sorry, Gavin—she grieved. —Please come home. Come back to us. Come back now.—

The grief that squirted through her also tamped down her panic. Somewhat quieted, she walked past the YES hippie house and then, closer up near the corner, past the Women's Commune where she suspected liberated ladies hid behind the upside-down American flags which served as curtains on the front windows to watch nonemancipated, yea, counterrevolutionary middle-class mothers rolling their children toward the park in a caravan of various two-, three-, and four-wheel vehicles, victims and veterans of some battle by Brecht. But, like Mother Courage, Coco straightened her shoulders and stood a little taller. —Go ahead, laugh, you bitches—she thought bitterly, stopping herself at the last minute from silently calling them dykes. For what indeed was there to feel prejudice about? So what if some of them did look sort of butch? So what? What was so great about heterosexuality anyway? What had it done for Coco, huh?

"Mike, watch Nicky," she yelled. Because now, right there in front of the Women's Commune, the uphill sidewalk turned into a sharp downhill slope. For seven years Coco had had recurrent nightmares about one of her children inadvertently picking up speed at that point—in buggy or on bike—and suddenly rolling down the hill, one fingertip out of reach, onto Columbia Road to die instantly beneath the wheels of a Railway Express truck.

"Okay," Mike yelled back.

So then Coco had one more free moment to look sideways toward the cracks between the flags to see if anyone was really watching her. Because Coco always felt sublimely self-conscious in front of the Women's Commune, like a living example of a pre-lib, pre-pill, pre-legal abortion, pre-zero population-growth freak. And today her children, plus one extra, scattered and spread along the sidewalk, seemed so devastatingly old-fashioned, so counter-counterculturish, so reactionary a statement about her 1950-

ishness—planned or otherwise—that she felt her soul
shrivel with shame as she turned to latch onto the
stroller that Jessica was trying to slow down in the last
lap of their perilous journey to the corner.

"God, it's hot," Coco murmured when they were
all safely braked and parked along the curb. Then she
smiled at Mike, who had used his bike as a barrier
near the street.

"How does Mrs. Marshall get everyone across
here?" she asked casually.

Coco would obviously have to push the stroller and
hang on to Nick's trike (with him riding on it or else
running alongside holding onto the other handlebar)
while Mike got the wagon down off the curb and took
Jessica and Sarah across. But then who would take
Mike's bike? Or did he just leave it? And then who
watched the kids on the other side when he returned
for the bike if it was still there since no one had
stayed behind to guard it?

Coco stood on the curb. "You know what?" she
asked outloud so that everyone turned their faces
upward to listen. "This is like the riddle about the
man who had to take a wolf and a sheep and a piece
of cheese across the river on his ferryboat. But he
couldn't leave the wolf alone with the sheep or the
sheep alone with the cheese. Or something."

Suddenly Coco began to laugh. Sick, pathetic,
helpless laughter came dancing up like bubbles out
of her mouth and nose. The children all stopped talking to stare at her and then Nicky smiled because he
thought his mother was happy and that was when
Coco realized she wanted, very badly, to die—right
there—to lie down on the hot dirty pavement, close
her eyes and expire so that the damn police would
have to cart her body away in a paddy wagon and put
out a dragnet to find Gavin and bring him back in a

squad car right here to this corner to assume and
accept his responsibilities as a father on 19th and
Columbia Road N.W. And then *he* could try to get all
his children plus Sarah, safely across the street with
their bikes and their trikes and their strollers and
wagons and picnic lunch and other paraphernalia.

"Listen. This is too much," Coco said with an un-
mistakable tone of hysteria. "I can't manage all these
shitty bikes. We're going home. You can just sit and
watch television all day if you have to drag every
goddamn toy you own to the goddamn park for a
stinking hour."

"Aww, Ma. Cool it," Mike groaned with disgust.
"I'll take them all across. You just grab Nicky."

—Oh, no—Coco thought wildly.

—Oh, no. I'm not going to become dependent on
Mike now. I'm not going to get into *that*.
He shouldn't even be here—she thought, feeling
more frantic. Why wasn't he out in some green field
playing softball or swimming in an Olympic-sized
pool? Why wasn't he having a normal boyhood
instead of letting his middle-aged, middle-class, middle-American Jewish mother make him into an
unpaid substitute baby-sitter, a poor exploited eldest
son—obviously destined to become an emotionally
disturbed adolescent now that there was no father
figure around the house. Was Coco any different than
the ugly, aggressive Mrs. Portnoy thwarting her son's
sexual, social and athletic development? Oh, Coco
should change her name to Ms. Portnoy or Ms. Take
or Ms. Fortune or even better, Ms. Calculation or Ms.
Begotten.

"Mikey," Coco moved forward to put her hand on
his shoulder, "why don't you call up Skip later on?
Maybe you can go over to his house and play some
ball."

"Sure. Okay," Mike shrugged. "If you don't need me this afternoon. But I thought Mrs. Marshall couldn't come this week."

"Oh, don't worry about that," Coco said penitently. "I'm going to be just fine. I can take care of everything. And I'll find someone else to help out later today."

Shut up, she said to chairman of the newly established Department of Economics in her brain.—Forget the money. If worse came to worst, she could always turn a couple of tricks at the Arlington Marriott Motel to pay for a baby-sitter instead of turning Mike into an emasculated nursemaid.

"As a matter of fact, I'll even drive you over to Skip's if his mother says it's okay."

Horrors were mounting upon horrors. There she was—stranded on the curbstone of Nineteenth Street not wanting to cross, not wanting to return and march in defeat back past the hidden, but judgmental, eyes of the Women's Commune—suddenly promising to spend hours on the telephone hunting for a baby-sitter to be paid out of some nonexistent emergency funds on the first day of her life when she had no income or source of support and not one cent more than the seven dollars and some odd cents in her wallet, promising to drive through the entire city of Washington (a gouache of heat and traffic) to deliver Mike out to the suburbs for a few hours of outdoor life before she had to return and pick him up again.

But then, God (looking a little like Dr. Finkelstein up in the sky on his golden throne) gave Coco a moment of grace. For without any effort she suddenly swallowed a huge deep gulp of rich-bodied air that went directly into the dried-out bags of her lungs so that she could draw a full breath. In and out.

In and out. Her lungs had begun working normally, independently. —Thank you—Coco said to some Higher Power and then, temporarily high on oxygen, she marshaled the children across the street to the park. Mike instantly found his way into a baseball game with some older boys. The girls played hopscotch, Nicky drove around the water fountain in furiously happy circles and Josh crawled ecstatically into the sandbox where Nicky had already relieved himself.

So Coco sat down on a bench, still breathing nicely, and began to watch a long-haired young mother, photogenically pale and slim in a faded cotton dress, push her fair-haired child high on a swing.

—Why am I so different from her—Coco wondered, painfully enamored of the girl's natural glamour. There was no way in the world Suede would have cut out on that chick if *her* old man split. Suede would have hung in with that braless beauty forever.

Mesmerized, Coco watched the young woman move like a ballerina, dancing with the swing. And slowly it occurred to her that the difference between them wasn't one of age—it wasn't that Coco was old and the girl was young—but that Coco was old and the girl was *new*.

Coco was definitely a fifties person, not even in the same ballpark as the truly liberated young women who let their children run barefoot and bareass through the park with their little pink rinky-dinks bobbing up and down. No, Coco was from a different generation, a different world. The little kid on the swing had been acculturated so long he probably wouldn't even answer if someone asked him whether he was a boy or a girl. He was at one with nature. He could probably fall asleep anywhere—on the floor of a commune, on the back seat of a renovated hearse, on a grassy hill covered with a cloud of grass smoke, and he probably didn't give a damn if his mommy took naps with some guy who had a long pony tail and wore a necklace.

But Coco's kids were different. They thought men who wore love beads were weird and they couldn't fall asleep anyplace in the world except in their own little beds or on airplanes immediately after vomiting. Each one *needed* his own bed, blanket, pillow, address, drawer, corner and telephone number. Each one liked his own TV programs, place in the car, chair at the table, bench in the park, Kool-Aid flavor. Each one had his own hiding places, shelves, closets, combs, friends, toilet, cereal and individual stall for his toothbrush.

Coco couldn't wander from hippie pad to Vermont commune. Her kids wouldn't eat vegetables—fresh, cooked, canned, frozen or organic. They wouldn't eat Cream of Wheat—let alone crunchy granola— and they wouldn't touch peanut butter unless it was Skippy's plain, not crunchy. They didn't like homemade bread because it wouldn't slice straight enough to fit in the toaster. They thought health foods were for sick people and they would never miss *The Dating Game* or *What's My Line?* to weed a field of corn with members of some extended family. They never went to the toilet without shutting the door and they wouldn't take off their shoes at the park because they were afraid of stepping on broken glass and having to go to a crowded emergency room for stitches. They definitely were not swingers like the little kid swinging through the air. They were clearly prerevolutionary, middle-class, middle-American, middle-of-the-road Dr. Spock-type kids.

—So what's wrong with that?—asked some public defender suddenly on the scene in Coco's head.

—They're nice kids and they like people. They're smart and sensitive and decent. —

—Yah? Then why so uptight?—a post-lib prosecutor countered.

—I don't care if they are square—Coco said defensively to a rather long-haired jury. —I never wanted them to be any different. I never carried any of them on my back in an orange papoose when I marched on the White House. I always hired a sitter.—

—Then you shouldn't have broken up your family.—

(Was that Mrs. Silverman hiding behind the pre-lib legal counsel's table?)

But suddenly a shriek filled the air and Coco was on her feet and running before she saw it was Nicky who had fallen off his trike. He was lying in a puddle of water that had sloshed out of the fountain and his left ear was bleeding. Gobs of blood hit the pavement, splattering like red ink. Nicky began to scream louder as kids gathered and flocked crazily around him. And then the pretty young hippie mother came over, wet a wad of Kleenex she took from her pocket, and neatly held the compress against the raw flesh of Nicky's earlobe while Coco fought to keep down her chocolate doughnut. Ten minutes later Nicky was happily driving his trike around the fountain again with the little hippie boy riding on the rear, avoiding puddles with exaggerated full-wheel turns. At two o'clock the children and several new friends shared their picnic lunch. Coco was feeling semi-successful when a fight broke out between Jessica and Nicky about who should carry the garbage to the trashcan, and then, humiliated, she said good-bye to the young woman, gathered up all their equipment, and took everyone back home again.

It was ten to three on the kitchen clock. And it was still Saturday.

During the next hour Coco bathed Nicky and Josh, put Josh down for his nap, called Georgetown Hospital and found a nursing student who could baby-sit, talked with Skip's mother, who invited Mike to spend the night, settled the girls down to paint with a box of water colors she kept hidden on top of the Frigidaire for emergency distractions, and then went upstairs to her own bedroom, flooded with despair and panic. —I must learn to love peace and privacy— Coco thought, shutting the door and trying to remember advice Dr. Finkelstein had given her during her false emergency in June. —I must cherish my own quiet times, protect my own solitude and pursue my own interests. —

—But what interests did she have?—Coco plunged face-downward on the bed. —What in the name of God was she interested in? Why did Dr. Finkelstein always lobby for a hobby? What was there to be interested in? Horticulture? Foreign coins? The Divine Light Mission? Political posters? Ceramic potting? Est? Esalin? Student Demonstrations?—

Coco turned her head on the pillow and looked around the confusion of her bedroom. Perhaps it would be therapeutic to redecorate her house. Perhaps she could convert her bedroom into a combination sleeping, sitting-room and study. Maybe she should go out and buy several ugly round tables at the Salvation Army so she could disguise them beneath gay felt cloths. Then she could grow paper daisies in ceramic bowls on the tables and surround them with hot-pink-and-orange cardboard boxes full of non-functional drawers and lots of small silver-framed photographs of the children. When summer was over the room would become her study. Then she could have fuchsia wicker baskets full of personal mail and bigger avocado-colored wicker baskets full of *Vogue*s and *Harper's Bazaar*s or pussy willows and some Mexican paper flowers. Then she could bring friends upstairs to her sitting room. She could even have a party there—a goddamn gang-bang on her king-size bed.

"It won't work," Coco said to the ceiling.

The Burman house was an insoluble decorating problem because it had more than enough closets and storage space. It didn't pose the small-apartment puzzles solved every Sunday in *The New York Times Magazine*. Coco didn't need any sleeping lofts built halfway up in the air or form-fitted storage drawers built under beds. She didn't need shelves and filing cabinets hidden under radiators and staircases or above windows in the kitchen to be painted in marvelously coordinated tenant-decorator colors. Coco simply didn't have any nice, hard space problems to work out.

Standing up for a moment, she took off her clothes, aimed the air-conditioner vents toward the bed, and lay down again. What she had to do now was figure out what she should do. But even before that, she had to try to understand what had happened. All day long Coco had subliminally been trying to remember the cause of her complaint against Gavin. Her quarrel with him had lasted twelve years, but now in her confusion she couldn't recall the subject of their de-cade-long discussion. Although Gavin had always been the primary irritant in her life, now that he was gone he had vindictively removed both the source and object of her rage so that Coco couldn't even remember what she had been angry about.

—Don't panic—she cautioned herself. —Think positively.—Even if hysteria kept welling up every few minutes, it could still be channeled into creative writing. Panic itself could produce a brilliant panoramic epic of the sixties and instead of eating compulsively or calling up friends or looking for lovers, Coco could now choose a new theme for her book and outline all of the chapters on a long yellow legal pad. Then she would not scream at her children. Then she would not be too tired to melt cheese with bacon crumbs on top of their hamburgers for dinner. Then she would really *want* to take Joshua with her every time she went to the supermarket so he could ride in the jump seat of the shopping cart which he dearly loved to do.

Tears came to Coco's eyes. Maybe if she spent more time with Josh he would learn to say bye-bye. He was almost thirteen months old and he still didn't know a single word. Hot, stinging tears rolled down her face. Her baby. Her last baby. Joshua. She had neglected him. No wonder he was speechless.

And what about Jessica? What could Coco possibly do about Jessica? Was it really nuclear family life that had made Jessica so difficult—both wild and withdrawn? Or had Coco also failed her only daughter? Perhaps if they went to the park alone and lay in the grass feeding pigeons like those old ladies from the schizophrenic halfway house on Ontario Road, Coco could soothe Jessica. But only Mike understood Jessica's moods and knew how to quiet her tantrums. Mike. Mikey. He knew how to comfort and love the babies better than Coco did and he always ran outside to help Coco carry in groceries. So what was so great about that? Did she want him to be a permanent mother's helper?

Coco cried steadily.

Why didn't Gavin call? Where was he? She thought about phoning Suede in New York to say that Gavin had found out about their affair and was starting instant divorce proceedings, that he had left her alone in the world in a house with broken locks on the doors that could turn the toilet into a tomb, four children and mice in the kitchen. Coco would sound so seductive over the telephone that Suede would catch the next shuttle back to Washington and the children wouldn't even be suspicious when he moved back into the house.

—He'll never come back—a post-lib choral group began to sing. —He'll never come back. He's afraid of you because you're afraid . . . afraid . . .

Coco reached for the telephone, dialed Suede's number in New York, and hung up after fourteen rings.

Oh, yes, it was true. Coco was alone, all alone, just her and her children and her fears and her needs, most of which remained mysteriously unspecified. But it was becoming patently clear that she would never be passionately pursued by many men and that for her there would be no illicit liaisons or promiscuous passions. Her future was a vast wasteland. She thought about *Take Heaven by Storm* and decided that it was no longer relevant to her life—no longer a subject she could deal with.

Last month Dr. Finkelstein had suggested she write a book called *Vengeance Is Mine Saith the Lord*. Then he wasted a good half-hour telling her a long tedious tale about those Jews who remained behind in Egypt to avenge the Pharaoh and were thus destroyed along with the Egyptians. Coco, in all fairness, had to concede that it sounded like a major theme, certainly heavy enough to warrant explication in a graduate English seminar, but it wasn't exactly what she felt like writing. She wanted something that *sounded* heavy but was *easy* to handle.

"Hurry up, Ma," Mike yelled.

Coco jumped off the bed and went into motion. Instead of taking a shower, she sprayed her body with lemon scent and then slipped on a sheer low-cut sundress. After brushing her hair and putting on makeup, she decided that she looked quite young and rather beautiful framed in her own familiar mirror.

After the babysitter arrived, Coco drove Mike out to Kensington, Maryland. The car was stuffy and smelled slightly of mildew—an odor which had permeated the upholstery since she'd left the windows open during Hurricane Agnes. Out of the corner of her eye, Coco could see that the car floor was even dirtier than the kitchen linoleum and she wondered if the Sanitation Department could ticket moving vehicles. Wrapper peelings, sandwich crusts, toys, sweaters, a broken car seat, several old brown-bag lunches, highway BINGO cards, matchbooks, crushed Kleenex boxes, library books, spilled Crackerjacks, empty soda pop bottles and mixed up, crisscrossed, seat belts surrounded her.

But despite the smell and the confusion, Coco tried very hard to pay attention to Mike during the ride and engaged in an animated discussion about Washington losing the Senators. When she screwed up by calling the N.F.L. the N.L.F., she pretended she was just teasing him. When they reached Skip's house, she kissed Mike good-bye and drove away quickly so that none of his suburban friends would discover he had a mother.

CHAPTER 21

Coco drove slowly back down Connecticut Avenue, disturbed by the fact that she had a baby-sitter at home and four free hours with nothing to do and no place to go.

—Why don't you stop and have a drink over at the Shoreham?—a pre-lib orientation guide suggested hospitably. —You can always get your shit together when you're sitting in a bar. —

So Coco stepped on the accelerator with an old, familiar feeling of expectancy.

At the hotel, she treated herself to a stall in the underground parking garage and then floated skyward in a mirrored elevator, her heart racing against the floor numbers flashing on the control panel. Something was wrong. Something had changed. Coco no longer felt like a swinger readying to raid a bar. Now she was something else. . . . Now she was a desperate, ring-less, unwed mother in a miniskirt dress with a French bra underneath working valiantly to collect enough tired tits to create some cleavage.

"But I'm still going to make it," Coco promised the sisterhood. She stepped off the elevator into the thickly carpeted lobby, smiling and swishing the fringes of her false eyelashes. Invariably, over the years, each time Coco had reactivated the hunt for her P.L. and/or an alternative lifestyle (which simply meant daring to walk through the doorway of a dizzyingly fearsome bar) her identity was critically endangered. On each occasion when the compulsion to find romance overwhelmed her normal timidities, she risked psychological annihilation at the hands of some barfly who didn't realize that she was a J.A.P. in disguise. And since illicit pursuits demanded a false identity, each adventure imperiled her anyway-shaky self-image.

So Coco walked quickly toward the cocktail lounge while her heart muscles squeezed out twinges of terror that moved like cramps through her soul. She tried holding her breath Lamaze-style, but the tail end of each panicky feeling made her cringe, and she could no more ignore her fear than she could overlook labor contractions. Her marriage had fallen apart and she was hurting.

But when she reached the cocktail lounge, social and cinematic standards claimed her attention because there were so many things that needed doing. First off, she had to transmit a classically traditional air of desperation, because she could not bear, even for a moment, to appear common or ordinary to the live audience already seated in the darkened theater. Her entrance had to convince everyone that her unescorted arrival was warranted by some mysterious but terribly dramatic event.

An amazingly long-legged hostess who looked glamorous, intelligent, and ten years Coco's junior accosted her in the dark cavernous doorway of the cocktail lounge.

"Are you alone?" she asked sadistically.

"Not permanently," Coco smiled as her heart plummeted. How cruel women could be to each other.

"Would you like a table?"

Coco tried to make a logistical survey of the room, but it was too dark. So she shook her head. "I'm waiting for someone; I'll just sit at the bar," she lied coolly.

The hostess motioned her forward.

But by the time Coco's eyes adjusted to the darkness, she discovered the bar was an island unto itself far from the mainland of tables. This isn't working out, Coco thought grimly, as she walked forward in a blind panic, still ignorant as to whether she would ask the bartender to change a dollar for the cigarette machine or actually slide her buttocks up on top of a clammy leather bar seat. But in one surprising motion, Coco mounted the first stool she saw, leaned an elbow on the bar, lit a cigarette and found herself facing a rather raunchy-looking bartender.

"Good afternoon," he said.

"Hello." Coco gave him a soulful, preoccupied smile. "A G-and-T please."

The bartender set down a glass. "With a tan like that, you must have been out at the beach," he said approvingly.

Coco smiled vaguely and donned an expression that indicated she was expecting a specific person at a precise moment.

The bartender swirled his wet bar rag near Coco's elbow for what seemed an insultingly long period of time.

So Coco looked away, toward the dark horizon of a distant bandstand, sobered and sad. She shouldn't have come here. She should have gone shopping for fall pantsuits in Georgetown or a pair of Gloria Steinem tinted aviator eyeglasses out in Chevy Chase. Although there was a constant changeover of men at the bar—most of whom looked like ITT lobbyists or retired brigadier generals—Coco remained unmolested. No one had heard the thunderous announcements of her terrible loneliness. She decided to remain aloof and spend her free time with her P.L. in a favorite mini-fantasy that featured them quarreling and then reconciling in a small *pensione* on a little Greek island. But the fight ended quickly as they fell on the bed in a wild embrace and Coco felt gypped because even her fantasies featured premature ejaculations—leaving her to her own devices, much too soon, again.

I'm going to die, Coco thought. All my adult life my strength came from hating Gavin, and now that he's not around to hate anymore, I haven't got any life force left. For a brief moment Coco decided Gavin was only deluding himself, that he could not voluntarily stop loving her. Beneath his hate there had to exist an eternal, unalterable, unconditional and immutable love. Some things in life had to be permanent.

"May I have another G-and-T please?"

The bartender slid Coco a fresh drink and she gulped it down like a glass of lemonade. Then she opened her purse to take out her notebook. She flipped through the pages and decided that in many ways her notebook had now become obsolete. Her

Current Condition would obviously necessitate the
removal of certain Permanent Friends who would
have to be crossed out and recopied under Acquaintances since they clearly belonged to Gavin. And
how long would it take until she found out which way
their friends would split? Who would belong to
whom? Who liked whom more? Who would be *in*
and who would be *out*? Would Gavin get the Presti-
gious and Coco the Lightweights? Of course, some
Acquaintances would have to be switched to different listings under new headings, such as: Possible
Affairs or Potential Second Husbands or Occasional
Companions or Who to Call When Things Really Get
Bad Until Dr. Finkelstein Returns like a Swallow
from Capistrano Early in August. Flushing with embarrassment, Coco printed: People I Must Entertain
if I Want to Get Invited to Their Parties Where There
Might Be Some Interesting Men and hid it behind
XYZ. Then, with the tip of a quivering finger, Coco
pressed the ring release and inserted a clean paper
under M.

> *Men with Money—CEOs?*
> *Men with X-L* _____
> *Important Men*
> *Available Men*
> *Single Senators and Congressmen*
> *Men Who Have Indicated Interest*
> *Married Men I've Always Liked?*
> *Political activists*
> *Creative types*

How pathetic, she thought with disgust. Flipping
to the front of the notebook again, she started another page:

WHAT KIND OF WOMAN SHOULD I BE?

a. *An earth mother—have more children—live on commune in Vermont—bake breads, buy Honda, burn bras (save one strapless), get very thin, dye own yarn. Meditate, wear no synthetic fabrics, eat no chemicals.*

"I'll have one more," she smiled as the bartender passed by.

b. *Become serious novelist but also big commercial success like John Updike. Hang in with arty set. Write for Esquire. Summer in Hamptons.*

c. *Radical-Activist-Intellectual—work hard to end war. Get indicted for conspiracy. Organize demonstrations and street actions. Check out Weathermen types. Work with draft resistors. Cut hair like Jane Fonda. Use grass for aphrodisiac and to relax. Make it once with a priest.*

d. *Become companion to international financier or multinational conglomerate executive corporate president from military-industrial complex? Infiltrate. Inform.*

e. *Become tough "new" journalist—eventually join Washington Bureau of N.Y. Times. Buy new attaché case (avocado green). Use silk scarves tucked through suit-jacket buttonholes as trademark. Get assignments which necessitate traveling overseas. Hook up with Oriana Falaci.*

f. *Remarry! Buy large country home in West Virginia. Hire staff for formal dinner parties. Teach children to ride horseback and ski.*

The third gin-and-tonic arrived. Coco smiled gratefully and took a deep breath. Bored with her laundry lists for the future, she decided to dredge up some of Dr. Finkelstein's technical advice. Like a good basic black that could be worn anywhere, it should be applicable now to her Current Condition. Neglecting Dr. Finkelstein's therapeutic insights was like buying a Chanel suit and never wearing it. Coco closed her eyes, nibbled on a refreshing particle of lime, and decided to try updating one of the thirty-dollar lectures that she repressed the moment she left his office.

"All right, now, Mrs. Burman. You don't have to go around acting frivolous or superficial or self-hating anymore. You can be your own woman now. You can take yourself seriously. You can throw away all those false eyelashes and begin to pursue your real interests. You are an extraordinarily beautiful woman, Mrs. Burman. You don't need all that makeup and crap. Develop some new friends. Find genuine pleasure in being with your children. There are many enjoyable things for you to do. There are trips to take. Places to see. Books to read. You don't have to waste your life persecuting Gavin Burman. He is no longer your sole and exclusive access to an identity. Now that you are free, you can become yourself."

Free? Coco shrieked silently.

She opened her eyes and saw an attractive man, momentarily illuminated by light from the lobby, enter the bar. He paused long enough to look around with the proper amount of nonchalance and curiosity. His hair was graying at the temples and he wore his suit in a style that suggested he always hung it up when he stripped, thus indicating he was a mature man.

A cold shiver slid through Coco's body.

—Listen, Dr. Finkelstein—she said—I happen to
have a number of hangups and a great variety of
needs that are not being met. But that doesn't neces-
sarily constitute an Identity. In fact, Dr. Finkelstein,
when I'm all alone, my *me* disappears. It just van-
ishes. My identity tends to evaporate so that all that's
left is a lot of anxiety. And I happen to know that's
what will happen if I don't get married again.—

The man sat down at the nearest table.

—I don't want to live alone the rest of my life.—

Coco was speaking more rapidly to Dr. Finkelstein's remembered face now. Her words were arriving at a faster clip.

—Why should a woman like you *have* to get married?—Dr. Finkelstein asked in his usual fifty-minute
seminar tempo.

—Well, why don't you live alone if it's such a
groovy idea, Doctor?—

Agitated by the development of her silent sce-
nario, Coco glanced over toward her new neighbor.

Nothing doing. He was staring toward the door,
waiting for his wife.

No. The only thing left for Coco was work. She
must now write not only fiction, but also frequent
articles studded with insight and intelligence, at least
until she became an authority on something. Literary criticism was out of the question, but muckraking
was very in. She could choose or carve out some new
subject area where she could squat and homestead.
But what should it be? Non-verbal Behavior? Com-
munity-Controlled Schools? How to Dismantle the
National Security State? Methadone Treatment for
Heroin Addicts? What? Ethel Kennedy and Her
Kids?

Coco's values and interests obviously needed sorting, like the hundreds of mixed-up playing cards in

the middle drawer of the desk in the den. One constructive thing she could do right away was start cleaning out all the drawers in her house. Now, since the children no longer had a father, there would be plenty of time for them to sort cards into decks and put a rubber band around each pack. Even Nicky was old enough now to match up suits even if he didn't know all his numbers. Together they could introduce order into chaos. This would be healthy for everyone.

And when they were finished with the cards, they could stick all the loose snapshots into their photograph albums—in chronological order—and put all the records back into their proper jackets and then Mike could file Coco's recipe cards behind the dividers in her recipe box, and Jessica could hunt for missing earrings in Coco's jewelry case to reunite separated pairs, and Nicky could line up the children's books according to height and stack the oversized ones in nice horizontal piles. And then they could start sorting the hundreds of unmatched socks stuffed into pillowcases in the linen closet, and snag all the spools of thread so they wouldn't unravel in the sewing box, and someone could re-organize the spice cabinet into some kind of order, and all the while they could listen to Elementary French lessons on the phonograph.

—Nonsense—Coco's post-libby lobby interrupted. —The only sensible thing to do is finish *Take Heaven by Storm.* Quickly. There is nothing else as important, including the man at the next table who is obviously not waiting for his wife but for Raquel Welch to join him. Coco must instantly finish a first draft that would be very close to final form. Then she could take the shuttle to New York, wearing a Pucci print, while hordes of literary agents, fiction editors and publishing-company executives, alerted to her arrival, clustered together at the Shuttle gate eagerly waiting to thrust large advance checks into her hands. Suede, of course, would be down in the crowd, milling around, trying to move out front. But Coco would pretend not to see him and concentrate on psyching out the sexual potentials of the various publishing industry executives. She would choose her high-class hardback publisher right there at La Guardia, with her skirt lifting in the breeze of the still-spinning propellers (did jets have them?) before rushing off for cocktails to talk about movie sales.

Within a few months Coco would come out figuratively and literally speaking. Once published, she would appear on the *Johnny Carson Show,* looking glamorous and less abrasive than Germaine Greer and with total unselfconsciousness tell that she wrote 1973's best selling novel because her husband had abandoned her to run off with a professional libby who had huge tits, a fat ass and a big mouth. Unlike Debbie Reynolds and Sybil Burton, Coco Burman had no Liz Taylor to explain away. Unlike Maria Callas, Coco didn't have to swallow Jackie. She could come on as flip or as coy as she wanted.

But perhaps too many talk shows would spoil Coco Burman.

Perhaps it would be better just to move to Los Angeles and live in the foothills right down by the ocean, accidentally renting the property right next door to a handsome, well-known West Coast artist who loved children. They would all be poor—of course—but *together* and the children would never suspect that Coco made love five or six times a night with their husky virile "uncle" after they went to sleep.

Coco slipped three plastic swirl sticks into her

purse to give to Nicky who used them as tomahawks for his Indian braves.

But, of course, the L.A. trip was absurd too, because Coco would not have enough money for plane tickets and would have to get a job. Now, in her old age, she'd have to take a hideous job to support her children. She tried to picture herself as a bank teller or a receptionist in an employment agency, but Radio Free Coco immediately began jamming the fantasy waves so that static prevented reception of any more jive about jobs like those.

Aware of a slight tingly sensation about her mouth, a familiar sign of intoxication, Coco clenched a cigarette between her lips. Then suddenly, dramatically, she was confronted by a flaming match. Although she was startled, Coco had certainly seen enough late-night movie reruns to know she should light the cigarette before slowly lifting her eyes to smile, speechless with gratitude, up at her provider.

Instantly she recognized the well-shaped head of the man from the next table. So Coco took a deep sigh of relief, along with her first inhalation of smoke, because yes, yes, yes—there were still strangers in the world who used the opportunity and ritual of an unlit cigarette to ignite a flaming affair which, in later years, would evolve and be consummated by marriage.

CHAPTER 22

"Thank you," Coco said huskily in an appropriately appreciative tone—more for the man's dramatic approach than for the light he'd offered her.

"Are you waiting for someone?"

"No." Coco smiled alluringly.

"Well, maybe we can sit over at my table and have another drink."

"That sounds nice."

—See, Dr. Finkelstein—Coco cabled Europe in gloating triumph as she scraped herself off the stool to follow the man. —See? A person never knows in the morning whether or not to risk leaving the house without gluing on at least a few individual lashes on the bottom. A person could get careless and feel satisfied with well-applied double-fringe tops. A person could get lazy and maybe not want to bother, every day, with those tedious carefully torn-apart bottom clumps.—But Coco had been wise enough to know that in her newly precarious condition she could never afford to take such chances.

Puffing luxuriously on her cigarette, she sat down, looked toward the bar to see if the bartender had noticed the pickup, and then watched her handsome new friend settle himself back in his chair. His motions were very restrained. Instantly Coco decided that he would be a perfect lover—fortyish, rugged and with a corporate-executive style suggesting he preferred his sex straight-up rather than fancy—a type for which Coco had an unnatural fondness. Although it was dark in the bar, the first flare of his match had revealed the man's seductively light-colored eyes and ultra-white smile.

"Are you staying at the Shoreham?" he asked, setting his drink down close to Coco's and moving his chair nearer to hers.

Coco smiled. Of course he would think that, but it gave her a moment's pause.

"No. Actually I just stopped by for a little peace and quiet before going home."

Oh, no. That was wrong, she decided instantly. "Peace and quiet" announced the existence of a great number of unruly children as clearly as if she had suddenly rung a little bell to summon them in for a march around the cocktail lounge banging pots and pans like Miss Audrey on *Romper Room* suggested they do on rainy days.

—Change your tone—Coco's interior stage manager ordered.—Hurry before he follows up the kid bit. —

So Coco spoke before it was her turn. "Are you in town on business?"

"Yes. I came in last week for the APA meetings and

then I stayed on an extra few days to do some research at the L.C."

Oh, good, Coco thought. He's testing me to see if I know those initials. The right answer would instantly establish Coco as an equal even while she was being picked up at the Shoreham Hotel bar.

"Oh. You're a psychiatrist?"

"No. A psychologist. I run a clinic in L.A."

Down one point for not having read coverage of the convention and thinking it was the psychiatric meeting. Recoup, she ordered herself. Drop a name now. Some West Coast psychologist. A West Coast psychologist . . . But she couldn't come up with anyone, before it was time for her turn again. Down another point. Take a different line.

"What kind of research are you doing?" she queried him in an academic tone of voice.

"Well, actually it's not in the area of psychology." He inspected his glass. "Are you ready for another drink?" With sweet suave authority, he beckoned to the waitress. "Two more, please," indicating their drinks with official kindliness. "Actually," he said, returning his attention to Coco as if bestowing a federal grant upon her, "I'm researching the effect of the increase of gypsy moths on the cuckoo birds along the eastern seaboard."

Now there was a really protracted silence. A terrible one.

Coco was stricken dumb.

Vengefully she cursed herself for having assiduously avoided reading any newspaper or magazine article flying a conservation or ecology banner for the last three years. By shaving inches of newsprint to save time, Coco had now jeopardized any chance for remarriage and a new life. But how could she have known, way back then, what tests were to be

announced later on in the course of her life. And she
couldn't even try to cover up her ignorance with a
joke because ecologists, like professors, had no sense
of humor whatsoever and considered moths and
whale shit equally serious. Indeed, now that she had
time to think about it, what was funny about nature
anyway?

Coco lost her turn.

"I'm president this year of the L.A. branch of the
Sierra Club."

Wow. He was feeding her lines like Mike Nichols
setting up Elaine May, but Coco was too spaced out
trying to remember some basic ecological principles
to pick up any of his throw-away lines. She was desperate.

"Why are the gypsy moths increasing?" she asked
hurriedly, so as not to lose anymore ground.

"No more DDT."

No more DDT? That must be good. Coco at least
knew that no more DDT had to be a plus. So why was
he so worried?

But now he was watching her carefully, ready to
make a final judgment about her intelligence. If she
didn't pass this exam, she was finished. She had to ask
the next question correctly.

"Well, what do gypsy moths do," she began, "bad?"

He smiled.

Four gins-and-tonic plus the morning's tranquilizers had obviously blown Coco's mind. But when the
waitress reappeared she accidentally mixed their
glasses and this caused enough confusion to afford
Coco a slight reprieve.

It would be too much—too ironic—to have the day
end with this kind of failure. Here was Coco, the
smartest woman she knew, at a moment of crisis
coming on like a little Capitol Hill secretary

who couldn't remember the number of her boss's congressional district. Recklessly Coco sent a give-me-another-chance smile at the man and quickly transmitted a complicated message explaining the reasons for her current flustered condition.

—I do know all about psychology and ecology—she said through expressive changes around her eyes—but the trouble is that I've been under a tremendous strain lately.— She let flashes of troubled intelligence play across her face. —My husband and my lover have left me. So have my best girlfriend and my shrink. I happen to be in charge of four little children, one of whom may already be completely emasculated, another one who has enuresis, one who lisps and another who won't talk. At all. Not even bye-bye. Apparently I have few or no friends. Although I possess oodles of talent, I have no discipline so no one knows about it. I have enormous rats out on my patio, great sexual passion, and a broken lock on the back door. Please give me another chance.

But with a shock Coco saw that her companion was already shifting around in his chair, chafing from disappointment, and casing the bar for a means of escape.

Coco felt panic panting behind her.

"Washington's certainly a lot dirtier than the last time I was here," the man said, clearly trying to disengage now. Any body-language expert would have no trouble translating his motions into an exit urge.

"Well," Coco flailed, desperately, "actually Washington has a higher pollution . . ." (rate? standard? quota? level?) "Worse smog than L.A.," she blurted.

—Sure. Great. Come on competitive with the psychologist-ecologist you're trying to make. Terrific. —

"That's weird," he said, "since there's no industry here."

Blank. A total blank. Even the pain of her failure was erased for a moment.

"It's the cars," Coco said slowly. "The commuters."

But instinctively she knew that wasn't right. What was it? She had accidentally, inadvertently, read about it endless numbers of time. But what headline had tricked her into reading a story about smog? Traffic? Parking? Automotive-repair courses for women? What? It couldn't be that Washington was in a valley, since she never saw any hills around. Coco began punching at her mental Morse Code machine, anxious to get her SOS across the Atlantic. Dear Dr. Finkelstein: I am beaten. For me now, everything is over. I cannot remember one fucking thing about anything. I cannot come up with anything under the title of Ecology, Pollution or *Psychology Today*. All I can think about is Arlo Guthrie singing "Alice's Restaurant" because he got arrested for littering.

Is Littering a subdivision of Pollution?

A vision of her backyard floated before her eyes. Did disorder qualify as a pollutant? And what about the drawers in the desk in the TV room where they had once found maggots? And what about the rats in the alley who belonged to her because they took their meals on her property? Maybe I am drunk, Coco thought. Maybe the insufficient amount of oxygen reaching my brain has caused actual damage to the cells, plus deterioration of the central nervous system.

"What kind of clinic do you have?" Coco asked, squeezing her legs together under the table in an effort to assert bodily authority over her mind.

"Actually, it's quite experimental," the man answered, averting his marvelous eyes to case the room for other opportunities and women.

Coco felt totally reckless now. "Clinically experimental?"

He turned back toward her again with a more speculative expression. "Well, we're devoting ourselves almost exclusively to the psychological problems of women. All aged women."

—Thank you, dear Lord—Coco whispered. —Thank you, Dr. Finkelstein. I'm home free now. I've paid my dues and now I've hit pay dirt and I'm home free. Women. Women. Hurray.—

"Well, it's about time some mental-health people begin to focus exclusively on a specific problem area," Coco said briskly.

"What do you mean by that?" Instantly he was back in Coco's orbit, studying her, leaning forward, gravitationally held in time and space by the acuity of her questions.

Coco smiled, remembering how Jessica had run into the house after her first day of kindergarten yelling, "I'm here now." Flushed with success, Coco suddenly understood what her daughter had meant. The surprise of survival necessitated a public announcement of the fact.

"Well, it's been perfectly clear to everyone that there are specific problems females face that orthodox therapists simply disregard—an oversight, which to say the least, has had a rather catastrophic effect upon American women."

"Be more specific."

Now he was lighting another cigarette for her, bringing the flare of the match high enough so that they both watched his large tanned hand, covered with a sheer, furry coat of dark hair, move seductively close to her face.

Pleasure rumbled through Coco's body.

"I certainly wouldn't quarrel with the fact that

women have hangups, but most of them are cultural
rather than personal. For instance, if a woman can't
get a decent job," Coco continued, "it's not because
she has work hangups or because she's paranoid or
because she's ambivalent or afraid of employment.
It's simply because men don't like to hire women. So
at least if therapists are clued into some of these facts,
it will save women a lot of pain, time, talk and
money."

Now he was smiling excitedly and beginning to
explain in detail the design plans for his female group
therapy program organized according to specific issues.

Suddenly Coco felt tired. How much could she
possibly put out on so little sleep? How much
strength could she possibly have left after so many
pills and so much alcohol, after pulling the stroller,
the trike, and the bike up and down the stairs twice?
Where was her energy supposed to come from? But,
luckily, male chauvinists liked to hear themselves
talk, so now that she had proven herself a worthy
audience, she was off the hook. Her adrenaline, triggered by desperation and determination, began to
subside.

After a while the man interrupted his own narrative to announce that his name was Charlie O'Connor, that he thought Coco was beautiful, that he had
left his family and was living with one of his formerly
schizy patients in a marvelous house out in Pasadena
with three avocado trees in the backyard, that he had
tripped with Timothy O'Leary ("O'Really?"), that he
had been to Esalen eleven times, that he believed
the world could be saved only through the new Divine Light Mission plus a coalition of ecology groups,
that he was working with the L.A. Amnesty for Draft
Resisters, and that he belonged to a nudist club

where he and his mistress spent one weekend every month. Eventually he pressed his thigh against Coco's leg and moved in closer to whisper that he was also raising money to make a movie early next year about a drug rehabilitation center and that—confidentially—Peter Fonda was interested in playing a small bit part.

By now Coco was floating through the Straits of Nausea. The outer rims of her lips felt frostbitten; her ears were playing a light buzz into her head; her eyes were dilating and contracting, making the world drift in and out of focus, while the tips of her fingers turned numb so that twice she almost lost a grip on her glass. Internally her program director was providing equal airtime for various public-service announcements such as a missing-persons lookout for Gavin Burman (last seen wearing a determined expression on his face) and an encouraging spiel about how student nurses could provide first-aid treatment for any cuts, chipped bones, concussions or convulsions suffered by wards in their care.

Meanwhile, Coco was slowly realizing that the man next to her was a foppish fool, but still a decent person to know on the West Coast if she really decided to resettle near the Pacific. Silly as it seemed, it would be through just such a schmuck as Charlie O'Connor that she might very likely meet a suitable second husband, since other hip people would also know him in the same casual way she did. So while not responding to his thigh, she also didn't avoid it and instead concentrated on trying to counteract the tranquilizer-plus-alcohol sick sensation swimming through her system. She had already discovered that if she remained completely silent and motionless she could maintain life with the residue of air already in her lungs.

"Would you excuse me for a moment, please?" she asked suddenly, taking herself so much by surprise that she didn't even have her purse firmly clenched in her hand before she rose from the chair. Clearly some higher power was telling her it was time to urinate. The table seemed to shrink as she grew taller and the handsome head of her companion was clearly sitting just to the left of his neck.

At the end of a tunnel of blackness she could see a pinpoint of light identifiable as the Shoreham Hotel lobby. But her journey to the powder room took a long time and, when she finally stood in front of a full-length mirror, the environment began to play games with her senses and she had to fight to restore authority over her rebellious body.

"Maybe I should vomit," she said outloud to the mirror, since there was no one else in the restroom.

—Why did you do this to yourself?—the disgusted face of her post-lib prosecutor inquired from behind the glass.

—Where is Gavin?—Coco asked her accuser. —Please tell me. —

—Gavin—she called silently. —Gavin. I'm sick. I'm really sick. I want you now. I *need* you. Please.—

Coco went into a toilet stall, clutched the crotch of her panties to one side, squatted over the bowl and listened to the comfortable splash of urine spilling from a great height straight down into the water. After what seemed like a long while, Coco walked back out to the sinks, splashed some water on her wrists, wiped her face on a roll of toweling coming out of a machine, and began to reapply mascara with a hand that seemed totally disconnected from her arm.

"It doesn't matter if the eye-liner is a little crooked," she said to one unanchored eye rolling

around in the mirror. "*Vogue* doesn't really expect us
to paste silver sequins on our lids. That's only their
way of suggesting an approach—an attitude—a reminder not to forget your Maybelline."

She smiled at her reflection and began making
plans for her return trip to the cocktail lounge.

—Why don't you just split?—the dazed-looking
post-lib prosecutor, peering out over the sink, suggested. —Go home. You look awful. You can keep the
nurse there for an extra hour—for just another dollar
twenty-five—and take a nap. —

—*No way,*— Ms. Burman, Chairwoman of the Department of Economics, replied promptly. —Pay to
take a nap? Are you crazy? Anyway, when you're
planning to open a branch office in California, you
can't afford to throw away any fresh contacts on the
Coast. —

—But in exactly three minutes he's going to ask
you to go up to his room. —

Coco shrugged nonchalantly.

—But you haven't even shaved your legs—her
mother piped up from some impossible location.

—So what? Charlie O'Connor's hip, Coco countered.

—But, Coco—Ms. Post-libby said—you don't *want*
to go to bed with him. You don't *have* to you know.
He's not going to make you feel any better. You'll feel
worse.

—Even he can't make me feel any worse—Coco
replied, replacing her cosmetic bag in her purse and
turning to push open the restroom door. She
skimmed across the royal scarlet carpet until she saw
Charlie O'Connor standing outside the cocktail
lounge.

"Are you all right?" he asked intently.

"Sure." Coco smiled. A single woman could obvi-

ously never confess to feeling sick. Illness was the
exclusive privilege of children and married people.
There was no one in the world who cared if an unwed mother developed a cold.

"Actually," Coco amended bravely, "I think I'd
like some coffee."

"How about ordering dinner up in my room?"
Charlie O'Connor suggested, somehow encircling
her by the way he positioned his body. Then he took
her elbow in a departmentstore-detective–clutch
and moved her toward the elevators. "Let's order up
some steaks. I'm starving."

So Coco allowed herself to be maneuvered
through the lobby, wondering how she appeared
from the rear, trying to pull in her bottom so she
wouldn't look like a hooker to any vice-squad plant or
hotel dick or Congolese linoleum salesman conven-
tioning at the Shoreham. She walked along dutifully
until they were on the elevator where she had to
fight back an unexpected swell of nausea that rose in
her throat. Gulping down the bile, she noticed that
she was panting instead of breathing. What's the
matter with me? Coco wondered. And why doesn't
this schlep who knows all about women see I'm sick?
Really sick.

They reached his room after traveling vertically
and horizontally for a long while. Once inside the
door Coco moved automatically toward her reflection on the far wall, placed her purse on the dresser
top, and looked back through the mirror at the green
bedspread and the green carpet and the floral draperies and the boxy TV and the green squarish chair.
Then she looked at herself again. Silently she requested the blurry reflection not to disappear in a
dead faint.

"Comeere a minute." Charlie O'Connor's voice sounded like a wink.

Coco released the strap of her shoulder-bag purse with reluctance and turned around.

"If you're feeling queasy, lie down here for a minute."

The word "queasy" brought another rush of salty liquid into Coco's mouth. She floated toward the bed, sat down, and then slowly flattened her body into prone position. No sooner had her head touched the pillow than the dark bulky shadow of Charlie O'Connor's head closed over her, blotting out reality, daylight and oxygen. She raised her hands against his chest to push him away so she could grab a mouthful of air, but he was involved in some grunty sexual advance that was so inexplicably noisy he paid no heed to her livesaving efforts.

"Please," Coco whispered against his face. "Stop."

The pimply visage of a rabbi's son at a Chicago-Winnepeg AZA convention floated before her eyes. —I'm drowning—she thought, trying to get some air down her throat.

Charlie started to kiss her as she went under for the second time. When he forced her lips apart to insert a fat bumpy tongue inside her mouth, she began to emit the sick helpless moans of a street-crime victim. But just like the ghostly rabbi's son who had suddenly appeared to haunt her, Charlie O'Connor misinterpreted Coco's moans of pain as pleasure. A moment later, traveling by his own private itinerary, he began nuzzling his way into the top of her dress.

Coco opened her lips and gulped some stale, artificially cooled air. With one hand she unbuttoned her dress before Charlie O'Connor could rip it open and then lay motionless, still concentrating on forcing the oxygen down into her chest, past Charlie O'Connor's head, which was making untranslatable sucking, rutting sounds, and down to the bottom of her lungs. Breathe in, she instructed her diaphragm. Now let a little air come out.

But her chest was too tight. She wondered if a clinical psychologist had to study anatomy in college. If she fainted right now would Charlie O'Connor realize she was getting insufficient oxygen or should she tap him on the shoulder, right now, and say, "Excuse me for bothering you, but I'm having a little trouble breathing?" In fact, she should probably tap him on his shoulder right now and warn him she was dying, so that he could split before the police and the press arrived and found him in such mysterious circumstances. Indeed, Coco was just drunk and drugged enough now to be able to die voluntarily if she chose to do so. If Charlie O'Connor would just stop jumping and lunging around, she could very simply close her eyes and, like some arctic explorer, lie back, in the snowy drifts of insufficient air, curl up, and fall into a warm cozy sleep, never to awaken again in her frozen white universe.

"Listen, honey," Coco heard the sound of his voice hissing in her ears. "Lately I've been having a little trouble making it when I'm with strange women. I mean, women who are still strange to me. Women I never made it with before."

Charlie O'Connor's voice sounded distant and tinny—like a poor transatlantic connection.

"Give me a little help, huh?"

Coco's lungs were getting tighter. Soon they would be involuntarily inoperative and she would be dead. Apparently lungs were not the kind of organs which, if threatened with annihilation, fought for their own survival.

"What . . . ?" Coco murmured vaguely. "What did you say? What do you want?"

"I need a hand-job," Charlie O'Connor said apologetically.

Your receiver is off the hook. Your receiver is off the hook.

"What?"

"Come on. If it works, I'll stop in time to give you a good fuck."

And then, through the bitter desert of desolation and a new surge of dizziness, Coco felt her hands maneuvered into position around Charlie O'Connor's butter-soft size-S penis.

"Move them up and down slowly," he said. "Not so hard. Not so fast."

Please, dear Lord, Coco began to pray, let me die right now, right here in the Shoreham Hotel jacking off some guy who can't get a hard-on, because it is only poetically perfect that this be the last scene of my third act. Her tingling appendages seemed to be drifting away from her body while her heart palpitated in sick little jerks. Just let me die, God. Right now. Please, Sir.

"Not so hard, honey. Not so fast," Charlie instructed a bit impatiently.

Coco stared at the face next to her on the pillow as she rhythmically and mechanically rubbed the loose skin of Charlie's penis up and down with the same motion she used to stretch leather gloves when they got mixed up with the dirty laundry and ran through several cycles in the washing machine. Meanwhile Charlie O'Connor lay flat on the bed with his eyes closed, apparently trying to send blood donations from other parts of his body down to the disaster area between his legs. His mouth was hanging open like someone receiving first aid at a rescue operation and he seemed to be in a trance of impotence.

But then, somehow, although Coco's pumping motions had no visible effect on Charlie O'Connor, they began to produce some positive results for Coco. Each time she bent to knead his little organ, a small quantity of air pressed between her lips and slid down her throat into her lungs. Crazy, Coco thought, I'm doing artificial respiration on myself. I'm making my lungs expand and inflate because I'm hunched over like this and my arms are pumping in a way that's pressing air into my diaphragm. Diaphragm? What was she doing here without her rubber diaphragm and with her organic one out of order?

—I'm going to be able to breathe again in a minute,—sang her heart. —I'm about to catch my breath. —Coco opened her eyes, rejecting sick darkness and gulped one deep mouthful of oxygen that went splashing down to the bottom of her chest, spilling through her lungs.

—Oh, yes—Coco thought silently, reverently. — Oh, yes, how fresh, how religious, how great was God's air. I'm all right, she thought joyously. I'm all right. I'm breathing regularly, normally now. I'm breathing again. —

So Coco stopped her manual labor and sat up straight in the bed. Quickly she fumbled around until she extracted her sheer little mini-dress from the wrinkled clump of sheets bunched up at the bottom of the bed and jumped to her feet. In a slithering motion she yanked on the dress, crumpled her bra in her fist, slid her feet into her sandals, keeping them on with curled toes so she didn't have to buckle them, darted to the bureau to retrieve her shoulder-bag purse and started moving toward the door.

"For Christ's sake, you little bitch," Charlie O'Connor groaned, sitting straight up on the bed, his face contorted with amazement and fury. "Where the hell do you think you're going?"

"Oh, Charlie, I'm sorry. But I've got to get home. It was just taking too long. I'm sorry, but you'll just have to finish by yourself."

Coco smiled and waved good-bye. Then she darted through the doorway into the liberated zone of the hotel corridor. It was in the elevator that she realized she had lost the belt to her dress, was missing one of her favorite Mexican silver hoop earrings, and that one of her eyelids felt suspiciously light. (Had her Revlon Double-Thickness Daytime Midnight-Blue Real-Hair Lashes fallen off and stuck to Charlie O'Connor's pillowcase like a dead scorpion so that in the morning he would awake and shriek with horror?)

After sitting in the lobby long enough to fasten her sandals, Coco began walking home slowly, enjoying the regularity of her breathing that was now in sync with the easy motion of her strides. Indeed, she felt momentarily suffused with physical well-being.

She was halfway home before she remembered she had left her car in the Shoreham underground garage.

CHAPTER 23

*I*t was almost eight o'clock when Coco reached home. Nancy Grant, the short little student nurse, looked somewhat harassed, having just put the children to bed. Coco paid her six dollars, mostly in coins from the bottom of her purse which were sticky from melted Clorets and sprinkled with tobacco jimmies. But when she picked up the car keys to drive Nancy back to Georgetown Hospital, the enormity of her plight struck her again with renewed force. Obviously one of the unanticipated and more horrid consequences of divorce was that there was no one to stay with the children when baby-sitters had to be taken home. Stunned and disoriented, Coco considered risking a quick round trip to Georgetown— even if Mike was away. But then she remembered an old baby-sitters' tale that the danger to unwatched children was not the untimely arrival of a child-mo-

lesting killer-rapist but the possibility that the parent
might never return. Coco paused to picture herself
dead on Wisconsin Avenue beneath a burning car
and her three little children, ever mindful of instructions not to go outside alone, drying up and dying,
their little bodies decomposing for months—since it
was clear that no one ever dropped in to visit divorced women and their families.

So Coco went to the telephone, ordered a taxi, and
rushed around looking through the children's various
banks, drawers and hiding places to find another dollar and a half for cab fare.

After the nurse was gone, Coco ran up to the third
floor, checked on the children and then went into
her room to stretch out on the bed. The preview
of Life as a Parent Without a Partner, the whole how
are-you-supposed-to-drive-the-baby-sitter-home?
syndrome, multiplied by a still unknown X, left Coco
feeling weak. It was apparent that her nightmare was
only just beginning. After all, the children didn't
even know the truth yet and their reaction to Coco's
announcement was happily unimaginable. Indeed,
Coco herself was nowhere near ready to believe in
the finality of Gavin's unyielding, unwavering, unilateral decision to cut out on all of them.

Worries rose to her head in little bubbles that
erupted like burps from the mouths of comic-strip
characters: How did this happen to me? What did I
do to deserve this? What am I going to do now? Why
did I drive away the father of my children? How will
my children survive? Will they ever forgive me? Occasionally the dialogue was cast in declaratory sentences such like: I am afraid to be alone. I will have a
life full of Charlie O'Connors and Suede Bellocks. I
will turn into a Sylvia Brydan. I am a failure. I am in a

great panic. I am a Victim. Terrible things always happen to me.

Tsk, tsk, tsk, Dr. Finkelstein cabled from Europe.

Fuck you, doctor, Coco wired back. What do you know about anything anyway? What do you know about being a woman or how that can screw up a person's life? What do you know about me or the Silverman family or corrupt Chicago Jewish culture or the real effect of dirty male-chauvinist-pig husbands or how four little kids can do a woman in with all their diapers to change, pins to snap, bows to make, buttons to sew, toys to fix, belts to buckle, ears to Q-tip, laces to tie, shoes to find, socks to match, Pop Tarts to toast, milk to pour, mouths to kiss or tookies to wipe? What do you know about all the crummy jobs working for crummy men or any of the other sociological, economic, political or psychological facets of women's lives which you always thought was my own private neurotic stock until it went public? What do you know?

Nervously Coco rose from the bed. She walked over to the dressing table and looked down at the two earrings, one silver, one gold, lying abandoned near her cosmetics. She had seldom lost earrings before, but today she had dropped one in the park and one in Charlie O'Connor's bed at the Shoreham. Two pairs ruined in one day. Coco felt a sweet sense of sadness possess her as she stared at the gold and silver hoops—lone survivors—useless, nonfunctional items that could never be rehabilitated. No occupational therapy could ever provide them with alternative careers. Their only value now were as symbolic objective correlatives for Coco's condition.

Picking up the telephone, Coco dialed Sylvia's number again. The unanswered rings produced a quick skin flick that flashed across the screen of Co-

co's mind. The stage set was a sparsely furnished
bedroom with a mattress on the floor. The camera
zoomed in on a naked Sylvia sitting totally unselfcon-
scious, with her thighs spread apart,—eating a juicy
Sunkist orange. The unflattering camera angle revealed not only her gross vulgarity but also her political opportunism, intellectual underdevelopment,
emotional duplicity and pathological need for someone else's husband.

In the next frame Gavin could be seen lying naked
beside Sylvia and giggling nervously as the telephone
jangled, occasionally reaching out to hug her when
the tension produced by the ringing became unen-
durable. Coco considered leaving her receiver off the
hook all night so that Sylvia's phone would never stop
buzzing and the lovers would be driven either to
answer it (sufficient cause for Coco to drive right over
and storm the building) or else flee the apartment,
rendered sexually impotent by aggravation, to rent a
motel room.

But, judiciously, Coco replaced her receiver just in
case Suede might be trying to call from New York.

Highly agitated by her home movie, Coco ran
downstairs to the kitchen. Since the chocolate-covered doughnuts—which by now were obviously
defused by twelve hours of abstinence—Coco had
not eaten anything. She opened the Frigidaire, decided to start Dr. Stillman's water diet first thing in
the morning, and then ate a container of creamed
cottage cheese and a half-pound of raw hamburger.

—I will eat only protein from now on—she swore
passionately. —Protein and water make you thin and
also produce great creative energy.— She sat down
next to the telephone, tried Sylvia's number again
and then Gavin's switchboard. Tomorrow she would
organize her telephone canvassing so that it would

be more systematic and provide better coverage throughout the day and night.

Pouring herself a cup of murky coffee, she returned to the big brave sketchpad on the kitchen table. No. She would never move it. The kids could eat in the dining room from now on, since they always wanted to anyway, but she wasn't going to move that sketchpad. And every night after dinner she would transfer notes from the little notebook in her purse onto the huge tablet, using that process to get a handle on her material. The monumental sheets of the paper would finally produce epic clarification.

Coco sat quietly, sipping her coffee, and letting a strong sense of The Man in the Brooks Brothers Suit Syndrome come to her mind. If Mary McCarthy had done it, masterfully knocked over a sitting duck, why couldn't Coco? Why not simply record the disastrous afternoon at the Shoreham and the deadly life-giving clinical climax she had achieved in Charlie O'Connor's bed. Oh, Charlie O'Connor was perfect, a perfectly magnificent symbol of the impotence that was running rampant across the country and all the ailing organs attached to silly, insincere and insignificant men.

"Wow," Coco said outloud.

That was it. A natural. For not only was Charlie O'Connor fucked up, but he fucked up plenty of women.

—Oh, move over, darling—Coco hummed to herself, thinking of Bellow and Roth and Malamud and Updike and Mailer and Styron and Jones—all as a single male entity. Move on over, darling, because the revolution started at 9:27 P.M., July 1, 1972, and it's our turn now. We've waited a long time. We've spent our lives going down on you and having live-organism sore throats for hours or walking around with sticky-stinky sperm dripping out of us all day, pasting the flabby skin on our inner thighs together like Elmer's Glue.

Coco wrote *The Sex Life of Gwensandra Rappaport* on her sketchpad and underlined it like a proper freshman English teacher. What she really should do was write a sexual autobiography. But then she would have to include her early years, wrestling with the devil alone in bed, seeking an end she wasn't convinced existed. No. That was too much. Let Roth jack off in public. The female thing was obviously much more private and complicated, too hard to confront with all the hairbrush handles, the empty Coke bottles, the carrots, the fingers, the hands, the pillows, the violent rockings, the shaking beds and quaking hearts.

She began to doodle, drawing small boxes fitted into other boxes joined by parallel lines, and tried again to think of a friend to call who would produce the right responses and provide insights, indignation and possible travel plans. Then she picked up her red Flair and wrote: "Wanted: A father for three boys and one girl. Regular part-time position. No experience required. Evenings after 6:00 and weekends. Live in or out. Close to bus line. Call 202-765-8431." But where could she place such a personal Personal? *The New York Review of Books? The Berkeley Barb? The Texas Observer? Playboy?*

Then jealousy beset Coco again and she began to quiver with pain. What she really should do was list all the great women who had made Big Jealousy trips. Instead of famous ladies publicly announcing their past abortions, what about an International Jealousy List? Now, that was a real trip, a gut issue, a put-up-or-shut-up kind of list. What if Simone de

Beauvoir produced a legally notarized statement
that she had written *The Mandarins* because she was
ravished by jealousy over Jean-Paul Sartre's indecent
indiscretions, and what if dear Shirley Jackson acknowledged she wrote "The Lottery" because she
had to put up, and put up with, girl graduate students
and if Doris Lessing confessed she wrote *The Golden
Notebooks* because she was hurting over Clancy's
fancies? Was it true that the finest women artists
were whipped into creativity only by lashes of jealousy? Were Sylvia Plath's last poems, scribbled in
that cold London flat, only the ultimate moans of a
woman betrayed? Was jealousy perhaps the only cat-
alyst for great female writing? Was Emily Dickinson
jilted rather than jolted, into brilliance?

Because whether or not a woman loved her man,
the result of conjugal betrayal was extreme, possibly
fatal, jealousy. The pain Coco felt now on the beach-
head of her heart—a potent combination of rage,
competition, love, revenge and rejection—was obviously an automatic reaction. It apparently stemmed
from some strange contractual state of mind that
married women developed to explain to themselves
their own puzzling situations. Whatever the cause,
women certainly couldn't tolerate husbands having
extramarital love lives. Jealousy instantly canceled
out all history and truth-in-labeling and immediately
activated the classical how-dare-you-do-this-to-me-
when-I-really-should-have-done-it-to-you-first-ex-
cept-that-it's-harder-for-a-woman-because-she-has-
to-pick-up-the-kids-at-three-etc.-etc.-etc. response.

Coco began to draw triangles. She covered half a
page with symmetrical triangles. Then she drew one
upside down, superimposing it on another, and
watched a Jewish star appear to taunt her. Next she
methodically began assigning triangle points to peo-

ple. She did a Liz-Dick-Sybil Burton triangle. She did a Mia-Andre-Dory Previn triangle. She did a Mrs. Rockefeller-Gov. Rockefeller-Happy triangle.

—Good Lord, why am I sitting here doing this?— she thought hysterically.—Why am I just hanging out in the kitchen like I'm sitting Shiva? Am I sitting Shiva for the death of my marriage? Should I run right out to the Safeway and buy a Yarhzeit candle?

Then a scene from Coco's past resurrected itself. Once, perhaps twelve or thirteen years ago, she had been visiting Helen's seventh-floor walk-up apartment in New York. Standing near the window, she had caught a glimpse of some commotion down below in the street that drew her closer to the dirty paint-spotted glass, and she had watched a miniature horror show that brought the sick taste of fear into her mouth.

A woman had gone berserk in the street in front of the apartment building and her shrieks were cascading upward like an inverted waterfall, splashing in a translucent spray against Helen's window. The woman ran, wailing along the sidewalk, back and forth in front of the building, caged in by her own delirium while children stood watching, fascinated rather than frightened, and someone must have called the police because finally a Black Maria appeared and, somehow, despite the cosmic disintegration the woman was suffering, once the cops had grabbed her, once they began to shove and push her toward the double doors at the back of the van, she must have realized that she was safe, that she was no longer solely responsible for herself, that some force stronger than her own madness had now seized her, claiming her for its own. Because once hands had been laid upon her, she ceased to bellow, ceased to scream, and cooperatively climbed up to disappear inside the paddy wagon. Now, years later, Coco suddenly understood the peace of submission and thought, as she rose from her chair, that even city hospitals have sheets and that private institutions probably have their linens pressed as well as laundered.

She went upstairs to bed.

The next morning the baby slept late and, unexpectedly, it was Jessica who climbed into Coco's bed first on that Sunday morning.

"Hi, baby snuckums."

Coco reached out and Jessica, still sweet from sleep, rolled over into Coco's crooked arm.

"Gee," she said, "Daddy sure leaves a lot of space when he goes away."

Coco's heart fluttered and she turned so she could see Jessica's light blue eyes with their Hollywood-thick lashes.

"When's he coming back, Mama?"

Temporarily the air escaped from Coco's lungs again.

"I'm not exactly sure." Should she tell her now while they were alone and feeling close? But perhaps Gavin would call today and then inflicting such a wound upon Jessica would be barbaric. As soon as Gavin called, and Coco convinced him to come home again, there would be no reason for the children to know anything about this.

"In a couple more days, honey. It depends how fast he can finish his work." But, oh, what if he never called? What if Gavin had fled to Pago-Pago like the man who wrote the story in *New York Magazine* and who felt sorry for his wife every evening as he watched the South Pacific sunset? Then what would the children think of Coco's blatant cowardly lying? But still . . . Gavin was essentially a responsible

Jewish lawyer; he wouldn't not show up in his office
after a long weekend. He hadn't fallen that far yet
. . . or had he?

"Is this Sunday, Mama?"

"Yes."

Coco lifted her free hand to press the slightly
damp hair off Jessica's forehead and for a moment
she saw the promise of her own features hidden
within the face of her little daughter.

"You know what I was thinking?" Coco asked casually, careful not to invest too much enthusiasm in her
suggestion since that would immediately cause Jessica to reject it. "Since Mike is going to be at Skip's all
day, maybe you and I could clean out some of our
drawers and make them nice and neat."

"Oh, ish," Jessica groaned.

"But it could be fun. Just you and me."

"You mean we wouldn't have to go to the zoo?"

"No. We'll have a treasure hunt instead."

"What's that?"

"Well, it's like that time I put a bounty on yellow
pencils that had points, erasers and didn't give sliv-
ers. If you can find your pink barrettes in that terrible
drawer in the den or the key to the basement or the
magnet that goes to the can opener—then you'll get
a prize. Each time I'll tell you what to hunt for—what
the treasure is—and then, after you clean the drawer
and find it, you get a prize."

"Does Nicky get to play too?"

"Well, we'll see. Maybe I'll give him a different
drawer to do it in."

A short silence.

"Mama, are you afraid to sleep in the house when
Daddy isn't home?"

Coco's tears were mobilizing more swiftly now.
The nearness and unusual niceness of her little

daughter seemed to test all her controls. "No, not at all," she lied.

"All right, Mama, I'll play that silly hunting game. Let's go down and start."

"Right now? Right this minute?" Coco squeaked, still limp from sleep and emotion.

"You said so, Mother. You're the one who wanted to play."

As the hard demanding look began to tighten Jessica's face, Coco collected her strength and began moving, desperate to avoid a confrontation that would sabotage the day.

And, for some reason, this Sunday turned out better than any of the previous ones in June. With Gavin and Mike away and the phone ominously silent, Coco's impatience shriveled up. Although Joshua knocked over an empty coffee can filled with Tinker Toys, Lincoln Logs and Lego bricks that rolled away into lethal hiding places, Coco's nerves were steady and her breathing regular. Cleaning made the time seem fluid so that the day didn't become combative. Nicky even agreed to be the mailman, which consisted of carrying trash to the kitchen garbagecan, so Jessica could maintain the lead role of treasure hunter.

Late in the afternoon, Coco put the children in the car, picked up Mike and stopped for dinner at a taco restaurant which accepted Central Charge cards. Later that night, when the children were sleeping, Coco sat in the living room, on the long blue couch where she had lain with Suede two nights before, and reread her entire manuscript. Occasionally she felt moved by a particular passage, but when she had finished reading, she buried her manuscript—with no intention of ever unearthing it—beneath the whiskey bottles in the lowest cabinet of the bar. Then she went downstairs to the kitchen, opened the huge sketchbook to a clean page, and began to write a review of her novel for the *Washington Post*—her own unsolicited literary obituary.

TAKE HEAVEN BY STORM BY CHARLOTTE BUR-MAN. PUBL. BY RANDOM HOUSE. $6.95, pp. 300. Reviewed by Karl Stankiewicz, Professor of American Literature at George Washington University.

And what have we got today? Well, it's another novel in the ever-growing list of female complaints by self-centered, egocentric, whining American women who clearly have nothing to feel badly about except their own egocentricity and narcissism. While the war in Vietnam continues to rage, while poverty, unemployment, crime, inadequate housing and ecological disasters plague our nation, a group of well-educated but giddy middle-aged women sit around writing bad novels in which they rail against easily identifiable men for various psychological and genital shortcomings. How boring . . . how obvious . . . how poorly done. Although the heroines of these clit-lit books are totally crippled by their own bitchery, they eclipse all the other characters—especially their pale Jewish mates. These books are spun out of authorial hysteria and thus do not have any fictive status.

The latest contender for the Ms. American Bitch crown is Gwensandra Rappaport. Sandy, as she is called in bed, was ill-conceived by a local lady—Mrs. Charlotte Burman—whose only show of subtlety was casting her book in the third-person singular, thereby ineffectively veiling her *roman à clef*. Ms. Burman's first novel,

Take Heaven by Storm, is a poorly disguised autobiography of a JAP (Jewish American Princess), from a small principality on the near North Side of Lake Michigan, who takes off on a Hunt for the Wholly Male with such an overdeveloped sense of expectation that her relentless and tireless chase is inevitably doomed to failure. Since she attributes her monomaniacal husband-hunting to the brainwashing of her Jewish parents (are there any other kinds these days?), she holds them totally responsible for all her Ms. Conceptions, Ms. Takes and Ms. Adventures.

Gwensandra Rappaport has deluded herself into thinking that if she tries out enough men, like dresses off a rack, she will find one that fits and thus attain eternal happiness. Her constant discovery that no man is quite right—that each needs some alteration—is viewed as either bum luck or sexual deficiencies peculiar to the Male Sex. What the author—who tries very hard to be witty, clever and caustic—never seems to understand (any more than her silly, superficial heroine) is that Gwensandra's tragedy is caused by a comic flaw in her character (if she has one). By sleeping her way through a cross-section of the male population (none of whom can rise up to the height of her expectations), she overlooks the fact that there is no man who can make her happy, because happiness is a self-created condition. Responsibility for oneself if a whole new ball game and it's tough teaching an old dog new tricks.

While the discontents of our heroine's catalog holds our attention as much as any well-organized laundry list, the reader does get some insight into Ms. Burman and a lot of her sullen, sulky sisters around the country. What exactly do these totally undisciplined women—who apparently have full-time domestic help to care for anywhere from one to ten kids while they write —really want? A good job? A better screw? A contraceptive pill for men? Divorce insurance? House and field slaves? The presidency? What? It is quite clear that America's women do not know what they want—so neither they, nor their men, can possibly provide it.

Why don't these bright, energetic ladies address themselves to the problems of their sisters —around the world—who are still living in starvation, disease, oppression or purdah—and stop writing novels they don't even bother to polish any more than their silver? But if their itch to bitch is irresistible, how about looking at some other ethnic groups for a change? (A Martian would think 97 percent of Americans are Jewish women.) Where are the novels about the Chicano women of Texas, the black women of Harlem, the Polish women of Pennsylvania who wait after mine explosions for their men's bodies to surface?

Ladies! Ladies! Open your false-lashed eyes and look around you! Jewish princesses are not the largest or most oppressed ethnic constituency in America and we are getting tired of hearing you *kvetch.* Down with counterrevolutionary princesses! Up Real Women!

Coco locked the back door and walked through the first floor turning off lights. On the second floor she opened the guest-room door, glanced toward the unmade bed full of tangled linens that Suede had left behind like a sick joke, and then walked outside onto her porch. Standing motionless in the darkness, she remembered the bright eager promises of June—with all their prerogatives and privileges.

The moon was shining behind the decaying apartment building across the alley and on the skyline she could see the illuminated dome of the U.S. Capitol. An enormous weariness began to wrap itself around Coco's body, pressing against her cheeks and eyes. Turning around, she gently transported her tired body up to the master bedroom.

CHAPTER 24

Gavin did not call on Monday.

Around noon Coco decided to risk tying up her telephone line for a short while and began calling baby-sitters so she could go to the demonstration on Tuesday. She made eight phone calls, but all of her prospects were either out of town, planning picnics or working holiday shifts at Georgetown Hospital the next day. Feeling like a hopeless, helpless shut-in, Coco sat at the kitchen table energetically despising Gavin for splitting before his July Fourth baby-sitting assignment.

"What's the matter with you, Mom?" Mike asked, passing through on his way to the backyard.

"Nothing, darling." Coco made her lips stretch sideways into the approximation of a smile. "But we're out of milk. I thought we could all take a walk up to the store."

"Okay," he agreed.

So Mike helped Coco drag a limited amount of equipment down the front stairs. But as soon as they started up the block, Coco saw several women sitting on the front stairs of the Commune call out to Nicky, who was peddling at the front of their parade. Innocently he slowed down and then, with his head shyly lowered, parked his trike to hear what they were saying. Coco, who was helping Jessica push the stroller, felt herself cringe, but she kept up her pace and her spirits until she reached the commune.

"Hi," one of the young women said.

She was wearing a man's shirt with the sleeves unevenly cut off.

"Hi," Coco answered and then unexpectedly, self-defensively, launched a first strike. "Listen, is there any chance that anyone in your commune might be able to baby-sit for me tomorrow during the day?"

The words tasted sour on her tongue. Why was she destined to see every woman under twenty as a potential baby-sitter rather than as an equal? "I was planning to march in the Women's Independence Day demonstration to the Capitol," she explained carefully, as an act of redemption.

"I doubt it," another young woman answered. She was thin and had pale blond hair and a tired, sad-looking face. Still, she was pushing Nicky's trike back and forth with her bare foot, in a friendly effort to entertain him while she spoke to Coco. "Most of us are going to the march, too."

Coco felt a flush of embarrassment leap into her cheeks at her own insensitivity. Of course they would all be going. Of course. That was their thing—a women's march; they too were a part of it all and probably for them it was more real than for Coco—less political and more authentic.

"I thought you probably would be," Coco said apologetically, rocking the stroller back and forth as Joshua began cranking up to cry.

"But why don't you come inside for a minute," the first one said. "Sheila's home and I don't think she's going to the march."

"All right."

Coco pressed her arms close to her body so that the sweat rolling down her arms wouldn't drop to the pavement like drops of pee. Jessica was studying the two young women solemnly and even Mike had come close enough to hear what was happening. Coco kicked down the foot brake on the stroller and started up the stairs leaving Josh behind so she wouldn't appear anxious or over-protective.

"I want to come in too," Jessica said.

"Me too," Nicky squealed, jumping to the sidewalk.

And then, of course, Nicky's trike, unleashed at the top of the incline, started to roll downhill.

"Oh," Coco screamed, even though the trike was riderless.

"I got it," Mike said, running after it and grabbing the handlebars.

"Honey, please hold onto Josh's stroller," Coco begged nervously. "I'm afraid it might roll away too."

"I'll hold the stroller," the blond girl said. Her voice was a soft whisper, sad as her face, and her lips barely moved as she spoke.

"Thank you," Coco said politely.

What am I doing? she thought. I don't dare take Josh out of there now, because I'm too fucking other-directed, but I am leaving my baby in the hands of a spaced-out, dope-smoking, acid-dropping, Woodstock-Weatherwoman communal living lesbian. But

she followed the first girl up the stairs, holding onto
Nicky and Jessica, and as she turned (under the pre-
tense of stopping the screen door from slamming)
expecting to see Josh hurtling down the hill, she saw
that the blond girl had lifted him out of the stroller
and was holding him in her arms while she talked to
Mike.

How nice, Coco thought, filled with a swell of gratitude because a stranger had understood her concern
and was trying to be helpful. Locked up in her own
neuroses, Coco had forgotten that the world still had
people in it who weren't either men or husband-
snatchers and that there were still women out there
who would instinctively lift a whimpering baby out
of a stroller and say hi to a three-year-old boy driving
past on a trike.

The front room of the commune was dark because
the American flags were drawn—or lowered half-
mast. There were no women's-liberation spies
crouched behind the Stars and Stripes. Instead there
were three young women sitting around on sagging
furniture reading newspapers, drinking coffee and
looking more sorority-like than depraved.

"I'm sorry. I don't know your name," the girl beside Coco reminded her.

"Oh, I'm Coco Burman. I live right up the block."

"Yes. We see you go past all the time."

Aha!

"I'm Judy. Sheila," she called out, "this is Coco
Burman and she's looking for a baby-sitter for tomorrow so she can go to the march."

One of the girls got up off the couch. She was the
prettiest one so far and seemed to have more vitality
than the others.

"Hi. I'm Sheila Parker," she said, and then she also
bent over and introduced herself to Jessica and

Nicky. "I should give you one of our Children's Commune handouts. We're organizing an all-day daycare
thing for the kids around here. But, anyway"—she
paused thoughtfully—"I could baby-sit for you tomorrow. Since everyone will be gone, you could
bring them over here."

Oh, oh.

"Well, I think it's probably best at my house," Coco
said, feeling ninety-five years old and two-hundred
pounds fat. "So the baby can sleep in his own crib."

There it was, right out front, right at the start, the
damning, damaging difference between Coco and
them. Joshua Burman could fall asleep only at home
in his own little crib, with his worn-away satin-edged
blanket, his pacifier, his brothers and his night light.

"That's okay. I'll come over there. What's your address?"

"2594."

"Swell. I could use the bread and I think your kids
look great to talk to. What time?"

"About ten-thirty if that's okay."

"Sure."

"Wow," Coco said, so sincerely touched that she
wanted to talk to the natives in their own language.

And then—suddenly—she felt as if she were beginning to melt, as if her inner organs were getting soft
and mushy. Gratitude—because the young women
all seemed very sympathetic and had actually spoken
directly to the children, looking right into their faces,
treating them as little people—made Coco feel weak.
After so many nights and days of frightening solo
flights, all at once Coco wanted to sit down cross-
legged on the floor, take off her shoes and her
makeup and her eyelashes and her bra, and tell them
that her husband had left, that her chauvinist-pig
boyfriend had split, that her only girlfriend was off on

a junket, that her shrink was on vacation, and that
she was all alone and unable to get it together. But
instead, she began to move toward the door, shyly
motioning Nicky and Jessica to follow. Outside she
hurried down the stairs to retrieve Joshua, hoping he
hadn't made his doodoo while the girl was holding
him, waved vaguely back toward the commune and
started off again to the store.

CHAPTER 25

Coco was awakened the next morning at seven when she heard Joshua screaming from his crib and Jessica yelling from her bedroom.

"Okay," Coco called. "Here I come."

She bounded out of bed and ran down the hallway into the boys' room. Instantly she was enveloped by a foul odor. Carefully Coco lifted Joshua out of his crib.

"Phewey, he sthinkths," Nicky said from the top bunk. "And he woked me up."

"God, **Ma,** change him," Mike chimed in with a disgruntled voice.

"Well, that's what I'm doing," Coco said.

Her stomach churned as she replaced Josh in the crib and unpinned the diaper filled with loose, messy stool.

"Mama," Jessica called.

"Jessica, will-you-please-wait-a-minute?"

"When's Daddy coming home?" Mike asked with a slight burr of suspicion in his voice. He was lying face down on his bunk.

"I don't know," Coco said, gagging around the two plastic Donald Duck diaper pins clenched between her teeth. Her stomach moved in a queasy motion as she wiped up her son's diarrhea, went into the bathroom, wet some toilet paper, returned to wipe off Joshua's buttocks and then ran back to kneel on her knees before the toilet bowl to rinse the diaper. Slowly the water in the bowl turned brown, leaving dark marks on both of Coco's arms when she finally stood up to deposit the rinsed diaper in the hamper.

Later, Coco went back to her own bedroom, opened the closet and began looking through her clothes. The day would be too hot for slacks and her mini-dresses looked too short and frivolous for the occasion. Finally Coco put on an African print shift, a modest amount of makeup and brown leather sandals.

When Sheila arrived, Coco spent half an hour showing her the house and the children's equipment. At eleven, she extracted a token from the bottom of her purse and walked out to catch the Connecticut Avenue bus. The moment she disembarked near the White House, she felt the vibrations of rally fever that preceded all Washington demonstrations. It was still early enough to catch all the aimless waiting and walking and talking, the repetitious speculations about tear gas, busts, heat strokes, comfort stations, chartered bus arrivals, television coverage, the whereabouts of the President, the percentage of blacks, the presence of food, shoes, Band-Aids, youth-contingent bum trips, riot squads and the official estimate of crowd size versus the police chief's version.

There was seldom any mention of the politics of

the protest, either because the principles were too
profound for small talk or simply because issues were
forgotten during actions. There would be no mention of oppression or liberation until everyone was
seated, picnic-style on the Mall, cooling their feet
and tempers in the Reflecting Pool, warmed by the
sun and the holiday humor. Then they would listen
to speakers expound on the reasons and objectives of
the gathering, always ending by exhorting the pro-
testers not to disappear after they dispersed.

But today the demonstration felt like half-forgot-
ten Fourth of July political rallies back in Chicago
when Daley-machine aldermen and congressional
candidates entertained constituents in Hyde Park
and the kids set off firecrackers (illegally smuggled in
from Wisconsin), released free balloons into the hot
sky, and ate hot dogs smeared with German mustard
while their fathers emptied kegs of Democratic beer
and mothers relaxed, content that their children
were safe at a Party party. Coco felt a resurgence of
excitement, an old Illinois State Fair high, but she
also felt a nagging need to locate a familiar face in the
crowd so she could have a base from which to stray.

The D.C. Women's Liberation leadership had
planned to meet on the northeast corner of Lafayette
Square, directly across from the White House, so
Coco walked slowly through the park, peering at the
women who stood about in small groups, reciprocally
feeling powerful as they watched NBC and CBS
watch them. But Coco knew that the cameramen,
high up on their scaffolds, faded in only on the faces
of the notables or on the notable bodies of the
unknowns and for the rest of the time focused on
whatever Lucille Ball qualities they could extract
and capture. Coco felt simultaneously serious and

silly, committed and frivolous, concerned and con-
spicuous, as she passed before the TV crews.

Near the center of the park, she saw a cluster of
familiar faces and she began walking toward them,
excited by their looks of excitement. Coco wove in
and out of the crowd, moving toward the Washington
contingent who looked super-responsible on their
hometown turf and who were busily providing hospitality to out-of-town women. They milled around,
trailing long lists of papers, maps, timetables and lists
of speakers.

Then a hand reached out and caught Coco's wrist.

"Hi, Coco."

It was Sylvia.

There was a violent wrenching cramp in the center of Coco's stomach.

Sylvia stood her ground, solid, stoic and sullen. She
was wearing a white Mexican blouse hanging out
over a pair of blue jeans, big hoop earrings, and a rosy
little sunburn on her turned-up nose.

"This looks like it's going to be a great march."
Sylvia sounded insincerely enthusiastic.

Coco nodded. Her knees were vibrating because
the sight of Sylvia had transmitted an electrical shock
through her entire system. Over the past two days,
Coco had totally repressed the idea that Sylvia was
still in Washington or planning to attend the march.
Hadn't she and Gavin run off to Latin America?

"I heard there's a couple units of pigs waiting on
the Fourteenth Street Bridge in case we commit any
civil disobedience," Sylvia announced.

"Oh." Coco couldn't think of an appropriate reply.
Her legs were trembling so athletically now that she
was certain Sylvia would notice.

"So, how have you been?" she asked, feeling both
defensive and homicidal.

The crowd of women was flowing around them.

"Pretty good," Sylvia nodded. "Say, Coco. I was wondering about something."

Pitipatpitipat . . . WouldYouMindGivingGavin ADivorceSinceWeAreMadlyInLoveAndWantTo GetMarriedAsSoonAsPossibleAndWeKnowYou Won'tMindLettingUsHaveTheChildrenBecauseWe HaveJustBoughtAnAppleOrchardInVermont AndWantToRaiseThemRurallyAndWouldYou MindPleaseJumpingOffTheMemorialBridgeSo ThereWon'tBeAnyAlimonyPaymentsOrCustody QuarrelsOrLeftoverLives . . . ?

"I was wondering if . . . I haven't been home much, because I've been into all that Steering Committee shit . . . you know . . . organizing the—"

"Yes. I know," Coco interrupted. Pitipatpitipat.

They shared a long silence in their cave of emotion near the rocking ocean of women. Then Coco heard a familiar gasp as Sylvia tried to catch her breath. It was the same sound she had been hearing during her own desperate four-day struggle to breathe. Sylvia's face had become mottled with pink splotches and beads of sweat broke out on her forehead as she struggled to swallow enough air to finally flush the words out of her mouth.

"Well, I was wondering, since I haven't been home much, if . . . well, I don't know, if Suede's been trying to reach me . . ."

Helen Blumenthal walked past and touched Coco's shoulder to greet her.

Coco waved and smiled.

So. It was Suede, then, not Gavin after all. Sylvia was so transparent that it was clear she had no idea Gavin was missing. It was clear that Sylvia had spent the last few days waiting for a telephone call from Suede—not knowing whether he was still in Wash-

ington, unaware that he had flown away into the wild
blue yonder on a Saturday-morning shuttle.

Now pieces of intuitive evidence were scrambling
about in Coco's head like an animated cartoon of
puzzle pieces reassembling themselves. So it wasn't
Gavin whom Sylvia wanted, but Suede. Somewhere
Sylvia had been lying flat on her back in the old
numero uno favorite position for sex or for life—just
as Coco had done—suffering, frightened, hurt, jealous, helpless and outraged. But it wasn't over Gavin.

Briefly Coco felt cheated because Gavin wasn't the
cause or object of Sylvia's pain, gypped because Sylvia had miraculously exempted herself from the battle Coco had been waging against her, making a
mockery of all the war games. Sylvia was no longer
an enemy because she had already been wiped out
by a common foe—by the ambidextrous, double-
dealing, two-timing finger-fucking Suede Bellock.

It was so terribly Jamesian that Coco felt overcome
by emotion, heat, information and aching empathy.

"Well, Suede left," she said very gently. "A few
days ago."

The words lifted an enormous weight off her heart.
Mysteriously she was beginning to identify with Sylvia—soul-mate, victim-sister, partner in a long spec-
trum of painful emotions.

"When?" Sylvia panted softly, trying to conceal
her breathing difficulties.

"Saturday. Very early," Coco said quietly.

Suddenly she wanted to grab one of the nearby
picket signs, turn it over to expose its clean side, and
india-ink a message in simple block letters: Dear Dr.
Finkelstein: Gavin not with Sylvia. Whereabouts still
unknown. Jealousy subsiding from disappearance of
co-star. Prognosis for Recovery Good. Wounds Mend-
ing. Paralysis Lessening. Patient now able to reach

out hand to other human being. WILL LIVE. WILL LIVE. Signed, Ms. Anthrope. Coco's spirits lifted as she waved the invisible picket sign high above her head.

"It looks like they're getting ready to start," Sylvia said after several minutes of silence observing the crowd.

Now they were being jostled by flurries of women pushing forward toward Pennsylvania Avenue. Helen Blumenthal, holding a bullhorn, was calling out the names of states to bring delegations forward. The NWRO women were to be up front.

"Listen, Sylvia," Coco said quickly, "Suede asked me to tell you good-bye for him. His editor telephoned him to come back to New York unexpectedly and he couldn't reach you."

Sylvia looked at Coco quizzically, trying to sift out some truth from the saving lie.

"Well, I guess it's just . . . par for the course," she said slowly. "I mean . . . Suede just seemed sort of different to me, but I guess he's really just like the rest of them." She began to draw a cold defensive expression across her face. "Oh, I don't mean Gavin, of course. He's not. He's doing a great job for us. But guys like Suede, they just come and go—and I guess I still believe all their same old bullshit."

"Come on," Coco said. "Let's walk together. We can walk behind National Welfare Rights."

Sylvia flushed, re-igniting the heat splotches on her skin, as contradictory emotions fought over the battlefield of her face.

"I'd like to," she said awkwardly, but then quickly withdrew her consent and began to retreat, "but I'm supposed to be with the Steering Committee. Maybe I'll see you later," she whispered.

Veiling her vulnerability behind the long spaniel

ears of her hair, she began drifting away until she disappeared among the other women.

"WALK EIGHT ABREAST, WALK EIGHT ABREAST," the bullhorn instructed.

So Coco moved out into the street, joined an incomplete line, and walked in the outside file. Still busy sorting information in her mental file drawers, she looked straight ahead toward the Capitol dome and didn't speak to the woman at her side. Although she was still not one hundred percent convinced that Gavin wasn't stashed away in Sylvia's apartment on Capitol Hill, the resurgence of compassion had diminished her own emotions. Both pain and suspicion had subsided.

The women marched up Pennsylvania to 14th Street, followed the jag of the avenue, and then started toward Capitol Hill. On the corner of 9th Street, Coco asked the woman walking in front of her if she might carry her baby. The woman looked grateful and silently handed over the child. So Coco wrapped her arms around the baby and walked along feeling the pressure of infant knees and elbows plundering her body. After several blocks, the mother insisted Coco had done enough. She reclaimed the little girl and Coco felt a chill of loneliness for Joshua.

When they reached the empty Capitol building, the women swelled up and over the front steps to petition a government that had already adjourned for a redress of their grievances. As impractical and symbolic as the gesture was, there was a sweet closeness among the women as they stood together in the heat and Coco felt reaffirmed and fortified. The speakers seemed less strident than usual; Bella's bellow was less abrasive, Steinem's vision more political, Shirley's charges less rhetorical.

—We're growing up—Coco thought.

We're all learning how to do things, put things together. We're all getting high on our first taste of feeling power and knowing that together we might be able to do all the things none of us can do alone. Like those girls in the commune. Maybe they feel stronger because they have each other and when you're strong you can help other people. Maybe every woman needs to know there are other women around to help—and then each one *can* do it alone.

Coco left the Capitol before the rally was over and walked fifteen blocks before she caught a bus.

She was exhausted when she reached home, but after dinner she put the children in the car and drove downtown. The traffic was tedious and she couldn't find a parking space near the Mall. Finally she abandoned the car blocks away near a vacant fire hydrant and then, boosting a cranky and tired Joshua into her arms so that her shoulder-bag strap kept slipping down into the crook of her elbow (making the purse bang against her leg), she took Nicky's hand and delegated Jessica to Mike. Already weary and worn, feeling like a martyred Joan of Arc, Coco herded them forward, on toward the biggest light show of the year. She knew she was overachieving again. The children would have been perfectly happy watching the fireworks from the second-floor back porch if Coco had made popcorn and used real butter.

Why do I do these things? Coco wondered helplessly, moving amidst the crowd with wobbling knees and aching shoulders. When they finally reached the Mall, Mike flung the old madras spread across the grass and Coco sank down, dumb and numb, amidst her children. Joshua instantly revived and, in full possession of his mute energy, began to half toddle,

half-crawl away, around other blankets, farther into
the crowd.

"Jessica, get him, honey," Coco begged.

"I want to watch the fireworks," Jessica said
calmly.

"But they haven't started yet."

"How do you know?" Jessica asked.

—Tune out—Coco's de-lib-erating voice said—
tune out.

"Peoples von't keep him, Mudder," Nicky said, trying to placate everyone.

So Coco lay down, flat on her back as usual and
looked up at the upper halves of people moving past
her with their bags and baskets and blankets and
babies, waiting for darkness in the hot muggy night.

After a while a man appeared directly above Coco's head. He was holding Joshua. In a nasty voice he
asked if the boy belonged to them. Mike confessed.

Slowly July Fourth turned into the longest day of
the year. The sky didn't begin to darken until 9:30.
Then the government finally capitulated and sent up
their first flare. Josh and Nicky were sound asleep.
Jessica and Mike cricked their necks back to ohhh-
hhh and ahhhhhhh about the finest, farthest-flung
explosions of color.

A strong scent of dope was in the air and Coco
breathed deeply, trying to get a contact high.

So, she thought, here we are. We're here because
we're here because we're here because we're here.
We're here because it's the Fourth of July—grand ole
Independence Day in America. And now Coco Burman, newly liberated from bondage (otherwise
known as deserted by her husband), lay stoically on
government ground staring up at the sky.

—Yea, though I walk in fear through the Valley of
Freedom, through the darkland of liberty where peo-

ple must take care of themselves (plus their children), I shall not fear.—

Gavin, Coco called wordlessly, please come back. Here we are. Right over here. On the Mall behind the White House on our old madras spread. Can't you see us? Over here.

And what is independence? Coco wondered, watching lights splash down through the darkness.

What does freedom mean?

Coco continued looking up at the sky. The answer was in a folder that was missing from Coco's mental filing-cabinet of information.

"Mama, let's go home," Jessica said.

"Jessica! It just started. Oh, look at that one. It's red, white and blue. Isn't that beautiful?"

"But my neck hurts."

"Well, lie down, honey."

But Jessica continued nagging. Finally Mike socked her on the shoulder and then Jessica threw herself, screaming and shrieking, upon her brother. Coco broke it up. The fireworks and the fighting went on and on, until Coco finally surrendered. Mike was so outraged at having to leave early that he refused to hold Jessica's hand on the way home. Coco woke up Nicky and lifted the sleeping baby into her arms. Then they began stumbling over the bodies of spaced-out spectators as they moved across the Mall. Nicky began to cry that he was too tired to walk. He wanted Coco to carry him. He sobbed and called, "Daddy, Daddy," weeping pathetically enough to make people turn around to watch him. Mike, furious about missing the fireworks, grumbled, complained and wouldn't help either Nicky or Jessica cross Pennsylvania Avenue. Coco's arms felt as if they were breaking. Her head throbbed.

It was almost eleven when they reached the house

and the telephone was ringing as Coco unlocked the front door. She laid Josh down flat on the floor in the hallway and ran wildly toward the kitchen.

"Hello."

"Hello."

"Hello."

It was Mr. and Mrs. Silverman coming in from Chicago over two extension phones in their Michigan Avenue apartment. Mrs. Silverman would be in the kitchen, leaning on the counter, while Mr. Silverman probably lounged on the bed using the powder-blue Princess that matched the bedspread and draperies.

"Darling, how are you?" Mrs. Silverman intoned. "We've been so worried. We've been calling all evening and no one answered."

"Oh, hi, Mom. Hi, Dad. I'm fine. I took the kids downtown to see the fireworks and we just got home."

"Oh, honey. We couldn't imagine what was wrong, why no one answered. And we've been expecting you to call all weekend. How are the children?"

"Fine, Mom. I just have to get them up to bed now."

"So what else is happening, sugarplum?" Mr. Silverman asked.

"Not much, Dad." Coco maneuvered around the kitchen table so she could open the door and release Happy into the yard.

"Where's Gavin? Did he go with you?"

"Well . . ." Coco took a deep breath and pulled the screen door shut so that the rats wouldn't come in.

Through the window she could see flashing flares and lights exploding in the patriotic sky above the apartment building across the alley. Liberation and

Freedom and Independence were shattering into millions of cascading stars.

"Well, actually, Gavin has gone away for a while."

"What?" Mrs. Silverman whispered. "Where?"

"I'm not sure, exactly. You know, we weren't getting along too well. I guess he just wanted a little peace and quiet."

"Coco, what are you telling me?"

"Wait a minute, Jenny. Hold on a minute. Now, tell me the whole story, Coco."

"Oh, Daddy," Coco moaned. "Not now. I'm really bushed. I had to carry Joshua for about ten blocks."

"Honey. We want to help you."

"I know, Daddy. Thank you. But I don't need anything now." It seemed true enough for the moment. "You know, we've been having some rough times and Gavin just got fed up and split. That's all. I don't know where he is, but I'm okay. I can take care of myself and things will just work out one way or the other. Whatever happens, it will be all right."

"I can't believe this is happening," Jenny Silverman wailed. "I just can't believe it."

"Mother, please. It's all right, I said. Everything is all right. Don't worry. Listen, I've got to get the kids to bed. It's eleven o'clock here. I'll tell you what. Tomorrow I'll sit down and write you both a long, long letter and tell you everything. Okay? Please don't be upset or worried. I've got to go now."

Coco hung up the telephone and went upstairs to put the children to bed.

CHAPTER 26

Coco was still up on the third floor when the telephone rang. She took her time answering it because she assumed it was Jenny Silverman announcing the estimated time of her arrival at National Airport to save her daughter and grandchildren.

"Hello," she breathed wearily into the telephone. A faint odor of old breath (her own?) rose from the mouthpiece, and mentally Coco jotted down: Buy Mr. Clean. Deodorize all three phones—esp. kit.

"Hello. Is this Coco . . . Burman?"

"Yes."

"Hi. This is Ann Carradine."

"Oh."

Instantly Coco felt the same tremor she experienced when she heard the voice of the assistant to the principal at Mike's school. Her inner ear wired dread to her brain which then transmitted terror impulses to all her vital organs. The fragile, delicate sense of calm that had been trying to assert itself all day began to dissolve.

"I hope it's not too late to phone. I've been trying for the last few hours, but there wasn't any answer."

"Oh," Coco said blankly.

"Well, let me explain why I'm calling. I'm doing a story on the Women's Independence Day March for *The New York Times Magazine*. It's supposed to be a complete evaluation of where the movement's at right now. You know . . . where it's coming from."

"Oh," Coco said again. The tape recorder in her brain jammed on Ann Carradine . . . *Times* Magazine . . . Ann Carradine . . . *Times* Magazine.

"But what I really want to do is personalize the politics of the thing a little. I . . . well, I thought we might get together and have a chat."

"I see," Coco said very carefully, uncertain whether the voice she heard was real or imaginary. "When?"

"Whenever it's best for you. I'm free now."

"Did you want to come over here?" Coco asked disbelievingly.

Had Ann heard about Gavin? Was she coming over to gloat, to taste her sweet revenge?

"That would be great," Ann answered quickly. "But actually, I thought we might just rap alone—without Gavin, I mean. I mean, I don't really think he'd be too interested . . . it's just about feminist stuff."

"You're right, he wouldn't be," Coco said slowly, "But anyway I'm home alone with the kids."

"Well, then, I could come over there. I've got your address and I'm right downtown at a restaurant. Is your place far out of town?"

"No," Coco said, pulling the telephone along the

dressing table so she could check her physical reaction in the mirror. "It's just about ten minutes from the White House."

"Swell. I'll leave right away."

Coco's hair had begun to curl—making a soft-edged frame for her face. Her eyes looked huge and had the glamorous glow produced by an emotional overdose.

Another test, she thought grimly, slowly replacing the receiver. She had thought she was just about ready to graduate, to collect all her credits, make up all her incompletes, and start to think about things outside her own head once again. And then—here came her past again. It was ironic. Just as Coco was ready to begin a mental-health recovery program, Ann Carradine turned up to torture her.

—No makeup—post-libby counseled from her office behind the looking-glass.

—Why not? I don't want her to think I'm a frump —that I'm a tired housewife suffering from the disease-with-no-name.—

—You look great. Just be cool. You might straighten up the living room a little.—

—I thought maybe we would just sit in the kitchen.—

—Well, then, run along and get things ready.—

So Coco stumbled out of her bedroom and down-stairs to the kitchen. By the time the doorbell shattered her shroud of ghostly silence, she had sliced up her last fresh lime, poured dry-roasted peanuts into a Mexican bowl and planted ice cubes in two matching glasses.

"Hi," she said almost before she had opened the front door.

"Hello, Coco," Ann Carradine smiled.

It was not that Ann looked more California-beautiful than before, but that now she *knew* how she looked and actually intended to come-on exactly the way she did. Gracefully she slipped through the half-opened door as a reminder for Coco to stop staring and move back.

But as Coco shifted to get out of the way, she caught a glimpse of an ignominious pile of something near the hall radiator. Instantly rattled, Coco tried to remember if some doodoo could have rolled out of Josh's diaper when she put him down on the floor to run and answer the phone-call from her parents or whether Happy had taken his revenge for being left home alone.

Strung out by domestic demerits, Coco felt a rise of resentment against Ann's unshackled performability —the childless woman who never unsuspectingly wore a strain of burped-up milk down the back of her blouse, who had no pets to defecate in doorways or husbands to abandon her on the Fourth of July.

"Would you like a drink?"

Coco's offer sounded preposterously premature since they were still jockeying through the doorway. A little more of her cool melted away.

"Yes. That would be nice."

Coco moved laterally until she saw that Happy had unloaded a mountain of totally undigested Alpo meatballs on the carpet. Planting herself in front of the dark mound, she cursed her dog for not having the decency to re-eat his barf as he usually did if no company was expected.

"Straight ahead," Coco smiled.

Then she followed Ann's long slim body through the hallway, trying desperately to spot some flaw beneath the white shantung safari suit. But Ann's back was straight, her waist small, her jacketbelt loose upon her narrow hips, and her California golden hair cut bluntly (who did it? Sassoon? Kenneth?) across her shoulders so that it swung out front with a come-fuck-me bounce.

"Oh, what a nice kitchen," Ann said, looking around and awarding Coco one of her dazzling California surf-white smiles. "It's marvelous."

"Thank you." Coco marched to the counter. "Would you like a gin-and-tonic?"

"Wonderful." Ann sat down at the table and put her white shoulder bag down on the floor.

Sneaking a side-view look, Coco received a spear of anxiety through her chest. A reporter's notebook—a classy skinny version of a stenographic pad—was jutting out of Ann's purse. Was everything Coco said to be recorded for *The New York Times?* Should she perhaps say at the start that this interview was off-the-record? Dare she ask not to be quoted? Dare she request attribution be made only to a highly placed source close to the women's-liberation administration? Was this actually an interview? But why would anyone want to interview Coco Burman? Totally disoriented, she finished making the drinks and then sat down across the table from Ann.

She smiled expectantly while her pre-lib fashion coordinator began to nudge her—You better buy a safari suit just like that one, although it's probably too late to find anything in white since it's already the Fourth of July. Maybe you can get it in brown for the fall. —

"How is Gavin?" Ann asked, pushing the two lighter-streaked frontlocks of her hair behind each ear.

"Oh, fine. He had to try a case in Atlanta tomorrow, so he flew down there tonight. We just took him to the airport. I know he'll be sorry he missed you."

"I'm sorry too, but I really wanted to speak with you alone."

—Oh, what does she want?—Coco's head hammered.

She can't still be pissed off at me for ripping off Gavin. That was thirteen years ago and it was damn lucky for her that I did, because otherwise she'd have to hide the dog puke and I'd be wearing that white silk suit.

"I think I mentioned over the phone that I very much want to personalize women's lib in this article and show how the movement helped me get myself together."

Coco was steadily gulping her drink and envisioning Ann bumping into Gavin downtown the next morning as he exited, sexually exhausted, from some hotel on Connecticut Avenue to return to work. — Oh, terrific. Wonderful. Had to happen. —

"You know, after Gavin and I broke up, I had some pretty bad times," Ann said in the seminar tone of voice used for recounting historical hysteria at consciousness-raising sessions. "First I went back to L.A. and then up to Boston and then, later on, to New York, but I couldn't find a decent job and I kept thinking that I had made a terrible mistake."

"A mistake?" Coco queried.

—Dear Dr. Finkelstein: I am in no condition for this. I cannot handle what she is about to lay on me. I cannot survive this chic little consciousness-raising session à deux. I don't know if you remember that Women's Commune on my block I once mentioned to you. Well, I was there yesterday and it felt very nice being there. It felt . . . sort of safe. Just women, you know, young women. They liked my kids. But I don't want to do this whole number with Ann. I don't feel like being intense. I am tired of all my old shit.

I'm tired of talking about it. I just feel like I want to
. . . be. I will send in the final installment on my last
months' bill next week. Sincerely yours, Ms. Appre-
hensions.

"Well, I kept thinking I should have given the marriage more of a chance. Because . . . well, I don't
have to tell you, but Gavin really is a great guy and I
thought maybe I shouldn't have split the way I did."

From far off on the third floor Coco heard several
thumping sounds. Instantly her body tensed with the
prospect of one of the kids waking up, running downstairs, marching into the kitchen and demanding to
know why they hadn't seen Gavin since last Friday
morning.

"Oh, you know the whole bit," Ann continued with
a weary shrug. "It all sounds like a cliché now, but
back in the early sixties, I thought I was the only one
going through it."

The golden-haired daughter of the West Coast began to unbutton her jacket.

Coco stared straight ahead while she winged a
prayer up through the ceiling. Oh, no, dear God, not
that! Anything but that, she begged. Any minute now
Ann was going to open up her jacket, expose her tits,
and ask Coco to go down on her—right under the
kitchen table. Of course. What else? Why else would
she come here? Ann was so with it she would come
out just because gay was in. Vainly Coco tried to think
of a properly worded refusal that wouldn't make her
sound anti-lesbian.

But Ann had a plain white sleeveless blouse beneath her jacket. The only thing she exposed was the
fact her breasts were still high, pointy and big
enough to make her midriff look miniature.

Ann smiled at Coco, lit a cigarette, captured sev-

eral peanuts with long graceful fingers, and lifted her
glass to her lips as if performing a Geisha ritual.

"Of course, way back then, I wanted to set the
world on fire and I was obsessed with the idea that
Gavin was holding me back. I thought I'd have to go
live wherever he decided to practice law and that I
would never be able to do what I wanted to, even
though I didn't know what that was. So when I went
home for Christmas that year, I thought it through
and when I got back to Chicago I just told him that I
wanted a divorce."

Slowly her Pacific-blue eyes began to cloud over as
she watched Coco's reactions teletype their way
across her face.

"I mean," she corrected herself, flushing like a lie
detector about to score, "we decided. I mean, we
decided to stay in the same apartment together until
the quarter was over, but . . ."

"Do you mean that when Gavin met me you had
already decided—you had already told him you were
going to leave?"

Coco's mind was self-protectively sluggish now.
There was a delay between each assertion Ann made
and the meaning Coco slowly dislodged from it.

Ann paused, puzzled. "It's all so long ago," she said
softly. "It's like another lifetime. You know, we really
should have talked before now. It's been thirteen
years. Nowadays wife number one and wife number
two get together right away and talk things over to
help each other." She laughed nervously.

"Gavin told me he left you because he wanted to
marry me," Coco said. "He always said how hard it
was to tell you that he was leaving you . . . for another woman."

Ann's face was twitching with emotion.

"Well, I can't really remember exactly how it happened. He certainly fell madly in love with you and I'm sure it wasn't any rebound thing. Actually, both Gavin and I decided together, although maybe it was at different times, but those things are always so unclear. I'm sure it was mutual. I'm sure he had tuned out long before I decided to get divorced, so it really couldn't have been a rebound thing with you."

Coco felt her heart begin to hammer, but then suddenly some electrical switch inside of her cut off. Her interest in keeping score had disappeared. Coco had turned off—the same as when she watched Sesame Street with Nicky and felt free to think of other things or not to think at all. Something had changed within her. The girls at the commune, the women at the march, Sylvia's pain, Ann's problems, Coco's own suffering—something had finally worn down the sick spirit of competitiveness within Coco. And everything seemed inverted now. Past obsessions had become passing observations. Competition had gone dead within her like the telephone when Gavin forgot to pay the bill.

To figure out why she had gained strength from the mistaken notion she had stolen another woman's husband or why Gavin had lied about it—if he did— or whether Coco had only caught Gavin on the rebound, actually marrying him while he still loved Ann, or why Ann wanted to go through all of this— seemed like a complicated math problem that was not part of any officially assigned homework. Coco did not have to cram any more kinky equations onto the messy page of her psychological equations. Mentally she crumpled up all her competitive computations and tossed the paper out of her consciousness.

There.

"Look, Coco. One of the reasons I came over, well, I did hear you were active in D.C. women's-libera-

tion things, but actually I really wanted to say . . ."
Ann paused to seek bravery at the bottom of her glass
like Nicky searched for the face of Willie Mays beneath the milk in his plastic tumbler. "I was so terribly jealous of you for so long. . . . It almost wiped me
out. Everytime I bumped into Suede Bellock somewhere in New York, at a party or some political wing-
ding, he always told me about you and Gavin—how
happy you were and how you had all these darling
kids. And, of course, I was still getting rushed by
creepy guys and working at second-rate publishing
houses. And the worse things got for me, the more I
wondered about you. I wondered if I should have
stayed with Gavin and had some babies and . . .
Oh, I don't know. That hassle in New York—all those
sick guys leeching around and all the messy affairs
and bad feelings—"

The enormous ocean-blue eyes misted over with
sympathy for her own past pains.

"Well, I guess we were suffering from cross fantasies." Coco smiled.

It was time for the women's liberation potlatch
ceremony. Coco was now compelled to offer some
personal intimacy to match Ann's confession. She
rose to her feet, collected the empty glasses and
moved back to the counter again.

"It's crazy because I've been jealous of you for
years, too," she said, without turning around. The
electric coffeepot winked its bright red eye encouragingly at her. "Whenever things got too heavy here
or I got spaced out"—she shrugged to indicate the
internal costs of domestic duty—"I used to feel like I
had liberated you by taking Gavin away . . . I
mean, well, he told me that . . . that he left you
because of me. Anyway, I thought it was because of
me that you were free to swing with all the Beautiful

People in New York and to write articles and get
famous."

Coco returned to the table, passed Ann one of the
drinks—indifferent about exchanging glasses since
now they were simulating sisterhood and sat down.
But what once would have seemed like a valuable
exchange of confessions now felt tiresome, tedious
and a trifle tawdry. Coco had retold her emotional
history too many times when it led nowhere.

"Of course, Suede always told *me* that you were
living with this writer or that sculptor or having an
affair with some network VIP and producing TV programs about women's issues and giving commence-
ment addresses at swish girls' schools and writing
course curricula for Women's Studies programs."

Admitting to envy was suddenly so simple that
Coco wondered if her confession sounded phony. Because what she was really feeling was an enormous
craving to be alone so that she could listen to some
vague ideas that were beginning to stir in her mind.
She felt as if she were about to discover or understand something and talking with Ann Carradine was
an imposition, an interruption of her real work.
Something was calling to her now. Her mind felt like
the lower back right before the onset of labor, something vague and undefinable was happening which
commanded her complete attention.

Ann readopted the earnest expression which indicated her soul-searching was about to rev up again.
"You know, it wasn't until I joined a C.R. group about
three years ago that I began to dig what was happening." She shook her head disbelievingly. "There
were usually eight or nine of us at those meetings and
there were always at least three other women, besides myself, who had been married in college and
who'd left their husbands when they graduated."

This time Ann didn't catch her oversight. Her version of the end of her marriage was so firmly established —by either truth or illusion—that she was unable to alter it enough to protect her successor which she genuinely seemed to want to do.

"We all helped each other get our heads together. It was only during the last five years that I had the guts to go into free-lance writing full time and hang in there. I've just begun to come to terms with a lot of things and I thought as long as I went through so many changes over you, I felt . . . well . . . I wanted to tell you about it."

So it goes, Coco thought. She didn't want to hurt Ann or be rejecting, but she could hardly follow her words any longer. Somehow Coco's spirit had moved beyond any need for intimate reevaluations and reappraisals. Haltingly Coco was moving toward something private, toward some state of internal integrity that was demanding her attention like bands of contractions ringing her body. She tried to appear interested in Ann's presentation, but her mind was now totally independent, moving involuntarily toward some other end. Her mind was gathering up loose ends like strawberries in a basket.

The silence that ensued, while Coco hunted for something to say, was too long and obvious to overcome.

Ann felt herself cut off, dismissed at some premature point in her confession.

"How . . . are your children?" she asked, trying to hide her hurt.

"They're fine," Coco answered, modulating her voice so as to sound pleased, but not proud—thankful rather than self-congratulatory. She then began a frantic foray for an equivalent inquiry, a question that acknowledged some aspect of Ann's life that was painful for Coco. But there were no glorious illusions left.

"Well . . ." Ann paused long enough to give Coco time to restart the conversation, but the silence kept spinning like an empty turntable.

Slowly Ann began making motions of departure, setting down her glass, closing her cigarette box, shifting slightly in the chair, "Well, it's getting late," she said. "It's after midnight. I just wanted to see you and say some of these things, but I guess I better get going."

Coco couldn't muster any reasonable objections. "It was nice to see you again," she said. "I'm glad that we spoke." She stood up in a way that forever fore-closed the possibility of any future encounters. "You've really been writing some great stuff. I always watch for your articles."

Very quickly Ann gathered her possessions and started toward the door.

"Do you think I can catch a cab on Connecticut?"

"Oh, yes. You won't have any trouble getting one up there," Coco said. "It was nice being able to talk like this. Thanks for coming over."

They shook hands.

Impulsively Coco leaned forward and touched her lips against Ann's face. Then she watched her go down the front stairs before she shut and locked the door.

CHAPTER 27

Coco returned to the kitchen, took the ashtray off the table and wet it down under the faucet so no live butts would burn down her house in the early-morning hours. Then she ran upstairs to her bedroom, turning off lights along the way. Belly-flopping down onto the mattress, she closed her eyes and lay very still. Yet even while she faked deep yoga breaths, she was listening for the arrival of her anxiety—preceded and announced by a roll of heartbeats drumming their stately salute.

But the Mau-Mau tom-toms remained silent. In a semiprofessional Finkelsteinian fashion, Coco wondered if she had been creating her own terror by expecting and awaiting it.

Indeed, Coco felt half-empty now without her companionable, familiar hysteria rattling around inside. Her heart rested, suspiciously quiet, in its nest.

—Maybe I've made a spontaneous recovery—she thought optimistically,—like a spontaneous abortion. Maybe the embryo of my incipient insanity has been ejected by Mother Nature from my body.— Coco turned her head gently, wary of moving so quickly as to jar loose any part of her newly assembled jigsaw puzzle of quietude.

—It's so quiet inside me—she thought. Slowly she opened her eyes and saw the street light shining through her madras curtains. Once in the *Chicago Sun-Times* she had read a Letter to the Editor from an impoverished old woman who wanted to thank Mayor Daley for giving her block a street light, because now she could sit by the window and read at night, which she couldn't afford to do if she had to use her own electricity.

Briefly Coco wondered if she had unplugged the electric coffeepot. She couldn't remember doing it, but the danger of an overworked appliance starting a fire seemed remote. She was feeling so brave even electricity didn't seem frightening at the moment. Indeed, she thought it might be a nice practice, a kind little act of charity toward her next day's self, if she brewed a fresh pot of coffee every night before going to bed and left it on so it would be hot when she came downstairs the next morning.

—Dear Dr. Finkelstein— . . . she wrote in the air above her head using little circles instead of dots over the *i*'s, which she always did on thank-you notes and party invitations. —Do you think leaving the coffeepot on all night is (a) dangerous? or (b) the kind of funny little institution only old-maids initiate? In other words, am I experiencing maturity or is this resignation? Blah-blah-blah. Sincerely yours, Ms. Givings.—

—Dear Ms. Taken: There is nothing wrong with

taking care of yourself. Sincerely yours, Dr. Finkelstein. —

—Dear Dr. Finkelstein . . . —This time Coco
used her regular irregular slanted-to-the-right, uphill
script. —I am glad to hear that it is all right for me to
be nice to myself, since at the present time, temporarily at least, there is no one else doing nice for me.
As you may know, Gavin did not telephone yesterday. I am still in the dark as to his whereabouts.
However, I believe I have achieved a certain amount
of understanding as to the nature of (a) our separation
and (b) his needs. These are things that you have
mentioned to me previously. I sincerely believe that
my new-found immunity is producing ingenuity so
that I can deal with my moods. Sincerely yours, Ms.
Understanding. —

—Dear Ms. Cellaneous: Good work. Carry on. Af-
fectionately, Dr. F. —

Coco closed her eyes.

Apparently she had been awarded a welfare grant
from some social-service agency. As the recipient of
an unrequested stipend for survival, she felt no reason to disqualify herself. She could even enjoy her
psychological-welfare benefits without identifying
the celestial service worker who had erroneously ap-
proved her eligibility and changed her from a victim
into a survivor. Although Coco still felt like a single,
lonely gold-hoop earring, she was no longer the *lost*
one. Now she was Coco Burman the Survivor—separate and alone, but at least with a known address—
even if it was only the junk pile on her dressing table.
Even that was something. It was definitely better
than being nowhere.

—Gavin—she whispered.

—Gavin—she called.

Suddenly Coco felt tremulous with love. She

wanted to give and take love. Love was tumbling
through her system. Perhaps if she had a live-in baby-
sitter she might have jumped up right then, driven
over to the Shoreham, found Charlie O'Connor's
room by following, bloodhound fashion, the smell of
her own hysteria, so she could finally lend him a
helping hand. That was how much love she felt. Not
exactly undifferentiated—just enormous. Coco
smiled.

She had let go. Incredibly, she had let go of her
own hysteria.

The only way to quit smoking is to quit smoking.

The only way to quit eating is to quit eating.

The only way to quit fearing is to quit fearing.

But what was it she had done right all of a sudden?
She still had no idea where Gavin was. She was really
worse off now than when she thought he was with
Sylvia. The idea that he had maybe split *alone*, without any woman in the wings, made his act even more
serious. Perhaps she would never see him again. Perhaps he would never let her love him again. That
would be too bad. She would like to be allowed to
love Gavin again. She didn't NEED to love him, she
just wanted to.

Suddenly Coco drew herself up off the bed and
padded down the stairs, through the guest room, and
out to her porch. The sky was busy sweeping clouds
around the darkness and Coco felt a brush of cool
night air encircle her. She looked around at the cozy
clutter of her possessions ringing the porch. Oh, yes,
she had used the porch to crump out. A porch was to
sit on—in the evening, with all the family around, in
old wicker chairs, watching a road or a river go by—
not for hiding.

Coco bent over, unplugged a cord and lifted the
Smith-Corona portable into her arms. Pressing it

close to her breasts, she carried it downstairs to the
kitchen. With one arm she swept the sketchbook
across the table, sending vitamin-pill bottles, salt and
pepper shakers, and unopened mail skating toward
the precipice. Then she placed the typewriter down
squarely at the head of the table. She made one more
run up to the porch for her box of typing paper,
leaving behind all the beauty aids and office supplies,
and then returned to the kitchen. Sitting down in
front of the typewriter she wrote:

The reason no American woman has ever written a Great American Novel is . . . ?

She pressed the carriage return three times and
then wrote:

I would like to write a novel about an American woman who, after a lifetime of psychological
dependencies upon men—fathers, brothers,
husbands, lovers, sons—self-consciously, but self-
confidently, moves out front alone, on her own. I
do not yet know the proper parable for this
story, because I do not yet know what form such
an experience takes. I do not know what scenes
will ensue, because it hasn't happened yet. But I
would like to transcribe the metamorphosis of a
female into a woman—of a woman into a human
being—honestly, without cuteness, snideness or
self-disparagement, and show how a woman
learns to live without a man, just like a pioneer
learns how to live in the wilderness—in order to
survive. I want to show how a woman learns
survival and then goes beyond it toward excellence and then beyond excellence toward cele-
bration.

Coco rolled the page off the typewriter, slipped another clean sheet into the machine, hit the lower-case *L*, and smiled at the number *1* which appeared on the top of the page.

Then she started to write.